MINOR GODS

SUMMONERS
BOOK ONE

A.M. YATES

For information contact; address www.amyates.com

Cover photographs: *Portland, Oregon Panorama/* Josemaria Toscano/123rf.com ; *Beautiful woman with long hair/* Coffee&Milk/istock by Getty Images

ISBN-10:1-943746-04-4
ISBN-13:978-1-943746-04-0

LS Print Edition: May 2016

10 9 8 7 6 5 4 3 2 1

For Ben,
who gave me so much more
than bread and cheese.

PROLOGUE

IT'S ALL THE SAME ceremonial rigmarole until a pissed off earth goddess busts in with a few minor gods and a cadre of phantasmal TemperMentals. Then everybody's screaming and running for their lives.

Before I can assess the situation, someone shoves me aside. I hit the wall, banging my head. I slide down to the floor.

One of the summoners is filling the room with fog.

Daisuke crouches next to me. His words sound garbled. My head is throbbing. Summoners go flying around us, knocked back before they have a chance to fight.

Up on the stage, Mom only needs a nanosecond to summon the mask of the Tripartite, but for some reason she's not moving. Come on, Mom, you're the Triune—Summoner of the Three-Faces, Voice of the Supreme Divine, Mistress of the Elements, and a host of other redundant titles—time to show this earth mama who's in charge.

Daisuke pulls out his mask—river god. The mask is elaborate, vicious looking, red-forked tongue and horns on its head. He brings it to his face. His body becomes encased in roiling green water.

An air god summoner appears next to us. His guise is a swirling mass of fog. Daisuke surges to his feet. The Fog God whips up a cannonball of air and slams it into Daisuke. Daisuke crashes into the wall. The plaster cracks. He slumps to the floor, unconscious. His guise vanishes as the mask falls off.

I reach for Daisuke, but the Fog God seizes my arm. Beneath the god's façade, the summoner's fingers are slender and digging. He yanks me up to my feet. "Pleasure's all mine, Lady Day."

I stumble. My head spins.

That's when I notice the gleaming hourglass in Earth Mama's hand. Where did she get a godsdamned time bender? Sacred tools of the divine aren't just stocked at every convenience store. And not just anyone is capable of summoning a demon to fetch them one either. Earth Mama knows how to wield it too.

Mom is frozen, unable to move. She's trapped in her own personal time disruption.

Not good.

Even worse, I can't do shit. I can't even summon a minor god like Daisuke, or handsy Fog God. My whittling tools are in my bag, but I doubt they'll do me any good. Fog God is sure to be wearing protective charms.

Summoners are scattered across the red carpet. Unconscious. Dead . . . I don't know. Everyone else is running. None of them stop to help. But why should they? Mom's the Triune. The Triune doesn't need help from anyone.

The tribal hall is tilt-a-whirling around me.

Before I regain my balance, the earth bitch plunges a sword into Mom's gut.

Time stops. Not for the rest of the world, just for me.

Then time resumes for both my mom and me. Blood soaks Mom's shirt—oxford, white—and her slacks—khaki, pressed. She crashes to her knees. Her eyes are wide. She falls.

No goodbye. No motion-picture last look at her eldest daughter. Dead. Gone. Just like that.

And nothing happens.

The earth bitch turns in my direction. On her face—her goddess face—flowers are sprouting, blooming, decaying, and then are consumed into a churning vortex, like some art student's nightmare video installation.

"Well?" she demands in her dual voice. The voice of the goddess—cavernous, deep, dark, earthquaking. The voice of the summoner—high-pitched and a little whiny.

Fog God turns me around. I can't see anything of the summoner beneath the blue shroud of mist. His eyes are empty holes of air.

"Nothing," he says. His own bifurcated voice sounds hollow and annoyed.

"That can't be!" Earth Mama shrieks.

Her TemperMentals swirl around her in a muddy mass of phantom irritation and then swoop down on me.

The Fog God has enough sense to let me go before Earth Mama's manifestations of divine orneriness reach us. They cyclone around me, slapping against my skin like willow switches, stinging and drawing blood. This is no backwoods earth goddess. TemperMentals that can get this physical require serious godly juju and more than a couple of recent sacrifices—of the bloody mammal variety.

Still, no mask. No divine intervention. Where the hell are those three-faced jerks? I'm supposed to be the next Triune, with all the redundant titles and crappy responsibilities and lackluster interpersonal skills. And, most importantly at this moment, the incontestable power.

A bubble of hope forms in my TemperMental-addled brain—Mom's not dead. That's why I'm not in contact with the Tripartite. That has to be it.

The TemperMentals peel off, one by one, and return to Earth Mama. They flap and circle around her. I can hear them murmuring in their breathy snickers and low groans, like leaves rustling and branches bending.

Not her. Not her. Not her.

I look at my mom. She's flat on the ground. A pool of glistening maroon spreads around her. If she's alive, she won't be for long.

"She's not the Triune!" Earth Mama's roar shakes the building.

The plaster falls off the ceiling in chunks. Plumes of dust thicken Fog God's haze.

Fog God swears under his breath.

Earth Mama turns and kicks my mom. Mom flops onto her back. My hope bubble bursts. Mom's eyes are big, open, glassy—dead. Acid pushes into my throat. I start towards her, but Daisuke grabs my hand as he pulls himself up.

"No, Josie-san," he says.

Earth Mama is shrieking in rage. The ground is shaking. The cracks in the wall behind us grow wider and wider.

"Run away," Fog God says.

I don't know if he's talking to himself or to us, but I can't. A Triune doesn't run away. A Triune summons the power of the Three-Faces and rips Earth Mama's mask—and head—off her body.

I'm not going anywhere. Even without the mask of the Tripartite, I'm racking my aching skull for some way to destroy that earth bitch.

Daisuke hooks me around the waist and hauls me out as the gilded ceiling collapses. I kick and struggle, but it's no use. Daisuke is stronger and my head is pain-filled and spinning.

You may be asking, where are the details? Where am I, who am I... what color is my hair? Here's a detail for you. My mom's dead. Who gives a shit about the scenery?

Blood and fog, that's all I remember.

CHAPTER 1

JANUARY 27TH

JOSIE STOOD ON THE PORCH, shivering and dripping wet. The numbers above the mailbox blurred and came back into focus and blurred again, 7325. Were those the right numbers? Was this the right street? Was it the right city?

The drizzle and craftsman-style houses suggested Portland, but she'd been zombie-walking through airports for the last twenty-four hours. This could've been Maine for all she knew. Right name, wrong coast.

She forced her eyelids to blink. They resisted. Once they were closed, they stubbornly refused to open again. She rested her forehead against the door jamb.

This had to be her dad's house. The stained glass panel in the front door, porch swing the color of raspberries, meticulous zen-scaping in the front yard—it was all the same. Of course, it had been four years since she'd been back. He could've moved. He hadn't mentioned it the last time they'd talked, but that had been two months ago.

She lifted her head, peeling back her eyelids. "You're a terrible daughter, Josie Day." She flipped open the mailbox and took out a letter. "Maybe that's why the Tripartite blew you off."

The name on the envelope: Marc Day.

If she'd been able to cry, she would've. But she couldn't. Somewhere between Brunei and here, she'd forgotten how. At least she'd made it to her dad's. Too bad he wasn't home.

She stuffed the envelope back into the hammered-copper letterbox and turned, giving the swing a considering look. She hadn't slept on any of the three planes—probably because she was in shock. Daisuke had put her on the first plane, somehow. If not for him, she'd still be in Brunei, either murdered by Earth Mama or crushed under the rubble of the tribe's assembly hall.

When she'd left the bus to walk to her dad's house, the driver had given her a look like he might refuse to let her off. Now she understood why. Shorts, a tank top, and flip-flops were perfect for the tropical humidity of Brunei but not so much the frigid mists of a Portland winter.

"Josie?"

She tensed.

On the sidewalk was a young man straddling a bright-orange bicycle. He pushed back his hood, tattoos on the backs of his hands, a ring on every finger—like most summoners. So he was part of the tribe. Dark hair sheared short, spacers in his ears, eyebrow pierced, good-looking in a punk-kid-next-door way. Then she remembered. He *did* live next door.

She came down the steps. "Beech, right?"

He smiled a crooked smile—cute. "You remembered."

Yes, she remembered. She'd been trained to remember. People didn't expect the Triune to remember them usually, unless they were a member of a tribe's Eye or a matriarch. But Mom had been strict about it. If Josie hadn't remembered an important name, it had meant days of catching crabs and giving them names and then reciting those names when Mom had pulled the slimy clackers out of a tank weeks later.

Beech was easy to remember. Not many people were named Beech, and his algae-green eyes not only reminded her of the beach but were pretty much dazzling.

"Do you know where my father is?" she asked.

"Yeah . . ." Beech looked her up and down as she strode towards him. "Aren't you cold? You know it's freakin' raining out here, right?"

"Where is he?"

Her mom hadn't taught Josie tact. How could she when she didn't have any herself? A Triune only needed so much diplomacy. Managing the tribes was what the Eyes were for. The Triune's primary job, besides ceremonial duties, was to administer justice. Josie wanted to bring that earth bitch to justice so badly that the mere thought of doing so warmed her frozen body.

"With the Eye. With your sister." Beech leaned back on the seat of his bike. "Everybody thought you were dead. You know, since Tessa . . ."

"Since Tessa what?"

"Since she's the new Triune."

"Tessa is the—" No, she couldn't say it.

How could Tessa be the Triune? The drama queen who dissolved into tears watching sappy greeting card commercials?

How could Tessa wield the power of the Tripartite? They'd run her over and make sacrificial hamburger out of her.

Josie pressed her fingers to her forehead. Time for freaking out was never. Breathe.

"Her brains will be pouring out of her ears in two days," Josie muttered.

"More like hours from what I hear," Beech said. "Word is she's not handling her new responsibilities too well."

"No shit." Josie took a deep breath and looked around, trying to get her bearings.

"Are you sure you're not cold?"

"I'm freezing, okay? Who cares?"

Beech's eyes widened.

"I'm sorry," she said. "It's been a rough—"

"No worries," he said. "If you want, we can go back to my house. I'm sure there's something you can—"

"Thanks," she said, "but all I care about right now is finding my dad."

He removed his raincoat. Underneath he wore a black hoodie. "Here." He handed her the coat.

She hesitated. Why was she such an ass? Living on an interdimensional island for the last twelve years with no one but her mom and a bunch of cranky crabs hadn't done much for her social skills. "Don't you need it? Someone told me it's freakin' raining out here."

He smiled. Definitely cute. "You need it more."

"Thanks." Residual body heat and musky boy scent wrapped around her as she pulled it on.

"Can you ride pegs?" He cocked his head towards his rear wheel.

"Do you have a car?" From what she remembered, he was at least her age, seventeen, maybe older.

"Nope."

"How far is it?" She came around the back of the bike, putting her feet on the pegs and bracing herself on his sturdy shoulders. Her feet slipped in her sandals. The thin leather straps of the thongs cut into her skin. Not that it mattered; she was numb from the neck down already anyway.

"The way you're dressed?" He started pedaling, picking up speed as they hit the road. "Too far."

Too far was about twenty minutes. She didn't get much use out of a watch. Every time she and her mom had returned to the mortal plane, they'd come out in a different time zone. A boy in Prague had told her once that watches made good charms to ward off unintended releases of gas—she hadn't been able to tell if he'd been joking or not. She'd never been able to produce a charm other than the run-of-the-mill protective circle.

The streets of Portland passed in a drizzle-shrouded blur. It must have been late in the day, the light was fading fast. Hands clutching Beech's shoulders, she tried not to dig her nails in as he maneuvered through cars and across parking lots. She could tell he was avoiding curbs and puddles, which she appreciated; nonetheless, she was thoroughly jarred and sprayed.

Nothing looked familiar until they rounded the corner and the tribe's community center appeared. A huge industrial building of red brick with big blocks of tinted windows. The ground level housed a coffee shop, a yoga studio, a spa, a ceramic café. Each one was owned and operated by a tribal member.

Beech took another corner and pulled up to the building's main entrance.

Josie stepped off the pegs tentatively. Beech dismounted and pulled open the door for her.

Red rugs in amorphous designs, lots of big potted plants, leather couches, and a sweeping receptionist desk like a pool of honey warmed the lobby with its basic foundation of concrete floors and high ceilings gridded by exposed vent ducts. The manicured young man behind the desk stood, frowning. She didn't remember his name, but she noted the constellation of moles under his right eye, the long stretch of his neck, the fashionable style of his blondish hair. She'd remember him later.

"Really, Beech? You know you can't bring that in here." He pointed at the bike.

"Why not? It's no wetter than either of us," Beech said.

Josie pushed back the hood of the raincoat and scanned the lobby. Elevators sat before her, stairs flanking. "Which way?"

It seemed a strange question. This was her tribe's center. She should've known where everything was and how to get there, but she hadn't been here since the renovations had been completed. Besides, her mom hadn't liked coming home. Her mom would've never said it like that, but Josie had known.

"What's going on?" the receptionist asked, hands flat on the desk, scowling at Josie.

"Third floor for sure." Beech parked his bike by the door. "They'll be in the Eye's sanctum."

She nodded, heading for the elevator.

Behind his horn-rimmed glasses, the receptionist's eyes rounded. "Wait a minute." He raced around the desk and intercepted her. "You can't go up there."

"I *am* going up there," she said.

He crossed his arms over his smart white shirt and red suspenders. "I told you—"

"You heard the lady, Ty, piss off." Beech placed a hand on her shoulder. "Don't you know who she is?"

Ty looked saucy. "Should I?"

"She's Josie Day," Beech said.

Ty snorted. "Josie Day's dead..." His arms dropped. "Oh. I guess . . . let me call up first."

"Do that. I'll wait upstairs." She moved around him, stalked to the other end of the lobby, and hit the elevator button.

Ty hurried back to his desk, picking up the phone. The doors opened with a pleasant bing. Josie boarded, Beech close behind her. Her teeth chattered, but she refused to allow herself to think about hypothermia.

Third floor. Going up.

Beech seemed to watch her from the corner of his eyes, but she refused to let herself think about him either. A Triune didn't think about things—or feel things—that weren't useful to her.

When the doors opened, they stepped out into an airy hallway with the same modern look as the lobby—white walls, stainless steel lights, glossy concrete floors. Beech hooked her arm and guided her to the right. The office suites they passed were all darkened. Accountant, graphic designer, architect, therapist—all conveniently housed within steps of the Eye's ritual space. Josie's gaze caught on one of the plaques: Marc Day, Attorney-At-Law.

They turned a corner and came face to face with a golden-haired Adonis.

He frowned at them. She couldn't recall his name either, but something about him was familiar. He looked like he expected to be remembered. The way his right eyebrow was fixed in an upward tilt set her on edge. Or maybe it was the sculpted planes of his handsome face. Or maybe it was the fact that he wore only one ring, which meant he was damned cocky. Only one other summoner she knew wore just one ring—her mom.

Behind him were the doors to the Eye's sanctum, and beyond them, her father.

"What are you doing here, Beech?" Adonis asked.

Beech held up his hands like he wasn't looking for a fight. "Just along for the ride."

Josie attempted to slip around the god of male beauty, but he sidestepped into her path.

She glared up at his deep-set eyes. "Move."

He gazed back at her, motionless. "You forgot to say please."

Her mother had been murdered; she'd been traveling for days . . . all she wanted was to see her dad. Her patience, if she'd ever had any, was long gone. She squared her shoulders. "I forgot to say get the hell out of my way."

"You can't go in there."

"Watch me." She moved again, but Adonis moved with her, like they were engaged in an infuriating dance. Her hands clenched around the wet cuffs of Beech's coat. Adonis stared coolly down at her, his eyes hard as sapphires.

Beech stepped up next to them. "Look, maybe I ought to make some introductions—"

"I don't need to be introduced," Adonis said. "No one is allowed inside."

"Yeah, but—" Beech started.

Josie cut in. "Well, then why don't you trot on in to your masters, Fido, and tell them that I'm here. Good boy."

The sharp angle of his brow steepened. "Wow, you're a real bitch."

"Not yet, but I can be."

"Okay." Beech took Josie's shoulders and forced her to step back. "Judah, this is Josie. As in, Tessa's sister, Josie."

Judah's face remained impassive. "We were told you'd died."

"Sorry to disappoint you."

"If you're alive, then why is Tessa the Triune?"

She raised her fists, wishing she had taken more martial arts training. Seeing pretty boy splayed out on the ground right now would've done more to sooth her aching soul than just about anything else she could imagine.

Before she could break her knuckles on Judah's chiseled jaw, one of the doors behind him opened.

Judah stepped aside.

A lean, balding man with rimless glasses and a tidy goatee stared at Josie like he didn't recognize her.

"Josie?" he said.

She wanted to cry. "Dad."

Then the screaming started.

CHAPTER 2

January 27th

"You!" Tessa shoved past their dad. Her hazel-gold eyes were huge, dilated, like she was on drugs. Mascara ran down her cheeks. "What did you do to me?" She clawed at her mess of dirty-blond hair. "I can't make them shut up."

Josie seized her little sister's arms—except Tessa was taller than Josie now. Strange.

"It's okay, Tessa."

"No." Fat tears rolled down Tessa's face. "No, it's not. You don't understand."

A bitter burn scoured Josie's throat, but she swallowed it down. She had to help her sister. Time for resentment was never.

Tessa pawed at Josie, at her coat, at her face, like a drowning puppy. "They're all in here, and they're saying things you wouldn't believe ... I can't even understand, and it's like, explosions going off in my head, and they keep getting louder and louder ..."

Tessa continued working herself into a state that was definitely going to lead to brain splatter if Josie didn't do something.

Josie looked from Beech, chewing on the metal chain of his necklace, to her dad, who was holding Tessa up from behind as she blubbered and blathered, then to Adonis . . . Judah. He was dressed in upscale mall fashion, jeans, T-shirt, hoodie, brand names stamped everywhere, but around his neck was a blue crystal that was all Core.

She pointed at the necklace. "Give me that."

He didn't move.

Again, she imagined knocking him flat on the ground. "Please."

He lifted the leather cord over his head and put the pendant into her palm.

She looped the necklace around Tessa's head and steered her to a bench next to the doors. She knelt in front of her little sister, who was still babbling, overcome by the power of the Tripartite.

"There's no end, there's no beginning, it all goes and goes and goes and goes . . ."

Josie squeezed her sister's arms. "Tessa."

"Death whispers, like shaking rattles and soft kisses an—"

"Tessa!"

Her sister blinked, tears spilling from her eyes.

Josie put Judah's crystal in Tessa's hand. Tessa's lips parted to speak, but Josie put her finger to them.

"Look into the crystal, Tessa."

Tessa's eyes lowered to the spear of quartz.

Their dad knelt next to Josie. Tessa had his eyes, green with a gold starburst center. "We've tried everything, nothing's working. A simple crystal meditation isn't—"

Josie shot him a sharp look. His lips sealed.

Tessa's hand trembled in Josie's. Josie wrapped her icy fingers around Tessa's warm wrist and steadied her sister. Josie's eyes were drawn to the crystal too. Within the stone was a sliver of light, a white flame. Gazing at it, the biting chill inside her abated. The tight coil that was her body loosened. The flame seemed to speak to her. *You're safe here.* Another sob tried to free itself from her chest, but she pushed it back down.

"Do you see the fire?" she asked Tessa in a soft voice.

But Tessa was already lost in the quartz. Her panicked breaths slowed, her strained face, smoothed. After a few seconds, she seemed fully immersed in the meditation.

Josie bowed her head and let out a sigh of relief. No brain-splatter. Not today anyway.

Josie eased back from Tessa and stood up. She ran her hands over her face and then back through her damp tangles of black hair. It wasn't supposed to be like this. Why was Tessa the Triune? Something had gone horribly wrong.

She glanced over at her dad. Two women hovered in the doorway behind him.

One was thin-lipped, hair a silver bob, dimple in her chin, gray pants suit: Nancy. The Eye of the Future. The other was middle-aged, frazzled hair dyed various shades of garish red, dark circles under her eyes, tiny wringing hands: Lily. She'd lost weight since the last time Josie had seen her, but she was still doughy-looking in her gypsy skirts and peasant top. The Eye of the Past.

She was about to ask where Caroline, the third member of their tribe's leadership was, when her father gathered her up and hugged her. She stiffened. Her mom hadn't hugged her since the onset of puberty. Before Josie had a chance to lift her arms and return the gesture, her dad pulled back.

"We thought..."—he smoothed her wet, tangled hair—"something had happened to you."

"Something did happen," she said, fighting against the knot in her throat, "Mom's dead." Looking up at her dad, she felt a pressure build around her eyes again. She couldn't remember the last time she'd cried. She felt like she needed to, and yet the tears didn't come. She wanted to collapse against him and let him hold her, but she couldn't. She didn't know how. "I'm not the Triune. How is that possible?"

Her dad looked as lost as she felt. She pushed back against the feeling. She knew just where she was, who she was . . . didn't she?

"We were hoping you could tell us," Nancy said in a tight voice.

Her dad stepped aside so Josie could face the two women. Every sister tribe had its own Eye, three women who presided over day-to-day tribal matters.

"Forgive me, Honorable Mother, but where is Caroline?" Josie asked.

The two women looked at each other, then away. Lily to the floor. Nancy back at Josie.

"That's not your concern," Nancy stated.

Josie may not have been the Triune, but she'd spent most of her life on the island training and studying Core laws. Without Caroline, Nancy and Lily were merely two highly skilled summoners. She wasn't technically required to address them formally or even to follow their directives. Still, they were elders and due some degree of respect. She reminded herself of that as her gaze clashed against Nancy's.

"Mother of the Future, as a witness to the murder of a Triune, I'm obligated to report to the Eye of my natal tribe." She held

Nancy's sharp stare. "So, I guess we'll have to wait until the Eye shows up."

"Murder?" her dad said, forehead crinkling. "They told us it was an accident . . ."

Lily leaned heavily against the threshold, like she might faint at the thought. "A Triune hasn't been murdered since Gansu, China, 1718."

"Don't be ridiculous," Nancy said. "Melinda wasn't murdered. The building collapsed."

Inside, Josie was on fire. Outside, her teeth were chattering. "What else do you call it when some bitch earth goddess guts you with a sword . . . Venerable Eye?"

Her dad's hand went to his bald pate, his color whitening to something like paste.

Nancy's taut features pulled tighter. Her gaze flicked over to Judah and then to Beech, who was lingering behind Josie.

"I could leave," Beech said, sneakers squeaking as he took a backwards step. "Yeah, why don't I do that?"

"I'm not going," Judah said.

"It doesn't matter who stays," Josie said. "Everyone should know the truth. We were in Brunei. I had to . . ." Her words tangled up in her throat. Judah was giving her critical brow, like he didn't believe anything she was saying. Her words pushed out, stronger. "I had to leave her. I had to run. I don't know what you heard, but my mother was murdered. I saw it."

Lily gasped. Nancy looked as if she'd sat on something sharp and probe-like.

"Oh no." Lily wrung her pudgy hands. "No, no, no . . ."

"Do you realize what you're saying?" Nancy said in a restrained tone.

Josie took a step towards her. "Do you, Eye of the Future? Forgive my bluntness, but why the hell didn't you see this future? Why didn't someone see a rogue summoner, with the power to produce tangible TemperMentals and the ability to access immortal devices, murdering my mother?"

Nancy's lips pursed, white and thin. "I needn't remind you, young woman, that you are not the Triune. From what Melinda told me, you're not capable of summoning at all. And since you wear no rings, I can see that is, indeed, the case."

Well, that was a salty finger in an already bleeding eye. No, she wasn't the Triune. No, she couldn't summon any gods and never had. Her lack of rings displayed that painful truth for every Core member to see. Her mom had often said that Josie was just a late bloomer and, since she was heir to the Triune, it didn't matter if she could summon any other gods. One day, Josie would summon the most powerful gods. Except Josie wasn't a late bloomer. She wasn't the Triune either. Turns out, she was a drudge—a non-summoner. In the tribal world, drudges were pitied and disdained, more often the latter.

Nancy continued in her imperious tone. "You cannot speak to me—"

Josie seethed, dispensing with the respect. "You're right. I don't have to speak to you at all. Without Caroline, you're just a stuck-up old—"

Her dad inserted his arm between them. "Wait. Stop." He took Josie's shoulders and turned her towards him. "Josie, you have to tell us everything that happened, whether Caroline is here or not."

"Where is Caroline?" she asked again.

"We don't know," Judah answered.

"Judah!" Nancy snapped.

Josie turned, remembering now who Judah was: Caroline's son. She might've seen him at Caroline's induction into the Eye ten years before, but she'd been so busy trying to memorize every detail of the ceremony that she hadn't taken note of anyone who wasn't a matriarch or an elder.

"We don't," Judah said with the same impassive expression.

Josie turned back to Nancy. "The Eye of the Present is missing?"

"It's not the first time. Caroline is... always living for the moment." Lily gave Josie a weak smile.

"When was the last time you heard from her?"

"I talked to her three days ago," Judah said. "She left for a climb. Smith Rock."

"And you haven't talked to her since?"

He gazed at her like it was a stupid question.

"Aren't you worried?"

Are you a moron? seemed to scrawl over his face.

"Has anyone gone to look for her?"

"Of course we have," her dad said. "One of the rangers out there is Core. Caroline was going to meet him, but she never arrived."

"And I don't guess anyone saw that coming either," Josie said.

"You well know that prophesizing the future is no simple matter. It's not like watching the morning news," Nancy said.

"Do I? For someone with no standing I sure do know a lot, don't I?"

"Then how come you don't know why you're not the Triune?" Judah asked when Nancy was left retortless.

She turned on him, burning from head to toe. "What are you doing here anyway?"

"I came because Tessa wanted me to," he said.

Her stomach twisted. "You're not dating her, are you?"

"What if I am?"

She drilled her fingers into her forehead, struggling to maintain focus. "That figures."

Tessa had always been attracted to pretty, useless things.

"Honey, you shouldn't do that to your third eye," Lily said.

"Who cares about my third eye?" she snapped. "Our tribe's Present Eye is missing. The Triune has been murdered."

She gazed around at them, but they were just standing there, staring at her. She wanted to scream. Why weren't they doing something? If she'd been the Triune . . . oh, the misery she would've inflicted on them for gaping at her like she was some lunatic who had wandered in off the street. She wasn't crazy. She wasn't lying. She was the Triune's daughter. Or had been. The Triune, the leader of the Corpora Deorum—commonly called the Core—and the voice of the Supreme Divine, had been murdered and what were they doing? As far as she could see, nothing. Unacceptable. If they couldn't figure out what to do, then she'd have to take charge herself, Triune or not.

"Get a scribe down here, now," she said to Nancy and Lily. "Assemble the matriarchs. Call the messengers. Prepare to convene a godsdamned tribal council. In the meantime, get every charm-maker you have to protect my sister, our house, this entire freakin' city, and yourselves, for that matter. While you're at it, wake up your warriors and tell them to dust off their most blood-thirsty gods. Because if you think this earth bitch isn't going to show up again, then you're just asking to be the next one who gets a sword plunged into your gut."

No one moved. Josie was clenched so tightly she was trembling.

"Um." Lily twisted her rings around her stubby fingers. "She might be right . . ."

"We'll take the girl's statement," Nancy said tersely. She reached into her pocket. "I'll call Brunei."

CHAPTER 3

FEBRUARY 4TH
A WEEK LATER

SHE PANTED. SWEAT SLUICED down her face, sheeting her back and chest. She unzipped the rain jacket. The hood bounced between her shoulder blades, keeping time.

She didn't know how long she'd been running. Long enough for the rain to start and stop, then start and stop again. She'd run the trail loop so many times the black-billed geese that seemed to own the park—based on how much of their fecal matter was splattered over everything—had given up hissing at her and simply moved off towards the pond, glaring at her with beady menacing goose eyes.

When she felt that wave of too-much-running nausea for the second, or maybe tenth time, she veered back into her dad's neighborhood. The streets were patch-worked, lines of black sealant straining to hold them together. Sodden brown clots of leaves collected on the iron grates, muffling the constant rush of water from the sewers and tingeing the air with a decaying scent.

Tidy, well-loved bungalows huddled beneath their peaks, dark-eyed on a Monday afternoon. She ducked under grasping bushes and low-hanging branches. Everything felt too close here—the houses, the plants, the people.

Stretching her legs further, pounding through the last few blocks, her lungs picked up pace, but her pulse remained stuck in the same heavy throbbing gear. She could run for miles, whittle for hours, meditate all afternoon, but her heart continued to sink—encased in grief like concrete—deeper into that dark place where she shoved all thoughts and feelings that weren't of any use. She'd never had much use for her emotions, but she seemed to have even less use for them now, except for her anger. She held onto that, refusing to let it abate even for a second. When Earth Mama had paid for her crime then, maybe, Josie would dredge up her pain and set it free.

She cut across the street, slowing as she approached the pale green house with the dark green trim and the shadowed front porch. An urge to turn around and keep running came over her. Inside the house, she knew it would be more frustration for her and more tears for her dad and sister. They'd been crying nonstop since the funeral on Friday.

Rounding the fence into the driveway, she almost smacked right into a golden-haired god.

She stumbled, bumping into the tall fence behind her. The fence groaned and pushed her back towards Judah. Her chest continued to heave as she glared.

"You again?" she asked.

Judah crossed his arms, standing at the back end of Josie's dad's Volvo, eyeing her in that way he did—that silently critical and completely infuriating way—like he was wondering how she could've gone out of the house looking like she did; which at the moment probably fell somewhere on the attractiveness meter between drowned rat and mangy street dog.

All she'd found to wear while running was one of her dad's old painting T-shirts and a pair of Tessa's yoga pants that were the worst shade of chewed-bubblegum pink Josie had ever seen. Josie's clothes remained stuck on the Triune's Island, for good, or until Tessa got enough of a handle on her powers to translocate there.

In the week since Josie had arrived, shopping hadn't been on her list of priorities. But squeezing into Tessa's hand-me-downs was becoming tiresome. Even Tessa's running shoes were too small. How could her little sister be taller, thinner, and have smaller feet? Josie was considering penciling in a shopping trip, right below: Find Earth Mama. Execute Earth Mama.

"Josie?" Her dad came around from the driver's side.

She glanced at him and then away just as quickly. His eyes were reddened—tear-stained—and full of concern. She was starting to understand why her parents had split up. Her mother's emotional pipes may have been clogged up and shutdown, but her father's seemed to be overflowing and riddled with leaks.

"How long have you been running?"

"No idea," she said, breathless. "Did you come from the center?"

He took a cleaning cloth from his back pocket and removed his glasses, wiping the lenses. "I did."

"And?" she asked.

His lips pressed into a thin line. "And nothing."

"What do you mean? Nothing?"

"The investigators in Brunei still haven't turned up any evidence of this . . . earth goddess."

"You mean besides Mom's corpse?"

He winced and gave her another fret-filled look.

She set her teeth, pulling heavy breaths through her nostrils, glaring off towards the slick dark street.

Days before, a tribal council had finally been convened. The matriarchs and elders assembled. A scribe recorded Josie's testimony. Daisuke backed her up via webcam, but none of Brunei's tribal members would admit to seeing any earth goddess or even that they were attacked. Josie wasn't sure if they were lying because they were afraid or if they were conspirators.

She demanded the council give her a truth-charm, so they would know she wasn't lying, but they claimed to believe her story. After the autopsy had confirmed her mother had been stabbed, they didn't have much choice. Still, all they did was sit on their butts and argue.

A summoner guilty of the highest crime in the Core, assassinating a Triune, was strolling around with weapons of the gods in her pocket. After a week, all the Core had done was send investigators to Brunei to "look into the facts." Josie didn't need to look. She'd seen enough. She knew everything she needed to know.

"We are doing everything we can, Josie," her dad said.

"I sincerely hope that's not the case," Josie said.

"What do you want—?"

"I want to find that psycho who murdered my mother and bring her to justice," Josie said. "What do you think I want? And if the Core can't do that, then I will."

Her dad looked as if he was going to start crying again. He moved towards her, arms out, like he might try to hug her. She stepped back.

"Josie, please—"

"I mean it, Dad. I am not going to sit here and do nothing—"

"What do you think you can do?" Judah asked in his patented impassive tone.

Fists. Curling. "Excuse me?"

"You and your boyfriend claim this 'earth goddess' has a time-bender and a crew of henchmen, not to mention material TemperMentals—"

Blood. Boiling. "I don't 'claim' it, I saw it. She does. And Daisuke is not my boyfriend. He is my friend. Neither of us is lying."

"So then what are you going to do? How are you going to 'bring her to justice' exactly? You can't summon a god, so you can't fight her or even pacify her long enough to take custody of her. You'd get yourself killed. Besides that, you don't know where to find her or even where to start looking. And if you do, then that's something you should've included in your official statement to the Council."

Even though he was five inches taller, fifty pounds heavier, and muscled like an Olympic swimmer, she was tempted to take him on. Just one good punch.

"Judah's right."

She cringed. She hoped she didn't have to hear those words again. Ever.

"You have to trust us," her dad went on.

"It's not that I don't trust you," she said. "It's that I can't sit here and be useless. Even if I'm a drudge."

Her dad winced again. "Don't call yourself—"

"I may not be able to summon a god. I may not be able to fight. I may not even know where to start looking, but at least I'm willing to start. The Core can't even decide if they should convene a council of the Eyes. After the murder of a Triune! It's insane. You can all sit around and buff your nails"—she glanced at Judah's neat and shiny fingernails—"or whatever it is you do, but I can't. I have a passport and a bank card. I'll get a plane. That's where I'll start. I'll meet with every tribe in the entire world if I have to. Someone knows something."

"Sure they do," Judah said, "but why would they tell you?"

"What are you even doing here? Wait,"—she held up her hand—"don't tell me. Tessa wants you here."

"Josie, I know you're upset—"

"You're right, Dad, I am—"

"And that's completely understand—"

"Yes, it is."

"But you're not thinking—"

"Wrong, Dad," she said, leveling her voice. "I am the only one here who is—"

A wail issued from the house. Judah was the first to bound off, up the front yard and onto the porch—good boy. Josie was close at his heels. Judah left the front door open behind him. Josie rushed into a tidy house filled with pale godly light. Tessa stood between the living and dining areas, clutching her head, her skin glowing.

"*Kuso!*" Josie swore. "Tessa! Get it under control!"

"I can't! I can't!" Tessa cried.

Josie pushed by Judah and seized Tessa's trembling arms. "Look at me."

Tessa looked up. Her copper-green irises were fading to white. Not good. Visions of brain splatter played across Josie's mind, but she shut them down. She needed to distract Tessa, quickly.

Josie fixed a frown on her face. "Oh my gods, what happened to your hair?"

The color burst back into Tessa's eyes, the glow diminished. "My hair? What's wrong with my hair?"

"There is a salon at the center, right?" Josie asked. "Are they open?"

The glow receded and then was gone.

"Oh gods, is it that bad?" Tessa asked, distracted, for the moment, and grounded, once more, in the mortal world—her mortal world, where the state of her hair was paramount. Josie wondered at her sister's normal upbringing sometimes. If only Josie could be so easily distracted.

"Go upstairs and get dressed. We are going to the salon, right now," Josie said as if it mattered to her. In fact, all that mattered to her was keeping those three-faced pricks from redecorating the living room with the contents of Tessa's skull.

Tessa nodded and turned, disappearing into the kitchen.

Josie let out a long breath.

"I can't believe that worked," her dad said. "If only I had known—"

"It probably won't work again," Josie said. "It's only going to get worse." She turned to Judah. "Your mother is the tribe's charm-maker, correct?"

Caroline, the tribe's Present Eye, who had been missing, had called the day after Josie had arrived. Apparently, she did live for the moment because, at the last minute, she'd ditched her plans to climb Smith Rock and had taken a week long cruise to Alaska instead. She'd lost her phone somewhere between Seattle and Dutch Harbor. She'd shown up just in time for the funeral.

"Yes," he said.

"Call her. We need more grounding and centering charms, the most powerful ones she knows. We have to do everything we can to keep Tessa in the here and now."

After a moment of seeming consideration, Judah took out his phone and thumbed over the screen. His hesitation irritated her, but she let it go—this time. She turned to her dad.

"Dad, I'm sorry for blowing up at you out there," she said. "You're right. I am upset. I'm upset that no one seems to be taking the threat of the Earth Goddess seriously. And I really can't just sit here. I'll buy a ticket to Osaka. Daisuke is there. He'll help me. He knows I'm telling the truth—"

"We believe you, Jo—"

She held up her hand, stopping him. "I know you do, Dad, but I cannot stick around and be useless—"

"What about Tessa?" Judah said, taking his phone away from his ear.

Why did his every word chafe her? "What about your mother?" she asked.

"She's not answering." He slid the phone back into his pocket. "She probably forgot to charge her phone, or lost it, again. I'll talk to her as soon as I can, but you're not really going to leave now, are you?"

"Why? Because you'd miss me so much?"

He stared, not amused. "Because your sister needs you. You have a duty to her."

The word duty was like a punch in the gut. It was one of the words her mother had used every day. The ghost of her mother's smoky voice floated up from the depths of her mind, so clear and real that Josie could almost feel her mom's breath on her ear,

Duty to the Corpora before all things, Josie. That is the right way. That is the only way for the Triune.

"Judah's right."

Damn. Those words again? Already?

"Tessa cannot do this on her own," her dad said. "You must realize that. You are the only one who can help her. You need something to do? Train your sister. Teach her everything that your mother—" His voice hitched.

Oh gods, please no more tears.

Thankfully, he collected himself. "Everything your mom taught you," he finished. "Trust us. Trust the Core. We want to find whoever did this to your mother, to our Triune, just as much as you do and bring them to justice." He grasped her arms. "We need you, here, Josie. Your sister needs you. Your Triune needs you. You have to stay."

"*Kuso,*" she muttered.

Shit.

CHAPTER 4

FEBRUARY 25TH
THREE WEEKS LATER

JOSIE TOSSED DOWN THE dry erase marker. The Invocation circle for the Fates was left half-drawn on the white board behind her. "That's it, I'm done."

Tessa broke away from Judah. "Good. Go away."

"My pleasure." Josie knelt stuffing her notes into her bag.

Tessa had the entire second story to herself. Years ago, their dad had transformed the attic into one long partially divided room: bedroom, bathroom, and a sitting area big enough for a desk, sofa, chair, and a huge TV. Josie had set up a whiteboard in the sitting area which Tessa occasionally glanced at when she wasn't batting her lashes at Judah.

For the last few weeks, Josie had spent almost every moment attempting to teach Tessa all that their mother had taught her, but Tessa wasn't a particularly interested or apt student. Once she'd figured out how to tune the Tripartite out, she'd stopped paying attention. It didn't help that Judah was always draped in some chair nearby. Whenever Josie turned her back, Tessa would sneak over and curl into his lap like a needy kitten.

Josie stood, slinging her bag over her shoulder. "Don't blame me when your brain explodes."

"Real nice," Judah said. "It's not your sister's fault she's the Triune and you're . . . not."

Josie looked around. "Did you hear something? Like the obnoxious sound of someone who should mind his own business?"

"Why can't you two get along?" Tessa pouted, playing with the leather cord around Judah's neck.

"Why can't you pay attention? Damn it, Tessa! This is important."

Tessa's face darkened. "Why? I'm never going to invoke the Fates. That would be crazy."

Josie dug her fingers into her forehead. "You never know what you're going to need to do. You have to be ready, just in case. You're the Triune. Do you get that? Do you have any idea what that means?"

Tessa wound Judah's necklace around her finger. "I know it made Mom into a huge bitch."

The worst part was that Josie couldn't deny it, but it still felt like having her knee caps ripped out.

"Don't you care at all that she's dead?" Josie asked.

"Do you? I haven't seen you cry once, not even at the funeral."

"You cry enough for both of us."

"I'm trying, okay?" Tessa slumped back. "But I haven't spent my whole life studying for this like you have. You can't expect me to learn it all in a month." The back of her hand draped against her forehead like a swooning Southern belle. "I need a break. We've been trapped inside forever." Suddenly, she sat up. "I know, let's go to the beach." She grabbed Judah's shirt. "Let's take a hike like we used to and have a bonfire. That would be so great."

"No way," Josie said.

"Why not?"

"It's not safe."

Tessa rolled her eyes and held out her arms. They were bangled in charms: braided leather ones with feathers and stones, chain mail cuffs, sparkling strings of glass beads. Some of them helped her control the Tripartite, others protected her from various physical dangers. "I'm safe, Josie. Look at me. I'm drowning in safety."

Josie shook her head. "Those may protect you from here to the tribal center, but a summoner like her—"

"The mysterious earth goddess, you mean?" Tessa clawed her fingers at Judah and bared her teeth. He smirked.

"That's not funny."

Tessa dropped her hands. "You don't think anything is funny."

Josie slung her bag over her chest and started towards the stairs. "What's funny about witnessing the murder of someone you love?"

"Josie, wait," Tessa called.

She caught up with Josie at the top of the steps, grabbing her hand. Josie pulled it away. Tessa was like Dad, so touchy-feely. Josie had been touched more in the last month than she had in the last ten years.

"I know you're trying to help me," Tessa said, "and I appreciate it, really. I couldn't do this without you."

"You're not taking this seriously."

Tessa sagged. "I am taking it seriously, but I'm burned, okay? You don't know what it's like—"

Josie turned away. "You're right. I don't." She started down the stairs.

"Josie, that's not what I meant!" Tessa called after her.

But Josie knew what Tessa meant. Josie didn't know what it was like to be the Triune. She never would. She was trying not to be bitter about it, but how could there have been such a huge mistake? She'd studied a lot of Core history and had never once read about a mix-up concerning the Triune's heir. How had she won that crap lottery ticket?

On her way down, she passed a mirror—of course Tessa would want to gaze at herself as she walked up and down the stairs. Josie turned her shoulder towards her reflection, pulling down the collar of her shirt. The circle tattoo—surrounded by symbols for the Corpora Deorum, Covenant, duty, amongst others—was like an old blood stain. The mark of the Triune.

Though it had hurt like nothing Josie had ever experienced, she'd kept silent throughout the marking ritual. In the end, the tattoo had remained on her skin which meant the Covenant had accepted her, the gods had acknowledged her as the heir, and her destiny had been set, except . . . she wasn't the Triune.

"What happened?" she murmured.

"Maybe you're defective," Judah said, somehow having descended the constantly groaning stairs without making a sound. Maybe he was light on his feet because he inclined toward the air elements. Maybe he was the Fog God; he seemed evil enough. Why were the most attractive guys such jerks? But she pushed away any thoughts she had about his good looks. Firstly, he was her sister's boyfriend. Secondly, he was an arrogant ass. It didn't matter what he looked like.

She moved quickly into the dim hallway. When she reached her door, she turned. "Leaving so soon? Got other places to be useless?"

He reached into his pocket and took out his keys. "I'm going to pick up my sister, Simone. She's been on a mission for the last month."

"How ... human." She opened the door to her tiny bedroom that had once been her dad's home office.

"You should try it sometime," he said.

"You're one to talk."

"You're just pissed off because you're not the Triune. That must suck. One minute you're Miss High-and-Mighty, and now you're Miss Nobody. Worse than that, you're the Triune's older sister who was passed over. You can't summon the Tripartite. You can't summon anything. No wonder you were sent the rejection letter." He bounced his keys in his hand like he was testing their weight. "You'd think someone would've realized it sooner."

Her desire to see him flat on his back knocked out cold was quickly evolving into an urge to push him off a very high tower and watch him fall a long, long way.

She leaned back against her bedroom door. "I'm sorry. I was wrong about you."

He spun his ring around his finger. One ring. No decoys to make it harder for some crafty summoner to steal it and thus any masks he might've had in his stash.

"It's not going to work. Whatever you're about to say. I don't care," he said.

"No. Why would you? In order to care you'd actually have to be a human. My mistake."

She shut the door, cursing under her breath. What did Tessa see in that goat scrotum, besides his pretty face? Not that she was acknowledging that he was good-looking. For her sister's sake and her own, she was staunchly curtailing all thoughts about Judah other than the ones that involved putting him in his place, which ideally would've been out of her life entirely.

She tossed her bag onto the bed, a saggy futon that her dad and the goat sack had brought up from the basement. The former office was hardly big enough for the futon and the old dresser that, in its most recent past life, had been in the garage filled with tools her dad hadn't used since he'd completed the house's renovation.

She moved aside the stacks of books she'd borrowed from the tribe's archives, dropped onto the bed, and stared through the French doors to the deck out back.

Dad had been momentarily hesitant about giving her a room with its own entrance, but Tessa had laughed and reminded him that Josie was probably more responsible than he was. And she was right.

Dad was too laissez-faire as far as Josie was concerned. He let Tessa do whatever she wanted and he was never around. Too busy working and being a puppy dog to his girlfriend, the dental hygienist. Even though Mom had dissolved their marriage by Core laws and they'd been officially divorced for thirteen years, it still irked Josie that her dad was shacking up with some perky little teeth-scraper—Ashley.

She slipped on her shoes—Dad preferred they didn't wear them in the house. Thankfully, he had found time to pick her up a few pairs. He kept saying that Ashley would love to take her shopping for clothes, but Josie preferred squeezing into Tessa's cast-offs over bonding with Dad's girlfriend.

She couldn't understand how any of them could continue with their lives, shopping, snuggling, and dreaming about trips to the beach, while the Earth Goddess was at large. Hardly a minute went by in which Josie wasn't haunted by the memory of her mother and her mother's murder. Every time she closed her eyes she saw fog and blood.

But she had decided that Judah was right (damn him). Tessa did need Josie's help, even if she didn't always act like she wanted it. Training the Triune for the trials was Josie's duty now. Earth Mama had been after Josie—assuming that Josie would be the next Triune—for whatever reason. To kill her too? If that were the case, why hadn't Earth Mama just done it when she'd had the chance? Josie didn't know. One of the dozens of unanswered questions that kept her up at night.

Whatever the answer, Tessa was in danger. Earth Mama would turn up again. Josie had to make sure Tessa wasn't caught off guard, like their mom had been. One more reason Tessa's lack of dedication was so frustrating. Not only could the Tripartite kill her if she didn't take her training more seriously, but Earth Mama was out there too—waiting.

Josie retrieved her whittling tools and the figurine she'd been working on, a crab, and went outside. As she ran her knife along the jagged teeth of the crab's claw, she was surprised at how much she missed the stupid little clack-clack-clackers. And the island.

She'd never liked the Triune's Island. It was only supposed to be a repository—not a permanent residence. This was evidenced by the crumbling architecture and the lack of life, other than the vegetation and the crabs. Mom had done her best to spruce it up—

curtains, pillows, oil lanterns, and lots of batteries, so Josie could listen to music or watch movies when she wasn't studying or training—but it remained a forlorn place. The island was out of time, between the mortal world and Beyond, shrouded in mist. No day, no night. And always the mutter of primordial gods in the forgotten distance. Mom had claimed she couldn't hear them, but Josie was sure her mom had just been trying to shut her up. Josie had opted to keep her headphones on most of the time to drown out the gods' constant complaining about being taken for granted.

As surprised as she was by her occasional nostalgia for the island, she was just as surprised by moments like these in Portland. Out on the redwood deck, she experienced an odd sense of ease. Instead of blaring music to drown out the primordial gods' bitching, she could lose herself in the birds' songs and the soft patter of water dripping off the deck's roof. The air was thick, heavy with oxygen, like it wanted to be breathed—not like the air on the island which tasted acidic, sulfurish, alien. And unlike the gray, ghostly ruins of the island, she was surrounded by thick, spiraling evergreen trees.

In these moments, she felt like she was on the verge of understanding something, some sense of place she'd once known about but had forgotten. Everything was permanent here. The buildings, the trees, the people, they ... stayed. That had a certain appeal.

She had attempted to maintain her strict routine of training and studying, and had even coaxed Tessa into joining her for a few days, but that had quickly proven pointless. Portland managed to thwart her every effort at reestablishing her Triune-training regimen. Something was always interrupting.

"Hey. There you are." Beech appeared in the gap between the back edge of the house and the front of the garage.

He grinned that crooked grin of his that had, lately, been leaving her a little muddled.

She guessed she was developing a crush on him, but she'd never crushed on anyone. Not anyone real. Movie stars and manga characters probably didn't count.

Her mom had stomped out all flickers Josie might've felt for anyone over the last few years. *For your own good,* her mom had said. *When it's time, I'll introduce you to a select few young men who, you can be assured, understand what it means to be with a Triune.*

Josie had trusted her mom, so it hadn't taken long before Josie was extinguishing any errant sparks for herself. Lately though, her mom had been allowing Daisuke to meet them more often whenever she and Josie were on the mortal plane. Daisuke was probably one of those young men who would've been suitable for a Triune, but Josie and Daisuke had decided years ago that they were only friends.

So Josie wasn't entirely sure what she was feeling. Beech stopped by every day, sometimes multiple times, to say hi and see what she was doing. And she was sort of starting to like that about Portland too. The freedom to feel something and not have to worry that it might interfere with her duty, that was new. And a bit overwhelming. She was keeping herself as tightly controlled as she could. She still had a duty to her sister, her Triune. Nothing was more important. Anything that might interfere with that she banished into the dark forgetting place of her mind—the oubliette. In spite of her frustration, she would keep training her sister until Tessa was enough of a Triune to command Josie to stop.

Beech hopped over the step onto the deck and plunked his skateboard down, rolling it ahead of him. He slid onto the bench, close enough that his knee touched hers, even though there was twenty feet of seating on the deck.

"The whittling thing is cool." He draped his arm behind her. "I told my mom about it. She wants you to come down to the art lab."

Josie blew away the shavings, running her thumb over the soft basswood. "Why would I want to do that?"

"It would get you out of the house."

"Yeah, but not away from my sister and her shithead of a boyfriend."

"Judah is a chode," Beech agreed. "But he and Tessa don't hang out in the art lab. They wouldn't want to ruin their manicures and overpriced shoes."

She snorted, still carving and still very aware of his leg touching hers.

He leaned forward. "Come on, Josie, you need to get out of here."

"So everyone at the center can gawk at the girl-who-was-supposed-to-be-Triune? Sounds like fun."

"Screw them. You don't really care what they think, do you?"

She worked the blade into the crab's claw, sharpening the points. "It's not that I care. I just don't want to deal with it."

"You're going to have to deal with it sooner or later." His hand wrapped around her arm, squeezing. "If I were you, I'd be stoked."

"Stoked?"

"Hell yeah. You're free. You don't have to be the Tripartite's slave. You don't have to spend the rest of your life overseeing every stupid ceremony and ruler-slapping naughty summoners every time they drink a little blood. You can do whatever you want. Go wherever you want. If I were you, I'd give these mofos the finger and hit the road."

She smiled a little. Beech made it easy to smile.

"Oh, yeah? Where would you go?" she asked.

"Wherever I want. I'd hop a train. Or hitch a ride. Go wherever the road leads."

The glint in his eyes was like sun-sparks on green water. As much as she enjoyed it, and just being around him, what he was saying didn't speak to her. She'd spent the last ten years hopping all over the world, to every sister tribe on the globe.

"Sounds like you'd rather be somewhere else," she said, returning to her carving.

He squeezed her arm tighter. "Right now, there's nowhere else I want to be."

Her smile widened, all on its own.

"That's pretty amazing," he said. "You should do that more often."

The weirdest thing was happening; her skin was growing warm. Was she actually blushing? She couldn't remember the last time that had happened.

She straightened her face. "I'm going to be honest. I'm pretty inept with all this ... personal interaction stuff, so ... are you flirting with me?"

"Uh, yeah."

"Oh." She smiled again, looking down at the flat little crab in her hand. She hadn't given the crab a name yet. She'd have to wait until he was finished to learn his name.

"But I need to tell you something."

"That sounds ominous."

"Not really. I just don't believe in monogamy, as a general rule."

She stopped carving. "So, what do you believe as a general rule?"

"Nothing," he said. "I don't believe in generalities and I don't really believe in rules either, other than believing that there are always exceptions."

"What are you saying? You like me, but you don't want to get married? There go my plans."

"I just want to be up front with you," he said, "because I do like you. I don't want any hurt feelings later on."

"Who says there's going to be a later on?"

"Nobody. That's why I'm telling you this now. So you can decide if you want there to be a later on. Some people are cool with it and some aren't. There's nothing wrong with that. I'd be a hypocrite if I said there was. But I know what doesn't work for me. If you're interested in finding some dude to give you the fairy tale ending, that's not me."

"Then who are you?"

He leaned back again, grinning. "I'm Beech."

She smiled in spite of herself. She didn't know what to think about his bluntness or what he was telling her.

"It must be nice to know what you believe." *And who you are.* "I'm not sure I do anymore."

"Exactly," he said. "You've just been blown out of a super-heady relationship. You put in all the time and all the investment and the Tripartite screwed you over. Not cool. You played by the rules, you did what you were told, and what did it get you? So forget about all that. Forget about them. Forget about your sister and the tribe and everybody. Screw all of them. Do what you want to do, whatever it is. And if you want to do it with me . . . all the better."

"So you're the man of the moment, is that it?"

He prodded her arm with his finger. "That is exactly it. Live in the moment. Live for this moment. Forget the past. Don't worry about the future. Just be here now. And relax." He grabbed her shoulder and shook her playfully. "You're so damned tense all the time."

When he stopped, his hand slid down from her shoulder to her lower back and stayed. It felt good.

"I don't know," she said.

"Don't know what?"

"Anything. Everything I thought I knew turned out to be a lie."

"Maybe not everything," he said. "But so what if it was? Like I said, screw them. Now are you coming to the center with me or not?"

"Right now?"

"Yeah, right now. This very moment. Stand up." He took her arm and pulled her to feet. "Here we go."

"I should tell someone . . ."

"Tell who? I just saw your sister leaving with Prince Chode, and I know your dad's not home."

She stopped, planting her feet. "Tessa left?"

"Yeah, and she didn't bother to tell you, did she? So screw her. Let's go."

"She can't just—"

"Don't worry about her. Judah's as tight over the rules as the Tripartite. He won't let her go anywhere without every tribal member's stamp of approval. He probably took her straight to the center. Do not stop. Do not pass go. Do not collect two hundred dollars. Dude needs to relax almost as much as you. You can yell at Tessa when we get there. Or not. If she can't figure out how to protect herself, it's not your fault. She's the Triune now. Let her worry about protecting herself."

Maybe some of what he said spoke to her.

She smiled, bemused. "Can I grab my bag first?"

"If you have to."

She gazed at him. "Are you going to get me in trouble?"

He grinned. "Only if you let me."

CHAPTER 5

FEBRUARY 25TH

AS SOON AS THEY OPENED the door, the room went silent. Everyone stared at them.

As much as Josie had thought this would bother her, she found she was accustomed to the staring. People had always stared at her. The only thing that had changed was the reason. Before, they'd thought she was someone important. Now, they just thought she was a reject. A couple of the tween girls at the easels whispered and snickered, but the rest simply gaped.

Upstairs from the ceramic café, the art lab was large—white walls and concrete floors. Cabinets lined both sides. Tables clustered in the middle. Across the room, near the windows, sat easels and ceramic wheels. A dozen tribal kids were there, most of them under the age of fifteen. Core kids were generally homeschooled—in the countries where formal schooling was an option. In Portland's tribe, homeschooling meant studying with tribal elders.

"Hi, Baby Bear," Beech's mom, Gretchen, said from behind a stack of coils on one of the tables. She straightened up, her exposed arms defined and tattooed with Core designs. A wide smile spread over her lean square face. Her eyes were the same brilliant green as Beech's. "Josie,"—her grin was almost as crooked-mischievous as her son's—"about time. I've been hassling Beech to get you down here for weeks. I was beginning to think he'd lost all his charm."

"Charm? It was more like coercion," Josie said.

"You're uncharmable," he said.

"Too bad for you."

"Well, whatever works," Gretchen said with a wink. "I hear you whittle."

"It's just a hobby."

"Ever tried your hand at weaving?" Gretchen held up a coil of dark reed. "I'm just about to give a tutorial. Care to join us?"

"Sure, I guess."

"I've got to hook up with Ty at the café for a few minutes," Beech said. "He wants me to post flyers for his band. I'm supposed to pick them up."

Josie frowned at him. "You're leaving?"

Beech grinned and lowered his voice. "They're more afraid of you than you are of them." He caught her hand and gave it a tug. "I'll be back in a few."

Gretchen took Josie by the shoulders. "Why don't you sit with . . . Kai." She ushered Josie to a table in the back. Its occupant was a teen about Josie's age, whose bangs hung in dark chunks over one eye. His other eye, traced in black eyeliner, tracked Josie as Gretchen propelled her down into the chair next to him.

Josie searched her memory but couldn't pull up anything on the rail-thin kid with the dramatic cheek bones and long fingers—nails painted different colors. His vivid polychromatic fingertips struck her, reminding her of the colorful sheds at Brighton Beach, especially since the rest of his outfit was all one hue—black. His leg bounced at rapid fire.

Something about him was familiar. She was sure she'd met him before, but she'd met so many people over the years. A few of the other kids in the room were also familiar to her, but only in relation to their parents or grandparents who were elders or matriarchs. None of them said hello or greeted her.

Gretchen returned to the front of the room, clapping her hands to get everyone's attention. "Okay, my fledglings, weaving. By the end of the day, you'll love it as much as I do."

"Don't bet on it," Kai muttered, giving Josie a sideswiped half-grin.

"I heard that, Kai," Gretchen said. "And I'll take that bet."

Gretchen proceeded to walk them through the basics: soaking the reed until it was workable and stank like an old hippie resale shop, then dividing the reeds into spokes and weavers, punching holes in the spokes to create a base. Once Gretchen had helped them with the base and showed them how to work the pattern, Josie fell into the rhythm of weaving. Kai ignored her and that seemed about as good as it was going to get with him. Josie was fine with it.

After a time, Gretchen squatted next to the table. "Josie, that's beautiful. You're a real natural. Let me show you how to finish."

As Gretchen helped Josie complete the rim of the basket, Josie glanced up at the clock. She wondered what Beech had meant when he'd said he'd be back in a few. A few hours?

Then her basket was done.

"Nice work," Gretchen said, smiling widely and patting Josie on the shoulder. Josie smiled back. Another thing she hadn't done much of, but thanks to Beech, and now Gretchen, she was doing it more often too.

Gretchen left to check on another table.

"Since you're done with that one"—Kai pushed his splayed, hardly touched basket towards her—"why don't you finish mine too?"

He pulled his phone from his pocket and leaned back.

She put her own basket aside. Just then, a petite, pixie-faced girl with spiky, pink and purple hair opened the door. Her face fell. "I missed weaving?"

"Simone!" Gretchen held out her arms and swept the girl into a tight, rocking squeeze. "How was your mission?"

Simone mirrored Gretchen's wide smile. "Great."

"She's lying," Kai murmured. He shoved his phone back into his pocket and stood up.

Gretchen plucked Simone's chin. "Don't worry about it, kiddo." She gave Simone another hug and then let her go.

Simone toyed with the plastic bead bracelets around her wrists, looking crestfallen. Josie couldn't help but notice that Simone was the only other person in the room not wearing any rings. Even the younger kids wore them, which meant they'd been able to summon at least one god. Not that they had any masks in their stashes, but they still wore the rings as a marker of their accomplishment.

Simone saw Kai and brightened. They met halfway. Kai kissed her . . . really kissed her. Two of the younger basket weavers started gagging and turning red. One of the painters in the back called, "Get a condom!"

Even Josie looked away. She heard Kai say, "I missed you so much." It sounded like he really meant it.

Simone's face matched the pink parts of her hair by the time she'd come to Josie's table with Kai. Josie busied herself taking Kai's basket apart and starting another shape entirely.

"Hey," Simone said, hazel eyes big and shining. Her cheeks were lightly freckled and her nose upturned. She reminded Josie of a manga-pixie. "You're Josie Day."

"Guilty."

"I'm Simone."

Simone. Her name was familiar . . . Josie's heart sank.

"You're Judah's sister."

"Also guilty," Simone said, sitting down next to her.

"Foster sister," Kai corrected, pulling up another chair. "No blood relation."

"Judah is my brother," Simone said. "Blood or not."

Kai looked grim, but he didn't argue. Josie appreciated Simone's willingness to stick up for her brother, even if he was Judah. She wasn't sure her sister would've done the same for her and they were definitely blood-related.

Foster kids were common in the Corpora. Summoning the gods was dangerous under the best of circumstances. Having the power to control water, earth, air, and fire often led to the inability to control them, which also often led to dying. When kids found themselves without parents, sometimes they were sent to other tribes, especially if they were young. The tradition kept relations between the sister tribes strong and the bloodlines from getting too thin. People didn't have to marry within the Core, but it was encouraged, as introducing a civilian—terrae, as they were called—into the world of the Core was both a tedious and dangerous process. If the Covenant did not find a nominated terrae able or worthy, the nominee could be killed. Many tribe members chose to give up their attachment to the Core when they fell in love with terrae, rather than put their loved one through the rites of conversion.

"Judah is the best brother a girl could have," Simone said to Josie, since Kai clearly didn't look interested in the topic. He was staring up at the ceiling like he'd heard her say this many times before. "Really."

"Are you a foster kid too?" Josie asked Kai as a way of changing the subject.

His dark eye fixed on her. "Why do you think that?"

"I don't remember you," she said, ignoring his defensive tone.

"Yes, he is," Simone said, defusing the tension with a few simple words. "Did you make that?" She reached over and plucked the little basket from the corner of the table. "Cool."

"Keep it," Josie said.

"Thanks," Simone said with grin. She turned to Kai. "Where's yours?"

"Your new BFF is tearing it apart," he said.

"No, she's not," Simone said. "What are you doing to it?"

Josie looked down at the oblong, amorphous shape forming before her. "I don't know. Just messing around." Her gaze caught on the bracelets around Simone's wrists. The cheap rainbow-colored beads were carved with tiny symbols—some intricate and powerful. She leaned in closer. "Did you make these?"

Simone plucked at her bracelets. "Uh-huh."

"She's the best charm-maker in the tribe," Kai said.

"No, I'm not," Simone said. "I learned everything from my mom and brother. They're the best in the tribe." Simone fiddled with a bit of discarded reed, winding it through her fingers. "But they're powerful summoners too. Charms are the only thing I can do."

"Don't take it for granted. Skilled charm-makers are rarer by far than summoners," Josie said. "The power a charm can channel, without all the blowback and godly BS? That's worth something. I know tribes who would kill to have a talented young charm-maker like you. It's an underrated art and crucial to the safety and functioning of the Core as a whole. Our tribe is fortunate to have you. I hope they realize it."

Simone and Kai gazed at her. Simone looked like she was about to cry—happy tears. And Kai's dark eyes were less brittle-edged than they had been earlier.

"I realize it," Kai said, his sideswiped grin widening.

The room had gone quiet. Josie realized then that everyone had been eavesdropping on them. She hunched over the reeds. Her hands moved faster and faster, but her mind was elsewhere. She hadn't meant to make a speech. She'd only said what she knew to be true.

Simone beamed. "Well, I would be proud to be able to weave like you can. Look at this awesome basket."

Josie arched her eyebrow. Simone's smile was the kind that couldn't be refused. Josie smiled back.

"I'm looking forward to a long life full of basket weaving," Josie said.

The noise in the room seemed to be returning to its normal teenage levels.

"Are you insulting the basket?" Simone cradled the basket to her chest and rocked it like a child. "It's okay. She didn't mean it."

She stroked the glossy reeds. "I'm going to call him Henry." She set the basket neatly on the table in front of her. "Maybe he'll grow up to be a plant holder. A mother can hope."

Josie snorted. "You're weird."

Simone sagged a bit. "I know."

"I like it."

Simone's face brightened again.

At that moment, Beech returned, loping into the room.

"Look at you." He sat on the edge of Josie's table. "Making friends."

"And baskets," Simone said, displaying the basket on her palms.

"Nice."

Josie picked up the utility knife and cut into the reeds she had woven.

"Where have you been?" Beech asked Simone.

"Mission," Simone said. "Up at Crater Lake. Three weeks."

"Any luck?"

Simone shook her head. "I prayed, I fasted, I burnt offerings. I tried about a dozen masks. Nothing."

"Maybe you should've killed a couple a tourists, spilled a little blood," Beech said with a wicked grin. "That always brings the gods out."

Simone's mouth fell open. "You shouldn't talk like that..." Manga eyes flicked in Josie's direction.

"Josie doesn't care, do you?" he said. "She's not the deputy anymore. She's turned outlaw."

Josie didn't like to hear anyone talk about bloodspilling, jokingly or otherwise. But she didn't have to be so duty-bound that she couldn't let a casual remark pass.

"Even if you don't summon a god, it doesn't matter because as a charm-maker, you're more valuable than half the summoners out there. But I'm sure you'll summon a god sooner or later, most charm-makers can," Josie said to Simone. "You just have to find the right one."

"How about this one?" Beech said.

Josie frowned up at him. "What do you mean?"

Beech gestured to the mask in front of her, the one she'd been weaving without realizing. She stared down at the face staring back up at her.

"Too bad you can't make a mask for real," Kai muttered, not looking up from his phone.

"Yeah, you could make me the face of a god who would actually show up when I call," Simone said, dropping her chin to her hand. "When was the last time the actual face of a god was made material?"

"Before the last demigod died." Josie studied the mask in front of her. Something was missing. "A thousand years. Maybe longer."

"It's crazy to think that all the masks we have are a thousand years old," Simone said.

"And the ones we have aren't even the really ancient masks," Kai said. "You should hear my 'brother' wax poetic about the tribe's archived masks, all smashed to smithereens, abandoned and unappreciated, except by him, their sole curator and guardian. Guy really needs to cultivate a hobby." Kai made a jerking-off gesture with his hand.

Crude as it was, Josie couldn't help but grin a little. She straightened her face. "Most of the ancient masks were destroyed for a reason," she said, thinking of Earth Mama.

Earth Mama's mask must've been very old, possibly ancient—from one of the early eras of the Core, before it had even been called such, possibly from the Age of Manifestation even, which could make it almost two thousand years old. The older it was, the more inherent power the god possessed. Blood sacrifice couldn't make a god more powerful, only bring forth more of a god's power to the mortal plane. And Earth Mama had a lot of power. Thinking about Earth Mama caused a swell of fury to pass through Josie that was so strong her vision warped.

On the table, the dark strands making up the mask seemed to slither. The gaping mouth appeared to smile.

"And the rest of the ancient masks are locked away from all you mischievous little bunnies," Beech said. "You might have too much fun with them."

"Do you have any masks, Beech?" Kai asked.

"Do you?" Beech asked.

Only the Eye and the matriarchs knew who possessed masks in the tribe. Each tribe only had so many available. A great deal of training and trust was required for a person to earn full possession of a mask, even if that person was the only one who was able to use it. Gods could be picky that way. They chose who they liked and didn't like. A mask that worked perfectly well for one summoner might not work at all for another. Other times, a summoner might've been in possession of a god but not fully capable of using the god's power. Mom had called those situations "bad fits." Like gods were shoes.

"Yeah, I have loads of the masks," Kai said with that same half-smile that Josie was starting to find sort of endearing. "You know—one for sunny days, one for rainy days . . ."

An image flashed in Josie's mind. A symbol—like a broad tree, branches dripping with water, surrounded by a circle. A Core symbol. Without thinking, she carved it into the forehead of the mask.

The symbol glowed and then vanished. She blinked. What the—

"Me too," Beech was saying to Kai. "In fact I've got my own personal mask-maker right here." He picked up the mask before Josie could stop him and brought it to his face. "How does it fit?"

The reeds came alive, wriggling like snakes. They shot out from the mask and mummified Beech. Thunder rolled. Oxygen filled the air—greener even than the air of a Portland.

A second was all it took for Beech take possession of the god.

Josie stared, stupefied.

Simone and Kai jumped out of their seats, scrambling away.

Someone screamed. Chairs clattered as they fell. People were shouting.

The god, a rainforest god, Josie knew without knowing how she knew, smiled down at her. Its voice was like a massive tree groaning in the wind.

"He's a bit loose," the god said.

Beech's tattooed hands appeared through the tangled guise of green-black vines. His fingers stuck under the edge of the mask, straining. The mask came free, flying through the air, hitting the cabinets, and falling at Kai and Simone's feet. Simone squealed and cowered against Kai. Beech fell back, landing on his butt. Josie jumped up, leaning over the table.

"Are you okay?" she asked.

He stared up at her, wide-eyed.

Gretchen ran over to him. "What was that? What happened?"

Everyone else had retreated to the corners of the room.

Kai reached down and picked up the mask. Simone grabbed his T-shirt, like the mask might hurt him. He gazed down at the mask and then up at Josie.

His sideswiped smile returned. "I think I'm starting to love weaving."

CHAPTER 6

FEBRUARY 25TH

THE EYE SAT AT THE front of the sanctum.

Over the years, Josie had seen sanctums of every variety: incense and charm-filled, dark and mysterious; vast and august, marble pillars and sun-filled windows; primitive and simple, a cave or a hut or just a spot under a sacred tree.

In Portland, the sanctum had a classroom feel, plastic chairs and folding tables, except the latte-hued walls were painted with white symbols, protective circles and ritual praises. Crystals and stones hung in the windows, charms of various types. The Eye, fully assembled, looked like PTA members.

Caroline, the Present Eye, sat in the middle. She was a golden-haired beauty like her son, with the same cleft in her chin and blue eyes. But her eyes were alive, dancing and flickering, warm, unlike Judah's cool and critical ones. At the moment though, Caroline's were darkened by concern. Nancy, to her right, was stern as steel.

Lily looked paler than ever, her hair even more garishly red against her pasty complexion.

The rest of the witnesses, kids who had seen Beech go into possession of the god, had already given their testimony and been excused. Gretchen, Beech, Kai, and Simone remained, clustered to Josie's right, near the wall. Her dad stood behind her. To her left was Tessa. Judah was posed behind Tessa in bodyguard fashion. A handful of matriarchs sat in the chairs, most of them white-haired and skeptical-eyed.

"I think," Caroline said after she, Lily, and Nancy had conferred quietly, "we would like to see it for ourselves."

"You want me to make another, Honorable Mother?" Josie asked.

A pregnant silence filled the air.

Caroline leaned towards her, eyes alight. "Do you think you could do that?"

Josie pursed her lips. Not sure how to answer.

"Of course she can't." Nancy leaned back in her chair, speaking for all the skeptics in the room. "It's not possible."

A murmur of assent issued from the matriarchs behind Josie. Frankly, Josie was inclined to agree with them.

"Why don't we start with this one?" Caroline touched the rainforest god's face lightly. "I think we can all agree that she did make this one, can't we?" she asked Nancy.

"It's a stunt," Nancy said. "It's well-known that the Triune possesses countless confiscated masks. The girl must have stolen it and brought it with her."

"That's not true," Josie blurted out. Hastily, she added, "Forgive my interruption, Venerable Eye."

Nancy's nostrils flared. Her eyes forgave nothing. "No doubt the girl wants attention. Being out of the spotlight must be a difficult adjustment to make for a young lady."

Josie ground her teeth but held her tongue. She looked at her sister. Tessa twisted her hair around her fingers, looking uncertain. That figured.

"Please, Honorable Sisters, may I speak?" Gretchen said. "We saw Josie make that mask, and we saw Beech go into possession of the god."

"You didn't say you saw her produce the mask," Nancy corrected.

"That's true, but—"

"Righteous Mothers, pardon me, but we saw her," Simone spoke up. "She did make it." She gave Kai a punch on the arm. "Right?"

"What does it matter? They don't believe us," Kai muttered, not looking up from his phone. "We already told them. Why would they believe a couple of foster kids?"

The matriarchs grumbled.

Nancy's hands flattened on the table. "Watch yourself, young man."

"Serene Mothers,"—Beech stepped forward—"if I may, I saw it too. Josie didn't pull that mask from some secret stash or smuggle it into the room. When I came in, it was just a bunch of reeds on the table. I saw her weave it. She made it. She made the face of a god."

Maybe Kai had been right about foster kids, because Beech's testimony seemed to hold more sway than either his or Simone's— among the matriarchs anyway. Nancy still didn't look convinced.

"First," Caroline said, lifting the mask with her fingertips, "let's see if it works." She held it out to Lily. "You're tied most strongly to the earth, Sister. If this is a tree god—"

"Rainforest, Mother," Josie murmured, though her voice carried anyway.

"One word out of turn, young woman, just one." Nancy lifted her finger at Josie. "You have earned nothing in this tribe. You will remain silent before the Eye, and once this ruse of yours is proven, you will be punished accordingly."

Josie's hands clenched at her sides.

Lily gave Josie a sympathetic look as she took the mask. Tentatively, she brought it to her soft, round face.

Nothing happened.

Nancy let out a soft *um-hmm*.

But then, slowly, the reeds flexed, like they were stretching. Again, thunder purred. A soft rustle, like the whish of rain, breezed through the room. Lily clearly had more control than Beech. Though the appearance of the god's guise was just as quick as Beech's, it wasn't as dramatic. The writhing reeds that surrounded her were more subdued, less like snakes and more like vines gently swaying.

Lily stood up from her seat. In the god's guise, she appeared thicker and taller.

"We are in possession," Lily said in her nasal squeak and the god's groaning voice.

"We can see that," Nancy said. "And what do you say, God of the Trees?"

The god's face turned towards Nancy. Its eyes were vibrant jungle green, pulsing faintly. A grumbled response issued from the god.

Josie let out a short laugh.

Everyone frowned at her.

"You heard him?" Lily asked.

"Yes . . ." Josie looked around.

Apparently, no one else had heard the god's reply to Nancy's question.

"What did he say?" Lily asked.

"Oh, tell them," the god groaned again. The reeds of his guise twisted into a grin.

Josie hesitated, but then met Nancy's fierce, doubt-filled gaze.

"He said, as a tree god, he could help you get that stick out of your ass—"

Simone, Kai, and Beech laughed. Gretchen tried to hide her grin behind her fist. The matriarchs grumbled.

Nancy shot up. "That's it—"

"No, Sister," Lily cut in. "That *is* what the god said." She reached up and removed the mask. The vines blew away, vanishing like smoke. She laid the mask on the table and then sagged into her seat, looking even more exhausted than before, but her gaze was fixed on Josie, bright and probing.

Nancy's face remained implacable. She turned to Josie's allies, who were still chuckling. "We've heard your testimony. You may leave. Now."

Gretchen tugged on the sleeve of Beech's hoodie and led them out. She gave Josie a wink as she passed. Simone and Kai followed. Simone mouthed the words, *It's okay.* Kai flashed his half-smile. Beech clasped her wrist briefly, running his thumb over her skin. Then they were gone.

Josie had thought she'd felt alone before, but she'd been wrong. Now she felt alone, even with her dad and sister in the room.

Nancy turned towards Lily. "Were you able to learn the truth from the god concerning the origin of its mask?"

Lily stopped scrutinizing Josie to look at Nancy. "No. He was unwilling to share that with me."

Thanks a lot, Josie thought. Gods could be such jerks.

"May I say something?" Tessa asked, looking more like an uncomfortable fifteen-year-old than the leader of the Core.

Nancy frowned.

"Of course, Divine Mother," Caroline said, smiling. "Please."

"Why don't we just have Josie make another one?" Tessa asked.

Caroline nodded. "I was just about to suggest the same thing." She turned to Nancy. "Sister?"

Nancy didn't reply. A web of pucker lines creased her face.

Josie rubbed her thumb against her forefinger, her pulse skipping beats. She didn't know how she'd made the first one. She wasn't sure if she could do it again. Or even how to start.

Lily was already nodding her head before anyone asked. "I agree."

The matriarchs murmured their general assent.

Caroline turned to Josie. "What do you need?"

Good question.

"Ridiculous," Nancy said. "We've been here for two hours. How much longer are we going to allow this farce to continue?"

Caroline set her coffee mug on the table. "Josie?"

Various crafting supplies were spread before her: clay, branches, leaves, stones, more reeds. Josie hadn't touched them.

She glanced over at Tessa, who was immersed in her phone. Judah was sprawled in a chair beside Tessa, staring at Josie with a smug look that said, *I knew you were lying.* Josie's hand closed around a smooth river stone. It wouldn't kill him, just bloody his pretty face a little. Maybe break his perfect nose.

She released the stone. Better not. She was already in enough trouble.

She looked at Caroline, no one else. "I can't, Honorable Mother."

"Of course you can't," Nancy said. "Now, if you admit the truth and apologize, perhaps we will be lenient."

Josie's hand closed around the stone again. "I wasn't lying, Venerable Eye."

"Then prove it," Nancy said.

"I can't," Josie said. "It doesn't work like that . . ."

In fact, she had no idea how it worked or why it had worked in the first place. Maybe it had been a fluke.

She couldn't deny she'd made a mask. She'd been there. She'd seen it. She *had* brought forth the face of a god, but how and why and if she could again, she had no idea. There were no mask-makers. They were ancient history. If she'd been in Nancy's position, she would've been just as skeptical, although she hoped not as viciously so.

"Because it doesn't work at all," Nancy stated.

No throwing rocks at the Future Eye, Josie reminded herself. That was definitely against the rules, no matter how much she's asking for it.

"Maybe we should take a break. Try again tomorrow?" Lily asked softly.

"And waste another day? Not all of us spend our days idle in the garden and escorting the youth on nature hikes, Lilith. Some of us have lives to lead." Nancy stood up. "I'm not going to sit through any more of this girl's performances. Once you are ready to deal with her properly, I will happily return. For the moment, Sisters, you'll have to excuse me."

"Nan—" Lily called as Nancy grabbed her purse and coat and stormed out of the room, leaving a trail of frost and orchid-scented perfume.

"We'll try again," Caroline said to Josie kindly. "Not tomorrow though, I have to go to Eugene for a conference," she said to Lily. "I'll be back Monday."

Lily nodded, looking wistfully at Josie, like she was secretly wishing Josie had been able to produce another mask. She wasn't alone. Josie wished she could too. She wished she knew how she'd done it in the first place.

"Monday then."

Great. Now the tribe had all weekend to hear about how she was not only a reject but a liar and drama queen too. She was sure that was what Nancy and the matriarchs and Judah would be telling everyone.

Metal chair legs scraped across the floor as the room cleared out. Josie continued to sit, staring at the supplies arrayed before her. How had she made the mask? She hadn't been thinking about it. She'd just done it. It was as if the god had been inside the reeds, waiting to be found. She hadn't so much made his face as discovered it, like some forgotten relic buried in the thick grass.

Her dad put his hand on her shoulder.

"Let's go, honey," he said.

"You believe me, don't you, Dad?"

He gave her a weak smile, but didn't answer.

Even her father thought she was a liar.

CHAPTER 7

MARCH 3RD
A WEEK LATER

"**Y**OU'RE NOT WEARING THAT, are you?" Tessa's nose crinkled when Josie came into the kitchen Sunday morning.

Josie looked down at the skintight shirt and painted-on jeans. "If you don't like the outfit, don't blame me, it used to be yours."

"It looked better on me," Tessa said.

"No argument here," Josie muttered.

She shuffled around Tessa to the coffee pot. She frowned at Judah, who was sipping coffee at the corner table. "Don't you have a home?"

"We need to go shopping," Tessa said to her.

"I already ordered new clothes online."

"Without me? Well, next chance we get, we're going anyway. But today, we're going to the beach."

Josie almost dropped the coffee pot. Steaming black liquid slopped onto the counter. "What?"

"I told you yesterday. Dad said it was okay, but only if you came with us. And the Eye agreed. Caroline gave me this" —she lifted the giant crystal hanging on her necklace, like Josie couldn't see it. The stone was the size of a golf ball—"for extra protection."

Josie shook her head as she sopped up the spill. "I don't believe this."

"Why not?" Judah said. "It's not the most unbelievable thing that's happened around here lately."

She spun on him. "Just say it. I know you've been dying to."

He set his cup down. "Say what?"

She turned away from him, burning all over. "I know what you're thinking." She shot Tessa a dark look. "Both of you. You think I tricked everyone at the art lab. You don't think I made that mask. Admit it."

Tessa twined her hair around her finger. "I don't know what to think, Josie."

Josie wrung out the dish rag, wishing she could wring her sister's neck. "Why don't you ask the Tripartite? See what they have to say about it."

Tessa's pink cheeks paled. "I'm not asking them about that."

"Why not? You have been talking to them, haven't you?"

Tessa's bagel popped out of the toaster. As she reached for it, a small roll of paper appeared in her hand. Anyone in the Core could send the Triune a message if the proper rituals were followed. Tessa could send a message back too, if she wanted. The godly form of texting.

Tessa scowled at the slender scroll and then shoved it into her back pocket. Josie gripped the edge of the counter.

"You should read that. It could be important."

Tessa's delicate chin firmed. "I'm not reading anything today." She snagged the bagel from the toaster.

"Tessa—"

"Oh, leave me alone! Can't we just have one day that doesn't involve the gods?" She smeared cream cheese across her bagel in sharp swipes.

"No," Josie said. "You can't. You're the Triune, Tessa—"

"I know that! Better than you—"

"Do you? Then act like it."

"Act like what? You? Mom? No, thanks."

"I'm sick of hearing you bad mouth Mom. She did the best she could—"

"Then her best was shit." Tessa tossed the knife into the sink. Steel clattered against steel. "Look what she did to you."

"What the hell does that—?"

"You're a bitch, Josie. A cold bitch, just like her. And you know what I think? I think you made up the whole mask thing. I think you used a charm on everybody or got them to lie for you somehow. I think you brought that mask from the island and only pretended to make it."

Josie dumped her coffee into the sink. Apparently, her sister knew how to circumvent all her emotional controls because Josie's anger was spilling over, unchecked.

"Think what you want," she said, "but I'm not a liar and I'd rather be like Mom than a shallow, vain, blubbering uber-brat like you. I know why you're not talking to the Tripartite. You're weak. And you're scared. And you ought to be. You think they're going to let you ignore them forever? You thought it was bad before? Just wait. Only the next time, when your frontal lobe is leaking out of your nose, I'm not going to be there to save you, because that's just the kind of cold bitch I am."

"What is going on here?" Dad said from the threshold of the hall.

Josie tore away from the glaring contest with Tessa. Judah continued to lounge in the corner, watching coolly. Another flare of anger shot through her. She was more than sure he was the reason Tessa doubted her. Tessa had always been a follower. She listened to whatever her friends told her.

Josie held down her hurt. Bad enough that Nancy had half the tribe thinking she was a liar, but that Tessa believed it . . . Josie didn't even know how to deal with that. She'd never been accused of lying before. Her mom hadn't prepared her to be doubted or disbelieved. The Triune's word was law. She was the Voice of the Supreme Divine. To doubt the Triune was to doubt the gods. Core couldn't doubt the gods. But of course, Josie wasn't the Triune.

Josie took a deep breath.

"Nothing's going on, Dad," she said. "I was just telling Tessa that I'm not going to the beach."

Her dad yanked down the hem of his sweater. "Well, if you're not going, then neither is Tessa."

"Dad!" Tessa spun around. "That's not fair!"

He reached around Josie to the coffee pot. "I'm a dad. It's my job to be unfair." He poured himself a mug of coffee. "If you want to go the beach, Josie has to go with you. It's time the two of you learned how to act like sisters." He tucked some of Josie's unruly hair behind her ear. "You only have one."

He headed towards the living room, pulling his phone from his pocket.

"Dad!" Tessa called after him.

"Figure it out, Tessa." Then he was gone into the living room.

Tessa's glare trembled with tears. Her voice was a growl. "You ruin everything."

She stormed out of the kitchen, into the hall, stomping up the stairs.

Judah's calm voice was chili powder on Josie's raw nerves. "This is important to her, you know."

She turned to him. He sat, posed on the stool with one knee bent, looking model perfect and useless as always. No wonder she hadn't been able to keep her cool with Tessa; she was expending all her energy crushing her every thought that related to Judah—just for Tessa's sake. If only Tessa knew how difficult that was for Josie, she might not be so quick to accuse her of being a cold bitch.

"You want to help my sister?" she asked.

His eyes narrowed. "Stop doing that."

"Doing what?"

"Turning it around on me. You can't push me around. Stop trying. You're wasting your time."

"I'm not trying to push you around. I'm trying to push you out. You're a distraction. You're not helping my sister become who she needs to be to survive."

"You think it's my fault your sister doesn't listen to you? Maybe you should try listening to her first. You still act like you're the Triune. You storm in and boss everybody around. You expect them to do what you say. But they won't, because you're not." He stood up, coffee mug in hand. "If you want people to listen to you, you should try being nicer."

"Good idea," she said. "Would you *please* go to hell?"

He shook his head. "I told you. It's not going to work. You can't push me out, around, or at all. I'm not helping your sister? What about you? Can you honestly say that you're helping her right now? Or do you have as much trouble with honesty as you do with simple courtesy?" His eyebrow lofted at her, provocative, as he left the kitchen and followed Tessa up the stairs.

Josie sat on the floor in her room, stabbing a block of white pine with her pocket knife, when someone knocked on the patio door.

She stood and opened the door, still holding the knife.

Beech held up his hands. "Whoa, don't hurt me. I'm unarmed."

"I'm not in a very good mood right now," she said.

"So I hear," he said.

She frowned. "From whom?"

"Chode. He came over and invited me to the beach. I thought it was a bit forward of him myself. I know I said I was an open guy, but he's not really my type."

Josie left the door ajar and sat down on the floor again, driving the knife into the wood so it stuck. "Judah invited you to the beach?"

Beech came in, looking around. "Yeah, I think he thought it would get you to go."

Josie hugged her knees to her chest, frowning. No matter which way she looked at it—searching for something to be annoyed with—she kept coming back to the thought that it was, actually, pretty smart. And almost nice. Not words that she'd been associating with Judah.

"Is it going to work?" Beech asked.

"Are you going?"

Beech grinned. "I love the beach. How could I not? It's my namesake. It's who I am."

"Even if you have to go with Judah and my sister?"

"Ah,"—he held up his finger—"don't forget the most important person, you. And I think he invited Simone and Kai, so he must be in a really good mood, or he's just desperate to get laid."

Simone and Kai? This was almost starting to sound like fun. Now she was suspicious again. Tessa wasn't friends with Simone and Kai, was she? Had Judah invited them just for Josie's sake?

She pushed up from the floor and went to the dresser, rifling through the clothes to find something warmer.

Tessa had given Josie bags of clothes that had been destined for the consignment shop. Some of them fit. Most of the jeans had to be fastened with rubber bands. She couldn't wait for her new clothes to arrive.

As she searched, Beech's offhanded remark about Judah wanting to get laid itched at her.

"Do you think they're sleeping together?" she asked.

He leaned against the wall beside her dresser. "You're her sister. Don't you know?"

"We're not those kind of sisters." She took off the tank top and tossed it at him.

Tessa's hand-me-down bras were much too small, practically nonexistent on Josie, but she wasn't bashful, even in front of Beech. In some tribes, people wore little to nothing. Her mom had instituted no-clothes days on the island just so she'd get used to walking around naked.

Beech's grin widened. "Wow, I didn't know we'd progressed to this stage already."

"We haven't progressed anywhere," she said coolly. "Haven't you seen a girl in a bra before?" She tugged on a long-sleeved shirt and then a tunic over that.

"Not this girl."

"Careful, you might make me feel special," she said, pulling on a pair of warm socks and some boots. She'd been informed that she couldn't live in Oregon without a decent pair of boots.

He sat down next to her on the bed. "You are special, Josie, and not just because you can make masks. Which reminds me—"

He caught her chin and kissed her cheek. A flood of warm needles washed through her.

"Thanks," he said. "Being in possession of that god was like . . . unreal. It's one of the best things I've ever experienced."

He grinned and took her hand, pulling her to her feet. "Let's get out of here."

CHAPTER 8

MARCH 3RD

"SORRY KAI COULDN'T MAKE IT," Josie said to Simone as they walked along the beach, picking up trash.

"He's not a big fan..."—Simone's gaze flicked down the beach towards Judah and Tessa, who were walking ahead of them, hand-in-hand—"of the beach."

Josie smiled, stopping to pick up a tiny plastic airplane. "I'm glad you came anyway." She held the toy airplane out to Simone, who was carrying the recyclables bag. Simone held open the bag, and Josie dropped the toy in.

Simone glanced behind them. Beech was dragging a stick through the sand. The end caught clods of brown seaweed and gelatinous bits of gods-knew-what. "Are you sure I'm not a fifth wheel?"

Josie wiped her cold fingers on her jeans and pushed her hands into the pockets of her hoodie. She should've worn another layer. The wind off the gray water was frost-fingered. Underfoot, the damp sand was hard as concrete, making prying half-buried cans and plastic bottles difficult.

"Beech is . . ."

"Beech?" Simone laughed, her faux fur-lined hood curled against her cheek. "He's not exactly boyfriend material."

"He told me as much," Josie said. "But I'm okay with that. I'm not exactly girlfriend material either."

"Why do you say that?" Simone asked as she scooped up another plastic water bottle.

Josie's gaze flicked to Tessa and Judah. Their long legs were propelling them farther away. Not that Josie was interested in keeping them company. She was more than happy to spend her day cleaning up the beach with Simone. "Apparently, I'm a cold bitch."

Simone stopped, her mouth gaping. "Who told you that?"

"My sister and her boyfriend."

Simone's brow fell. For her, it must have been a pretty menacing expression, but to Josie it looked more cute than threatening.

"Judah said that to you? I will kick his butt."

Josie laughed at the image of tiny Simone trying to kick Judah's butt. "Can you even get your leg up that high?"

"I'm a black belt in tae kwon do." She kicked her leg up into the air to demonstrate. Josie was impressed.

"I appreciate the thought," Josie said, "but don't bother. They might be right."

"Don't say that." Simone hooked her arm through Josie's and tugged her closer. Simone had a powdery clean smell that made it easy to be close to her. Her ever-sympathetic nature didn't hurt either. "I'm going to give him a talking to, you watch. He won't be calling people naughty names after I'm through with him."

"Tessa was the one who said it," Josie said. "Judah only... seemed to be in tacit agreement. Not that I care what either of them think."

"Darn tootin' you don't."

Josie smiled a little and let the ocean air fill her lungs. The sky was as gray as the water, the sun a distant white orb beyond the veil of clouds.

"I never got to say it," Simone said, still holding onto Josie's arm, "and I know it doesn't mean much, but I'm sorry about your mom."

Josie's gaze tracked over to the grassy berm. It reminded her of the island. Grayish grass, gray sand, gray sky. Her heart throbbed and sank deeper. She let it go. "Thanks." She eyed her new pink-and-purple-haired friend with the manga eyes and pixie face. "You lost your parents too."

"My biological ones, yeah, but I was a baby. I don't remember them," Simone said. They stopped again to pry a crusty shoe out of the sand. "But I remember my dad a little bit, I mean, my foster dad, Judah's dad. Judah is just like him."

Josie held out her garbage bag and Simone tossed the old sneaker in, wrinkling her nose.

"He was a firefighter, right?" Josie asked.

Simone nodded. "He was trying to rescue a little kid from a fire. They both died."

They walked in silence for a minute. The ocean murmured and sighed as it rolled in. The chill wind worked its way into the gaps of Josie's coat, up her sleeves, down her neck, making her shiver.

"I know it doesn't mean much," Josie said, "but I'm sorry too."

Simone smiled. Josie had quickly determined that this was what friendship was, someone whose smile made you smile reflexively without having to stop and think about why they might be smiling, what the smile might be hiding, or what they might really be thinking.

"Do you stay in touch with your natal tribe?" Josie asked. She bent to scoop up tiny bits of plastic that seemed as numerous as the sea shells and the gulls. "Which is it?"

"Southern Atlantic tribe. Their center is in Savannah. Do you know them?"

"I've been there." Their Present Eye reminded Josie of Nancy, only golden instead of steel, and with all that Southern charm to hide her intractable nature.

"I have a great aunt I talk to sometimes," Simone said. "She sends birthday cards and stuff, but my parents died when I was a baby and she's older and couldn't take care of me. I'm glad she sent me here. My mom and Judah... I wouldn't trade them for anything."

Josie kept her less than flattering thoughts about Judah to herself. Apparently, he was nicer to his sister than he was to Josie. "Kai doesn't seem so happy."

Josie dumped the plastic bits into the garbage bag. They started walking again.

"He gets along with his parents all right," Simone said. "It's his brother ... anyway, Kai was older when he came here, and he never really felt accepted, not like he tries very hard to be. He's always kept to himself."

"How did you two start dating?"

"Lily has this youth group. She takes kids out for hikes and teaches them about plants and trees and animals, gets them in touch with nature—"

"Kai was in a youth group?" Josie asked dubiously.

"I think his parents made him," Simone said with a smile. "Anyway, one time, Lily put us together. You know, because you always have to have a buddy when you're out in the woods. I finally got him to start talking and . . ." She shrugged, cheeks turning pink. She bumped her shoulder against Josie's. "So what about you and Beech?"

Josie glanced back where Beech was now picking up various things out of the sand and pitching them into the gray expanse of water.

"I thought we covered this," Josie said.

"We covered that Beech is Beech," Simone said. She kicked at a stubbornly buried tennis ball with her well-worn boot until it started to come loose. "But do you like him anyway?"

"I like him," Josie said noncommittally. She liked the warm sensation she had experienced when his lips had touched her skin. She liked the wild gleam in his eyes and the way he smelled, like pine and a warm, oft-worn T-shirt. She liked how differently he thought and how easy he was to be around.

Simone freed the tennis ball finally and tossed it into Josie's bag. "How much do you like him?"

"Like you said, he's not boyfriend material, and I'm not exactly looking for that right now. I'm not sure I'd know what to do with it if I found it."

"I'm not asking what you're looking for," Simone said, "I'm asking you what you feel."

"I feel as much as I want to feel," Josie replied, stopping to pick up a discarded beer bottle.

Simone laughed. "Feel as much as you want? What does that mean? You can't control how much you feel."

"You can if you really want to." Josie dumped the sludge inside the bottle onto the sand.

"You're not serious."

"A Triune can't afford superfluous or distracting emotions," Josie said, flinging out the last of the liquid. "Maintaining control over the Three Supreme Deities is taxing—emotionally, mentally, phsycially—not to mention dealing with the Eyes of every tribe in the Core. Duty over self. Emotions are liabilities that can and will be used against you if you're not able to keep them in their place. Rule your emotions or they'll rule you."

Josie's gaze cut up the beach towards Tessa, who was laughing and leaning comfortably against Judah's side. Tessa had zero control over her emotions as far as Josie could tell. Just another reason she was in danger of being overwhelmed by the Tripartite.

Simone was staring at her. "You're serious?"

Josie put the bottle into Simone's recyclables bag. "It's just part of being a Triune," she said.

"But you can't really control what you feel."

"Why not?"

"Because. You feel what you feel."

"You might feel something, but that doesn't mean you have to acknowledge it or allow that feeling to continue."

Simone crossed her arms. "So you're saying you don't have to feel anything you don't want to feel?"

"I'm saying there are ways to curtail distracting and potentially harmful emotions."

"How?"

"Practice. Training. Just like anything else."

Simone spun her bracelets, looking worried, like Josie had just said she had a chronic disease that could kill her at any moment. "So you're saying that if I trained enough I could stop myself from feeling . . . anything? Like I could just stop being in love with Kai?"

"Why would you want to do that?"

"I'm just using it as an example."

"I doubt you could do that at this point. You're already in love with him. You know it, he knows it, everybody knows it."

Hot pink splotches flared on Simone's cheeks. "Everybody?"

Josie grinned. She started walking again.

Simone fell into step next to her. "So you could stop yourself from having feelings for Beech, if you didn't want to have them?"

"If having feelings for Beech interfered with my responsibilities to the Core, I might try. That doesn't mean I'd be successful. "

She frowned at Judah's back. Every time he opened his mouth, Josie felt like she was losing her ability to control her emotions. The boy seemed built to make her angry. And she'd already blown up at Tessa earlier, which was not helpful to anyone. Her duty to Tessa, as the Triune, should've been enough to keep Josie's frustration in check, but Tessa was also her sister, and something about that relationship seemed to circumvent Josie's ability to keep her cool.

"Guess that sort of does make me a cold bitch," Josie said with a wry smile.

Simone bumped Josie's shoulder with her own. "No, it doesn't. It just makes you . . ."

"Weird?"

Simone smiled. "Join the club. I'm the president. You can be vice president."

"Look at this," Beech said, jogging up beside them. He caught Josie's hand and placed a smooth quarter-sized piece of translucent blue glass into her hand. "Sea-glass. Think you can make a mask from it? For me? Please?"

She ran her fingers over the satiny surface. "Even if I did, no one would believe it."

"We believe it," Simone said. "We saw it."

"You'll make it happen again," Beech said, giving her arm a squeeze. "So you don't perform on command. Neither can half the guys in the world." He grinned. "Do you realize what it means though, Josie? You're a freakin' mask-maker. That's . . . huge."

"He's right," Simone said.

For some reason, they were speaking in whispers, even though they were alone. Tessa and Judah were nearly out of sight. The rest of the beach was deserted. Judah's silver crossover gleamed, lonely, in the parking lot, which was already some distance behind them.

"I overheard Mom on the phone last night," Simone went on. "She wants to believe you, Josie. She was all excited, talking about the possibility of fixing some of the tribe's ancient masks, the ones in the archives. You should've heard her. She was giddy."

"It's nice to know she wants to believe me," Josie said, "but she doesn't. And I'm not sure I can make a mask again. I don't know how I made the first . . ."

Her words dried up in her throat. Behind Beech's shoulder, rolling over the grassy embankment, obscuring the parking lot and Judah's car, was a bank of fog.

Josie's heart stutter-stopped.

"What's wrong?" Simone asked.

"Josie?" Beech reached for her.

The fog swelled and grew, barreling towards them faster than a charging bull.

Fog God. He was back.

CHAPTER 9

MARCH 3RD

J OSIE SPUN, DROPPING HER GARBAGE BAG. "Tessa!"

Tessa and Judah turned.

"Watch out!" Beech shoved Josie, who toppled into Simone.

They both fell as a snickering TemperMental swooped down on them. The dark phantom sideswiped Beech as it flew past, spinning him and leaving a bleeding red gash on his cheek. Beech stumbled and staggered and was swallowed by the fog.

A second later, the miasma was on Josie and Simone too.

Josie pulled Simone back to her feet, barely able to see Simone's vivid hair through the opaque mass engulfing them. "We have to get to Tessa."

She dragged Simone behind her, running. She wasn't worried about Beech. He wasn't the one Earth Mama was after. The fog was already ahead of them, thick and blue-tinged. Josie couldn't even see her feet.

"Tessa!" she called.

She collided with Judah. Simone slammed into her back and the three of them nearly toppled.

"What's happening?" Tessa cried, voice pitched high in panic.

Josie disentangled from Judah and Simone but kept her hands on both of them, not wanting to lose them. Tessa clung to Judah's arm. They huddled in a tight knot. The fog seemed to want to fill the cracks between them.

Josie drew Simone right up against her, so they were almost nose-to-nose. "Draw a protection circle around Tessa. The strongest one you know." Simone nodded and knelt, finally dropping her plastic bag of recyclables.

Josie turned to Judah. "Do you have a mask?"

"Yeah, but—"

"Summon it!"

The fog began to clear, swirling back from them like the widening eye of a hurricane. She wasn't sure why until she heard the familiar snicker-whishes and looked up.

In the sky, a flock of TemperMentals gathered, ghostly streaks, like brownish-green phantom vultures. The clearing formed a bulls-eye. Tessa stood right at the center.

Josie tried to disengage Tessa from Judah, tugging him outside the circle. The circle would be stronger if it only had one person to protect. Simone hastily traced symbols in the sand with her fingers, grimacing—probably from the cold—but never stopping.

Tessa sobbed and clung to Judah's hand. "Stay with me!"

Josie searched the fog. The clearing around them continued to grow. The mist thinned. Where was the Fog God? Where was Earth Mama? She couldn't see either of them. Worse, she couldn't find

Beech. She let go of Judah and ran back in the direction she thought she had left him.

"Josie!" Tessa cried after her. "Where are you going?"

"To find Beech! Stay in the circle!"

Shrouded by the mist, a hulking figure appeared ahead of her. She slowed to a stop, heart thundering in her chest. Was it Fog God? If so, there was nothing she could do. She couldn't touch a summoner who was in possession unless she was also in possession or unless he touched her first. The thought of letting him escape again filled her with rage. She had to think of something.

"Josie!" Judah called in warning.

One of the TemperMentals had broken from the circling mass and was plunging towards her. The hulking, mystery figure sprang up, leaping impossibly high over her head, and slammed into the diving TemperMental. Not the Fog God after all, unless he'd decided to change sides.

She caught a glimpse of bark-skin and a head covered in green leaves as the god sailed above her. A tree god.

"Beech?" she called.

He and the TemperMental tumbled away, tangled, on the far side of Tessa. Tessa continued to cling to Judah, begging him to stay with her. Josie raced back towards them.

Judah pulled free of Tessa. His left hand flicked. A pale mask appeared in his fingers. Before he could bring the mask to his face, another TemperMental peeled out of the sky and knocked the mask from his hand. Two more came at Simone. She shrieked, punching and kicking as they swarmed her. Josie stopped at the edge of the protection circle. Tessa was hyperventilating.

"Tessa! Breathe! It'll be o—"

"Should I summon the Tripartite?"

"No!" Josie hands flew up to halt the idea. "It's too risky! Call—"

Judah dove at one of the TemperMentals tormenting Simone. The TemperMental spun on him and threw him into Josie. They sprawled.

Judah lifted his face. It was crusted with wet sand. The tide was coming in. The protection circle would be washed away. Tessa needed to move. Before Josie could call to her sister, another thought pushed into her head.

Judah reached for his face. She grabbed his wrist, stopping him from wiping his face clean. In the wet sand on his forehead, she drew a symbol: three wavy lines below a curl of a wave, contained in a circle, along with Core characters that she'd never seen before but somehow knew anyway. The symbol glowed gray for a moment and then vanished.

Judah's flame blue eyes disappeared under a flood of gray water. Josie hurried away, back towards Tessa. Beech, still in possession of his tree god, was far down the strand, surrounded by TemperMentals. The phantom battering Simone suddenly flew off. Josie grabbed Tessa and beckoned for Simone.

"The tide's coming!"

Tessa stared over Josie's shoulder. "What did you do to Judah?"

Josie glanced back.

Judah, in possession of an ocean god, had doubled in size, cocooned in a blue-gray cyclone of water. He summoned a geyser from the ocean. The jet of water soared upwards, splintering the throng of TemperMentals. Half of them turned and attacked him. The others descended towards Josie and Tessa.

"Hurry!" Josie yanked Tessa's arm. Simone had already run ahead, stopping near the berm and dropping to her knees to draw another circle. The remaining fog floated around them in heavy white drifts, but there was still no sign of Earth Mama or Fog God.

A few feet shy of the circle, Josie and Tessa were knocked flat.

Josie landed with a thud and a cringe, the wind thumped out of her. Before she could catch her breath, Tessa slipped away from her.

"Josie!" Tessa cried.

Josie groped for Tessa, thinking her sister was being dragged off. Except . . . Josie was the one moving. The TemperMentals were pulling her towards the ocean.

"Josie!" Tessa stumbled to her feet, chasing after Josie.

Josie clawed at the hard, cold sand. She kicked against the TemperMentals wrapped around her ankles. They held tight. Their grip chafed and burned, even through her jeans. Seriously material. Earth Mama had been sacrificing more than goats and cows.

More TemperMentals swarmed her, looping around her waist and jerking her up off the ground. She tore at them. Her fingernails were ripped as she clawed at their rough, flickering forms—like tearing at the bark of a tree, except nothing came away. Her struggles seemed futile. Why her? She wasn't the Triune. She wasn't anybody. She couldn't even summon a god. Was it a trick? A diversion?

She spotted Tessa again, racing after her, screaming her name. The TemperMentals weren't attacking her or Simone, who had stopped drawing her circle to join in the pursuit.

The TemperMentals yanked Josie five feet above the ground. She yelped as her head whiplashed. Then more appeared, winding around her chest. She thrashed as the ground grew more distant, but they only tightened their hold, writhing like snakes.

Below, Tessa jumped, swiping for her. "Josie!"

Josie managed to pull one of her arms free from the TemperMentals. She reached towards Tessa, straining. Their fingertips bumped. Josie was jolted upwards again. Ten feet, then more. Tessa vanished from view. Water unfurled beneath Josie—white edged, gray as slate.

"No!" Tessa's roar echoed across the beach.

A white light flashed, blinding Josie. Tessa had summoned the Tripartite. Josie didn't know if she should be relieved or scared to death. Tessa had never summoned the Tripartite. They could kill her. Josie twisted against the TemperMentals.

"Tessa!"

More TemperMentals joined the others, coiling around her face, blocking her vision, filling her ears with groaning whispers and dry snickers.

Mask-Maker. Mask-Maker.

She heard a crack, like a lightning strike. The rasping and rustling cradle of the TemperMentals broke open. A serene ceiling of sprawling clouds appeared above her.

And then she fell.

CHAPTER 10

MARCH 3RD

HITTING THE WAVES WAS LIKE plummeting onto a bed of swords. Swords of ice. They cut through her. She gasped, inhaling water. Everything vanished.

Darkness.

The next thing she heard was Simone calling her name.

Her eyes shot open as the water was sucked from her lungs, burning like lava. The air in her next breath felt even worse, too dry, inhaling sand. She retched, vomiting salt water and breakfast and bile after that.

A wavering gray-water face hovered over her. A hand appeared out of the water and tugged off the mask. The ocean god vanished.

Judah scooped her up.

He was warm, painfully. She wanted to push him away, but didn't have the strength.

Rain lashed her skin, stinging. Lightning zigzagged across the sky. The wind howled, tearing at her. She shivered, uncontrollably.

"Beech, help Tessa! Stop her!" Judah shouted over the tumult as he ran.

"How?" Beech's distant voice was mixed with the tree god's, which was deep and groaning.

"I don't—Knock her out!" Judah cried. "Simone, help me!"

His shouts hammered through Josie. At once grasping for and pushing against him, she sucked panicky breaths. His every step jarred her. Her body felt limp and clumsy, on the verge of coming apart, as if the ocean had torn her limb from limb and she'd been hastily stitched back together. Inside, it was worse—so much worse. Inside, she was porcelain, fissured by delicate cracks, so close to breaking apart. One wrong word, one wrong step, and she would shatter.

She couldn't stand it. Not the unresponsiveness of her body, not the fragility within. She didn't lose control like this—it just didn't happen. It couldn't. Not to her.

Judah stopped moving, thankfully. "Keys. Right pocket. Open the door," he ordered.

A high-pitched beeping made her wince. Judah put her down in the back of his crossover. She grabbed for him reflexively. The loss of his heat stole her breath. Her shaking fingers slid over his slick, wet jacket. He climbed in behind her, grasping her wrist in a way that promised he was there, he wasn't letting go.

"Start the engine. Crank the heat," he said to Simone, whose pink and purple hair was a tiny flicker of color in an otherwise bleak, drowning world.

Drowning. She had drowned. Just thinking the word brought it back—the engulfing darkness. The instant of panic before the impact. She struggled to breathe.

Judah shut the hatch behind him. He straddled her.

"We have to take off your clothes," he told her in a firm, but urgent tone.

Not waiting for a response, he yanked her soaked shirt off over her head, bra too. Her arms snapped over her chest. Her teeth chattered. The shaking wouldn't stop. The harder she tried, the worse it became. She ached deep down, like she would never be warm again.

Judah tore her jeans away, cursing when he had to twist around and pull her boots off. When he turned back towards her, he held a rolled fleece blanket in his hand.

Music filled the car as the engine purred to life. A female singer's soaring voice cut through the siren song of the ocean murmuring in her ears.

"Gods," she said in a shuddering voice that was barely hers, "I died."

Judah shook open the blanket, giving her a dark look.

"Tessa," she said, forcing herself to focus on something other than her own traitorous body, her own precarious emotions, the lingering sting of salt and bile on her every breath—the taste of death. "Tessa summoned the—where is she?"

She wanted to move, to sit upright, but she couldn't stop trembling. Gods, it hurt. And she was so cold.

He peeled off his jacket and wet shirt. He seemed so focused, so in control. She wanted to regain that feeling for herself, but it kept slipping away. She couldn't get a hold of it. She was out of step.

She couldn't tell if her quaking body wanted her to drop back and give up—sink into that place of silence and darkness. Or if it was trying to shake her out of her shock, like when she'd had one of her nightmares, usually about waking up and finding herself alone and trapped on the island with no escape. Her mom would shake her gently to wake her up.

It's not real, Josie. It's not real.

That's how this felt. Not real.

Outside, the world was hazy, distant—like that place between dreaming and wakefulness. Inside the car, Judah glowed. Wet hair like melting gold, blue eyes burning, skin sculpted bronze. Too vivid, surreal.

Her teeth clenched, her jaw ached. Black blotches ate away at the edges of her vision. Harbingers of unconsciousness . . . groping fingers of death.

"Gods, no." Her pleading thoughts snuck out of her head, through her too-tight lips. Little traitors. A Triune never let errant thoughts escape. She slammed her eyes shut. Her eyelids seemed to be the only part of her body under her command. She was in control. She would be in control.

A whimpering sound filled her ears. Had that been her?

Judah wrapped the blanket around her and pulled her onto his lap.

"No," she said, not sure what she was protesting. Being moved, which only drew attention to how much she was shaking, how much she hurt? Or his warmth, which only made her aware of how cold she was? Or his help? She didn't want his help. Where was Beech? Simone? Tessa?

"Move your arms," he said, forcing her hands away from her body.

Her arms moved stiffly, the muscles screamed as they were forced into action. He crushed her bare chest to his. Her breath shuddered as his heart slammed against her frozen skin, hot and fast.

Her frozen, rigid body huddled awkwardly against his warm, giving one, like a corpse laid out on sun-warmed sand. He kept adjusting, moving her, trying to hold her closer, make her fit.

Her fingers dug into his chest. Her lips skimmed his burning throat. "Stop . . . please."

He went still.

Her forehead pressed hard to his neck. She hated this . . . weakness, helplessness, neediness.

Slowly, very slowly, his heat slid under her skin. Teeth of fire gnawed into her body of ice.

The faintest traces of cologne lingered on him, a fresh, clean-sheets scent, but mostly, he smelt of sweat and a resinous heat that was distinctly male. It worked into her lungs, easing her breaths.

The tension began to release, the quaking ebbed. Her lungs sputtered and hitched, and then her breath fell into sync with his. Her heart took up the rhythm of his. She gave in to it, grateful that she was no longer cold, that the shivers were retreating.

For a few intertwined heartbeats, she forgot to hold herself back and to remain always in control. She forgot about her sister and her mother, about Earth Mama and Fog God. She forgot how awkward it was to be pressed naked to a guy who, moments before, she would've paid to disappear. She forgot everything. Their joined breath rocked her like waves, but this time the water was warm and safe. She was safe.

The door opened and shut. A cold gush of air made Josie flinch. She heard the rustling of plastic and clinking of glass.

"How is she?" Simone asked, breathless. "Gods, Josie, are you okay?"

Josie started to lift her head, but Judah held it firmly in place against his chest.

"There's another blanket under that seat. Give it to me," he said to Simone. His tone darkened, "You went back for the trash?"

Josie almost laughed.

"I couldn't just leave it there," Simone said, as if it made complete sense to go back for the bags of litter they'd collected. "I picked up your air god mask too," she said. "Here."

"Thanks," he said. "Hold onto it for me, will you?"

Judah's voice rumbled through Josie. She could feel it working deep down into her, flashing light across the cellar places. She retreated from it. She may have died, or almost died, but she couldn't let herself fall apart completely. Now that the shivering was subsiding, she was aching and weak, but she was starting to feel stronger again, more like herself.

He continued to hold her against him as he draped the second blanket over her bare legs. Her left ankle had begun to throb.

"Now do you believe me?" she asked into the hollow of his throat.

A hand touched her tangled wet hair. "He believes you," Simone said.

"She needs to go to the hospital," Judah stated, like Josie wasn't there or couldn't hear him.

"Tessa," Josie said.

Judah tensed around her—his chest, his arms. His pulse missed a beat, breaking their joined cadence.

"Wait," Simone said. "Oh gods—"

Another gust of chilly air made Josie clench and burrow closer to Judah.

"Is she okay?" Simone said.

This time, Judah let Josie lift her head and look over the seat. Simone was tugging Tessa into her lap, while Beech guided her legs in from outside. Tessa was soaked and limp and nearly as pale as the translucent ribbons of jellies that had been washed up all over the beach.

"Simone, check her pulse," Judah instructed. "Beech, get in and drive. We need to go to the hospital now."

"Check her pulse," Simone said as Beech closed the door. "Okay, how?"

Judah's voice was strained for the first time since the attack had begun. "Simone—"

"You're the one who's taken every Red Cross training course in the world, not me," Simone said.

"Just make sure her heart is still beating," Judah said, cool again. "Feel her neck."

Another surge of shivering overtook Josie as Simone's fingers prodded at Tessa's neck, searching.

Please, Josie prayed silently.

"I found it," Simone said, triumph in her voice.

Relief washed through Josie, but the shivering continued.

The car rocked as Beech opened the driver's door and jumped in. "I think I saw him," Beech said, ignoring the car's persistent bing-bing, reminding him to put on his seatbelt. He twisted in his seat as he backed the car out, meeting Josie's eyes. Water trickled down the taut, flat planes of his face. "That fog dude." His gaze dropped to Tessa. "How is she?"

"Her pulse seems steady," Simone said, one hand still on Tessa's neck and the other wrapped around her shoulders, holding her protectively. Josie loved Simone for that.

Beech turned away as he shifted the car into drive, but his eyes flicked into the rearview. "What about you, Josie-pie?"

Josie gazed at his reflection, but her throat was stuck, clenched.

"She's hypothermic." Judah closed his arms around her, bringing her head back to his chest. "Drive."

Judah held her steady as they bumped out of the parking lot and onto the road. Heat continued to pour into her. She clung to him, eyes closed, choking on the sob that was attempting to escape from her chest. But she wouldn't let it.

A Triune feels only what she wants to feel. Everything else is a distraction. Distractions can be deadly.

The echo of her mother's smoky voice only made the sob thrash wildly within her, like a caged animal desperate for freedom. She would not let it go. Even if she wasn't the Triune, she wouldn't forget. She would not be ruled by her emotions.

Judah's voice was soft, barely audible, far down in his chest. His breath was warm in her hair.

"I believe you."

CHAPTER 11

MARCH 3RD

"**I** DON'T BELIEVE THIS," Nancy said after listening to their stories.

"Nancy," Lily said. She sat in a chair near the door. She was pale and sweaty, looking like she might lose her granola. "Maybe this isn't the time to—"

"You drag me all the way here for this?" Nancy snapped at her. "I thought we'd settled this matter."

"I saw Josie make the mask," Tessa said from her wheelchair by Josie's hospital bed. "And we were attacked."

Somehow Tessa had convinced the nurses to wheel her over to Josie's room. As soon as Tessa had arrived, she'd taken hold of Josie's hand and wouldn't let go. Her grip was strong. That was good. When Tessa had regained consciousness in the emergency room, she'd puked twice and passed out again. Her skin had the same bluish hue as her thin cotton gown, but considering that she'd summoned and wielded the power of the Tripartite for the first time with almost no training, she was doing pretty well.

Tessa even managed to shoot Nancy a semi-threatening look. "Are you saying I'm lying too?"

Nancy's back straightened. "Of course not, but you are her sister—"

"She's also the Triune," Josie said, pausing deliberately before adding, "Serene Mother."

"What happened to the ocean god mask?" Beech asked.

Judah's jaw flexed. "I left it behind."

"Nice." Beech shook his head.

Judah's brow sharpened. "I was a little bit distracted."

Distracted . . . right. Saving Josie's life. Very distracting.

"I'm not listening to any more of this." Nancy held up her hands like she might cover her ears. She shot Lily and Caroline each a sharp look. "And if the two of you have any sense, you won't either."

She sidestepped away from Simone, who was busy drawing protective symbols around the door in invisible ink. Josie appreciated Simone's efforts, but the burn of citrus, one of the ingredients in the ink, was giving her a headache. Or it might've been the way Nancy's teeth clicked together every time she looked at Josie.

"Obviously, something happened, Nancy," Caroline said. "Look at them." She gestured to the small cuts and scrapes on Judah's face and arms, where the TemperMentals had touched him. "You think they did this to themselves just to perpetuate some silly prank for Josie?"

A shadow passed over Nancy's face and it seemed, for a brief moment, she might be wavering, but then her shoulders rolled back and her eyes hardened. "I think there are untold devices of power on the Triune's Island, any one of which this girl could have stolen and used to do any manner of things, including staging this entire . . . situation."

"That's the stupidest thing I've ever heard," Beech said, "Your Honorable Eyeness."

"Beech," Josie's dad said warningly. He looked about as exhausted as everyone else. He'd been in depositions all day—mind-numbing stuff. A glaze dulled his eyes.

Caroline lifted her finger at Beech. "Disrespect the Eye again and I will personally suspend all of your summoning privileges."

"I'll do worse than that," Nancy said. "This situation has become entirely out of control and considering the other, legitimate, concerns of the moment, you, Mother of Mothers"—she inclined her head curtly towards Tessa like someone had their boot on her neck, forcing her to do so—"should not be squandering your time with trips to the beach or with your sister's . . . stories. The Core needs its Triune now. With masks being stolen and—"

"Nancy," Lily cut in.

Josie sat up straighter, wincing as she accidently put pressure on her twisted ankle. "Masks were stolen?"

Nancy pursed her lips, scowling as if it were Josie's fault the info had slipped.

Nancy pushed open the door. "We may not be what we once were, Sisters, but this is not the way forward. That much I can tell you." Then she was gone.

"Nancy, wait." Lily pushed out of her chair with a groan. She spared Josie and Tessa an uncharacteristically hard look before she followed Nancy out the door.

Caroline's gaze swept around the room. From Tessa, sagging and bleary eyed in one corner, to Judah, rigid as a beefeater in the other. To him, she said, "How are you?"

"I'm fine."

"You were in possession of a serious deity, you were attacked, Josie almost died, and you're fine?"

Simone stopped drawing and turned to her mom. "You believe us?"

Caroline cupped Simone's face and then drew her into a hug. "Of course, I believe you, Simone, honey." She kissed Simone's forehead. "I'm just glad you all survived."

"Are we sure it's safe here?" Josie's dad asked. He lifted his head from where he'd been hunched over, rubbing his eyes. He tucked the curved stems of his glasses around the back of his ears. "Maybe I should take them home tonight." He slumped back. "Gods, what is happening?"

Caroline looked around the room again. "I'll make sure they'll be safe enough tonight, Marc. Why don't we have a word outside?"

Her dad nodded and stood, giving Josie's hand a squeeze before he left. "I'll be right back."

"Meet me outside in ten minutes," Caroline said to Judah. She gave Tessa and Josie a lingering look before leading their dad into the hall.

Judah closed the door behind them. "You know what this means? Don't you?"

"You owe Josie an apology?" Beech asked, sitting on the edge of the bed.

"I owe Josie an apology," Tessa said before Judah could respond. "I didn't believe you and I should have."

"I don't need anybody to apologize," Josie said, although, it was nice to hear it. She was just glad that Tessa knew that Earth Mama was a real threat. Now maybe they could actually do something about it. "What did Nancy mean when she said masks were stolen?"

Tessa pulled her hand into her lap, running her finger over the white tape where an IV needle was buried in the skin. "I've been getting messages for a while now, from all over. Masks being stolen."

"The Earth Goddess?"

Tessa sighed. "I don't know. It could be. I didn't think it was really that important. The stolen masks were old ones, broken ones. It didn't seem that big of a deal—"

Josie sat back against her thin hospital pillow. The fabric of the case rustled in a plasticky whisper that reminded Josie of the TemperMentals. *Mask-Maker. Mask-Maker.*

Josie pressed her fingers into her forehead, taking a deep breath. She would not lose her cool, no matter how much she was trembling inside.

"She knows. Somehow, Earth Mama found out. She knows I'm a mask-maker. That's why she's been stealing broken masks. She must think I can repair them—"

"That's why the TemperMentals came for you," Judah said.

"Repair them for what?" Simone asked.

"Building an army?" Beech offered.

Josie sank deeper in her bed, twisting the coarse white sheets around her hands. "*Kuso.*"

"Whoa, I was joking," Beech said.

"Let's talk about what happened today," Judah said, coming to the end of her bed.

She released the sheet and tucked her arms close over her chest. She didn't really want to think about what had happened, at least not the part where he'd saved her. Being around him had been hard enough when he'd just been Tessa's arrogant boyfriend. Now he was Tessa's arrogant boyfriend who had saved Josie from drowning and hypothermia. Apparently, he wasn't as useless as she'd thought.

"Those TemperMentals were seriously scary," Simone said, moving closer to Judah. "And seriously rough." She touched the bandage on her forehead that was covering a nasty gash.

"You were right. This earth goddess, whoever she is, is powerful," Tessa said.

"I didn't see an earth goddess, but I got a glimpse of Fog Dude," Beech said, "right before he translocated."

Judah gripped the fake wood footboard, leaning forward, looking right at Josie. As much as she wanted to, she couldn't look away. "You know what this means?" he asked.

No one answered.

"There's a traitor in our tribe."

Simone's brow crumpled. "What? No. No one in the tribe would—"

"Who else would know Josie's a mask-maker?" Judah said.

Beech tugged at the wooden spacer in his ear thoughtfully. "I don't know, man. You know how rumors get around in the Core. It's worse than VD." He grinned.

Tessa made a face at him. "Ew."

"That's a lot of effort and energy to expend based on a rumor," Judah said. "Whoever sent those TemperMentals won't be going for any more walks on the beach any time soon."

Judah was right. The TemperMentals were much bigger and badder than they had been the last time. Even if Earth Mama was a badass summoner, she would need some major recoup time after that little display.

"Unless she's making human sacrifices," Josie thought aloud.

Chilled silence greeted her words. If Earth Mama fed her goddess human blood, then she wouldn't need as much of her own energy to control the goddess. It made sense. Besides, Josie had already seen Earth Mama murder a Triune. For that Earth Mama's soul was doomed to Oblivion. What were a few more human lives on her conscience? Nothing.

"Why?" Simone said, spinning her bracelets, eyes sheened with worry. "Why would anyone do any of this? Why kill the Triune? Why try to capture Josie before and let her go, only to try again now, even if she is a mask-maker? And why would anyone want an army anyway? To do what with?"

Josie drew her knees up, feeling a resurgence of cold coming on. Her ankle twinged, but she ignored it. What was Earth Mama's plan? What did she want?

"Something to do with the old wars?" Beech ventured.

"The wars ended like . . . forever ago," Tessa said.

"Five hundred years," Josie affirmed.

Fighting within the Core, between sister tribes, was as old as humanity. But this didn't feel like the same old animosities bubbling to the surface, which they often did, even though the wars had officially ended.

The wars had mostly been about territory and personal slights—people in the Core knew how to hold a grudge, for generations. The violence bloomed and died back and bloomed again like weeds. Factions formed alliances and then betrayed them, feeding into the hostilities. No doubt fights would break out, they probably already were. Without a strong Triune to stamp them down and maintain order, some of the tribes would seize the opportunity to take care of business they felt was unfinished. But Josie wasn't convinced that this was the case for Earth Mama.

Simone's hands went to her head. "I don't get it. Why won't Nancy believe us? She's the Eye of the Future. Why didn't she see any of this—?"

"The Eye is blind," Tessa said in a soft voice.

Josie grabbed the rail of her bed. "What?"

Tessa's eyes slid away towards the off-white linoleum. "I shouldn't be telling you. You're not supposed to know. No one is—"

Josie's stomach lurched. She threw back her covers. This was bad.

The Eyes' ability to receive visions of the past, present, and future was rooted in the Covenant, the sacred contract that bound the powers of Life, Death, and the Other together and to the Triune. If the powers of the Eye were disrupted, if they were blind, then they were effectively powerless. If people found out, there could be upheaval, chaos. Worse, it meant that someone—Earth Mama—had figured out a way to interfere with the power of the Covenant, which was way worse than anything Josie had imagined. If murdering the Triune was akin to assassinating a president, then interfering with the Covenant was like hijacking the entire power grid and holding it hostage. No wonder Nancy was so on edge.

Very bad.

"Whoa." Beech put his hand on her shoulder, stopping her as she slid to the edge of the bed. "Where do you think you're going?"

Josie pushed his hand away. "I have to do something."

"Like?"

"I—" Her mind went blank. Her first thought had been to return to the island and consult her guides. But she wasn't the Triune. She couldn't translocate to the island, and she didn't have any guides.

She turned to Tessa. "Why are they blind? Do you know?"

Tessa shook her head.

"Tessa, look at me," she said.

Tessa's eyes moved sluggishly. She was exhausted, that much was clear. Josie felt a pang of guilt for pressing her, but the situation had just gone from stomach-upsetting to projectile vomiting. Earth Mama wasn't some crazy lone gunman, content to take down the Triune and then go down in a blaze of glory. She had followers—Fog God, primary among them, but there had been others in Brunei, a handful at least. She had godly weapons—the time-bender, but Josie also suspected Earth Mama's sword wasn't some run-of-the-mill medieval replica. And she had power—power enough to have followers and procure sacred tools and to create material TemperMentals, which was practically unheard of, and power to blind the Eye of Josie's tribe.

Very, very bad.

"Is it just our Eye? Are others blind too?" Josie asked.

"Just ours," Tessa said, "from what I know."

"What you know?" Josie spoke her words as carefully as she could, though she really wanted to shout.

She wished Caroline, Nancy, and Lily were still in the room, so she could ream them too, especially Nancy. How could she act as if she didn't believe Josie had been attacked when she herself was under constant attack? Blinded? More importantly, how had Earth Mama disrupted the connection to the Covenant? Did she have another godly device? Had she discovered some charm, some magic, some disruptive symbol? Josie racked her brain. But she couldn't remember reading about anything, device, charm, or otherwise, that had the power to come between an Eye and the Covenant.

"Have you talked to the other Eyes?" Josie asked.

Tessa's lips curled, like she'd gotten a whiff of curdled milk. "If they were blind, they would tell me, I am the Triune."

Josie measured her breath. "They might not."

"Why?" Tessa snapped. "Because I'm not a good enough Triune?"

"Because they don't know you. They don't trust you—"

"They have to trust me, I'm the Triune."

"It doesn't work like that. Just having the mask doesn't make you the Triune. You have to own it, Tessa. Why do you think the new Triune goes on a tour after she's completed her trials? It's not just a meet and greet. You need to show them that you're no slouch. That you're serious. That they should fear you. You have to put in the work—"

"I have been working—"

"I know you have, Tessa, but—"

"But it's never enough, is it? I summoned the Tripartite today. For the first time. I stopped those TemperMentals. I saved your life."

"I know, Tessa, and thank you," Josie said. "Thank you for saving me."

Tessa's chin remained firm, her eyes narrowed. "But?"

"But if the other Eyes are blind, they're not about to go blabbing it, not even to you. This may surprise you, but not all of the tribes enjoy being governed by the Triune."

"What would you do?" Judah asked. He had resumed his folded arm bodyguard stance. "*If* you were the Triune?"

He just had to remind her that she wasn't the Triune, didn't he?

She met his cool gaze with one of her own, wondering how someone with such cold eyes could be so warm. Just thinking about his heat brought warmth back to her. "I would go to the Fates."

Beech's eyes popped. "Whoa."

Tessa recoiled, sinking deeper against the black vinyl of her chair. "I can't do that."

Josie turned back to her sister. "Why not?"

"Because it's suicidal," Judah answered.

She glowered at him. "Maybe for you, but not for a Triune . . . necessarily."

Plenty of Triunes had died attempting to summon the Fates. But a Triune didn't think about her own life when the lives of others were at stake.

"I couldn't," Tessa said. "I can't."

Josie twisted, yanking the tubes and machines with her. "Stop saying that! Yes, you can. You are the Triune. You are the blood of the Daughter of Death. You are the only one who can summon Fates. If I were you, I would've done it a month ago, as soon as Mom had been murdered. I would've gone to the Fates and demanded they tell me who this earth bitch is and where to find her. I would've tracked her down and delivered her the justice she deserves."

Tessa wheeled her chair back. "I don't even know how to find the island. I haven't tried. And the Fates . . . If I go to them . . . won't they take years off my life?"

Josie gazed at her sister—so pale, so thin, so unprepared. It wasn't Tessa's fault she hadn't been trained. It wasn't her fault she'd been taught to fear the Fates while Josie had been taught to seek them out.

Josie swallowed back her fury and frustration. Not useful. Not to her. Not to Tessa. Helping Tessa was her priority. Really, it was the only thing she could do.

She inhaled. A Triune must maintain focus. Calm. Control.

"Yes, they would," she said. "The Fates would take whatever they thought was fair, and you would have to give it to them. And you would do so, gladly."

"No, I—"

"Tessa, please," Josie interrupted, wishing that Tessa would call her out for it. Interrupting the Triune was not allowed, but Tessa just sat there. They had so much work to do. "The most important thing at the moment is making sure you come into full possession of the Tripartite. Summoning them today was a great step in the right direction, but you have to keep pushing, especially now—"

"I will," Tessa said, "I swear."

"You know she's out there now," Josie said, careful to conceal any bitterness she might've felt about the fact that her sister had doubted her. "You know how dangerous she is. Material TemperMentals. Blinding the Eye—"

"I know," Tessa said. "I'll work harder. I'll do whatever you think is best."

"Anything."

"Just not the Fates."

"I can't make you go to the Fates, Tessa. That has to be your decision, but if that's what you have to do, then you'll do it, because you're the Triune. You don't get to be selfish. Not even with your life. Your duty is to the Covenant and the Core above all things."

Tessa looked like she might puke again.

Josie gazed down at her hands. Her palms were scratched, red, and swollen from being dragged across the beach. "Mom might've been a cold bitch, Tessa, but she wasn't selfish. She gave up everything... Dad, you. She knew you'd be happier if you didn't have to live with her, with the Triune. She didn't leave you behind because she liked it or because she wanted to. She did it because it was the right thing to do. For you. That's who Mom was. That's who you have to be now."

Tessa gazed at her for a moment and then dropped her head, nodding.

"And what about you?" Beech asked softly.

Josie shifted back to face him. "What about me?"

"You're a freakin' mask-maker, betty. You didn't see what Judah did. That ocean god was badass. He sucker punched those ghost-dicks. And when you hit the water, he parted the waves Moses-style and the tide delivered you right to him. Sick with a college degree." He lifted his eyebrow at Judah. "Wasn't it?"

Judah wore his impassive mask. "Water's not my element."

"It was amazing," Simone said, as she sketched more symbols on the foot of the bed. "I've never seen anything like it."

Beech pushed the tip of his finger gently into Josie's shoulder. "You did that. No wonder this earth goddess chick wants you so bad. If you could do that on the fly, just think about what you'll be able to do once you've earned your chops."

"And how am I supposed to learn? It's not like there are any other mask-makers around to teach me." Josie hugged her knees. "And ... maybe I shouldn't try to learn."

"What are you talking about?" Beech said. "You have to make more masks."

"No, I don't," Josie said. "It's dangerous. I don't know what god I'm going to make material. And if I don't make any more masks, then maybe that earth bitch will lose interest."

Beech's mouth dropped open. He held his hand out to the others. "Help me out here."

Tessa looked away. Simone squatted down, like she was drawing more symbols on the floor, even though she had already circled the bed twice.

"Come on, Judah. Ocean god? Water may not be your element of choice, but power like that had to have been a pretty sweet ride," Beech said. "Tell me it wasn't one of the best experiences of your life."

Judah's gaze turned upwards, as if he were weighing being in possession of the ocean god against everything else he'd ever done.

"I don't believe this," Beech said, shaking his head. "Dude, even you can't be that repressed."

Judah's eyes narrowed, but Beech didn't see it. He'd already turned back to Josie.

"Josie, you beautiful hardass, don't you get it? This is why you're not the Triune. The gods had another plan for you. This is it. You can't ignore this any more than Tessa can ignore the Tripartite. You think the gods are going to be cool with you blowing this off? You said it yourself. There hasn't been a mask-maker for centuries. The gods gave you a gift. What do you think they'll do to you if you don't use it?"

Josie drew the sheet back over her legs, which were breaking out in goose bumps again. She had the worst feeling in the depths of her stomach, almost as bad as drowning. A feeling that he was right.

"Besides, you gave him the ocean god?" Beech notched his thumb back at Judah, who was scowling. "Come on."

CHAPTER 12

MARCH 11TH
EIGHT DAYS LATER

"**A**RE YOU OKAY?" Tessa asked, breaking her standing meditation pose.

Josie lifted her head, pulling her fingers from her hair. "Yeah," she said, rolling her shoulders. "I just haven't been sleeping that well."

In fact, she'd been having nightmares. She hadn't had nightmares for years. And these were worse than any of the old ones—the ones about being abandoned and trapped on the island. Much worse. Sometimes they were about her mom's murder, sometimes about being kidnapped by TemperMentals, but always they ended with drowning—hitting the water, stabbing cold, suffocating darkness. Every night for the last week, she'd woken up gasping for air, hands clawing at her chest like they were trying to rip open her skin to let the air into her lungs.

"You look terrible," Judah said without looking up from the tablet screen. "Maybe you should take something."

Josie pushed off of the living room couch, grinding her teeth. "I need a break."

She went into the kitchen and started another pot of coffee. She heard Tessa's soft shuffle across the tile, but she didn't turn around.

"You haven't thanked him, you know," Tessa said. "I was hoping you'd be nicer to him, since he saved your life."

Josie leaned on the counter, rubbing a circle into her forehead.

"I am being nice," she said. "I haven't told him to get the hell out of here, have I?"

"Josie! I've done everything you've asked me to do, haven't I?"

Josie straightened up, turning around. "Yes."

"And?"

"And you're doing . . . well."

Since they'd returned home and resumed training, Tessa had been in daily contact with the Tripartite, had summoned them again for a few minutes, and had only puked once afterwards. Not bad. But Josie could only put Tessa through a fraction of the training exercises that their mother had put Josie through, because they were locked in, either at the house or the center, and because Tessa could only handle a couple of hours of training a day. If the Tripartite didn't exhaust her first, then she exhausted Josie with her whining.

"And since I've done everything you've asked," Tessa said, "I'm now asking you to thank Judah for saving your life. Is that so hard?"

Yes. Every time Josie looked at him all she wanted to do was translocate back to the Triune's Island and spend the rest of her life naming crabs. He may have saved her, but nothing had changed between them. He was still an arrogant ass. Saving her life hadn't softened his attitude towards her. If anything, he'd been more brusque and dismissive. But maybe that was because she hadn't thanked him. She'd been focusing all her energy on pretending nothing had happened, which mostly meant looking through him like he didn't exist. Not exactly the most grateful position to take, she knew.

Tessa crossed her arms. She'd been working on her authoritative face, and it was coming along nicely. Josie would have congratulated her, except she didn't want to be the one on the receiving end of the Triune's scolding.

"Don't you think he deserves it?" Tessa asked. "Isn't it the right thing to do?"

Josie let out a heavy breath. "Yes, you're right. It is." She pushed away from the counter. "I'll do it now."

"Good," Tessa said with a less than Triune-ish smile.

Even though it will kill some small part of me, Josie thought as she trudged back into the living room.

Judah lounged in the Mission-style chair, leg hanging over the wide wooden arm. Josie stopped next to him, stuffing her hands into her back pockets and choking on the words in her throat. Tessa stood next to her.

Judah looked up at them, from one to the other and back again. "What?"

Tessa prodded Josie with her elbow.

But the words wouldn't come.

Judah put the tablet aside—the slant of his brow turned suspicious. Gods, had she spent so much time with him that she could decipher the emotional degrees of his eyebrows? Ugh.

"What are you up to?" he asked.

"We're not up to anything," Tessa said. "Josie?"

Oh, just get it over with.

She took a deep breath and looked up at the ceiling. "Thank you for saving me."

There. That hadn't been so bad. She met his remote gaze.

"That almost sounded like you meant it." He leaned over and slid his tablet into his worn leather bag. "Maybe you would've rather drowned? Or died of hypothermia? I was there, you know. I heard what the doctor said."

She cursed under her breath. In the emergency room, the doctor had told her that she was lucky Judah had known what to do—strip off her wet clothes, hold her body against his—because even though she'd been saved from drowning, if Judah hadn't acted so quickly to warm her core temperature, she could've frozen to death.

"What do you want me to say? I thanked you, didn't I?"

Judah stood. He slung his bag over his head and across his chest. "If that's what you call it."

"Does it have to be like this?" Tessa stomped her foot in five-year-old fashion. "Don't I have enough to deal with without playing referee for you two?"

"Forget about it," Judah said. "I didn't do it so you would thank me anyway." He turned to Tessa. "You'd better get ready, if you're coming."

Tessa's eyes widened. "Oh, right, I forgot. Just a second." She ran out of the room and back through the kitchen to the bedroom hallway.

"Wait a minute," Josie called after her. She turned back to Judah. "Where are you going?"

"To the center," Judah said, taking his phone out of his pocket. "Simone's having one of her soup kitchen days. She didn't tell you?"

Josie pressed the heel of her hand to her head. "She did. I forgot too."

Simone was planning on feeding the homeless that afternoon. She'd asked Josie to come help.

Judah didn't comment, engrossed in his phone.

Josie eyed him. "Can I catch a ride?"

Judah looked at her from the top of his eyes. Then he slid his phone in his pocket. "It's killing you, isn't it?"

Her head dropped back. "Never mind."

"What's the big deal?" he asked as she started to walk away.

She stopped. Don't turn around. Don't turn . . .

She turned around. "You know what the big deal is. You saved my life. That's a pretty big deal."

He crossed his arms. "I'm glad you think so."

"So what do you want? A card? A medal? A statue?"

He smirked. A surge of heat swelled up in her. Gods, she wanted to hit him. No matter how many times she told herself she wasn't going to let him get to her, he found a way.

"It really bothers you," he said, "to feel like you owe me, doesn't it? But if it makes you feel better, I would've done it for anybody. You're not special."

"Oh, yes, that makes me feel so much better."

He looked down at the floor between them, smirk fading, brow turning serious. "We're never going to be friends, Josie."

"You're right about that."

"But we both care about Tessa, so why don't we just . . . stay off each other's toes?"

She held up her hands, taking a step back. "My pleasure." She started to turn away again.

"But first . . ."

She stopped and turned back.

His eyes glinted, sapphires in firelight. "Say it," he said. "Say it and mean it."

Her fingernails dug into her palms. "You are such an asshole." She smiled. "And I really mean it, from the bottom of my heart."

"Scared?" he asked.

"What would I be scared of?"

"Of being honest. That's why you think I'm such an asshole, because I've told you the truth. You just haven't wanted to hear it."

"Truth? I had to almost die for you to believe I was telling the truth—for Tessa to believe me. And I know you're the reason she didn't believe me in the first place. That's what makes you an asshole. You've been sticking your nose where it doesn't be—"

"You're unbelievable," he said. "All this bullshit is just you avoiding the fact that you can't say it, can you? Was Tessa right? Are you really so frigid that you can't even say thank you and mean it?"

She threw up her hands. "You're right. I can't. Not to you. Not that you care, because nothing I say matters to you anyway, right? So why should you care if I thank you?"

"I don't," he said. "I just didn't think you could do it. And I was right."

"And that's what really makes you happy, isn't it? Being right?"

"You just can't handle it, can you?"

"What the—?"

"The fact that you're not the Triune. The fact that you're going to have to depend on other people to help you and protect you, to save you. That drives you crazy, doesn't it?"

"Where do you get—?"

"Get over it. It's not the worst thing in the world to have to depend on other people. Welcome to the human race, Josie."

A twisting mass of curse words churned in her gut, but before she could let any of them loose, Tessa's bouncy footfalls sounded, down the stairs, through the kitchen, into the living room.

"I'm ready."

Judah opened the front door. Tessa breezed by, smiling and rosy-cheeked. She stopped in the threshold and looked back at Josie. "Are you coming? Simone is like your new best friend now, isn't she?"

Judah leaned against the door, expression blank. So what if she hated him? She didn't have to like him to help Simone.

"Yeah, she is." Josie grabbed her bag from the bench by the front door. "Let's go."

CHAPTER 13

MARCH 11TH

JOSIE LUGGED ANOTHER MASSIVE, empty pot into the kitchen, greeted by the mingled scents of dish detergent and black bean soup. Not her favorite perfume. Kai was at the sink, up to his skinny elbows in suds. She set the pot down on the cluttered counter next to the deep industrial sinks.

"Need some help?" she asked, surveying the piles of dirty dishes.

"Nah," he said. "The longer I'm back here, the less likely I am to be dragged out there where I might have to pretend like I actually care."

"Big fan of charity, huh?"

He pushed the pot into the soapy water, drowning it. "It perpetuates weakness," he said. "I believe in survival of the fittest."

"That's pretty brutal." Josie loaded up one of the dishwasher trays with plates and silverware.

He shrugged. "Nature's brutal. Our mistake is thinking we're separate from it."

"And what does Simone think about that?" She shoved the tray into the dishwasher and yanked the handle down. A gush and whoosh filled the big kitchen. Next door, the cafeteria-like room, also the tribe's meeting hall, was crammed with a wide array of Portland's hungriest. Simone was in her element, grinning from ear to ear as she loaded up bowls with soup.

Kai's signature sly smile appeared as he scrubbed the pot. Aloof as he was, Josie enjoyed the rare moments when he would converse with her. Usually, he had something interesting to say. And, frankly, he was one of the few people who would actually talk to her. Most of the tribe was giving her the cold shoulder. Nancy's influence appeared to be greater than Caroline's.

"Simone thinks the same thing about me that she does about all those schmucks out there," he said. "That we can be saved." He hefted the pot out of the sink to rinse it. "That's why I love her."

Josie started loading another rack for the dishwasher. "You really do, don't you?"

"Do you think I'd be wearing this,"—he gestured to the bright yellow, full-length rubber apron he wore over his dark clothes—"if I didn't?"

She smiled. That was another reason she liked Kai, one more person who could make her smile.

The dishwasher finished its cycle with a clunk and a sigh. She opened it, releasing a cloud of steam, and shoved the next rack in, pushing the clean one out.

She hadn't needed to ask Kai if he loved Simone. She knew he did. She could tell, not just because of the way he'd kissed her the first time Josie had seen them together, but because of all the little things. The razor-sharp edge to his smile disappeared when she was around. He was always looking at her and errantly touching her. And why shouldn't he love her? Simone was generous and open and warmhearted. She was easy to love. Josie was sure no one had ever called Simone frigid.

Not that Josie cared what Judah thought. She was doing her damnedest to forget he existed at all. Most of the time she was successful, but his words were insidious. They'd burrowed under her skin, leaving her sore and irritated.

Did she still want to be the Triune?

Not really.

She just didn't know how *not* to be the Triune. She didn't know how to give up everything she'd been taught. So much of it had been ripped away from her already. She felt like she was hanging onto scraps as it was. Did he really expect she could simply forget it all and become a normal teenager? Did he think she would be able to exchange duty to Covenant and Core for Friday night keggers and Saturday night bonfires as easily as Tessa exchanged an ill-fitting sweater at the mall?

Why was he pushing her so hard anyway? Why wasn't he pushing Tessa? She was the one who needed to be pushed. Everything depended on her now. After all, Tessa was the Triune. Maybe it wasn't easy for Josie to accept, yet she didn't have any choice. And she really was trying to help Tessa. As different as they were, as little as Josie understood her sister, she still didn't want anything to happen to Tessa. The thought that that earth bitch might do to Tessa what she'd done to their mom made Josie's ears ring with fury.

It wouldn't happen. It couldn't. Josie would do whatever it took to make sure it didn't.

But that was the trouble, wasn't it? As far as Josie could see, there wasn't much she could do to help Tessa. She'd always assumed that when she started training the next Triune, the heir would be, in all likelihood, her own daughter. She'd anticipated raising her daughter the way she'd been raised, with an understanding that, at the end of the day, a Triune stands alone.

Did Josie have a problem depending on other people? Yes, she did. A Triune couldn't depend on other people. That's what she'd been taught. Except, the more she thought about it, the less convinced she was that it was really that simple. Her mom had always seemed omnipotent, but in the end, she'd been as vulnerable as anyone else. She'd been human.

It shouldn't have been such a shock. But it was. More and more, Josie was realizing just how naïve she'd been, about so many things.

The kitchen's back door swung open. Beech strolled in, grinning as always.

"I've been looking all over for you," he said to Josie. He slid behind Kai, slapping him on the shoulder. Kai stiffened, his lip curled. Even Josie knew not to touch Kai. But Beech persisted in flouting all rules. Josie wasn't sure how she felt about that or him. She wasn't doing anything to control her feelings for Beech, yet they remained elusive.

"I've been here for hours," she said.

"Then it sounds like you're ready for a break." He hooked her wrist and pulled her away from the dishwasher, leading her through the swinging doors and into the crowded hall.

The garlic aroma of black bean soup mixed with the pungent funk of a couple of hundred unwashed bodies. Josie kept her face neutral, though one table she passed stank worse than a public park port-o-john.

Simone didn't seem to mind the stink. She was collecting dirty plates from the tables, chatting it up with the locals, hugging people like they were long lost relatives. She didn't seem to notice Josie and Beech as he dragged her along the back wall towards another door. This one led into the center. In order to access it, he had to punch a code into the keypad.

"Are you supposed to know that code?" she asked.

His green eyes glinted. "Are you going to turn me in?"

Her eyebrow arched at him.

"Still haven't given up being the sheriff, huh?" Beech said, turning back to keypad.

Josie glanced back at the crowded hall, but no one was paying them any attention.

Tessa stood behind the serving table, ladling thick black soup into bowls. Her eyes wore purple shadows of fatigue, sweat glistened on her forehead. She'd been working hard lately, and Josie hadn't even really been pushing her. A pang of worry shot through Josie. Tessa wasn't prepared for the Tripartite, not in the least.

Judah appeared behind Tessa. He leaned over her shoulder, speaking close to her ear—intimately.

Tessa said something back and gave him a weak smile. He brushed her cheek with the back of his fingers.

Josie went cold.

No one had ever touched Josie like that.

No one had ever looked at Josie the way Kai looked at Simone.

Seventeen years had passed and it had never occurred to her, it had never bothered her. So where, all of a sudden, had this ache come from? She turned away from them and the ache. Another useless emotion, another thought to be stuffed into the darkness and forgotten.

Beech pulled her into the bright corridor and led her to the stairs.

"Where are we going?" she asked.

"My mom has something she wants to show you," he said as they came to the top of the flight. "But first." He stopped on the landing, turned, and stepped into her.

He kissed her. Under the harsh fluorescents, in a stairwell that smelled vaguely of pine-scented antiseptic and wax, with a boy who had promised nothing but to never make any promises, Josie had her first real kiss. Not like that quick peck he had given her in her room, or the kiss she'd given Daisuke all those years ago that had been awkward for both of them. This was warm and alive and touching that ache inside of her that she hadn't been able to quite lock away from her consciousness.

He pulled back, grinning. "Hope that was okay. I was going to wait for you to give me the green light, but patience . . . not my favorite game."

She had to remind herself to breathe. "It's okay."

"Good." He pulled his necklace into his mouth, biting the chain. "Want to do it again?"

She nodded.

"Me too." He dropped the chain and kissed her again. This time she was ready. She kissed him back. In a few minutes, she was pressed between him and the wall, forgetting about the ache. And it was good. Really good.

A throat-clearer interrupted.

Their mouths broke apart. Josie glanced over Beech's shoulder and shrank back, arms sliding away from him.

Beech turned and let out a groan. "Come on, Mama Bear."

Gretchen leaned a shoulder against the wall, grinning. "Forgive the intrusion," she said, "but Caroline sent me to find you. Some of us do have other things to do today."

Beech's fingers threaded through hers. She felt herself smiling, for real smiling.

"This better be good," he said, leading Josie towards the next flight of stairs.

Gretchen's eyes sparkled. "Just wait."

Josie floated into Caroline's office, overcome with a flushed, disembodied sensation.

The office was bright, airy, messy: a big window to the left, under it a desk, a monitor on one corner, a laptop in the center, to the right, a wall of shelves, packed with books. The longest wall was covered in cork. Pins held up rough sketches, bold graphic designs, and cartoonish doodles.

A darkly clad young man dominated the corner of the room. A sudden rush of self-consciousness flooded Josie. She touched her lips, like she could cool them with her fingertips. Her hand disengaged from Beech's.

Caroline jumped up from the light table under the cork wall, smiling widely.

"Josie, I'm so glad you're here." Caroline hurried to the door, shutting and locking it. "Lily wanted to join us, but she wasn't feeling well."

Josie glanced again at the young man with the pouty lips and honey-hued skin, trying to remember if she knew him, but for some reason looking at him made her mind go blank. He watched her with a reserved expression.

"Risky business," Beech said. "My favorite kind."

Gretchen took his arm and made him step back. "Cool your porridge, Baby Bear."

Caroline ushered Josie to the glass table, which was glowing softly with bluish white light. She gestured towards the young man. "Josie, this is Russell. He's one of the tribe's archivists."

It came back to her then.

"I remember," Josie said. "Russell Vale."

His dark eyes sparked a bit. People liked to be remembered, especially after such a long time. The last time she'd seen him, she'd been seven. He was older by a few years. He'd been eleven or twelve when they'd last crossed paths. At one of the tribe's weddings, all the older girls had been giggling over him. Josie remembered thinking they were silly. In fact, she was feeling a bit silly herself at the moment.

"You're Kai's foster brother," she said, piecing together the last names, and Kai having mentioned an older brother.

At the mention of Kai's name, Russell's expression turned grim. He shifted his dark, dark eyes to Caroline. Were they brown or black?

"With all respect, Glory of the Present," he said to Caroline, his tone belying his youthfulness even though he exuded a much older presence, "are you sure this is a good idea—?"

"They're not doing any good down in the archives, Russell," Caroline said. "Lily and I have both agreed it's worth trying."

Josie didn't fail to note that, whatever was happening, Nancy had not agreed. More dissension within the Eye. Not good.

"What's going on?" Josie asked.

"Here, look." Caroline ushered Josie to the table. Eight shallow wooden boxes sat side-by-side, dark rectangles on a bright flat plane. "Russell?"

He slid the lid off the first box. A milk-white crystal flashed from under his shirt cuff as his hands moved—a charm of some kind. Otherwise, his appearance was professional and neat, dark slacks, a maroon button-down. Was it synthetic or silk? Her thumb ran over her fingertips. She had an urge to touch his shirt to find out.

He caught her eye and smiled a little, like he could tell what she was thinking. Yes, he was attractive. No, she wasn't attracted to every guy she met. She'd met plenty of good-looking young men in the Core. Few of them had that inexplicable force surrounding them that compelled her to give them a second thought. But when she encountered someone with that invisible charge, she found it difficult not to take notice. Beech was like lightning, dazzling in a sudden, unpredictable way. And Russell... Russell had his own mysterious aura.

Josie and Caroline stepped back as Russell moved down the table, removing the lids. Within each box was a mask. Or most of a mask. They were all broken. Josie's heart hurt gazing down at the shattered faces.

Most were made of wood. Two appeared to be clay. One seemed to be chiseled from stone. Their jagged fragments were nestled in thin curls of wood shavings like broken egg shells.

"These are the ones we thought might be salvageable," Caroline said in a soft, reverent voice.

Josie's gaze ran over the faces. A black clay mask drew her attention. It had presence too. Even though it was broken, it spoke to her.

Josie forced her eyes up to Caroline. "The tribe's ancient masks?" It wasn't really a question.

Caroline nodded.

"You want me to repair them?"

Caroline's face was lit up from within. "Do you think you can?"

Josie's eyes returned to the mask.

It was broken down the middle. One half was intact, sharply featured, with long eyes and a slanting brow. The other half was splintered further in two, along the cheekbone. A triangular fragment was missing from the forehead, where the two halves of the face would've come together.

Compared to some, the mask was plain, without an exaggerated expression to represent the god's personality, or the ornate decoration to celebrate the god's greatness. Just a smooth burnt black face. The longer she looked at it, the more something stirred within her. A hot something.

She reached for it.

"Careful," Russell said, stopping her.

"Of course, she'll be careful, Russell," Caroline said.

"Just because it's broken doesn't mean it's not priceless," Russell said, not harshly, but with anxiety. "It's still the mask of a god."

Her fingertips grazed the mask's lower lip—and were singed. She snatched her hand back, more from surprise than pain. A flicker of flame appeared in the god's eye and then vanished again.

"What is it?" Caroline said.

Josie's lips were dry. Her fingers throbbed from the heat sinking beneath her skin and winding up her arm, spreading all through her.

"Josie," Caroline said, prying her attention from the mask, "what do you think?"

"I don't know." Was it her imagination or did she hear a faint crackle?

"Well, whatever you need, Gretchen will help you," Caroline said.

"Wait a minute," Russell said.

"Russell, this is not your decision," Caroline said.

"But—"

Caroline turned on him. "This can happen with or without your involvement, which would you prefer?"

Russell withdrew, but he didn't look happy about it.

Josie's hands started to sweat. "Can . . ."

"You can do whatever you need to do, if you think you might be able to repair them and bring our gods back to us," Caroline said.

Josie slid the lid on and swept the box off the table. The flush returned, but this time it was far below the surface. Some deep down heat within her had been awakened.

Russell's dark eyes—black—looked like they might pop out of his skull, but he kept his lips pressed tight.

"Can I take this one with me?" she asked.

Russell stepped forward as if he might try to snatch it from her. She stepped back, cradling the box. Caroline put a hand against his chest, stopping him. "Yes. If you think you need to."

Her hands tightened around the box. The wood felt warm. Was the god's power seeping out of the mask somehow? Had it really burned her? She refused to let go of the box to inspect her fingertips. Russell tracked her every movement.

Need. Yes, that's what this feeling was. A need.

CHAPTER 14

MARCH 19TH
EIGHT DAYS LATER

"ALLISON," ONE OF THE GIRLS working at an easel, Fiona, hissed. "Look."

Allison, a pretty girl whom Josie recalled had once been a close friend of Tessa's, but didn't seem to be any longer, peeked around her easel. "What's he doing here?"

"Good question," Kai muttered, sinking into a deeper brood as Russell entered the art lab. He and Josie were hovering at the back of the room, keeping Simone company as she shaped a bowl on the kickwheel.

"I told you," Fiona whispered. She and Allison were stationed close enough that Josie could hear everything they were saying.

Allison finger-combed her platinum hair. "How do I look?"

"Gorgeous as always," Fiona said. "But I hope you're going to make him grovel before you take him back."

"Of course I'm going to make him grovel. And pay. Big time. But who said I'm going to take him back?"

"Are you?"

"He's been blowing me off for the last week. What do you think? Shut up, he's coming."

She and Fiona ducked behind their easels again.

Josie hugged her messenger bag to her chest. Inside was the mask.

Russell started towards the back of the room, but Gretchen intercepted him with a big smile. "Russell! How nice to see you back in the art lab. It's been too long."

"I think he has the hots for you," Kai muttered, leaning against the counter next to her.

Josie's eyes darted over to Allison, who apparently had been dating Russell. Allison didn't seem to hear Kai's remark.

Simone looked up from the pottery wheel. "You didn't tell me that."

"Because I've been trying not to think about it," Kai said with an air of disgust. "He's asked me about her every day for the last week. He moved back home a couple weeks ago, because his roommate bailed on him." Kai growled. "As if that wasn't bad enough, he's been harassing me for days. Are you going to see Josie today? What's she doing? Is she going to the art lab?" He leaned closer to Josie. "It's obnoxious. Keep me out of your love life, please?"

Josie turned her back to Russell. "He doesn't have the hots for me."

"I hope not," Kai grumbled. "He's getting his master's in douche-baggery, just so you know."

Josie watched Allison, who was pretending to be totally engrossed in her painting, but didn't seem to be paying them any attention. Josie hoped that Russell really was here for Allison.

Not that Joise wasn't attracted to Russell, she was, but it felt strange to be attracted to another guy when she'd been making out with Beech every night. She liked Beech, a lot. As much as she enjoyed kissing him—and she did—sometimes she found her mind wandering. Most often to the mask. Sometimes to Russell. She wondered if her detachment stemmed from Beech's beliefs on monogamy or her Triune training or something else entirely, but she didn't give it too much thought. Beech made it easy not to think too much, which was another reason she liked him.

As usual, her mother's throaty jazz singer voice was in the back of her head,

No matter whom you love, how well you love, a Triune stands alone, Josie. Between the gods and humanity. It is your duty. Let nothing come before that.

"Josie," Russell said from behind her.

Allison peered around her easel. Her icy blue eyes bulged and her cherry red lips pursed. If Allison's eyes had had laser sights, Josie was sure there'd be little red dots bouncing around on her forehead. Simone's would-be vase folded into a wet brown crumple in her hands.

Josie turned, still hugging her bag.

Russell's eyes were so black she couldn't tell the iris from the pupil, as black as the mask. They tracked down to the bag.

"You're carrying it around with you?" His lips barely moved they were so tight, but his tone remained polite.

"Do you realize—?"

"I won't let anything happen to it," she said.

He didn't look convinced. "May I see it?"

She leaned back from him, bumping into Kai. She had no reason to say no, and she didn't want to create animosity with Russell, but she didn't want to give him the mask either.

"What are you two talking about?" Kai asked.

The acrimony between Kai and Russell was palpable, a tense, ugly feeling that made Josie's shoulders bunch.

"May we speak in private?" Russell leaned in closer, his voice lowering. His cologne was cool and crisp, his eyes sparking. "Please?"

Josie nodded.

Russell gestured for her to go before him. She did, ignoring the stares of just about everyone in the room, but most pointedly the ones behind her—Simone, Kai, Fiona, and Allison.

She headed out towards the hall, but he caught her arm and pulled her into the kiln room. He shut the door behind her. Two electric kilns—one a stainless steel cylinder and the other a big metal box—took up most of the tiny space, which was constructed of concrete blocks. Racks, half full of fired pieces, sat in the midst of the room. Too dry, the earthy air stuck in her throat.

In such a tight space, his presence pressed heavily against her. He gave her a small smile, but it was hiding things; she could tell. She just didn't know what, and maybe that was part of his allure. Secrets seemed to haunt the dark recesses of his eyes.

"I realize Caroline gave the mask to you and that she trusts you," he said in a gentle, friendly tone, "but I was just hired to oversee the collection last month. I'm not even out of grad school yet, so . . ." He swallowed, looking a bit shy and pleading.

Josie wondered if this was the kind of groveling Allison had wanted. Josie could see how it might have some appeal.

"Please understand," he said, "I'm trying to establish myself in the tribe. You get that, right? I mean, there's a time in all of our lives when we have to leave behind who we were, you know, as kids, in order to become who we would like to be as adults. I don't want the matriarchs to think that they made a mistake allowing someone as young as I am, not out of school, to curate the tribe's ancient mask collection."

Josie's hold on the bag never loosened. "You're worried about the mask."

"Yes," he said, showing relief, seeming to be glad she understood. And she did.

"I'm taking care of it, I promise." She held the bag tighter. Even in the box, through the denim of her bag, she could feel the mask's heat, like a hot pan felt through an oven mitt. "Caroline said I could keep it."

"Not forever," he said.

"For as long as I need to."

His sparking eyes snuffed out. "And how long is that exactly?"

"I don't know," she said.

His face hardened, but then smoothed over again. He reached out and touched the strap of her bag. "May I just—?"

The door to the kiln swung open, Gretchen propped her fist on her hip. "I hate to interrupt—"

"Then don't," Russell said.

Simone peeked around the door. Kai took the door and opened it a little more.

"Is my brother bothering you?" Kai asked, like he hoped the answer was yes so he could do something about it. Not that Kai looked like he could do much of anything to his brother, who had a physique that appeared almost as well tuned as Judah's.

A few others had gathered behind to spy, Allison and Fiona among them, giving Josie more loaded-gun looks. Gretchen turned.

"Nothing to see." Gretchen waved her hands at them, shooing. "Get back to work."

One after the other, the gawkers disappeared. Simone slipped into the kiln room, frowning at Russell's fingers on Josie's bag. "What are you doing?" She slapped at his hand. "Let go. That's not yours."

He drew his hand back. "I wasn't going to take the mask—"

"Mask?" Kai asked, taking a step inside as well.

Gretchen cursed and shut the door, crowding in with the rest.

"You weren't supposed to say anything," she said to Russell. "Simone, Kai, I really think we should—"

"Now isn't a good time," Josie said to Russell.

"Can't have what?" Kai asked. "You have a mask in your bag? Not the best place to keep it."

"My point exactly," Russell said.

Kai cringed, as if agreeing with Russell caused him pain.

"I don't have a stash," Josie said, "and I wasn't going to leave it lying around."

Truth was, she didn't want to share the mask or give it back. The thought of being away from it, even for a minute, made her queasy. She even slept with it—in the box—but she wasn't going to tell them that.

Russell held onto his patience, though she could tell it was fraying. "I thought you were supposed to be fixing it."

Simone's eyes lit up. "You're fixing a mask?" Then her face fell. "You didn't tell me?"

"I haven't figured out how to fix it," she said, "yet. But I will, I just need time." Until then she'd just enjoy looking at it and touching it . . . and snuggling with it.

Okay, so it was weird. But ever since she'd brought the mask home, all her nightmares—plunging through the slicing waves, sucking in briny water, thrashing, panicking, helplessly sinking into the darkness—had been transformed.

Now, before the darkness swallowed her—before she would have awoken gasping and clawing and terrified—a light appeared in the swelling murk. A wavering flame. Instead of floundering senselessly, she was able to swim. She swam towards the flame. Thus far, she hadn't reached it, but she wanted to. She needed to.

When she woke in the morning, she wasn't flailing in panic. Instead, she had this sort of hopeful, warm feeling. And the mask was too hot to touch. The god might have been trying to send her a message, or maybe he was just trying to make her feel better. Either way, she wasn't giving up the mask. Not until she had no other choice.

"Why don't you let me store it in the archives until you've figured out if you can actually repair it?" Russell offered amicably.

"I can repair it," she said flatly. She knew what everyone was saying, calling her a liar behind her back. She saw the looks in their eyes, felt the chill of their whispers.

Russell held up his hands in surrender, that mysterious smile playing over his lips like shadows cast by flames.

"Good, great, amazing," he said. "I look forward to it, but until then, don't you think it would be safer in the archives? It's ancient, Josie. Delicate. It really should be handled with the utmost care. The archives are temperature and humidity controlled. That mask is a rare composite of volcanic—"

Kai rolled his eyes. "Don't be a jerk-off, Russell. She'll take care of your precious little mask."

A dark cloud swept over Russell's features. "This doesn't involve you, you twisted little—"

"Okay." Gretchen stepped up between them. "Josie, why don't you give me the box? I'll open it and Russell will see that you're taking as much care of it as he would."

After a moment, Josie opened the flap of her bag and pulled the box out. An already familiar heat met her touch and coursed through her. When she handed Gretchen the box, it felt like handing her heart over to a stranger. Gretchen took the box and slid the lid open. Russell crowded closer, leaning over to examine the three pieces of the mask. Kai and Simone peered around him to see. Josie stood by, her chest tight and her stomach in knots.

Simone turned to Josie. "Do you think you can fix it?"

Josie nodded. She knew she could. She wasn't sure how she knew, but she was certain it would happen—that it *had* to happen. She hadn't realized she had known until the moment Simone had asked. Maybe it had something to do with the dreams she'd been having, or maybe it was just instinct. Whatever the case, at the moment her only concern was having the mask back in her possession.

Russell eyed her. He didn't seem immediately dismissive of the possibility that she was a mask-maker, which made her feel all the worse for butting heads with him.

"That's a tricky bit of repair work, *ma belle*," Gretchen said. "What's the plan? Epoxy?"

Russell blanched. "Gods, please tell me that is not what you intend to—"

"I'm not going to glue it," she said, pushing the lid back over the mask and taking the box from Gretchen. Actually, she had thought about gluing it, except it was missing a piece. Glue wouldn't fix that.

"I don't know how else you'd go about it," Gretchen said. "It can't be refired."

Fire. Josie's hands began to tremble.

"Why not?" she asked, trying to sound as if she was asking out of mere curiosity.

"Pottery just doesn't work like that," Gretchen said. "You'd risk destroying the entire piece."

Russell had drawn back, giving Josie a deeply appraising look that made her face feel like it was being fired. "Have you studied mask-making?"

Josie had done a bit of research, but between attempting to train Tessa—without killing her always-lurking boyfriend—and spending time with Beech, she wasn't left with much time or energy for anything else. And frankly, the resources at the tribe's archives were minuscule compared to the Triune's archives. Mask-making was such an ancient art that there was really very little written about it in modern texts.

"You think she needs a degree in order to do it?" Kai asked.

"I've read up on it," Russell said, his voice taut as he addressed Kai. "Mask-makers were extremely rare, even in the age of demigods. In fact, most mask-makers were—"

"Thanks for the lesson, bro," Kai cut in. "But I think you should piss off now. You're not getting your little mask back so why don't you go spread your disease elsewhere?"

"Why don't you suck my—"

"Okay!" Gretchen clapped her hands. "My kiln room isn't rated for this kind of heat. Time to go." She opened the door and gestured them out.

Simone went first, since no one else was moving. She plucked at Kai's sleeve. After a moment of glaring at his brother, Kai followed.

Russell let out a leveling breath as Kai exited. Then he looked back at Josie, his flinty features softening. "If you want to talk about mask-making, before you attempt to repair our friend, you know where to find me. I'd be happy to help you, Josie."

He strode out.

Josie watched him leave. Gretchen rolled her eyes after him.

"Do you know where Beech is?" Josie asked as she stepped out of the kiln room.

"Hardly ever," Gretchen said, closing the door. "But I'm sure he'll answer if you call him. He seems to be all about you at the moment."

Josie ran her hands over the box, absorbing its creeping heat. "At the moment."

Gretchen offered her a tight-lipped smile. "If it bothers you, you should tell him," she said, putting a gentle hand on Josie's back, wrapping Josie in the smoky scent of patchouli and charcoal. "Not everyone is interested in an open relationship and that's okay. I'm not saying it will change him, but you should be honest if you want more. Who knows? I was in a committed relationship myself for a long time."

"And then?"

"Then it became an open relationship, and then it was over. We went our separate ways. But I don't regret it. I was happy in it and I was happy when it was over and I'm happy now. I was true to myself and honest with them. You should be too. Whatever that means for you."

"And what if I don't know what that means?"

Gretchen gave Josie a side squeeze. "So long as you're honest with yourself, you'll figure it out. In the meantime, don't be afraid of getting hurt. Everybody gets hurt. Some of the best art comes out of being totally crushed and brokenhearted."

"I'm not an artist."

Gretchen's pierced eyebrow shot up. "No?" She hooked her finger around the strap of Josie's bag, her voice lowered to a whisper. "I wonder what our fire god friend would say about that."

Josie gaped. "How did you know he's a fire god?"

"I've seen a couple. Their masks are usually austere. Fire doesn't need frills. They'd probably get burnt off anyway." Gretchen ran her finger over her lip thoughtfully. "He?"

Josie looked away. Although they were in the far corner, away from the others, it seemed like everyone was leaning in their direction.

"Fire is a dangerous element, Josie," Gretchen said, fixing her bright green eyes on Josie in a way that made her shift—sometimes it seemed like Gretchen had X-ray vision, like she could tell what Josie was thinking. "There's a reason so few summoners are allowed to be in possession of the fire gods."

"I know."

"I'm honestly surprised Caroline allowed you take it. Considering..."

"You mean the stolen masks?" Josie asked, keeping her voice in a hush.

Gretchen glanced over shoulder. Eyes dropped, voices raised.

"Or are you talking about the Eye being blind?" Josie added.

Gretchen, for the first time since Josie had met her, looked stern. "You shouldn't know about either of those things."

"Why not? What difference does it make? Even if I said something, most people in the tribe would think I'm lying, like they do about the mask-making."

"I don't think that, Josie," Gretchen said. "I know you'll fix that mask. The question is, what will happen to it afterwards?"

He'll be whole again. That's all that matters.

CHAPTER 15

MARCH 22ND
THREE DAYS LATER

I'M IMPRESSED, JOSIE-SLICE," Beech said, flipping on the lights in the art lab. "I didn't think you had it in you. Sneaking out in the middle of the night. Breaking and entering. It's hella sexy."

"Thanks for sharing," Kai grumbled as he came in behind Beech.

Josie went straight past them, the box hot in her hands. Simone was on her heels.

"Are you sure about this?" Simone said, twisting her bracelets frantically.

Josie set the box on the counter and shook out her hands, which were shaking and sweating.

"Mix the clay," Josie said.

Simone nodded and started to haul one of the five-gallon buckets away from the wall. Kai came over and lifted the clay-filled bucket onto the table for her.

Josie wiped the sweat off her forehead. Sneaking out had been a big risk, especially if she was being followed, or if Judah had been right and there was a traitor in the tribe. If Earth Mama attacked with only Kai and Beech around to summon up a defender god, Josie's protective charms, which were up to her elbows thanks to Simone, would still disintegrate in minutes. The risk was even greater since none of them had cars. She'd ridden peg-style with Beech to the center, while Simone and Kai had biked over separately. At least cars could be bulwarked with charms. On bikes, they were totally exposed.

Thankfully though, they'd made it without any problems.

"Now what?" Beech asked from too close beside her.

She pulled a pillowcase from her bag and laid it next to the box on the counter. Tugging off her jacket, she combed her sweat-damp hair back from her face. "Get me the hammer."

From behind her, Simone said, "Does this seem a little crazy to anyone else?"

"Yeah, but in a good way," Kai said.

"I just don't want you to get in trouble," Simone said.

Josie turned, forcing a smile on her face. "Neither do I."

Wrist deep in clay tempered with volcanic ash, Simone stopped kneading the clay body for a moment. "Then maybe—"

"Don't talk her out of it," Beech said, returning from a cabinet on the other side of the room with a rubberized hammer.

Josie took the hammer. "She couldn't. I have to do this."

"How do you know?" Simone asked.

Josie looked at each of them. "I just . . . do."

She turned back to the box, setting the hammer aside. Next to her, Beech was like a kid waiting in line for his first ride on a roller coaster. Jittery crackles of energy snapped and popped off of him.

"No offense," she said, "but you need to back off."

He held up his hands. "No problem. I'm stoked, that's all." He retreated from her, taking a seat on a table not far away.

Josie would've preferred to do this alone, but Beech knew all the codes to enter the tribal center. And once she'd started asking Simone about mixing clays and firing the kiln, Simone had quickly realized Josie was up to something and had pestered her until she'd confessed her plan. Once Simone knew, she wasn't about to be left out. For some reason, Kai had to tag along too. Josie guessed that's just what it meant to have friends, and she wasn't totally opposed to the idea, but she didn't want them getting in trouble either. As exciting as Beech found the rule breaking, Josie was only doing it out of necessity, not because she enjoyed it. In fact, a part of her was dead set against it, but that part had been overruled by the new mask-making part of her, the part that needed to see this mask, in particular, whole again.

She took a deep, shuddering breath. Even the air in her lungs felt overheated. With the tips of her fingers, she slid the box open. Smoke poured out as the wood shavings began to catch.

"Shit," Beech said, jumping off the table. "It's going to set off the alarms."

She grabbed the pillow case. As quickly as she could, she picked up the pieces of the mask, tossing them into the pillow case. She pushed the smoldering box into the nearby sink and turned on the water, letting the cold rush run over her sore fingertips. Beech stood next to her again.

He touched her arm. "You're burning up."

She splashed the frigid water on her face, scooping it into her mouth. "As soon as it's done, I'll be better." She hoped.

Somehow, the fire god was infecting her with this heat, like he was possessing her. The same way he'd been able to enter her dreams. She didn't know how it was possible. This felt different from when she'd created the other two masks, although the same inexplicable certainty had taken hold of her. She knew what she had to do, without knowing how.

Sweat dripped off her nose and down her neck. She pulled one of her bracelets off. Sweeping her hair up, she twisted it into a hasty bun, securing it with the bracelet.

She wadded up the end of the pillowcase and grabbed the hammer. At the back of the room, beneath the dark windows, she knelt. Against her shins, the concrete was blissfully cold. She laid the pillow case in front of her. The others watched.

When she raised the hammer, the door opened.

Judah came in, brow said, *You are so busted.* Tessa was close behind him. And then Russell. Apparently, she was being followed.

Russell pushed by Tessa and Judah. "Josie, what are you—?"

She brought the hammer down, again and again, as fast as she could. In the pillow case, the mask sighed and hissed as it was pulverized. Beech intercepted Russell when he rushed at Josie. Russell swore and shouted, but she barely heard him.

Each hammer strike rebounded up her arm and all through her, jarring and painful, like she was breaking herself in the process. When the largest pieces were crushed, she took the wooden end of the hammer and ground the pieces into powder. Sweat ran over her face, her clothes were soaked through, her head spun. Her vision blurred, clouded as if by steam.

"Josie, what are you doing?" Tessa said when Josie finally pushed up to her feet. The pillow case swung in her hand.

Beech was grimacing and holding his stomach, a pukish hue on his face. Russell must have hit him. Beech continued to stand between him and Josie, but Russell had stopped struggling. Fury roiled in the shadows of his face.

Blood ran from his nose. "You—you—what have you done?"

"Is it ready?" Josie asked Simone.

Simone pulled her hands from the glopping clay body. "Yeah—"

Josie turned the bag over into the bowl. Russell let out a strangled gasp. He started towards her again, but she pulled the bowl back and lifted the hammer again. "Don't interfere."

"You destroyed it." Russell sagged against the nearest table. "You—"

"I had to," she said, tossing the hammer down and digging her hands into the half-formed clay body. She worked the remains of the mask into the clay, grimacing as the heat began to build again. "It's the only way."

"Josie?" Simone asked uncertainly.

Josie grabbed the cup from the water bowl and poured a splash into the clay. The rest she dumped over her head.

"Fuckin' A, she's steaming," Kai murmured.

"Josie." Tessa came towards her.

"Stay away," Josie said, picking up the bowl of clay.

She gave Judah a particularly pointed look. She could tell he thought she was crazy, but he made no move to stop her.

A dry murmur of fire grew, burning lips whispering into her ear. The room swirled around her in a heat-warped blur. Her legs shook, weak, like the fire was breaking up her bones. She couldn't stand any more.

Dropping to her knees, she turned the clay out on the floor.

And then her hands began to work. She would make him again.

This time, he would be perfect.

She bent over the clay, her nose brushing the floor. Every few minutes, she had to stop and rest her forehead against the cool concrete.

"I need, uh ..."

Simone knelt next to her, the bowl in her hand. "Water?"

Josie nodded. "And ... smoothing ..."

"Kai, the tools, over there." Simone set the bowl down. Josie dunked her face in it. The water hissed.

Simone dumped a dozen tools on the floor next to the water. Josie picked up one, hardly knowing which, and began to shape the cheeks—sharp, long. Pressing her fist against the inside to hold the shape, she wanted to scream. Her skin burned where it touched the clay, but she couldn't lose focus. She had to finish. Screaming would only waste time.

As she sharpened the eyes, multicolored flames flared in the narrow gaps, dancing, smiling, laughing. Then she defined the lips. The top, twin peaks. The lower lip was full, a swell of magma.

Perfect.

His symbol came to her then.

She picked up another tool. She drew the circle and within it a cleft peak. Between the peaks, an arcing swell, like the sun, like an explosion—an eruption.

A volcanic god.

Then she added the lost symbols denoting the god's name in Core language. The mark glowed, traced by a ghost of orange flame, and then vanished.

She bit her lip as she went over the lines again. They had to be right. They needed to be right. She frowned as his lips began to turn red, dotted with crimson.

"Josie, stop, you're bleeding," Simone said, her voice distant and pained.

Gently, though her hands burned as if she'd had an acid dip, she picked up the mask. And then, somehow, stood up.

"Kiln."

They watched her as she passed, she knew, not that she could see them. All her focus was on the mask. The journey across the room was agony. The fire ate away at her, and yet seemed to be the only thing moving her forward. She laid the mask onto the kiln shelf. Beech closed the lid and flipped the switches.

The fire inside her eased. Head in a haze, body limp, hands throbbing, losing heat, her knees buckled. Someone caught her, lifted her up, and carried her out.

"No," she said weakly. "I have to wait for him."

"Turn on the water," Judah said. "Fill up the sink."

"Did she really do it?" Tessa asked from somewhere far away.

"Fire god," Kai said, a smile in his voice.

"Bring that table over here," Judah said. "Anyone know where I can get some honey?"

"Honey?" Tessa's voice was drowned out by the squeal and groan of table legs dragging across concrete.

"I think Mama Bear keeps some for her tea," Beech said.

"Get it. And the first aid kit by the door."

Judah set Josie down on something hard—the table that had been dragged over. Her head felt half melted. Her vision, heat blasted. Then her hands were submerged. The pain dissolved into the cool water.

She sagged against Judah. He held her upright, keeping her hands in the sink. His pulse thumped, familiarly, against her cheek. As the fire subsided, her vision cleared.

Simone appeared in front of her, pressing a cool rag to her lip. "You freaked me out," she said.

"Sorry," Josie said.

Tessa slid in between Simone and the counter, peering into the sink at Josie's hands. "Will she be all right?"

Judah lifted her arm up from the water. The skin was red. He lowered it into the water again, gently. "It's not as bad as it looks."

"It looks bad," Tessa said.

"That was way more intense than the rainforest god," Beech said, reappearing with a plastic bear filled with honey and a first aid kit.

"What do you expect?" Kai said, standing further back from the group. "Fire god."

"You shouldn't have done it," Russell said, lingering near the center of the room. "I called the Eye. They'll be here soon and then—"

"Shut up, Russell," Judah said.

His eyes flickered dangerously at Judah. "Stay out of this, Goodwin. It doesn't have anything to do with you."

Then his gaze darted towards the kiln.

A surge of fire licked up inside of Josie. She twisted in Judah's grip, pulling her hands out of the water. "If you go anywhere near—"

Russell dug his hands into his hair. "You destroyed the face of a god! Do you realize—?"

"It's what he told me to do," Josie said.

Russell gave her an incredulous look. "He told you? You can't summon the gods. You can't—"

She lifted her reddened hands. "Do you think I did this to myself?"

Judah gripped her forearm. "Josie—"

"Here's an idea," Josie said to Russell, "why don't we wait until he comes back. Then you can ask him yourself?"

"Yeah, I'll be happy to take possession of him," Beech offered.

"You need to put your hands back in the water," Judah said calmly, as if he didn't really care one way or the other what she did, which was probably the case.

She threw her elbow into his side. He stepped back, eyebrow cocked in a now-you've-pissed-me-off slant.

She plunged her hands into the sink again. Under the water, her skin glowed red as radishes.

Now that her task was complete and the fire god's heat was evaporating away, leaving her trembling and weak, she started to wonder if maybe bringing back an ancient volcano god wasn't the best idea. Very few summoners were allowed to possess fire gods. The gods of fire were notoriously difficult to control and known for hurting their summoners as much as helping them. Then again, he wasn't a typical fire god—she didn't know if that was a good thing or not. But she did know that Russell was wrong. She had been able to summon a god, in a way. At least, she felt like she'd been temporarily possessed by him. He'd infiltrated her dreams, filled her with heat, shown her how to shape his face, and provided her with his symbol that would transfer the power of his mortal aspect to his new mask. And now that he was gone, she was left hollowed and cold.

"Having second thoughts?" Judah asked softly, setting the first aid kit on the counter next to the sink.

She scowled at him.

"The human body shouldn't be able to handle heat like that." Judah said, seemingly to himself. He picked through the first aid kit. "Non-summoners anyway."

"I may not be a summoner," she said to him, "but I'm still Core."

He frowned, but didn't say anything more, though she could tell he was holding back.

She looked down at her submerged hands. He was right, of course. Normal humans couldn't have handled the kind of godly heat that she'd just experienced. That was part of what it meant to be Core and, more specifically, a summoner. Something in the Core's bloodlines allowed them to wield godly power that would have killed terrae—nonsummoners. Even well-trained summoners were occasionally overwhelmed and killed by the power they channeled.

"It was an ancient god, wasn't it?" Tessa said, twisting her hair around her hand thoughtfully. "Resurrecting the ancient gods . . . that's . . ."

"Awesome?" Beech said.

"Dangerous," Judah said, pulling out a roll of gauze.

Tessa nodded. "You know, that mask looked sort of like—"

The lights flickered.

"What the—?" Beech started.

An explosion rocked the building. Josie tumbled off the table into Simone and Tessa. Fire alarms blared. Smoke filled the room.

CHAPTER 16

MARCH 22ND

"I HAVE TO GO BACK," Josie said the moment Beech shut her bedroom door behind them.

"We just got you out," he said.

"I know, but—"

"No one's allowed in the center until the firefighters clear it and it's not safe for you to be sitting around in the street." Beech took her arm and propelled her backwards onto her futon.

"But the mask is—"

"The Eye will be there, with all their little monkeys." Beech flopped down next to her. "Do you think they're going to let anyone touch it?"

No, but she didn't want them touching it either.

"How are your hands?" he asked.

Wrapped up in mittens of gauze, her hands had gone numb after Judah had smeared them with honey. She didn't know how he'd had the presence of mind to grab the bottle and the gauze and her and get them all out of the center before the fire department had arrived. He'd hidden her in his car and instructed everyone to lie about her presence. And then, while the others intercepted the firefighters, he'd treated her wounds and told Beech to take her home. She supposed it was good that he was a useful jerk.

"I don't know," she muttered, slumping back against the futon, feeling helpless. It was a feeling she was becoming far too familiar with, and she hated it.

He lifted one of her arms and looked it over. A glob of honey glistened on the inside of her wrist. He licked it away.

"You're trying to distract me," she said.

He kissed her neck. "Is it working?"

She let him pull her onto his lap.

It did work—mostly.

MARCH 23RD

"Something's wrong," Josie said as her dad drove her to the center before dawn the next morning. "What is it?"

His eyes glittered, hard as polished agate, behind his glasses. "You mean apart from your irresponsible behavior last night?"

"Dad—"

Her dad's tone dropped into a low, still place, a place where bodies were buried and forgotten. "I am extremely disappointed in you right now, Josie. I would prefer if you didn't speak."

Josie lapsed into silence, gazing out at the empty streets that were gray in the pale light of dawn.

Once they parked in the underground garage, he got out of the car and opened her door for her, since her hands were still swaddled in gauze. His mood hadn't been helped by Beech's presence in her room that morning. Or by the fact that neither of them had been fully clothed. Her dad had turned from livid-purple to deathly-white and then, in a terrifyingly calm voice, had asked Beech to leave and told Josie to get dressed because the Eye wanted to see her.

He led her to the elevator and up to the third floor. An acrid sulfur stench hung in the air. Everything had a hazy quality to it. She couldn't tell if it was due to the early hour or the remnants of the fire.

He pulled open the door to the Eye's sanctum. Everyone else turned to look at her. Everyone but Judah. She shouldn't have been surprised he was there, or that he was still wearing the same clothes. Tessa, Simone, Kai, and Russell hadn't changed either. No one looked like they'd slept. The burning stench was stronger here, clinging to them. Soot smudged their faces and darkened their hair. The only other person in attendance was Gretchen. Josie was surprised the matriarchs weren't present. If they were planning on meting out some punishment, the matriarchs should've been there. They'd be pissed if they missed out on the fun.

Her dad put a hand on her shoulder and guided her to the front. The Eye sat behind their table, watching her.

Lily was wringing her hands again. Caroline's face was weary, but kind. Nancy looked like she was thirsting for blood.

Her dad sat down, leaving Josie standing alone.

Caroline gave each of her Sisters a look. "Well?"

Nancy's voice had a dull knife-edge quality. "Where is your son, Gretchen?"

Gretchen opened her mouth, and then closed it, shaking her head.

"Forgive me, Sisters," Josie's dad said. "I saw him. I didn't realize that you—"

"He'll turn up," Caroline said, "eventually."

"Or he won't," Nancy said. "If he's the thief."

"Pardon my tone, Honorable Eye, but my son is not a thief," Gretchen said.

Josie's heart started to hammer. "Forgive me, Mothers," she said, "but was something stolen?"

"You are not forgiven," Nancy stated.

Caroline's normally light face darkened. "There is nothing to forgive," she said. "Josie only did as I requested."

Nancy slapped the table. "Behind my back!"

"You were being entirely unreasonable—" Caroline twisted in her chair towards Nancy.

Nancy's cool eyes burned. "And you're irrational, as usual—"

"I'm irrational? What about you? You're acting like—"

"Like what, Caroline? Like what?"

"Like a petulant child!"

While the argument grew more heated, everyone in the room seemed to shrink in their seats, even Lily.

Josie looked towards Tessa, who was slumped in her chair apart from the others, half asleep. She glanced up at Josie.

Stop this, Josie mouthed at her.

"I'm a child? Ha! You're one to talk," Nancy was saying.

Tessa's eyes widened. She shook her head.

"I am one to talk. You may not like it, Nancy, but you're not the only one here with an opinion."

"I might give your opinion more credence if I thought you were capable of logical thought—"

"What the hell does that mean?"

"Oh, you know exactly what it means. You're as impulsive as a toddler in a toy store and about as intelligent."

Caroline stood up. "You intolerant, narrow-minded, desiccated—"

"Stop!" Josie cried.

Caroline froze, like she'd been slapped.

Nancy whipped around. "How dare you—"

Josie plowed ahead. "You are the Eye of this tribe. The tribe of the Triune. And you're arguing in front of…"—she swept her bandaged hands out towards the averted eyes in the room—"us?"

Nancy surged up from her chair. "You have no place to speak!"

"But I do," Tessa said, voice weak and tentative. "And … Josie's right."

Nancy dropped back into her chair, rolling her eyes at Tessa.

Josie's hands curled in their bandages. She shot Tessa another look. Tessa held up her hands, mouthing, *What?*

Josie dropped her head back, wanting to roar. No one rolled their eyes at the Triune.

Slowly, Caroline sat down.

Since Josie had already blown past all decorum, she didn't see any need to continue with it. Besides, the Eye was blind. Technically, their power was invalidated. No special modes of address were required.

"Where is the mask?" she demanded.

Nancy fixed her with a piercing look, but Caroline ran her hand over her face. "We were hoping that you had taken it."

Josie's heart plummeted. "It's missing?"

Russell slid to the edge of his chair, face strained somewhere between anger and panic. "You must've taken it."

She stared at him until his hard features faltered.

"You have to have . . ." he said weakly.

"When would I have taken it? In the two seconds after the explosion and before Judah carried me out? He was with me the whole time until Beech took me back home."

They all turned to Judah, who'd been staring impassively at the floor, like he'd been sleeping with his eyes open. "She's telling the truth," he said dully.

Pain bubbled up from the dark places. For a second, her eyes burned, like she might actually cry. It seemed stupid to be so upset about a mask. But it wasn't just any mask. Not to her.

"I don't even know if it worked," she said more to herself than any of them, "if I really . . . I never even saw it."

"I did," Russell said in an almost comforting tone.

She gaped at him. "You did?"

Russell scrubbed his hands over his face. Ash was smeared on his cheeks, rendering them more dramatic. "I went back. I got a glimpse of it before the firefighters threw me out."

"It was intact?" she asked.

Russell nodded.

She let out a sigh of relief. "And . . . was it . . ."

He gazed at her in a new way, one that caused her stomach to squirm.

"It appeared to be restored," he said.

She smiled. She'd done it. She'd repaired the mask of an ancient god. She'd brought him back to the mortal plane.

Her smile died. But now he was missing.

"Maybe you took it," Kai said to Russell without breaking his slouch.

"You're a more likely candidate," Russell sneered.

Kai flipped him off.

"They should all be searched," Josie said to the Eye. "All of their sanctuaries."

Kai snorted, like he'd expected her to turn on them. But she wasn't turning on them. She just wanted to find the mask.

"They were searched," Nancy said with contempt.

"They submitted to having their sanctuaries searched, Josie," Caroline said with sympathy.

"One of them could have a secret sanctuary," she blurted out, desperate.

The Eye stared at her. Judah and Tessa gave her incredulous looks. Simone's was wounded. She probably thought Josie was accusing Kai, like Russell had. But Josie wasn't accusing anyone. They just happened to be the most likely suspects. No one else had known that she was repairing a mask. And even if someone had found out, the only people who'd known that it was in the kiln were sitting in this room now, except Beech.

Nancy's eyebrow quirked. "A secret sanctuary. Now there's a thought."

Caroline frowned. "I am the only one who knows our tribe's sanctuary charm."

"What about the firefighters, the police?" Simone interjected. "One of them could've taken it."

"Possibly," Caroline said with a heavy sigh. "But why would they?"

"Maybe one of them is from another tribe. Maybe one of them is working for the Earth Goddess?" Simone proposed.

Josie could tell, by the current of discomfort in the smoke-tainted air, that everyone else found this theory as unlikely as she did. She glanced over at Judah. His eyes remained glued to the floor.

When he'd said there might be a traitor in the tribe, Josie hadn't been entirely convinced. Earth Mama could've found out about Josie's mask-making some other way. Rumors, like Beech had said, but now . . .

"How many people knew I had the mask?" Josie asked.

"You're looking at them." Caroline gestured around the room. "Minus Beech."

Josie hated to ask, but she had to. "Did anyone tell?"

"I didn't, I swear," Simone said.

"Neither did I," Gretchen stated.

"I didn't know about the mask until I got to the art lab," Tessa said. "Neither did Judah, did you?"

He bowed his head over his interlocked hands.

Tessa frowned. "Did you?"

"He knew because he stopped by my office when I was choosing the masks to present to Josie," Caroline said. "The only reason he didn't tell you was because I asked him not to mention it. I'd intended to tell you myself, Divine Mother."

Tessa continued frowning, not looking appeased.

"How did you know I was at the art lab?" Josie asked them.

"I saw you leaving," Judah said without looking up.

"Saw me leaving from where? You were at my house in the middle of the . . ."

A muscle in Judah's jaw ticked, his brow plunged in annoyance. Tessa's feet lifted to her toes like she might pounce.

Josie's throat dried up, clenching. "Oh."

Her dad was turning unhealthy colors again. Josie turned back to Russell.

"And what about you?" she asked.

"I followed Kai," he said. "I heard him talking to Simone. I knew that if Simone was going out at midnight, then it had something to do with you."

"You were eavesdropping, is what you mean," Kai said in a threatening growl.

"This isn't getting us anywhere," Nancy said. "We need to find the other boy and bring him here."

The other boy. Beech. Like she didn't know his name.

The only people who'd known Josie had the mask were in this room—except for Beech. One of them must've taken it. Either they took it for themselves or . . . they took it for someone else, like Earth Mama. If that were true, then someone in this room was a traitor.

Josie hated herself for saying it, but the words rushed out before she could stop them. She wanted that fire god mask back.

"What about a truth-charm?"

Every gaze turned to her, from Nancy's shrewd one to Simone's, pained-looking, to Kai's, dark and cynically amused.

It was Gretchen's gaze that hit her hardest, right in the gut. Dark shadows of disappointment clouded their normally brilliant green depths.

"I am not submitting to a truth-charm," Gretchen stated.

Josie's chest ached, but she shoved the guilt down.

"You will if that is what the Eye decrees," Nancy said, a smile creeping around the edges of her lips.

Caroline drummed her fingers on the table, also looking disappointed and annoyed. A truth-charm was drastic, Josie knew.

Usually, forcing the truth out of fellow tribal members with a charm occurred only in the direst of circumstances. She knew that by suggesting it, she was basically saying she didn't trust them—her own tribe. But someone had stolen an ancient fire god mask and that someone might also have been working for Earth Mama. How much more dire did circumstances have to be?

"I really don't think that's necessary," Caroline said, hitching her eyebrows at Josie, yanking the guilty pang back into Josie's chest.

"This is a serious matter," Nancy said.

"I don't believe anyone in this room has any cause to be dishonest," Caroline said.

"Well, that can be easily enough discovered, can't it?"

"There is nothing easy about a truth-charm," Caroline said.

"What do you think, Sister?" Nancy leaned around Caroline to look at Lily.

Lily's pudgy fingers toyed with her beaded necklaces, eyes darting between her Sister leaders, like a child caught between two bickering parents. She looked like a red-haired hedgehog trying to curl up into itself.

"Well . . ."

"You did agree to have the girl repair the mask," Nancy cut in. The words, *behind my back,* never came, but Josie heard them just the same. "You wanted this mask, didn't you? Don't you think it prudent we do whatever is necessary to recover it?"

Pink splotches marred Caroline's golden skin. "A truth-charm isn't going to help recover it, because no one in this room took it."

"You are too trusting," Nancy purred.

"Not *too* trusting, just trusting," Caroline shot back.

Josie glanced at Simone, who was gazing back at her with that look of hurt. Kai glowered at Josie from the corner of his eyes. Judah stared at the floor, brow all annoyance. She could just imagine what he thought of her for suggesting a truth-charm—untrusting, coldhearted, frigid. And she could see how proposing that her friends be subjected to an inquiry while under the power of a truth-charm wasn't the best way to keep them as friends. While having friends had never been on her list of priorities, Judah had been right. She needed to learn how to depend on others, to trust them.

"Forgive me, Mothers,"—Josie turned back to the Eye—"I'm sure everyone here is telling the truth. We have no reason to think they wouldn't. A truth-charm isn't really necessary, I just—"

"There have certainly been enough lies by omission lately," Nancy said tartly. "I move we convene a full inquiry and require all witnesses to submit to a truth-charm."

"You can't," Josie said more strongly.

Nancy's eyes flashed, deadly. "Do not—"

"You can't force members of your tribe to submit to a truth-charm unless all Sisters of the Eye are in agreement," Josie said.

"And I will never vote for that," Caroline said. "Or make the charms for it either."

"I agree," Lily added softly. "I don't believe any of these children took that mask."

"Then who?" Nancy said. "The rescue workers?" She fixed her knife-sharp eyes on Caroline. "Your husband was a firefighter. Did he often steal while on the job?"

Caroline's cheeks burned red. "Do not talk about my—"

"Enough!" Josie cut in again, before the Eye exposed their crumbling leadership any further. "Excuse me, Venerable Mothers, but you cannot continue to argue like this in public."

Caroline hung her head. Nancy glared at Josie. Lily looked away, towards the windows.

"Of course, you're right, Josie," Lily said finally, in her gentle tones. "Thank you so much for reminding us. I think we've heard enough for one day, Sisters?"

"There is still the matter of a missing ancient mask, which allegedly, was restored," Nancy said. "Not that I'm saying I believe it, but in either case, we would be remiss not to do everything in our power to recover it."

Josie hated agreeing with Nancy.

"We will search for it, Sister," Caroline said, her tone careful. "I know a few locator charms. I'll start work on them immediately."

Nancy's mouth puckered. Josie knew her thoughts exactly. Locator charms were notoriously unreliable. And in the instance of a stolen mask, if the mask were hidden in a sanctuary somewhere, then it would be even more difficult to find. Even though sanctuary charms were unusual because they weren't tied to a specific summoner—making them accessible to anyone who had the ring, one of the arcane rules of the Covenant—they were bound with the blood of the charm-maker, and nothing was stronger than blood magic.

As the meeting convened, Simone gave Josie a smile. Instant forgiveness. Josie was glad, but she still couldn't shake the terrible sinking sensation pulling at her, a feeling too much like drowning.

The mask was gone.

She'd have to fend off her nightmares on her own. Again.

CHAPTER 17

"WHAT'S HE DOING HERE?" Josie frowned as Judah strolled into the living room behind Tessa.

From the other side of the room, over the top of his computer screen, her dad shot her a warning look. "I invited him back."

"Why him and not Beech?"

"Because Judah spoke to me, for one," her dad said. "We came to an understanding."

"Kissed your ass, you mean," Josie muttered.

For the last two weeks, she'd found herself missing Beech's evening visits, almost as much as she missed the mask. In spite of the locator charms and a discreet investigation into all the rescue workers who had been on the scene that night, the mask was still missing.

Judah and Tessa sat down on the couch across from her. Josie eyed him. Adonis, as always. He even smelled perfect—that ambery, clean scent; not too strong, but noticeable. She ground her teeth, wishing she had an off button for her sense of smell.

The only thing she'd enjoyed about a boy-free house was no Judah. She'd almost managed to forget he existed. In the rare moments she'd seen him at the tribal center, he'd been pounding away in the gym or organizing the younger kids for one of Lily's "Communing with Mother Earth" hikes.

Sadly, the holiday had ended.

He caught her gaze. "The hands look good."

She dropped her eyes to the tablet screen. Her hands, in fact, were fine. They'd been tender for a few days, but the skin hadn't blistered. She supposed Judah wanted credit or a thank you, but if so, he was going to be disappointed.

"I've been thinking about it," Tessa said, "and I'm ready."

Josie looked up again. "Ready for what?"

"To go to the island and meet my guides."

Josie set the tablet aside. She'd been scouring the tribe's digital library for information on the fire god mask. So far, she hadn't found anything, other than its archival number and annotation: *Mask, clay, black. Three fragments. Fire.* Nothing about how it had come into the tribe's possession, when it had been created or destroyed, or who the last summoner had been to wield its powers.

"That's great," she said.

"I'm a little nervous," Tessa said.

"Don't be," Josie said, forgetting to be annoyed by Judah's presence. "You'll be fine. And once you contact your guides you'll progress much faster. You may be able to assume some of your duties."

Finally.

And then Josie could return to the island as well and do some real research on the history of the mask-makers ... and volcano gods.

Tessa ran her hands over her jeans. "I don't know if I'm ready for *that*."

Josie refrained from saying that Tessa should have been ready. She should've been responding to the urgent messages she received every day, some of which concerned more missing masks and, worse, missing summoners, not to mention all her usual responsibilities as Triune. But Josie had learned not to push Tessa too much or Tessa would shut down and be completely useless.

Leaning back in her chair, Josie took up the tablet again. "That's great, Tessa. When are you going to leave?"

"After the concert tomorrow," Tessa said. "Dad's letting us go."

"Although I don't know why," he grumbled from the dining room table.

The tablet fell against Josie's thigh. "Is that a good idea?"

"No," Judah answered.

"He said you can go too," Tessa said to her. "Simone cleared it with the Eye."

Josie ran her finger over the screen, flipping the page back and forth. Simone had been talking about the concert nonstop for the last week; ever since they'd exhausted all discussion of the mask and where it might've gone and if there really was a traitor in the tribe.

Kai's band had a gig, opening for an almost-famous group, which also happened to have a couple of tribal members in it. The venue was owned by a tribal member. Simone had been helping Caroline and Lily beef up the club's defenses with circles and charms, some as strong as the ones that protected the tribal center. Simone had mentioned this to Josie's dad at every opportunity.

"I don't know..." Josie said.

Tessa shrugged. "Whatever. I just thought it might be good for you, since you've been moping around so much."

"I haven't been moping," she said, not even convincing herself.

"Moping over Beech?" Judah said, smirking.

"It's not Beech she misses, it's that fire god mask," Tessa said archly. "Isn't it?"

Josie lifted the tablet in front of her face, hoping to hide the blush. She'd been blushing a lot since she'd moved to Portland. No matter what she did, she couldn't get a handle on the creeping heat. "That's crazy."

"You should see it," Tessa said to Judah in a playful tone. "She doodles the mask everywhere. I saw her drawing it in ketchup with her french fry the other day."

"So I was drawing a mask," Josie said, letting the tablet fall to her lap again. "That's what I do, if you've forgotten."

"Looked like the fire god to me," Tessa said, tapping her forehead with a wicked gleam in her eye.

Damn. Josie really needed to stop drawing the fire god's symbol all over the place.

"You know it's not healthy to obsess over a god," Tessa said, leaning into Judah familiarly. "Haven't you read the demigod stories? God/human relationships never end well."

Josie's stomach soured watching Tessa run her finger over Judah's neck. He didn't seem to notice Tessa. His eyes remained fixed on Josie.

"How can you be obsessed with a mask?" he asked.

"I am not obsessed."

"I know, right?" Tessa said, as if Josie hadn't spoken. "It's one thing to have the hots for a god, but you haven't even met him, really. Or maybe you just fell for his face. Was that it?"

Josie's cheeks burned. "No—"

"You fell for the face?" Judah said, amused light dancing in his eyes. He seemed to enjoy watching her squirm. "The face of the fire god? The face you created?"

"Was it like your ideal?" Tessa asked. "Is that why you miss it so much? Because the mask was the embodiment of your perfect guy's face? The artist falls in love with her own sculpture? That sounds sad."

"I made it the way the god wanted—" She pursed her lips. She didn't like talking about mask-making, not with Tessa and especially not with Judah. It felt too personal somehow.

Tessa and Judah's eyes narrowed in unison.

"How does that work anyway?" Tessa asked quietly. "You never explained it. When you made that mask, you were burning up. And you were literally burned. But a god's power shouldn't work like that. A god's power should only appear when it's summoned, right?"

"I don't know how it works." Unfortunately. All the information she'd found concerning mask-makers was vague and buried in stories about the Age of the Demigods and the Age of Manifestation, stories from thousands of years ago that seemed to be more myth than fact.

"But the god communicated with you," Judah said.

"In a way."

"What kind of way?" Tessa asked. "The gods talk to you?"

"No . . ." Although, she had heard the rainforest god speak.

"So how could you make the fire god's mask the way he wanted if he didn't talk to you?" Tessa asked. "Did he show you, like in a vision or a dream?"

The burning spread from her face to her chest and then all through her. Ever since she'd completed the mask, her dreams had changed, but they hadn't reverted to terror-filled nightmares like she'd feared they would.

They started the same. Falling, panicking, drowning. The distant flame that had been her beacon while she'd had the mask no longer appeared in the darkness. Instead, arms of blue flame wrapped around her and pulled her from the water. When she turned to thank him, all she saw was fire. Blue fire. Bluer than anything she'd ever seen. Bluer than the azure church cupolas in Oia, a cliffside Greek town where her mom had taken her for her thirteenth birthday; bluer than the birds that skittered through the cedars in Westmoreland park, their feathers brilliant flecks of color in a world of gray and green; bluer even than the Hope Diamond, which she'd seen in the Smithsonian years ago.

Even during the day when she closed her eyes, she could see the ghosts of blue flames. The memory of the heat flooded through her. Inching, caressing, consuming heat.

She brushed her hair away from her neck. "Like I said, I don't know how it works. It just . . . happens."

Judah opened his mouth, but was interrupted.

"What are you three talking about?" her dad asked.

"Josie's in love with a fire god," Tessa sing-songed.

Her dad frowned. "What fire god?"

"I'm not in love with anyone," Josie said loud enough for her dad to hear.

Her dad continued to frown, even as his eyes tracked back to his computer screen.

"Not even Beech?" Judah asked, distracted from her when Tessa stole a kiss from him.

Josie hesitated long enough for Tessa to stop slobbering on Judah.

"Are you?" Tessa asked.

"No," Josie said. "That would be stupid."

"Yeah, it would," Judah said. "But you've done some pretty stupid things before."

Tessa slapped his chest. "You said you'd be nice."

"When?"

"So it'd be really stupid of me to go to this concert, right?" Josie asked him.

His amusement vanished. "Neither of you should be going."

Tessa blew a raspberry at him. "You'd send me to the island and make me stay there for the rest of my life if you could."

"I'm going to the concert, Dad!" Josie called, flashing a smile at Judah. If he thought it was a bad idea, then she had to go. On principle.

"Okay," her dad said, not looking up from his computer. "But I'm dropping you off and picking you up."

"And he'll be at the bar down the block," Tessa said. "With Ashley."

She and Tessa exchanged a look. One of the few things they shared was a dislike of their dad's girlfriend. Not that she deserved it, but Ashley made it too easy. She was just so perky.

"That's right," Dad said, standing, gazing down at the thick sheaf of documents in one hand, his coffee mug in the other. "With half the other parents of the tribe." He disappeared into the kitchen.

"You worry too much," Tessa called after him. She poked Judah in the side. "You too. You're like an old lady."

"I don't worry, I anticipate," he said, brow in full disapproval slant. Apparently, two weeks hadn't been long enough for her to forget how to read the coded messages sent by every varied degree of his eyebrows. "And I anticipate, based on recent events, that letting the two of you go anywhere in public is asking for trouble."

"You mean, letting *me* go anywhere in public is asking for trouble," Josie said.

He leveled his cool gaze at her. "You are trouble."

"Then it doesn't matter where I am," she said, pulling her phone out of her pocket. "I'll text your sister and let her know trouble's coming. At least she'll be happy."

"And I suppose she'll be happy to save you the next time too?" Judah asked, brow stating, *I'm not going to let you forget.* "Because you can count me out. I've helped my quota of ungrateful charity cases for the year."

"Judah," Tessa said in a near-warning tone.

"Oh please, Judah," Josie said, leaning towards him with her hand to her heart, "don't leave me bereft of your altruistic heroism. Oh what, what will I do without you?" She stood up. "Guess I'll just have to find someone else to wield the power of an ocean god the next time. Someone who isn't a huge prick." She started past them.

"Josie, really?" Tessa said.

Judah's voice chased her like a growling dog. "No skin off my back. I feel sorry for her. It's not entirely her fault she's socially maladjusted and emotionally infantile."

"Judah!"

Josie halted beside the dining room table, burning again, but this time from anger. "Don't act so surprised, Tessa. It was clear from day one, even to my socially maladjusted eye, that your boyfriend is a complete jackass."

Tessa pushed off the couch. "You two are so selfish."

"Tessa," Judah said, voice ringing with apology. He started to stand up, but Tessa pushed him back down.

"I need you two," Tessa said. "Both of you. Do either of you have any idea how hard this is for me? To have all this pressure, from the Core, from all the Eyes, from the gods? Do you have any idea what it's like to have the Supreme Divine inside your head every second? Life, Death, and the Other? All three of them pulling me in different directions. It's like they're trying to tear me apart inside. The last thing I need is the two of you doing the same thing from the outside. So if all you want to do is fight, then go ahead, but I'm not going to hang around for it."

She stormed past Josie. Tears shone on her peach-hued cheeks.

Now it was Josie's turn to be apologetic. "Tessa—"

But Tessa was gone, stomping up the stairs, slamming the door behind her.

Josie swore, plopping the tablet onto the dining room table.

"What was all that about?" her dad asked, coming back into the room, his brow furrowed.

Josie met Judah's gaze, only this time she saw something in the distant blue, a flicker of emotion. She hoped it was shame.

"Nothing," they said in unison.

Josie turned towards her dad. "She's just stressed, Dad. You know how it is. I'll go talk to her."

"No, I will," Judah said, brushing past her.

Her dad watched Judah stride into the kitchen, after Tessa.

"You're okay with that?" Josie asked, when she heard Judah's footfalls on the stairs.

Her dad set his coffee mug down. "Why shouldn't I be? I trust them."

Josie frowned and picked up her tablet again, wondering what Judah had slipped into her dad's coffee to make him suddenly so trusting. And where she could get some for her and Beech.

"Psst."

Josie looked up. Beech crooked-grinned at her from behind the garage, green eyes flashing, black hair hanging in wet spikes against his forehead.

She put the tablet on the bench, nearly squashing a fat slug that was oozing its way across the redwood. She peeked over at the kitchen window to make sure her dad wasn't peering out at her, like he did regularly whenever she came outside. Every twelve to fifteen minutes on average, though the week before it had been every five to seven minutes. Based on the last time she'd noticed him, she had anywhere between eight to ten minutes before he returned. But there was always the chance he'd come back sooner.

"You're not supposed to be here," Josie said softly, bounding down into the small swath of grass beyond the deck.

April in Portland was proving to be much like March in Portland, chilly and wet. But she must've been getting used to it. As a gentle, straight-down shower of fine drops began, she didn't even blink or pull up the hood of her coat.

"I know that," Beech said, glancing up at the kitchen window himself. "Why do you think I'm here?" He reached out, grabbed her wrist, and pulled her behind the garage, into the warmth of his body. He kissed her. Like always, he tasted sugary sweet. He ate way too much candy.

The space between the back of the garage and the fence was narrow and dim. Gravel crunched under their feet. Beech leaned against the garage, sliding his hands into her back pockets.

He broke from the kiss first. "Simone said you're going to the show tomorrow."

"I guess," she said, wondering why they were wasting time talking.

Strange how quickly she'd become accustomed to being kissed and touched when two months before she'd been so unsure, not knowing what to do with her lips or her hands. Now her fingers plucked at the metal chain around his neck, running over the body-warmed beads of metal. Her tongue skimmed over her lip, still buzzing from the touch of his.

"Aren't you stoked? Papa's finally loosening up the chains."

As much as Josie hated to even think it, let alone admit it, Judah had been right. Going to the show was risky, no matter how well it was protected.

"He's just worried," she said. "He has a right to be."

Beech's head fell back against the siding. "No serious Josie, please."

"Some things are serious," she said. "Someone stole the mask of a seriously powerful volcano god. Someone's been stealing ancient masks from all over the world. Eventually, they're going to want to use them. And since the Triune is practically incapable of summoning the Tripartite at the moment, the thief is probably going to want to use those masks before Tessa might actually pose a threat. And guess who is the only person capable of repairing said masks?"

"Yeah, but so what?" Beech said. "What are you going to do? Stay inside until the apocalypse? Why don't you just have the Eye throw you in the detention center? I bet Nancy would be game."

She pushed back from him. His hands slid away from her.

"That's not what I'm saying."

"Yes, it is," he said. "You want to lock yourself up in a tower until the war's over, but you're not powerless, Josie-pie. You're a freakin' mask-maker. Do you realize how sick that is?"

"Yeah, and Earth Mama and her cronies do too, which is why it would be really bad if they hauled me off to some for-real tower and forced me to build them an even bigger, more badass army."

"I feel sorry for anybody who tries to force you to do anything." Beech hooked her waistband and pulled her back against him. "They don't know who they're messing with."

He kissed her again. She would've been happy if he'd continued kissing her—he was good at it—but he broke away again.

"Speaking of masks, when do I get my badass ancient deity?"

She searched his vibrant green eyes. "Don't you already have one?"

"I told you I didn't take it." His face darkened. "You think I'm a liar?"

She shrugged. "Maybe I wish you were. If you had taken it, I wouldn't say anything. I'd be happy, really."

"Nice to know, but it wasn't me, Your Honor." He held up his hands. "I'm innocent, I swear."

"I wouldn't go that far," she said, deflated.

For all his protests, she wasn't convinced Beech hadn't stolen the mask. Or maybe she was holding out hope. The thought that the fire god's mask might be in that earth bitch's hands turned her blood to magma.

Beech's arms circled around her again. His hands slid under her shirt, up the curve of her back, giving her goose bumps.

She liked kissing him. She liked the feel of his broad shoulders and ropey arms, his big, rough hands, his earthy boy musk and sugar-dusted lips. She loved his energy, the way he couldn't sit still and seemed ready for anything, at any moment. If the apocalypse came, Beech would grab a surf board and ride the destructive waves for all they were worth. That's who Beech was.

But who was she? What would she do?

If she'd been the Triune, she would've fought. She would've tried to stop the waves of destruction from forming in the first place; and if she couldn't, then she would've tried to push them back; and if that didn't work, she would've planted her feet and taken their brunt. That's what the Triune would've done. That's what the Triune had to do.

But, as Judah had felt compelled to point out, she wasn't the Triune. She was a mask-maker. She had no idea what that meant. What did a mask-maker do when faced with impending disaster? Run? Hide? Was that who she was now?

The thought chased all of Beech's residual sweetness from her mouth, leaving a sour tang . . .

She put her hands on his chest. "I should go. If my dad catches us, he really will lock me up in a tower."

But Beech didn't let go. "You're almost eighteen, Josie. We're Core. We're adults. You can do what you want."

He was right. In the Core, fifteen was the age of adulthood. She could do what she wanted, with whomever she wanted.

"I want to show my dad I respect him," she said. "I live in his house. His rules."

"Then move out," he said. "Crash with me until you find a place. Gretchen won't care. She practically lives with her girlfriend anyway."

"You don't mean that."

"Would I have said it if I didn't?"

"I'm sure my dad would love it if I moved in with the boy next door."

"That's my point, Josie. It's not about what he wants. It's about what you want."

She lifted her eyebrow. "I think in this case, it's about what *you* want."

"And you don't?"

Brain-lock. What was she supposed to say? That she didn't know what she wanted? What she liked most about Beech was how easy he made it for her not to think. Too easy. When she didn't know what to do or what she wanted or who she was, he always seemed to have an idea. Most of the time she went along, but this time, when it came to the possibility of sleeping with him, she hesitated.

He laced his fingers through hers. "This is your life, Josie-pie. Nobody controls it but you. Not your dad, not the Eye, not even the gods. Don't be afraid to take control. Don't be afraid of anything."

He kissed her again and then jumped up, grabbing the top of the fence and hauling himself over. "See you tomorrow."

CHAPTER 18

April 6th
The Next Night

K AI'S BAND HAD A MOODY hard-pop sound. Josie might've enjoyed it more if Simone hadn't dragged her to the front of the stage, directly beneath Kai, and the speakers.

Sweat ran over Kai's face, smearing his eye makeup to rock star perfection. In spite of the jostling overheated crowd and loss of hearing, being with Simone, who was smiling so widely her mouth seemed about to touch her ears, was fun. And Kai had a good voice. When he started singing, plenty of girls in the crowd got a glazed dreamy look in their eyes. Even Josie had her moments.

When Kai's band, Minor Gods, finished, Simone allowed Josie to slip outside to catch her breath and attempt to regain her hearing.

The haze over the city glowed ghostly. The block reminded her of so many others she'd seen in the short time she'd been in Portland, a mix of the run-down and the renovated-trendy, old and new, funky and modern. The old brick building housing the venue seemed to lean over the smaller newer buildings. It might once have been a warehouse or a tenement. At the end of the street, a neon cocktail sign burned red through the plate glass window of the restaurant where her dad and Ashley waited. Beyond that, the street darkened suddenly, giving way to chain-link fences and empty-looking commercial buildings.

Josie leaned against the brick and inhaled the cool, moist air, gagging on the secondhand smoke drifting by from the huddles of smokers. A mix of tribe and terrae gathered on the broad sidewalk. For most people, being a part of the Core didn't mean much day-to-day. They'd been born into it, and they didn't have to think about it very often. But she could tell who the tribe members where, not just because of all the rings they wore. Their gazes snagged on her as they skimmed by.

"Wasn't that great?" Simone shouted, like they were still inside.

"Kai is really good," Josie said at normal volume.

She knew she should go back inside. Simone had promised that the sidewalk outside the club was protected, but being out in the open put knots in Josie's stomach. She spun her charm bracelets just like Simone did, watching cars pass by and eyeing every face.

Inside, the club was packed, stinking of beer, sweat, and clashing perfumes. She glanced back down the street towards the restaurant again.

She toyed with her phone in her jacket pocket. How lame would it be if she called her dad and told him she wanted to go home? After all, she'd seen Kai's band, and she wasn't interested in the other act. Simone had mentioned going back to find Kai. Once Simone had Kai, she wouldn't miss Josie.

"Where's Beech?" Simone asked, craning her neck. "Wasn't he with us?"

"He was," Josie said. Half way through the set he'd yelled something at her, making hand gestures she vaguely deciphered to mean he was going to talk to someone, and she hadn't seen him since.

"I'm dying of thirst," Simone said. "Let's go back in and get something to drink."

Josie left her phone in her pocket and followed Simone back inside. She would try to find Beech again before she called her dad.

After buying overpriced bottles of water, Simone led them towards the front of the club again. The concrete floors pulled on the soles of Josie's sneakers, tacky and slick with gods-knew-what. The lights over the stage were dim as the equipment was set up for the next band. Shouts and laughter bandied back and forth around Josie and Simone as they worked their way to the front.

When they reached the door next to the stage, the keyboardist, a kid she recognized by his horn-rimmed glasses and the constellation of moles high on his cheek, came out—Ty. When he saw Josie, he backed up a step.

"Hi, Ty," Simone said. "Great show!"

Ty eyed Josie warily. "Thanks."

Simone pulled Josie closer. "Do you know Josie?"

Ty leaned away from her, like she'd forgotten to put on deodorant.

"We met," Josie said, recalling how she'd nearly bowled Ty over on her first day in Portland. "Sorry about that. I hope I didn't get you in trouble."

Ty seemed to relax. "From what I hear, you specialize in making trouble."

"Not on purpose."

Ty smiled a bit. "Then I'd hate to see what you could do if you were actually trying."

"I'll give you a heads up if I intend on making trouble."

"Please do," he said. "I'd like to get my flight to Bora Bora booked before you burn down the entire city or bring on the end of the world."

"Is that what people think of me?"

He arched an eyebrow at her. "Do you really care?"

"No."

"I didn't think so." Ty ran his thumbs under his red suspenders. "To hell with them anyway, right?"

"Right," Simone chimed in. "Ty, you're such a sweetheart."

He shrugged, smiling.

"Oh, and I loved your solo during . . ."

Josie turned away as Simone went on about certain songs and how wonderful they'd been. Opposite the stage, over the bar, were two levels of balconies. The lower one looked as crowded as the main floor. The upper balcony was shrouded in haze, like it was packed with smokers.

"Have you seen Kai?" Simone asked.

"Last I saw he was loading the van," Ty said.

Josie took a drink from her water bottle. The haze clouding the upper balcony thickened, dropping in heavy coils over the metal guard rail. Not rising, like smoke, but pouring down onto the patrons below—like fog.

Josie gagged on her water, crushing the bottle. She grabbed Simone's hand, yanking her. Ty jumped back, like he'd been expecting her to attack.

"What—?"

"Look," Josie said, pointing up to the balcony. Other people in the crowd began to take notice too as the fog reached the lower balcony and the bar. They pointed, smiling and laughing.

"It's nothing. Probably just an effect, you know, part of the show," Simone said, though her hand tightened around Josie's. "They can't be here. It's protected. Caroline was here. And Lily too. They promised, it was safe—"

Josie wanted to believe her, but the fog kept getting thicker. The upper balcony was completely obscured.

"We have to find Tessa," Josie said, standing on her tiptoes to search the crowd. She looked for Judah. He was taller than Tessa, and frankly, he stood out. Not too many golden-haired prep-types in this crowd. Even still, she couldn't find him.

"That's odd," Ty said, frowning up at the tumbling tufts of fog. Then he was distracted by a handsome young man who was waving to him from across the crowd. "Sorry, Simone, got to run."

"Ty—" Simone called him, but he was already working his way through the crowd.

Josie's heart was jackhammering in her ears, she could barely hear when Simone said, "Maybe we should get out of here."

Josie didn't want to leave Tessa. Then again, Tessa was the Triune and she was with Judah. Neither Josie nor Simone could summon a god to defend themselves if Fog God showed up.

"This way," Simone said, pulling Josie towards the door leading backstage. She flashed a badge at the security guard. "Kai will be out back with the van."

Josie stumbled after Simone, fumbling for her phone. They snaked through the backstage labyrinth. Josie found her dad's number and pressed the phone to her ear. Straight to voicemail. She swore and tried Tessa's number.

They came to a big metal door with an exit sign mounted above. Simone stopped.

Tessa wasn't answering. She probably couldn't hear her phone ringing over the crowd noise.

"Maybe it's nothing," Simone said, her hands on the door. "We're just overreacting."

The power went out. Only the glowing red EXIT sign provided light.

"Or not," Simone squeaked, pushing open the door.

They rushed into the alley, straight into a wall of fog.

Josie staggered to a stop. Opaque clouds swirled around them, tinged streetlight orange. Simone spun, reaching past Josie.

"Don't let the door—"

The door shut. Simone grabbed the handle, yanking, but it was locked. Simone banged on the metal.

Josie backed up, seizing Simone's twig of an arm. Josie had to practically press her face against Simone's to see her. Josie pressed her finger to Simone's lips.

Simone nodded. She started to turn, but was suddenly yanked away. She let out a yelp as she disappeared into the mist.

"Simone!" Josie groped into the fog, but Simone was gone.

Screams issued from inside the building. A rumble followed. A huge crash sounded, as if the balconies had collapsed. The ground trembled. Josie prayed Tessa was all right.

Keeping her hand on the wall, she ran after Simone.

Her eyes combed the fog, searching for Simone, a car, a trash can, anything. There was nothing but white swirling clouds. She pressed her back to the damp concrete wall, running her hands over her bracelets. She wore two dozen or so, each offering a different type of protection.

"What do you want?" she asked.

"Not much, Lady Day," Fog God's smooth, detached voice replied from... somewhere. "Just looking for a repairman, or woman."

"Where's Simone?"

"You want to protect her?"

"Where is she?"

"Take off the charms and she'll be fine. Everyone will be fine ... for a while." His voice echoed off the alley walls, making it impossible to pin down. The voice of the summoner was buried under the god's hollow tone.

"And then?"

Silence. The fog churned in thick billows, playing tricks with her eyes. Where was he?

"You had your chance," Josie said, inching along the wall, hoping to find something, or someone, that might help. She stepped on a flattened cardboard box—real helpful. "Why didn't you take me before? In Brunei?"

"Who knew you were worth taking?"

"Why did you murder my mother?"

"I didn't murder anybody," Fog God said testily. The summoner's voice rang youthful. In a more even tone, he added, "The Triune had to die. Nothing personal."

"And Tessa? You're going to kill her too?"

"That all depends."

"Why didn't you take her at the beach?"

"What can I say? I like brunettes better. Actually ... there was a change of plans."

"Because I'm a mask-maker."

"Bingo."

Another rumble sounded from inside the building. A swell of distant screams, like people on a roller coaster. But their screams weren't being inspired by any fun-filled thrill ride. Her heart sank. She wished she could help. At the moment though, she would've been content to find a way to help herself.

She needed more protection. The bracelets would only hold up so long. She flipped open her purse's flap, digging for a marker or a pen. Anything she could use to draw on the ground. She knew she had a Sharpie. Where was it? Chapstick, hair ties . . . damn it.

She had to distract him, buy more time.

"This was a trap—" she said.

"Of course it was a trap," he said.

"So there is a traitor in the tribe."

Damn, Judah had been right. Again. Where was he now? If she screamed would anyone hear her?

She continued to fumble around in her purse. "Are you the traitor?"

No response. More crashes. More screams. Another rumble shook the ground, tremoring through her. Her knees wobbled and she slipped on the cardboard, but caught herself on the wall.

In her bag, her fingers bumped against her pocket knife. She took it out, flipping out the blade.

"What do you think you're going to do with that?" he asked.

"Grab me like you did in Brunei and I'll show you."

If he touched her through his guise, with his own hands, like he had before, she could hurt him, a little, maybe. It all depended on how many protective charms he wore.

"Oh, threats of violence. I like it."

"I should've stabbed you when I had the chance."

"Yeah, probably."

Searching the fog for any sign of him, her palms grew slick with sweat. She probably wasn't going to be able to hurt him, but maybe she could wait him out until someone found her. She dropped to her knees and started carving into the cardboard.

"There's a club full of summoners in there," she said as she hurriedly sawed a protective circle, the cardboard stank faintly of urine, "not the best place to set a trap." She hesitated, trying to get her bearings. Which way was north?

"Kids," he said. "Most of them don't have masks and the ones they do have are weak. Trust me, they're wetting themselves right about now."

More ominous rumbles. What was going on inside? Was Tessa all right?

She closed her eyes and visualized the street, the building, the alleyway. North was to her right. She cut an air symbol to the north.

"Not many masks of real power left in the world," he said conversationally, "which is why you bumped your sister off the number one most wanted spot. Even though she's looking like a pretty good target herself these days. Not handling her newfound destiny too well, is she?"

"You shouldn't underestimate her," Josie said, twisting so she was facing the wall. Water to the west. "She stopped you last time."

"Beginner's luck. Everyone knows summoning the Tripartite almost killed her. And how long have we been chatting now? Two minutes? Three? How long would it have taken your mother to sort out a few rogue summoners? Oh wait . . . I know the answer to that question."

Josie fumbled, almost dropping her knife. "You had a time bender."

"Are you calling us cheaters?"

"Why don't you just use it on me now, if you want me so badly?"

"Do you know how much juice it takes to power one of those things?"

Earth to the south.

"So you want some new gods, for what? What's the big plan?" she asked.

Her back was to the wall again. Fire to the east. She could've chosen one of a thousand fire symbols, but the one she chose was a cleft mountain, crowned by the arch of an explosion. *His* symbol. She circled it and sat back on her heels. The protection circle was complete. Not the most powerful, but better than nothing.

Fog God appeared, kneeling right in front of her. Two hollow eyes and a bluish white body barely distinguishable from the surrounding clouds.

"Sorry it took me so long," he said. "Had to make sure sweet Simone was all tucked away safe."

"Where's Simone?"

"You don't really want to do it this way, do you?" His hand of fog swept towards the circle. "Be a pal and come quietly, please? Do us all a favor."

"I'm not going anywhere with you."

"Well, that's a nice circle," he said. "Let's take it for a test drive, huh?"

She gripped the damp edges of the cardboard as it rose off the ground. "*Kuso.*"

She hated how specific protection spells needed to be. She'd made it to protect her from being removed from the circle; she hadn't thought that the circle itself might be moved. Normally, it wasn't a problem since most protection spells were drawn directly on the ground.

Fog God used his godly powers to propel her up into the air. Then he let her drop. As she plummeted, she clung to the cardboard, bracing for the impact. Her knees slammed to the ground. Pain rang up her body into her teeth. She was nearly thrown out of the circle. The pocketknife flew from her hand, skittering across the pavement.

Charm bracelets popped and vanished from her wrists—used up. They'd probably saved her knees from being shattered. But if he kept it up, her knee caps would still get broken. Only a handful of her charms protected her from physical injury.

The cardboard rose again. Higher. Higher.

Then down. She bit into her tongue, tasting blood. More ear-ringing pain. More bracelets gone.

She was lifted once more. The cardboard, even bolstered by the power of the circle, sagged in the middle. She pleaded to the gods for it to hold.

The gods can be such jerks.

The cardboard ripped, right down the middle. She fell through, plunging into the fog.

She crashed to the pavement on her feet, stumbling and banging her shoulder against the wall.

Fog God grabbed her and spun her, pushing her face-first to the wall, crushing her between the smooth stone and his mortal body. Her vision flickered in and out like a bulb in a faulty socket.

"Not many left," he said, plastering her hands to the wall like he was about to do a pat down. The sleeves of her denim jacket were rolled up, exposing her bracelets. "Once Simone joins our team, we'll put her talents to real use."

"She would never help you." Her tongue moved slug-like in her mouth, tasting of hot metal.

"Once the fun really starts, she'll come around, and she won't be the only one." His grip tightened around her wrists painfully. "Don't suppose you just want to take them off and come along quietly?"

"Screw you."

"Don't say I didn't offer."

He released her and disappeared from view. She prepared herself for a godly assault. Maybe more TemperMentals. Maybe, since he was an air god, a gale or tornado. Her remaining bracelets only protected her from TemperMentals and translocation. All the others were gone.

The fog shifted. He reemerged suddenly, seizing her arm. She twisted, shoving against him. Her fingernails dug into his mortal chest, but he didn't flinch. Hot pain seared up her arm as he slid a knife—her pocketknife—under the bracelets and cut them away, slashing her forearm. The plastic beads clacked softly as they rained to the ground. Blood ran down her arm.

"Don't fight, Josie," he said as he grabbed her other arm. "This doesn't have to hurt."

She kicked at the fog, trying to connect with some part of him.

She swiped just below the knife. She couldn't see the hand holding the blade, just a ball of fog. Still, she caught his wrist—the mortal one hidden under his guise. She wrenched on his arm, trying to twist the knife out of his hand. They grappled. He flung her away. She landed hard on her knees, wishing she had a couple more of Simone's injury-protection charms left.

His foot planted on her side and gave her a shove, sending her sprawling onto the ground.

His knee crunched against her shoulder blade. She yelped. He held her arm down. She continued to thrash and struggle, but he cut away the last of her charms, again slicing into her skin.

He yanked her up to her feet. She spun, her palm flat, aiming for the area where she hoped his mortal face was located.

A god's face in possession didn't always correlate with the mortal's beneath. Instead of smashing into his nose, as she'd wanted, her hand went straight through the fog into nothing.

The summoner whipped her around, wrapping one arm around her waist and the other around her throat.

She threw her elbows into him.

"Ever translocated with an air god?" he asked, grunting as she fought. "Sorry you won't be conscious to enjoy the ride, but I can't have you thrashing around in the air."

His arm squeezed around her neck. She gasped, choking and struggling against him.

Her vision began to fade. The world of fog, somehow, grew hazier. Shadows, black as oblivion, dark as drowning, devoured the swirling phantoms of mist that were white, tainted blue like a corpse and . . . glowing red?

Then she heard Fog God mutter, "Shit."

CHAPTER 19

April 6th

FOG GOD'S GRIP LOOSENED.

The world spun as her vision returned. Her lungs hitched, heart pounding, skull thudding and aching.

A dull cracking noise filled her ears. At first she thought it was coming from inside the building, but after a second, she realized it was closer. And the red glow . . . where was that coming from? She blinked, forcing her eyes to focus.

Below her, jagged lines of red sprawled. The glowing fissures widened and grew brighter. Heat licked at her legs. Fire. Breaking through the pavement

No. Not fire.

Lava.

The ground undulated. They stood stranded on an island of concrete. Six inch wide lava flows burned away the fog around them.

"I don't believe it," Fog God said just before their island of concrete pitched and they were thrown off it.

She flew through the fog, over the rivers of burning red rock, and into a wall. Or what she thought was a wall, until the dark mass steadied her. Flames—livid purple, blood red, chemical green—rippled up his arms and over the shadow that was his skin.

She looked up at the face of billowing black smoke. She couldn't see the mask underneath. As soon as the summoner had put it on, the mask had transformed into the god's mortal guise. The features were too fluid to be recognizable, but still, she knew it was him. His eyes were molten and flashing, core and explosion, breath-thieving and blue. Vivid, impossible, star-imploding blue.

Her fire god.

"That's not very nice," Fog God said, once again hidden in the mist.

The fire god, or his summoner, pulled her close, gripping her upper arm with a strong, mortal hand. As she passed through his guise, sweat-inducing fingers of heat slid over her skin. Her shoulder bumped into the summoner's chest. The thief's chest. Not a woman.

"Well, now, isn't this an interesting turn of events?" Fog God mused, though his tone was strained by anger.

"Leave." The voice of the fire god and summoner overlapped, indistinguishable—deep and warm, lighting fires all through her. "Quickly."

"Monosyllabic," Fog God said, "but to the point. Very Batman. But this isn't going to play like DC, hero. Besides, you're in possession of a fire god, a god of destruction, right? That's all we want. Some good old-fashioned destruction. A little rebalancing of nature. You understand that, don't you? The world's getting trashed. We're the cleanup crew. That's all. We just need Josie to help us get started. I don't want to hurt her. I want to enlist her. We need her talent. We could use yours too."

Fire Guy's hands were, predictably, hot. He touched her wrist with his fingertips gently. He lifted her arm. Her skin was sheathed in blood. "What do you call this?"

"I asked her not to fight," Fog God said tightly. "I'm asking you too. We don't have to. I'm not into spilling Core blood—"

Josie tensed. "What about my mother?"

"The Triune had her chance to do the right thing," Fog God said. "She chose to stand by and do nothing while the planet is destroyed and the gods are left weak and impotent. I didn't want to kill her, but this is war. Either you're with us, you're against us, or you're in the way. I'm not saying I like it, but that's how it is. No more sideline sitting. Time to pick a team."

The fog drew back—exposing the dark graffiti-covered walls rising up on either side of them—and concentrating in a tight cloud at the far end of the alley. Somewhere in that swirl of mist was a summoner—a summoner she wanted dead.

"You murdered my mother," Josie said.

Flares of fire danced around her, brushing her face, but like most guises of the gods, they were insubstantial to her. More like images of flames. Still, she felt the godly source behind them. The heat brought all the hairs on her body to attention.

Fire Guy's grip tightened on her arm. "Looks like we're against you."

The roof exploded.

She ducked. Fire Guy crouched over her as brick and shingles rained down on them, slapping on the pavement like dark dead fish. When the rubble storm subsided, she looked up. Wind ripped at her eyes, pulling tears from the edges.

"Bitch," Josie muttered.

Earth Mama rose from the hole where the roof had been. She was twice the size she had been in Brunei. Her godly guise was voluptuous, covered in fluttering robes of continually falling leaves. Ever-sprouting roots twined around her legs. Branches lashed out from her guise like tentacles. A dirty swirl of phantom TemperMentals flocked above her. Mud poured over the top of the building, falling in heavy black glops, stinking like feces and rotted flesh.

Lightning crawled beneath the thickening clouds, shooting towards Earth Mama in blinding flashes, stabbing at the TemperMentals. Ear-shattering cracks overpowered the roar of the wind whipping through the alley. A white figure appeared above the roofline, a towering slender form almost too bright to look at.

Tessa. In possession.

Josie surged forward, not sure what she was going to do, but sure she had to do something. Tessa couldn't face Earth Mama. She wasn't ready. She'd be killed. Either by Earth Mama or by the Tripartite.

Fire Guy yanked her back.

"No!" She struggled against him. "Tessa!" She screamed. "Stop!"

Tessa's lightning struck one of the goddess's branches. Ash spun up and away, drifting down on them like gray flakes of snow. But Earth Mama had more—many, many more. And it proved her guise was substantial. Blood sacrifice could change a guise that way.

Distracted by the battle above, Fog God's cover of mist dissipated. The form of his body emerged, hovering ten feet above the ground.

Josie's hands clenched. The wounds on her arms stung. She turned to Fire Guy, her hand sunk beneath his shadowy guise. Her fingers clutched the summoner's shirt—sweat-damp cotton. Against her hand, it felt as if his heart had broken out of his ribcage and was thudding directly against the thin barrier of his skin.

"You have to do something," she said to him. "Help Tessa."

The lava around them began to sink away.

Fire Guy drew her to him, burying her in his guise of crackling shadow and roiling polychromatic fire and core-melting heat.

"Time to go," he said.

Translocating through the paths of fire felt like being shoved through a blast furnace at supersonic speed. When they came through, wherever they were, she pushed away from him, gasping and pressing her fingers to her face to make sure it hadn't melted off.

When she was sure she was still intact, she took a moment to register their surroundings.

A clear black sky studded by sparkling swaths and swirls of stars. Close and gibbous, the moon cast silver ribbons on the tranquil sea and shone bright on the dark beach. The air was cool, but warmer than Portland. Behind Fire Guy was a cliff like a fortress wall. Threads of flame laced his shadow body.

"Where are we?" she asked.

"Some place you'll be safe," he said, "for now."

"You have to go back. You have to help Tessa. She can't control the Tripartite. She'll get herself killed."

He seemed to hesitate. "You're hurt."

"Who cares? That earth bitch is going to kill my sister!" She shoved him. Tongues of fire slid up her arms, licking at her stinging wounds. "Go now! Help her!"

With a soft whoosh, he was gone.

Josie turned. The small pocket of beach sat in a cove sheltered by high cliffs. The tide was going out, but she knew it would turn again soon, probably flooding the cove completely. Hopefully, Fire Guy would be back before then.

She took out her phone. No reception. Big surprise. Based on the lack of city glow, she doubted this island was populated. She guessed it was a volcanic island, not that she knew for sure, but where else would a volcano god bring her?

Cancer, that cranky crab, was almost directly above her, Gemini and Leo not far from him. It had been a while since she'd plotted any star charts, but she remembered enough to guess, taking into the account the black sand and warm weather, that the island sat somewhere in the Tropical Pacific.

The pain from the cuts on her arms—one on the back and one on the front—changed from sharply stinging to deeply aching. A large knot was forming on the back of her head too. She took off her jacket and the long tunic she wore over her tank top—all of which had arrived only the week before. She ripped the tunic into strips and wrapped the scraps around her arms, tightening the knots with her teeth.

Nervous sickness built in her gut as she waited. If Tessa were hurt, if Tessa were killed . . . Josie was afraid of what she might do.

Thoughts of building her own godly avenging army came first to her mind.

Then her thoughts turned to the fire god and his summoner—the thieving summoner. He'd helped her. Maybe he was part of her tribe after all. She couldn't help but hope. He obviously wasn't working for Earth Mama, which was something to be happy about at least.

Once she finished wrapping her wounded forearms, she pulled her jacket back on and huddled on the beach, hugging her knees to her chest.

Closing her eyes, she picked over the physical clues she'd gleaned from Fire Guy when he'd touched her. But being submerged in his guise had been head-muddling. The longer she thought about him, the hotter she grew until she couldn't focus on any details other than the heat.

She could still hear the faint hiss and pop of flames from his guise.

Fingers brushed her shoulder. She flinched and scrambled to her feet, wiping the frost of sweat from the back of her neck and shying away from his burning gaze.

"Is Tessa okay? What happened?" she asked.

"The Triune is alive," he said, less than reassuringly. "The others have fled."

Finally, she looked at his face—into his eyes. Her throat tightened as the globes of molten flame flared. So blue. Bluer than in her dreams.

"Who are you?" she asked.

He didn't answer.

"Why did you steal the mask?"

For a second, she didn't think he'd answer that question either, but then he said, "He belongs to me."

She frowned, not sure if the summoner was referring to the god or the other way around. The fact that their voices were so fully merged was unsettling. She strained, hoping to hear the god speaking to the summoner the same way she'd heard the rainforest god speaking to Lily, but all she heard were the waves lapping behind her and the faint whisper and hiss of his guise.

"You should return now," he said. "They're looking for you."

He held out his hand.

Another surge of heat swelled through her. She wanted to touch him. This was bad. Tessa was right. She did have a thing for the Fire Guy. And not knowing the identity of the summoner behind the mask only made it worse. It could've been anyone. It could've been her dad for all she knew. Gross.

That thought helped her compose herself long enough to take his hand. He swept her up, fast, like he was in a hurry, or like he was afraid she might pull away.

Cocooned in shadow and fire, her rational thoughts burned away as they traveled through the scorching furnace of the fire gods' pathways.

An instant later, they arrived on her deck, outside her room. The summoner disengaged her, almost roughly, taking his warmth with him. She sucked in a sharp breath as the cold rushed in.

He took a few steps back. He was leaving.

She caught his arm. He didn't have to, but he was letting her touch his mortal body beneath his guise. Her fingers pressed against his hot skin. Blue flame twisted around her wrist. Her pulse skittered and her mind blanked.

"I have to go," he said.

"I know, I just—" She just what? Wanted him to stay? She didn't even know who he was. She wanted the heat to stay, to surround and fill and melt her, all the way through. "How did you find me?"

He seemed to hesitate again. "You called me."

She frowned. The only people she'd called were Tessa and her dad. She released him. "Dad?"

His tone turned amused. "No."

The symbol on his forehead appeared for a second, traced by blue fire. She'd carved it into the cardboard, as part of the protective circle. Whenever a god's mark was drawn in a ritual way, a way that summoned magic, it would call to the god.

"The mark," she said.

He was silent.

"I guess it's lucky that you were in possession when I drew it," she said.

"I wasn't."

She frowned. "You weren't in possession? So... it wasn't the mark that called to you—"

"I have to go." He started to turn away.

"Wait."

He stopped.

Josie ran her hand up her arm, trying to warm herself. "I just wanted to... if you hadn't showed up... that Fog God snatched Simone—Simone! Oh gods—"

"She's not hurt."

"You saw her?"

He nodded. Flames etched his shadowy features, sharpening them. She stared at the smoky guise, feeling a sense of familiarity, though she couldn't see the mask itself or the mortal face beneath.

"Do I know you?" she asked.

He shifted back, like he was about to translocate.

"Wait—" She reached for him again.

Again, he let her penetrate his guise. This time her fingers plucked at his shirt. He didn't have to let it happen. His guise could've repelled her. It could've bounced her hand back, preventing her from touching him, so long as he didn't touch her first.

"Thank you," she said in rush, afraid that he would disappear before she had the chance to say it. "Thank you for helping me . . . for saving me."

Without thinking, she closed the space between them and kissed him, not sure where her lips would land—not sure how closely the billowing guise correlated to the summoner's face. It must have been very close, because her lips pressed against the corner of his mouth. She only missed his lips because he turned at the last second. Her fingers slipped under the guise, trying not to be too obvious as she touched his cheek and grazed the hard line of his jaw—a little rough.

She had trouble gathering much more. Buried in the god's guise of shadow and smoke, multicolor fire tangled at the periphery of her vision. The flames were ghostly, part of the guise, not wholly real. Yet heat wound through her. She rocked on her toes, tingling and feverish. Her hand trailed down his neck.

"Thank you," she said again.

He took her wrist and removed it before it reached his chest. He stepped back, silhouetted in blue flame, and then he was gone.

CHAPTER 20

APRIL 7TH
EARLY THE NEXT DAY

"WAS IT BEECH?" Simone asked under her breath.

The door to Tessa's hospital room clicked softly as it closed behind them. The light in the corridor gleamed too bright off the white walls and polished floors. Josie hated the air in the hospitals, too dry, too recirculated, too dead. It made her skin itch.

"I don't know," Josie said, glancing back at her sister through the narrow window.

Tessa looked terrible, her skin was the color of old glue, her head wrapped in gauze, her eyes hollow. At least she was alive. After she'd come out of possession, she'd plummeted three stories into a pile of rubble. Her charms had saved her from breaking her spine or dying, but she'd still suffered head trauma and deep bruising. Nancy, Caroline, their dad, and Judah remained in the room with her. They'd listened to Josie's story silently and then asked her to leave.

Kai looked up from the row of chairs at the end of the hall. "Is the interrogation over?"

"For the moment." Simone sat down next to him and looped her arm through one of his. He had his own gauze headband too, thanks to Fog God knocking him out and shoving him into the van.

"They didn't ask you any questions," Josie said to Simone.

"They did before you got here," Simone said.

"What happened to you?"

"Fog Dude put a choke hold on me. I passed out, and he tied me up in the van with Kai. A while later, Kai woke me up and freed me."

Josie plucked at Simone's bracelets, which all seemed intact. "Why didn't your bracelets protect you? Don't you have any to prevent you from assault?"

Simone looked away, sheepish. "Well . . ."

Kai gave Josie a grim look. "She doesn't make them for herself," he said.

"What?"

"They're for other people," Simone said. "You never know when you're going to meet someone who needs it. Like you. Look, you don't have any." She pulled her mini-engraver from her back pocket.

"Not right now." Josie held up her hands. Both of her forearms were wrapped in bandages. The doctor had considered stitching the long, thin wounds, but in the end had decided against it.

Josie had told the doctor she'd been cut on some glass from the explosion.

Gas explosion. That's what everyone was saying. That's what everyone would believe, although the police had asked about some kind of fight between masked gang-bangers, which must have been what some of the terrae thought they saw. It was surprising any of them had noticed the masks; usually they didn't. To nontribe, summoners in possession were invisible. In Japan, terrae were called, *moumoku*. Blind.

"You need to protect yourself, Simone," Josie scolded. "Promise me you'll make some charm bracelets for yourself. Things are too crazy right now."

Simone hung her head, nodding. "Hey, would you find me something to drink?" she asked Kai.

"Do you really want something to drink, or do you just want to talk about Josie's *hot* new boyfriend?"

"Punny," Josie said.

Kai side-smiled, shrugging.

"Just give us a minute, okay?" Simone said.

"Sure, but I am curious; did you recognize him?" Kai leaned forward, gazing at her with an eagerness that made her shift in her chair.

"No."

Kai continued to gaze at her, like he wasn't sure he believed her. "Too bad." He stood up. "I'll be back in a couple."

"Thanks," Simone said. After a quick kiss, he ambled away through a set of metal doors towards the elevator.

Josie watched him go. She hadn't ruled out the possibility that he had taken the fire god's mask, which would have been terrible for a whole host of reasons.

"So?" Simone turned towards her, her hazel eyes sparkling. "Who is it?"

"I really don't know."

"But you translocated with him. You must have gotten a . . . feel for him." Simone grinned. Josie couldn't help but smile too.

"I did, but I really couldn't tell much. Except he was male, or a steroidal woman. But I'm leaning towards male."

"Could you tell how tall he was?"

Josie thought back. "Taller than me."

"As tall as Beech?"

Josie tried to do a mental comparison. "Maybe."

"Well . . . Russell is taller than Beech. Do you think it was Russell? I hope not."

"Why not?" Russell was definitely on the list of suspects, especially now that she knew Fire Guy wasn't working for Earth Mama. Russell had known about, and had the opportunity to steal, the mask. She hadn't seen him at the show, which meant he could've been in possession when she'd drawn the god's symbol into the protective circle . . . except, Fire Guy had said he hadn't been in possession when she'd drawn the symbol. But that couldn't be. How had he found her if not through the god's symbol?

"Russell is . . . well, he was really mean to Kai growing up," Simone said.

"Not everyone has the perfect sibling relationship that you and Judah enjoy."

Simone crossed her arms. "Russell and Judah have a bad history too. They competed for a mask and . . . anyway, they don't like each other."

As far as Josie was concerned that was all the more reason to like Russell. "Is that all?"

"*And* he doesn't have a very good reputation. He's a player. Everyone knows it. He uses girls. Ask Allison. I heard they slept together and then—"

"If everyone knows he's player, then how can he use anyone? Don't they know what they're getting into before they get into it? Beech isn't exactly Mister Monogamy. And I'm fine with that. Besides, can't people change? Russell hasn't tried anything with me. Nor has he been a jerk..." she trailed off, "unlike some people I know."

Simone sagged when Josie mentioned people changing. Simone was too forgiving to hold someone's mistakes against them in perpetuity.

"Do you think it was Russell?" Simone asked.

"It could've been. I don't know, but he did seem familiar."

Simone slid to the edge of her seat. "Familiar how?"

Josie shook her head. "There was something... when I kissed him."

Simone's hand flew to her mouth. "You kissed him?"

Josie's cheeks started to warm. She really had to learn how to get this blushing thing under control. "I sort of missed." She touched the side of her mouth where her lips had landed on him.

Simone grabbed her hand. "How was it?"

Josie looked away, shrugging, face on fire.

"Oh my gods. Did he kiss you back?"

"No, he actually... sort of... turned away."

Simone sagged. "Bummer. If it were Beech, don't you think he would've kissed you?"

"Maybe not. Maybe he was afraid if he did, I would recognize him."

Simone nodded anxiously. "What else happened?"

"Nothing. I touched his face. His cheek and his jaw. You know, to try to get a sense of his face."

"And?"

"And he's got great cheekbones."

"Beech has great cheekbones."

"So does Russell."

"You really think it was Russell?"

"His cheeks might've been sharper than Beech's. But his jaw seemed stronger than Russell's, possibly. I don't know. It was so hard to think."

Simone's smile widened. "He made it hard to think?"

"Definitely."

"But you think it's someone you know?"

Josie dropped her face into her hands. "I don't know." She groaned and slumped back in the chair. "Where is Beech? Have you seen him?"

"Yeah, I saw him after the police and everybody arrived, but it was so crazy. He asked if I was okay and if I knew where you were. When I said I didn't, he took off. Have you tried calling him?"

"My phone got fried," she said, taking out the phone. The screen was dark. "It must have happened the second time we translocated."

"How did your dad know where to find you?"

"I messaged him from the computer." She dug her fingers into her forehead and then stopped, remembering what Lily said about the third eye. Josie's third eye must have been completely blind by now. "How could this have happened? The club was supposed to be protected."

"It was protected," Simone insisted. "Mom put down the circles herself. And if you think I'm good, you should see her charms. Maybe the Earth Goddess is just . . . stronger."

"Maybe," Josie said.

Breaking protection spells was exhausting, even for the Triune, though it would've been easier to break them if they'd been corrupted beforehand. Earth Mama had more than enough power to taint the earth around the club so that it wouldn't be capable of holding a protection circle. But in order to do that, she would've needed a major heads up—before any of the newer, more powerful circles had been laid down by Caroline and Lily. Once again, that pointed towards a traitor in the tribe.

"However she did it, this was one pretty big show," Josie said. "Whoever Earth Mama is, she must be in a hospital somewhere too right now."

"And pissed off," Simone said. "She didn't get anything she wanted. Thanks to tall, dark, and flamey—"

"And Tessa," Josie added. "She fought off that bitch. I didn't think she could, but she did."

"She had a little bit of help," Simone said. "Once the elders realized something was up, they came running. That's really when the Earth Goddess took off."

The door to Tessa's room opened. Judah came out, clothes covered in dirt and dust, golden face taut and tired. He looked like he'd had a building fall on him, which, from Josie's understanding, was exactly what had happened. Simone had said he'd been trapped under some rubble during the fight, even in possession of an air god, he'd had trouble digging himself out.

"I'm supposed to take you two home," he said.

"I'm not leaving," Josie said.

"Yes, you are," he said. "Your dad's staying with Tessa tonight, and you'll be safer at our house."

"Your house?" she repeated.

"My house too," Simone chimed in.

"Why can't I go home?"

Judah stared dully down at her. "You really want to do this right now?"

"If your dad's not going to be home, it'll be better for you to be with us," Simone said, hooking her arm around Josie's shoulders and giving her a squeeze.

"They're not going to attack again. Not anytime soon," Josie murmured, shooting Judah a dark look. He reflected it back at her.

"Famous last words." Kai came through the door, balancing two cups of coffee, one on top of the other. He handed one to Simone and the other to Josie. He glanced at Judah. "Sorry, friend, didn't know you'd joined the party."

Judah's eyes flashed darkly at him and then quickly returned to their usual, unreadable state. Apparently, Judah didn't care for either of the Vale brothers. Josie wondered if Simone had taken that into consideration when she'd started dating Kai. Or if Josie was the only one who was supposed to care about Judah's opinions concerning other guys.

"Can you give Kai a ride home?" Simone asked.

"Don't worry about it," Kai said. "My 'mom' is downstairs now."

"I want to see Tessa," Josie said, standing up.

"There's nothing to see," Judah said, standing in her way, again. "She's exhausted. She saved all our asses tonight, you know?"

"Not all of us," Simone said tartly, poking her chin over Josie's shoulder. "Josie has her own personal savior."

Judah's eyebrow lifted in amusement. "Is that what you call it? Sounds to me like she's got a criminal stalker who's packing way too much heat for anybody's good."

"He's not a stalker or a criminal," she snapped.

"He stole the mask. What else would you call him?"

"Maybe he didn't steal it. Maybe he just . . . took it." She glanced back. Even Simone and Kai were looking at her like she was crazy.

"You're defending him?" Judah asked, brow turning suspicious. "Why's that, all of a sudden? A few weeks ago you were ready to throw all of us under the bus for that mask." He tilted his head, thoughtful. "Maybe there's something you forgot to mention about your little adventure with your knight in flaming armor?"

"Like what?"

Actually, there were more than a few things she hadn't mentioned. Glossing would have been a generous description. She hadn't relayed any of the details of her conversation with Fire Guy. And she had left out kissing him and how it was making her weak-kneed thinking about it.

"I don't know," Judah said, crossing his arms in his usual bodyguard fashion, "like maybe you recognized him. Maybe you figured out who he is. After all, you translocated with him, twice. That's a lot of physical contact to have with a summoner. You're telling me you didn't pick up anything about him, nothing at all?"

Josie ground her teeth. "What should I have picked up?"

"He's got a point," Kai said. "You practically ordered the Eye to do a body cavity search on us when the mask went missing. Then the thief shows up and you let him get away without a pat down?"

"Kai, shush it," Simone said.

Josie's blush crawled down her neck, across her back. Completely out of control. She took a sip of her coffee, hoping the conversation would turn to other topics.

"You did find out something," Judah said, brow saying, *I knew it.*

"Stop pestering her," Simone said. "She didn't find out anything, okay? And anything that may or may not have happened is none of your business anyway."

"Simone . . ." Josie growled.

Simone paled.

"Happened?" Judah repeated, eyes flicking from Josie to Simone and back again. "What happened?"

"Nothing happened," Josie insisted.

"Shit, you kissed that guy, didn't you?" Kai said.

"Kai!" Simone swatted at him.

"Tessa was right," Judah said. "You do have a thing for the fire god."

"I do not have a thing for the fire god," she said.

"So you have a thing for the fire god's thief," Kai said, in spite of Simone's scowling at him.

"No. And what does it matter who I have a thing for? Why do either of you care?"

"I don't care," Kai said. "I was just hoping you'd figured out it wasn't me."

"Of course it's not you," Simone said.

"How could it have been? You were knocked out in a van the whole time," Josie said.

"Got the head wound to prove it," he said, gesturing to his gauze coronet.

Josie nodded, but she didn't want to tell Simone the truth—which was that she didn't know if it had been Kai or not. They all knew the most likely suspects were Kai, Russell, and Beech. She'd excluded Judah. Not just because he was Tessa's boyfriend, but because the idea that Judah would steal was unimaginable. Beech had been right; Judah was as tight over the rules as Josie was, or had been. Obviously, she wasn't as tight about them as she had been, or she wouldn't have been defending Fire Guy at all. Judah was right. Whoever Fire Guy was, he was a thief.

Simone seemed to relax. Josie wasn't sure she'd ever be able to relax. If Fire Guy wasn't Kai or Beech, then it had to be Russell. Who else could it have been? Someone she didn't know? Someone who wasn't a part of her tribe? If that was the case, then how had he known about the mask in the first place? How had he known where to find it that night?

Judah continued to scrutinize her. "You don't know who this thief is. You can't trust him. Your life is in serious jeopardy, and you're kissing thieving summoners? Are you crazy or just stupid?"

"Judah, that's not very nice," Simone said. "He saved her life. And it's not like they really kissed. He didn't even kiss her back so—"

Judah smirked.

Josie dropped her head back. "Simone, please stop talking."

"Sorry," Simone whispered.

"For a volcano god, that's pretty cold," Kai said.

"That's it," Josie said. "We're not talking about this anymore."

"Don't you think you should tell the Eye?" Judah asked.

"Tell them what? That I kissed somebody? Why would they be interested in that?"

"Because you're not thinking straight," Judah said. "You don't know who he is or where he comes from or what he wants. If he showed up at your door, you'd let him in, wouldn't you?"

"No."

Liar, his brow said. "You'd let him take you wherever he wanted. And what if he decides he wants to take you straight to the Earth Goddess?"

"He wouldn't do that."

"How do you know? He stole one of the tribe's masks. He's proven he's not trustworthy, whoever he is. And if you know who he is, then you have to tell the Eye."

"I don't know who he is."

"Then you don't know you can trust him."

Josie's hand tightened around her coffee cup. The lid popped off. Dark liquid splashed over the rim and onto her hand. Fortunately, it wasn't hot. She cursed and set the coffee down on the chair, wiping her hands on her jeans. "I don't have to listen to you. I don't see why you care."

"Don't you? Look at me." He gestured to his soot-smeared face. "Look at your sister. This happened because of you. The Earth Goddess had ten summoners with her. Did you know that? Do you know how many innocent people were there? Do you know how many of our tribe members are in the hospital right now? Twenty-two, last I heard. And I don't know how many terrae. And all of that was just a diversion so they could get to you. You're lucky no one died."

"What do you want me to do? Lock myself up in a tower?"

"It's a thought."

"What good would that do? Lock me up, bury me, shoot me in the head, it won't make a difference. They'll just go after Tessa.

That was their plan in the first place. I just looked like easier pickings. But blame me all you want. I'm sure it's easier for you to think that if I go away, then all of this will go away too. You'd like that, wouldn't you? Josie disappears and everything goes back to the way it was. Tessa gets to be the spoiled drama queen again. Judah can go back to lounging around, useless and arrogant, judging everyone who isn't as perfect as he is. And you know what? I wish that too. I wish that I had that kind of power. Because if giving up my life could make that earth bitch crawl back into whatever hole she came from, if it could heal everyone who was hurt tonight, if it could save my sister from a life of serving the Tripartite, if it could bring back my mother, if it could accomplish any one of those things, I'd do it. I'd find the nearest bridge and jump."

"Whoa," Beech said from behind them. He held open one of the double doors, frowning. "I hope we're talking like, extreme sports here." He came into the hall, letting the door click shut behind him. "I'm all for bridge jumping so long as it's all about the adrenaline rush."

Josie went to him. He hugged her tight.

"Where have you been?" she asked.

"Looking for you." His thumbs were on her cheeks. "What the hell happened?"

Before she could respond, he kissed her.

"Sorry, I didn't call," she said once they broke apart. "My phone is toast."

"Wonder how that happened," Judah remarked as he passed by them. He pushed the door open and held it. "After you."

"Where are you going?" Beech asked.

"Josie's staying with us," Simone said. "Tessa's pretty shaken. Marc's staying here with her."

Beech took her hands. "You can stay with me if you want."

As tempting as that sounded, she knew it would just cause more trouble. Her dad was already freaked out enough.

"Walk me to the car?" she asked.

His arm slid around her shoulder, warm, familiar. "Whatever you want."

CHAPTER 21

SOMEONE KNOCKED ON the guest room door.

Josie woke in a sweat, sheets tangled around her legs, face plastered to the mattress. She squinted against the light filtering through the swag curtains, not sure if it was almost morning or almost night. She'd fallen asleep sometime in the afternoon.

"Time to get up," Judah said, standing in the doorway, stone-faced.

She pushed her damp hair from her flushed forehead and grabbed at the twisted sheet, attempting to yank it over her bare thighs. Luckily, she preferred boy-short style underwear over thongs. She'd borrowed a clean tank top from Simone to sleep in, but none of Simone's pants had fit, not even the stretchy ones. The girl didn't just look like a pixie; she was as small as one too. Simone had offered to pick up some clean clothes for Josie, but by the time they'd gotten back from the hospital, and Judah had cooked them a late breakfast, Simone's pixie nose had nearly fallen flat into her buckwheat pancakes. Josie had just decided to sleep in her underwear.

Josie kicked, trying to work the sheets free. They fell in a knotted crumple to the floor. She hugged the pillow to her chest. Not that Judah made her self-conscious, but the lingering memories of her dream—about Fire Guy on the beach under the moonlight—clung fresh to her skin, like steam gathered on a bakery window before dawn.

"What time is it?" she asked.

"Six. In the morning." Judah's hard blue eyes gazed down at his tablet, apparently disinterested in how little she was wearing or how flushed she was.

"Where's Simone?"

"She went to your house to get you some clothes. We just got a call. We have to leave."

She twisted around, sitting up. "For what?"

His brow rose as he finally looked at her. "The inquiry."

"*Kuso.*" She fell back, grimacing as the knot on her head hit the mattress. She stared up at the ceiling.

An inquiry. Wonderful. Let the circus begin.

The morning light played weakly over the ceiling, gray and diffuse. Was it actually going to be sunny? She couldn't remember the last time she'd seen the sun, maybe the day her mother had died. A lump formed in her throat. She swallowed it back.

She'd been channeling most of her grief into helping Tessa; the rest had been pushed into the darkness. Time for grieving was after justice had been served and Tessa was safe.

A lot of good it had done. Tessa could summon the Tripartite, but every time she did, she ended up in the hospital. She needed more time and practice. If Earth Mama kept showing up, forcing Tessa to go into possession of the Tripartite before she was ready . . .

No. Josie refused to think about what could happen if those three-faced jerks overwhelmed her sister. Tessa would just keep working. Josie would just keep pushing. What choice did they have?

She sat up. Judah continued to stand in the threshold, gazing at her.

"What?" she asked.

"I talked to Tessa," he said.

"How is she?"

"She's been better. She wanted to know more about your volcano god."

Josie's eyes narrowed. "And what did you tell her?"

He leaned against the door jamb. "I told her to talk to you. But you know, after what happened, Nancy might get her way and her truth-charms."

"I'm not hiding anything."

Disbelieving brow.

"Nothing the Eye needs to know," she clarified. "If they want to use a truth-charm, fine. Then everybody will know I have the hots for some thieving god. Big deal."

"The god's not the thief; the summoner is. Which is it?"

"Which is what?"

"Which one do you have the hots for?"

Her chest was warm. Was she blushing again? Why? Just because he was asking her about Fire Guy?

She ignored his question and snagged her jeans off the chair in the corner. They left an ash and sand imprint on the powder-blue upholstery. Cringing, she brushed at the mess. Her efforts only seemed to spread the stain.

Great. She'd ruined Caroline's chair.

The sheets were dirt-stained too, since she hadn't had the energy to shower. The second floor guest room looked unused from the unblemished honey and blond wood floors, to the glossy cream trim around the windows, to the crisp bed linens—pristine. The Goodwin house was only three blocks from Josie's, but it must've been renovated more recently. Everything looked more modern and cleaner. That is, until she'd come along.

She sat back, frowning at the chair and the remaining crust of blood and sand on her jeans. She hoped Simone would be back soon.

"I don't get you," Judah said.

She scowled. Why was he still here? "The feeling's mutual."

"You're really telling me you have no idea who the thief is?" he asked.

"I'm sorry, officer. I didn't get a good look at him. You know, behind the guise of a volcano god."

"Are you actually this immature?"

Not usually, but Beech seemed to be rubbing off on her. "Only when I'm getting the third degree for no reason," she said.

"You think I'm giving you the third degree? Did you hear me say there's going to be an inquiry? If you know something and they make you submit to a truth-charm—"

She tossed her jeans down on the floor. The floors were wood, she could sweep. "I told you I don't know anything."

"You translocated with him, twice. You're not that imperceptive, Josie. You can't expect me to believe you didn't pick up any physical clues about him. And I don't believe you didn't talk to him in all that time either—"

"So what? I talked to him."

"So what did he sound like?"

"I don't know. His voice was ..." She frowned, lapsing into thought.

"His voice was what?"

"Merged," she murmured, scratching at the rolled up corners of tape on her bandages distractedly. "I couldn't tell the god's voice from the summoner's."

"Really ..." He shook his head.

"Really," she insisted, standing up.

She looked around, though she wasn't sure what she was looking for. Something was niggling at the back of her mind, but she couldn't grab hold of it.

She hadn't been able to tell the summoner's voice from the god's. That was strange. Usually, they remained distinct. Judah was right. She was perceptive enough to pick up on that much, at least normally. And then there was the matter of how he'd known where to find her in the first place.

If the summoner hadn't been in possession when she'd drawn the god's mark, then how had he found her? He'd told her that she'd called him. He'd led her to believe that when she'd included the fire god's mark in her protective circle it had gotten the summoner's attention, but then he'd said he hadn't been possession ...

"Stop messing with those," Judah said.

She stopped picking at the bandages.

"They need to be changed," he said.

She nodded, not really hearing him.

"What's wrong?" he asked.

She raked her hair back. Greasy and gritty, gross.

"May I?" she asked, pointing to the tablet he held.

He hesitated.

She gritted her teeth. "Please?"

He held it out.

She took it and opened the browser. She navigated to the tribe's archives as she went back to the bed, sitting down again.

"What are you looking for?" he asked.

She wasn't sure. In the search field she typed in: summoner and god's voice.

A hundred or so results came up. The first was from a book titled, *Eras of the Corpora Deorum: Myths of the First Ages.*

The next was a brief article she'd read dozens of times already, written by a modern Core scholar: *Manifestation and the Lost Art of Mask-making.*

She tapped on it, pulling up the paragraph the contained her search terms:

> In these instances of manifestation, numerous sources recall how the god's and summoner's voices rang in unison, one indistinguishable from the other.... Of course, this was due to the god's gradual subsuming of the summoner's body.... The end result being the god's complete assumption over the previously shared corporeal form and ultimate displacement of the summoner's mortal soul.

Her stomach crawled into her throat as she scanned the rest of the article. She dropped the tablet to her lap. "*Kuso.*"

Judah's frown deepened. "What is it?"

"It's not possible," she muttered to herself.

"What's not possible?" he asked.

Her heart slammed against her ribcage. The bright light of revelation sliced through her head, stunning her. The floor seemed to drop.

"Hi," Simone said, appearing in the doorway next to her brother. Her smile faded. "What's wrong?"

Josie looked at her. "I screwed up."

"Finally, something that makes sense," Judah said.

Simone came into the room, setting a bulging backpack on the bed next to Josie. "Screwed up what?"

Josie lifted the tablet again and scrolled through the articles.

"Um . . . Josie?" Simone asked after a minute.

"Listen to this," Josie said, reading from another article. "'It was purported that from the very first moment the summoner donned the mask, the god was seeded. Before long, the mask was no longer required. The summoner was in constant contact with the god, able to draw on the god's power, even out of possession, to hear the god's thoughts and words and to know when the god was called by the drawing of his mark . . .'" She tossed the tablet aside, digging all of her fingers into her forehead. "Fuck!"

Simone brushed Josie's shoulder. "What are you talking about? What happened?"

Josie stood. The world bent around her in warped curves, like when she'd stood in front of the giant bean in Millennium Park. "He's becoming manifest."

"Huh?" Simone said, looking to Judah. But he was just staring at Josie, his brow in blackout mode.

"Fire Guy. His voice and the god's . . . I couldn't tell them apart," she said. "Fire Guy said he'd been able to find me because I'd called him by drawing the fire god's symbol in the protective circle. That only would've worked if the summoner had been in possession when I drew the symbol, but he said he hadn't been possession. The god's mark can't call to the summoner unless he's wearing the god's mask, unless the summoner is in possession—"

"Yeah? So?" Simone said.

"Don't you see?" Josie said. "I drew the fire god's mark in a ritual circle. And it called to the summoner, even though the summoner *wasn't* in possession. That just doesn't happen, not unless—"

"The god's becoming manifest," Judah said, voice dull with realization.

Josie's stomach twisted. "Exactly."

"Manifest?" Simone asked.

Josie snatched up the tablet and thrust it into Simone's hands. "In the old days, masks weren't passed down through the generations, from one summoner to another, like they are now. In the early years, mask-makers found the god who best fit the summoner. They tailored the mask, so the god and the summoner would be harmonized. So they would be . . . one."

Her throat clenched, cutting off her air.

"Is that bad? It sounds good to me," Simone said. "Who wants something off the rack, when they can have it custom-made?"

"Yes, it's bad," Josie said. "It's worse than bad." She gestured at the tablet. "From the moment the summoner put on the mask, the god . . . infected him. The god was with the summoner all the time, regardless of whether or not the summoner wore the mask. And eventually, according to this, the god would push out the summoner's soul and seize control of the summoner's body. In effect, the summoner died. The god became manifest. The god took mortal form. The summoner's form."

"Wait a minute," Judah said. "How is that possible?"

She wanted to ignore him, but she couldn't. "What do you mean?"

"You said you don't know who this Fire Guy is," he said, voice as taut as his face.

"I don't," she said.

He let out a breathy huff of incredulity. "Then how?"

"How what?"

"Oh, I get it," Simone said, wide-eyed. "You said that the mask had to be fitted to the summoner. That's how a god becomes manifest. The mask-maker makes the mask specifically for the summoner."

"Right . . ."

"Hello?" Simone waved her hand in front of Josie's face. "*You* made the fire god's mask. If you're right, and Fire Guy got your call because he's all god-infected now, then that means you tailored the fire god's mask for him. Right?"

Josie stared at Simone. Her mind was a perfect blank.

"You must know who the summoner is," Simone said. "How else could you have tailored the fire god's mask to fit the summoner's face?"

Josie felt like she'd run up against a brick wall. "I . . . guess."

Judah scowled. "What do you mean, you guess?"

"I . . ." She brought up an image of the fire god's mask in her mind.

That night was such a haze. The heat that had filled her distorted her memories, rendering them blurs of sweat and clay.

Even though she'd been drawing the mask for weeks, it was just a mask. Some features were strong, but when she tried to fix on them, to match them up to some face she actually knew—Beech? Kai? Russell?—the features of the mask curled into smoke.

If Josie's theory was correct, if the fire god was becoming manifest, then Josie had modeled the mask for someone specific, which meant the summoner *was* someone she knew, or at least, a face she knew. It also meant if Fire Guy lost his soul to the fire god, it would be her fault.

Her fists balled against her thighs as she groped for the face, willing it to reemerge and become clear. Her back teeth set and clenched, but her mind seemed to be working against her. She was chasing a thought, something she felt she knew, but the harder she pursued it, the deeper into the darkness it delved, finally slipping away into those forgetting places.

Try as she might, she couldn't match the mask to a face. Straining for a recollection that wasn't there wouldn't help him.

She stood up, looking around. Her purse was slumped against the nightstand. She swept it up and started digging.

"What are you looking for?" Simone asked.

"A pen."

"Why?"

"I have to tell him. I have to warn him."

Finally, she found that elusive black Sharpie, buried at the bottom of her bag, under curls of whittling shavings and a pamphlet about enlightenment a Krishna had pushed into her hands at some airport.

"But isn't it too late?" Simone asked. "If the god started becoming manifest the moment Fire Guy put on the mask, then ...

what can he do? Will it make a difference if he stops wearing the mask?"

"No," Josie said, hesitating. "I don't think so."

"So . . ."—Simone's voice was pixie-small—"he's just screwed?"

Josie scraped her lip with her teeth. "I am so stupid. I shouldn't have been repairing masks or making masks—"

"It's not your fault," Simone said soothingly. "You didn't know what you were doing."

Josie's gaze roved around as she searched her memory for more information about manifestation. Her eyes landed on Judah and the crystal around his neck, remembering how it had helped Tessa retreat from the Tripartite's mental assault. Her heart leapt.

"Maybe there is a way to help him," she said, mind racing. "The god's already becoming manifest. We can't change that, but the summoner might be able to control the god, like Tessa does. The Tripartite resides within her; they're with her all the time. It's not exactly the same as manifestation, but . . . it might be similar enough that the techniques she uses, grounding, centering, may work for him too. The Tripartite is far more powerful than an ancient fire god. If Tessa can restrain them and keep her soul, then so can he. He has to. Once Tessa has recovered enough to take me back to the island, I'll search the archives. There has to be a way to prevent a god from manifesting fully. I'll find it."

"I think I might know a charm that could help him," Simone said, eyes brightening. "It's a memory charm, but I might be able to modify it to act like an anchor, you know, for his soul, except"—her face fell—"I'd need to know who he is for it to work."

Josie glanced around the room. She couldn't draw a protective circle in black marker on Caroline's gleaming hardwood. Besides, she couldn't stand there and wait for him either. But a protective circle was one of the few charms she could create that would possess any power. If she just drew his symbol on a piece of paper, it wouldn't call to him. Clearly. She'd been doing that for weeks. She needed to draw his mark in some meaningful way—a ritual way—for him to get the summons. Other than protective circles, there weren't many rites that would work for just anybody, except—

She sat down and uncapped the marker. She started drawing his symbol on her thigh.

Simone yipped and grabbed for the marker. "What are you doing?"

Josie held the marker away from Simone's grasping hands. "I'm calling him."

"You're not calling him, you're—you're . . ." Simone's cheeks glowed bright pink. "I know you like him," Simone said gently, "but don't you think it's a little premature to ritually give yourself to him?" She swiped at the marker again.

Josie scooted farther down the bed, holding the marker away.

"You walk around with his symbol on your body, he can make you do anything he wants. *Anything.*"

"This is important," Josie said. "He has to know what's happening to him. The sooner the better. I did this to him. I owe him."

"Why don't we just go outside and draw a nice protective circle on the driveway? I'm sure he'll come."

"Not if we have an inquiry to go to," Josie said. "We can't stand in the driveway all day waiting for him."

Simone gave her a sympathetic look. "So you draw his mark on your body and what? You think he's just going to show up at the inquiry?"

"I think he'll be there anyway. I think he's part of our tribe."

"Who?" Simone asked.

"I don't know—"

"That doesn't make any sense," Judah interjected harshly.

"I know!" Josie snapped.

"Maybe it's a subconscious thing," Simone offered, reaching for both of them as if she could bridge the gap. "You saw his face once and it just stuck with you. Maybe you don't actually *know him* know him. That could be, right? I mean, you've traveled the whole world. You've met practically everybody in the entire Core, right? That's a lot of faces. Totally Freudian."

Judah didn't look convinced, but Josie wanted to kiss Simone for being so understanding, especially since Josie didn't understand it herself.

Judah was right. Damn him. It didn't make sense.

"However it happened," Josie said, "I have to warn him. And I'm sure he won't . . . do anything."

Simone turned to her brother, pleading. "Judah . . ."

If he had any critical remarks or dire warnings, he kept them to himself. He watched Josie, like he was waiting to see if she'd actually do it.

She knew he thought she was nuts. And she probably was, but if she drew the fire god's symbol on her body, it would definitely get Fire Guy's attention, because basically, she would be making herself his slave.

Before Simone could stop her again, she finished the symbol in a few quick strokes, circling it fast. A pulse of heat throbbed through her. She capped the marker again.

"There. It's done."

"Yeah," Judah said, standing up straighter. "And I'm sure he's not at all interested in any virgin sacrifices. I mean, he's just an ancient volcano god. They're not known for being into that stuff, right?" He smirked and left.

Josie scowled after him. "I really hate your brother."

Simone whimpered and flopped back on the bed. "I really hope he's not right."

Josie touched the symbol on her skin. It was warm.

Me too.

CHAPTER 22

STEAMING WATER AND lavender-scented soap worked a miracle on her aching body. The raw knife wounds had stung at first, but by the time she'd dried and rebandaged them, the pain had dulled to a vague throb.

She'd been careful not to wash off the fire god's symbol, but after she'd pulled on her underwear and T-shirt, she sat on the toilet seat lid and refreshed the mark anyway.

"That's not necessary," he said.

She flinched. The marker flew from her hand and clattered into the wet tub, rolling back and forth on the curves.

Fire Guy stood in the narrow space next to the linen closet, in front of the door. His guise was all shadow, the blackest smoke. Only his eyes flamed. Since the god's symbol was drawn on her body, he'd been able to translocate directly into the house, in spite of any protective charms or circles that might've prevented him otherwise. Marking herself meant no circle, no charm could protect her from him—not that she needed protecting. She hoped.

"I needed to see you," she said, standing up.

"I gathered."

"There's something I need to tell you." She finger-combed her wet hair.

She sat back down, this time on the edge of the tub. She was having trouble standing with his heat filling up the already steamy room. In a rush, she told him everything she'd told Simone and Judah, about manifestation and his soul, everything.

When she finished, sweat dewed her chest and her heart fluttered—just from being in the room with him. This was so bad.

"Well?" she said when he didn't say anything.

"Thanks for the heads up." The air shifted, like he was about to translocate.

"Wait," she said, jumping up. "This is serious. You could be in real trouble."

The smoke of his guise churned as if fanned by her movement.

"I'll take care of it."

"But—" She moved closer. The granite vanity was cool under her fingertips. "Don't you want help?"

"From you?"

"Well . . ." She glanced at her reflection. Gods, she was flushed bright enough to light the room.

"Sounds like the Triune is the one I need to talk to," he said.

She tensed. "You could, but she'd be expected to punish you for stealing the mask in the first place."

"That doesn't mean she will."

True. Tessa wasn't in a position to punish anyone at the moment.

"But . . . am I right? Is the god becoming manifest?" she asked.

He was quiet for a moment. "It explains a few things," he said finally.

"I'm sorry," she said. "I didn't know what I was doing."

"Like now?"

She frowned. "What?"

"You should scrub that off." The symbol on her thigh burned when he mentioned it.

She bit her lip against the sudden sting.

"It's not really fair," he said.

The burn mellowed but crept outwards, and inwards.

"I only did it to get your—"

"I know why you did it," he said gruffly. "And since you know I'm losing myself to this god, it's not very considerate of you to put yourself under my control when I might not have control."

Now her face really was burning. She backed up, stammering in a way that made her voice unrecognizable, even to herself. "You're right. I'm sorry." She reached over and turned on the faucet. "I only wanted to . . . I've told you what I needed to. I'll wash it off."

She perched on the edge of the vanity and pumped soap into her hand, lathering it on her thigh. The suds turned gray as the symbol smeared. Her thoughts blurred with the ink. She'd never been so muddle-headed in her entire life. She'd never allowed herself to be, but something about him made it hard for her to maintain control of her Triune façade. His heat worked against her, melting the defenses she'd thought had been chiseled from stone but, apparently, were only ice.

"You took a big risk," he said, seeming to read her thoughts, "trusting me."

She was afraid to speak. These feelings creeping through her . . . stupid, reckless, unacceptable feelings, feelings a Triune couldn't entertain.

"I could be one of the bad guys," he said.

A Triune feels . . . only what she wants to feel . . .

But then, Josie wasn't the Triune.

She took a deep breath, clearing her throat. "If you're one of the bad guys, then why did you save me?" She wiped the suds away with a tissue, but the symbol remained—faded, but clear. The heat under her skin continued to deepen and spread.

"I could make you do whatever I wanted," he said darkly. "Rob a bank. Highjack a plane. Jump out a window. Slash open your wrists." Low blue flames coiled over his smoldering skin. "I could make you have that symbol tattooed permanently and turn you into my slave, forever."

"Is that what you want to do?"

"Are you asking me? Or the god?"

"It's good you can still tell the difference."

"It's good *for you* I can still tell the difference."

She turned off the faucet, crumpling the tissue in her hand. "Are you saying the god wants to do those things to me?"

The fire crawling over his body grew from spiraling trickles into flickering streams. His voice came out low and hushed,

"I think you know what the god wants."

She gripped the edge of the vanity. Was he saying the god had feelings for her?

She struggled to come up with something to say. All these feelings were so strange, so new, she wasn't quite sure how to respond to them or to him.

Judah's question came back to her then. Was it the god or the summoner she was drawn to?

The gods used emotion when it suited them, wearing feelings like tacky jewelry they could discard on a whim. Deep down, her mom had said, gods are as vacuous as black holes.

Josie didn't know if her mom had been right. Gods seemed to be tempests of emotion. Fickle, yes, but intense. Once, she wouldn't have doubted her mother about anything, but now . . .

Whatever the god felt, or didn't feel, he hadn't been real until the summoner had put on the mask. The mask contained the god's mortal aspect. It had been comforting to her during her nightmares, she'd felt possessive of it, but she hadn't felt anything like what she was feeling now. The fire god hadn't saved her the other night. The summoner had. And for now, he still seemed to be calling the shots.

Whether it had started with the mask or not, the god was now a part of the summoner. There was no going back.

This was so bad.

His fire had died out, like he'd shut off the burner. He was all black shadow again.

"Most of the time, I'm in control," he said carefully.

Me too. Except with you.

She slid off the vanity. "That's good—"

"Don't call me again," he cut in.

Knife. Heart.

All she could say was, "Oh."

"I can't see you like this anymore," he said.

"Anymore? This is only the second time I've seen you . . . like this."

Blue flames limned his fingertips. For a moment, she was afraid he was about to translocate. That's right—afraid. A double-twisted knot in her gut. Fear. She didn't want him to leave.

So very bad.

His words were whispered, "He can't stop thinking about you."

Her throat went dry. "The god? Or you?"

"When it comes to you, I can't tell the difference." The flames snaked up his arms. "When it comes to you, I'm not sure who's in control. That's the problem."

She touched the towel on the rack, straightening it. "You're saying I'm threatening your ability to control the god? You can't tell if it's you or the god who . . . can't stop thinking about me?"

She ached saying it. She wanted to hear him say it again. He thought about her. He couldn't stop thinking about her. Just one more time. Only don't say *he*, say *I*.

I can't stop thinking about you, Josie.

Please say it again.

Instead, he said,

"Why are you being like this?"

"Like what?"

But he didn't answer.

A terrible panicked clenching started up in her chest. The god was becoming manifest. The summoner, whoever he was, could lose his soul. And now he was telling her that she was not only responsible for putting him in this position, but that being around her was making it worse.

No matter what she felt, she had to do the right thing. Or because of what she felt . . . she couldn't let him lose his soul. That much she knew for certain.

Her lungs fought her, like her body was struggling against her decision, but she forced the air out so she could speak.

"If that's true, if being around me makes it difficult for you to control the god, then . . ."—she took a deep breath—"you shouldn't be around me. You have to maintain control. To keep your soul. Nothing else matters."

Blue fire flared along the lines of his body. "You mean that."

She crossed her arms tight under her chest.

"Of course I mean it."

The silence hissed. The heat grew oppressive, smothering. She couldn't look at him. If she did, she might do something rash and irresponsible, like try to kiss him.

She stared at the white subway tiles on the wall. Blue light reflected in the glaze, pure, pulsating.

And then it was gone.

Her eyes closed. Tears formed behind her eyelids, but she drew them back.

Down into the darkness.

Into the oubliette.

CHAPTER 23

APRIL 8TH

"Is everything okay?" Simone asked again, twisting around in her seat to give Josie another worried look.

"Everything's fine," Josie lied.

Judah's eyes flicked to her in the rearview mirror. "You saw him, didn't you?"

She hugged herself and sunk into her seat. "Maybe."

Judah's brow turned brutal. "You let him into our house? Past our protective circles?"

She sank further.

"I can't believe you—" Judah started.

Simone slapped at his arm, but he was unrelenting.

"It's one thing for you to risk your own life by playing whatever game you're playing with this guy—"

"I'm not playing a game," she snapped.

"But don't get me or my sister involved," he finished like she hadn't spoken.

"What did he say when you told him about the god becoming manifest?" Simone asked.

"He said he'd take care of it." Josie stared out the window again. The mist was making her nervous. Not that fog was unheard of in Portland, but it still set her on edge.

"And?"

"And . . . nothing," Josie said.

Simone's face fell. "I'm sorry."

"What are you sorry for?" Judah said. "She's lucky she wasn't burned. Giving yourself to a god like that is just—"

"Shush it," Simone said, pointing her finger at him threateningly.

Judah fell silent for half a second before he said, "Guess you know it's not Beech."

Simone frowned. "How?"

Judah snorted. "That kid has as much self-control as a puppy at a fire hydrant party. Some girl draws his god's symbol on her body—you think he's going to be able to stop himself?"

Simone gave Josie a sympathetic look. "He's probably right."

"Isn't he usually?" Josie muttered.

Judah's brow plunged in irritation, but she wasn't interested in sparring with him anymore.

After Fire Guy had left her, she'd used nail polish remover to take off the mark. She knew it was gone completely because the heat was gone too. Even in a thermal Henley and denim jacket, she was cold—all the way through. Colder than she'd been the day she'd arrived, colder than the day she'd almost died of hypothermia.

As they pulled up to a stoplight, Simone and Judah's phones sounded off—Judah's a reserved beep, Simone's chiming a little ukulele tune. Both of their heads bent down.

Josie sat up straighter. "What is it?"

"The inquiry is postponed," Simone said, frowning at Judah. "That's weird—"

Judah let out a heavy sigh. "Look."

Josie leaned forward to see Beech on his skateboard, coming towards them, waving his arm.

When the light turned green, Judah made an impromptu left turn and pulled over along the curb. A minute later, Beech rolled up, pulled open the door, and climbed inside. His hair and face glistened with moisture as the haze turned into drizzle.

"No inquisition," he said, huffing as he plopped into the seat next to Josie's, closing the door.

"We heard," Judah said.

"Why?" Josie asked.

"Lily's MIA," Beech said.

"What?" Simone squeaked.

"Everybody's going nuts looking for her," Beech said. "It's one thing for Caroline, Miss Flight-of-Fancy," he said, looking from Judah to Simone, "but so-grounded-she's-practically-sprouting-leaves Lily?"

Simone's cherry-hued cheeks turned milk white.

Josie unfastened her seat belt and gripped the back of Judah's seat. "Call Tessa."

"She can't do anything—" Judah said.

Josie grabbed his sleeve. "Just make sure she's okay. Please."

After a second, Judah's thumb moved over the screen of his phone.

"Summoners have been going missing all over," Josie said. "Tessa's been getting messages, but—"

"Tessa?" Judah said. In the quiet of the car, Tessa's voice carried from Judah's phone, a sluicing gush of high-pitched panic. "Tess, I know, I know," Judah cut in. "Yeah, she's here." He glanced back at Josie. Tessa spoke again. "I will," Judah responded in a low voice. "She'll be fine. I promise."

Beech touched Josie's wrist. His fingers were warm, but not warming. She hated to admit it, but Judah was right. Beech wasn't Fire Guy. If he had been, she would've been tangled up with him on a black sand beach somewhere in the Pacific at that very moment. Instead, she was stuck in Judah's crossover on a foggy side street in Portland.

"You okay?" Beech asked.

What was she supposed to say? A fire summoner had put a knife in her heart an hour ago? How would he feel about that? She wasn't even sure how she felt about it. How had she become so vulnerable to someone she'd only met once before? It seemed absurd, but she couldn't help it. When he'd told her he couldn't see her anymore, a wound had opened up inside of her and started bleeding, and she didn't know how to stop it.

"Not really," she admitted.

His grip tightened.

Judah hung up with Tessa. He looked at Josie again in the rearview. "Tessa's fine, except for all the messages that have been flooding in. She said they're bypassing her directives and appearing right in front of the nurses. She's had to tell the hospital staff she does magic tricks. She wants out, but they won't release her until the doctor signs off. Your dad's still there too."

Josie let out a deep breath. "Messages about Lily?"

"I guess," Judah said. "She didn't say."

"Lily can't really be missing," Simone said. "I mean, not kidnapped or . . . something, right?"

For some reason, they all looked at Josie.

"I don't know," she said.

"But to mess with a Past Eye?" Simone said. "And after they just attacked us? You'd think they'd need a break." She slumped in her seat. "I know I do."

"Maybe that's why they did it," Josie said.

"What do you mean?" Simone asked.

Josie glanced over at Judah, who was still watching her in the rearview. "Maybe Earth Mama needs a fresh virginal sacrifice."

"Whoa," Beech said. "First off, I'm fairly certain Lily's not a virgin. And secondly, are you serious? You think that psycho would nab a Past Eye just to suck her blood? I mean,"—he flopped back in the seat—"are we seriously talking human sacrifice?"

"They murdered a Triune," Josie said. "Do you think a Past Eye is any more important to them? And since Lily is an Eye, sacrificing her would give Earth Mama a big energy boost. Whoever she is, she is way too powerful to be doing all of this without making sacrifices of some kind. Even Fog God told me that the time bender takes serious energy to use. She has to be feeding the sacrificial fires, or she's . . ." Josie's words dried up on her tongue.

"She's what?" Simone asked.

Josie bit her lip. "Nothing."

"Or she's manifest," Judah finished her thought.

Josie frowned at his reflected eyes. "She can't be."

"Why not? You think your new boyfriend's so special?"

"New boyfriend?" Beech said, leaning forward, eyebrows raised.

Josie glared at the twin sapphires glinting in the mirror at her. "He's not my boyfriend."

"Obviously, otherwise you wouldn't have been pouting for the last hour."

She flared. "I haven't been—"

"Okay," Beech said, "I missed something."

"Yeah, you missed your girlfriend making a pass at another guy—god," Judah said.

"Judah! What did we talk about?" Simone said, glowering at him.

"You made a pass at a god?" Beech asked Josie, like he was almost impressed.

"No."

"What else would you call drawing his symbol on your thigh?" Judah said.

Beech's eyes bugged. "You did what?"

"It's not like that," Josie said to Beech. Then she growled at Judah, "You are such a dick."

Simone touched Judah's arm and reached for Josie. "We should all take a deep breath—"

"I'm sorry, I assumed you were planning on telling Beech how you threw yourself at some mystery fire god," Judah said. "If my girlfriend did that—"

Josie was off her seat entirely, ready to rip the rearview mirror from the windshield and smash it over Judah's head. "Well, I'm not your girlfriend and it's none of your business and I did not throw myself at him."

Judah's brow tilted. "Right."

"Whoa, stand down, amigos," Beech said, taking Josie's shoulder and nudging her back. "It's cool. Josie's a free agent. She can do whatever she wants."

Judah snorted and muttered something unintelligible.

"Although I'm not sure about this whole putting a god's symbol on your body thing," Beech said. "You know I love the body art, babe, but . . ." For a second, a look that might've been hurt flashed over his face. "You didn't really do that, did you?"

"I had to," she said.

Beech slid back from her. "Okay . . . even I know that's crazy."

"No, Beech, she had a good reason," Simone said. "See, she made the fire god's mask for him and—"

"You made the mask for him?" Beech was scowling now. "But you said you didn't know who took it."

"I don't—"

"Then how could you've made the mask *for* him?"

"That's what I want to know," Judah grumbled.

"I didn't do it on purpose," Josie said.

"So, you did it . . . what? Subconsciously?" Beech asked. "Like he's so deep in there you can't control yourself? How serious is your thing for this guy?"

Everyone was looking at her again. Simone guiltily from the corner of her eyes; Beech, full-on, scrutinizing; Judah, the reflective surface of the glass rendering the blue light in his eyes even more distant.

"O . . . kay," Beech said, grabbing the battered end of his skateboard and opening the door.

"Beech, it's not—"

"Whatever," he said with a shrug. "Like I said, it's cool." But he wasn't looking at her anymore. "I'll check you later."

"Beech . . ."

He hopped out of the car, into the milk-white haze. Before he could shut the door, the fog condensed and wrapped around his throat. Beech let out a strangled wheeze, dropping his deck as he clawed at the arm of fog choking him.

"Beech!" Josie surged forward, but Judah caught her arm, keeping her from leaping out of the car. She yanked against him, but he held on.

Fog God coalesced behind Beech, whose face was turning unhealthy shades of red.

"Salutations, Lady Day."

CHAPTER 24

April 8th

"**J**UDAH, LOOK." SIMONE POINTED through the windshield.

Josie stopped pulling against him. More summoners emerged from the mist: two air gods, three earth gods, and two water gods.

Judah unfastened his seat belt.

"Don't waste your time summoning whatever pathetic excuse of a deity the tribe spared you. You're not a complete idiot. You can see you're outmatched," Fog God said to Judah, the hollows of his eyes widening into dark pits. "Just let the mask-maker come with us and we're out of here."

Judah's hand was crushing Josie's upper arm. Pulling her closer, he leaned towards Fog God.

"Fuck you."

"Eloquence in the face of pressure," Fog God said. "What a hero."

Beech let out a gurgling sound. His eyes bulged. His lips turned grape-candy purple.

"Let go!" Josie yanked against Judah's grip.

Judah turned around in his seat and put the car into gear, still holding her with his right hand.

"Judah!" Simone cried, grabbing for the gear shift between them.

At the same time, Josie threw herself over the console. The flat of her hand smashed into the crook of Judah's left arm, breaking his grip on the shifter.

"Stop!" Simone got hold of the shifter and slammed the transmission back into park.

"Are you insane?" Josie wedged her knee against the console. She thumped his chest with the heel of her hand, struggling to tear free from his hold. "They're going to kill him!"

"She's right. I will kill him," Fog God said calmly from behind her.

Judah grabbed Josie's other arm, heedless of the knife wound opening under his burrowing fingers, and pulled her into his lap. "I promised your sister I wouldn't let anything happen to you."

Fog God snorted. "So I kill him and then we attack and eventually we break through all your protective charms, destroy your car, kill you, and then we'll take Josie and your sister." Fog God paused as he seemed to think. "Actually, that doesn't sound half bad."

"Josie . . ." Simone whimpered. "What do we do?"

Josie's gaze flicked from the hulking red-gold sandstorm god and the brown-black swamp creature beside him. Then back to Fog God and Beech, whose eyes were rolling back in his head, his complexion turning plum hued.

"I'd say he's got about thirty seconds," Fog God said, "and then he's dead."

She looked back at Judah, trembling from the tension. She was so close she couldn't look into both of his eyes at once. Her voice came out in a breathless hush. "Let me go."

His grip tightened. He pulled her even closer. "No way," he said through his teeth.

"They're going to kill him."

His brow plunged, saying, *Let them.*

"You have to let go," she said, prying at his fingers. "It's the only way. Please."

"Ten seconds," Fog God reported. Beech was turning pale. "Maybe less."

"Judah," Simone said, "Beech is dying."

Some thought crossed Judah's face, like a shadow, but it passed too quickly for her to decipher.

Then he released her.

She scrambled to the open door. "Let him go."

Fog God's free hand stretched towards her. In Fog God's other arm, Beech was slack, eyes closed, lips blue.

"Don't worry. Judah's capable of reviving him," Fog God said, "if he moves quickly enough. Or I could just crush his throat right now."

"No." Her fingers slid through the cool breath of the god's guise and to the summoner's slender hand beneath. His grip locked around her hand, and he pulled her out of the car, dropping Beech as he spun her around and against him.

Almost instantly, the fog swept over her. The last thing she saw was Simone's pale face shining with tears. And Judah, finger pointing at his forehead.

When she emerged she was trembling. Traveling via the air god pathways had been less like flying and more like falling, bringing back painful drowning associations she really didn't need. At least the trip had been short.

She squinted, eyes aching as they adjusted from the blinding white clouds of the air gods' pathways to the deep shadows of wherever she'd been brought. Fog God released her.

She tripped on the uneven floor and fell to her hands and knees. Her hands sank into a soft bed of moss. The floor was a tangle of vegetation—thick monstrous roots, decomposing leaf litter, black soil. The air was moist and oxygenated, alive and decaying.

Pushing back to her feet, her first thought was they'd come to the clearing of a forest. Fat, wet-looking tree trunks stood rank and file on either side, tangled with blooming vines and heavy with leaves. High above, branches interlaced, creating a lattice-worked roof. Light peeked through, flat and distant. Amid the chaos of growth, an odd orange circle protruded from one of the trees—the metal rim of a basketball hoop. Then she spied the chrome leg of an overturned chair poking up from a cluster of ferns. In a gap between the trees, a glint of glass. Rectangular rows of windows. She surveyed the clearing again. Not a forest after all. An old building, a school maybe? Overgrown. Or more like, overtaken.

Summoners began to appear around her. Along with Sandstorm and the Swamp Creature, there was an earth god of gold and red prairie grass and another of glistening granite.

As Granite God stomped towards them, the floor began to quake. He stopped moving, but the quaking only intensified.

At the far end of the room, a massive mound heaped with vegetation, like an old compost pile, stirred. Vines slithered away like snakes. Giant shining beetles and worms, the size of Josie's forearm, were churned up from the pitch-black soil. Creatures tainted by blood sacrifice and godly magic. An iron-tinged stench erupted as the earth moved, stinking worse than a backed-up sewer.

Josie's stomach lurched. Bile rushed into her throat. As the mound cracked open, something smooth and white rolled towards them, coming to rest in a bed of violets. Rows of bone, half covered in strips of gray and maroon—a ribcage. The head and the legs were gone, but Josie knew a human ribcage when she saw one. As she stared, a pet-sized worm wriggled out of the remains and burrowed into the floor, disappearing.

Josie retched, backpedalling and stumbling into Fog God. His fingers dug into her arms.

"Stiff upper lip, Lady Day," he said.

Sloughing off dirt and beetles, the earth bitch emerged from the mound, climbing out like a zombie from a grave. Crimson flowers bloomed on her face, then wilted and died, leaving behind black earth, ridden with pink worms, brown beetles, and white maggots. Her eyes were empty pits. Robes of flowers and vines dragged around her, performing the same birth and death cycle as the blooms on her face. Above her, TemperMentals began to form, like nightmares escaping her head.

"Josie," Earth Mama said in her fractured voice—echoing baritone of the goddess and nasal chirp of the summoner.

Earth Mama opened the rotting trunks that were her arms. Bark peeled away with each movement. Josie backed further into Fog God. She slid through his cool guise, bumping against his chest.

A voice whispered, but she wasn't sure from where, "This better make her happy."

Earth Mama's hands closed around Josie's wrists. The goddess's guise was wet, like sinking through mud. Underneath, the summoner's hands were damp, her fingers, short.

Her hands slid over the gauze on Josie's arms. "You're hurt."

Vines snaked up Josie's body from the floor, twining around her legs, along her sides, and up her arms. She stiffened, unable to move. The thin tendrils slipped under the gauze, ripping it away.

Earth Mama tsked, turning Josie's arms so both wounds faced upwards—thin red gashes. "We can't have that, can we?"

Her fingers dragged over the wounds. Josie gritted her teeth, wincing. The wounds burned and throbbed, but when the earth bitch's fingers slid away, the wounds were nothing but tight pink scars.

Josie felt like the floor had opened up and swallowed her, which she was a little bit afraid might actually happen. "You can heal?"

"Of course," Earth Mama said. "I am Mother Earth. I birth life, I heal life, I take life, I consume life."

"You murdered my mother."

Earth Mama seemed to grow another few inches. Her voice darkened. "As I said, I take life."

"Watch it," Fog God muttered close to Josie's ear.

"What do you want?" Josie asked.

"From you? All I ask is that you perform the task the gods have sent you here to perform." Earth Mama's tone turned light, almost pleasant. "When it turned out you weren't the Triune, I have to say, I was . . . nonplussed."

Understatement.

"We had hoped to use your inexperience with the Tripartite to take their mask from you and splinter Death from his enslavement to Life and the Other, bring about the end of the Covenant, allow the gods to seek their justice. So many plans . . . so much work . . ." The dug-up grave that was her face began to churn.

The TemperMentals circling overhead began to whip and dart lower, within reach.

Fog God drew back slightly, bringing her with him. Against her back, she could feel his pulse speed up.

"But then you turned up, and I couldn't deny the signs, the timing. I knew we had to dispose of the Triune. I thought it was so we could find a way to dissolve the Covenant, but when it spawned a mask-maker, I knew that you had been sent here to assist us in our righteous endeavor. The first mask-maker in 1,971 years."

Josie swallowed hard. "Has it been that long?"

"Yes, Josie. Aelius the Younger was the last verifiable mask-maker, although there have been assertions that a tribe in China possessed a mask-maker as recently as 1134—complete conjecture. Lacking any physical evidence, we can't possibly—"

"I've got to go, Mom," Fog God said, like he'd heard this history lesson before.

"Mom?" Josie repeated.

"Yes, yes, go," Earth Mama said.

Again, Josie heard the whisper,

"Let's hope Miss Mask-Maker doesn't piss off Mommie Dearest."

Fog God let go of Josie, stepping back.

She turned, frowning at him. She'd heard the god speaking to the summoner. Why could she hear him now, when she hadn't in Brunei, or in the alley? Could she use it to her advantage somehow?

"Wait, my love." Earth Mama reached out to him, stopping him from translocating as she seemed to touch his face.

Josie sidestepped away from Earth Mama's decaying stink. Granite God loomed beside her, like she might try to make a break for it, not that she would know where to break to. She didn't see any doors through the trees. Maybe she could climb up one and out the window, but then what? She had no idea where she was. The bizarre collection of trees wasn't helping her pinpoint her location either.

An enormous ceiba dominated the room, with its flat buttressing roots like the fins of some prehistoric swamp creature. Ceibas she'd seen everywhere from Mexico to India. Directly opposite the ceiba stood a Norway spruce. Tall and erect, deep green and beautifully full, the spruce looked ready for Christmas in Rockefeller Center.

"I am so proud of you," Earth Mama said to Fog God.

It might've been a touching moment, except she was congratulating him for kidnapping Josie.

"I told you it would work," Fog God said.

"And you were right," Earth Mama said. "That's my boy."

Fog God swirled away. Josie felt an odd pang, like a child being left at a stranger's house. At least she had some sense of Fog God. She'd dealt with him one-on-one. Earth Mama, on the other hand, was a total wild card.

"Now, Josie dear, tell me,"—Earth Mama turned towards her—"are you interested in ancient Core history? I have quite a collection of masks I would love to show to you."

CHAPTER 25

APRIL 8TH
BACK HOME WITH SIMONE

THE WALLS STARTED TO QUAKE. Simone clung to Kai as Tessa's eyes bleached out, totally white. Totally freaky.

Judah, gods love him, ripped off his grounding charm and held it in front of Tessa's face.

"Tessa, focus," Judah said. "Breathe."

For a second, the building continued to shake. The lights flickered. The plastic water pitcher tipped over and spilled across the floor. A cold wind swept through the room. It looked like Tessa would summon the Tripartite in the middle of the hospital, but then her irises returned to their natural color, the trembling stopped, the wind died. Tears welled up in Tessa's eyes. She buried her face against Judah's chest, sobbing.

Simone left Kai and picked up the water pitcher, setting it back on the bedside table. She squeezed Tessa's arm, wishing she had something comforting to say. But what could she say? She glanced at Judah. She'd never seen him so angry—his face looked like it was chiseled from stone, but his eyes were *en fuego.*

Marc, Josie's dad, looked like he was about to summon his god too.

"What do we do now?" he asked Simone's mom. "What do they want with her?"

"They want to use her," Tessa said, ripping away from Judah. "This is all part of that psycho manifesto that dirty skank sent me."

"What manifesto?" Marc asked.

Her mom sighed. She had serious raccoon eyes. Simone wondered when she'd last slept.

"A few weeks ago, Tessa received a very detailed scroll from an anonymous source. We assumed it was from the same people who'd killed . . ." Her eyes flicked to Tessa and then back to Marc. "Anyway, it was a rambling environmentalist tirade. Overpopulation, global warming, pollution, genetic modification, rainforest destruction, species extinction . . ." Mom sighed again, deeper this time. Beech grabbed the chair that had fallen and righted it for her. She sank down into it. She gave him a weary smile. "Thanks."

Beech stepped back. "What's so crazy about that?" he asked. "It's true, isn't it?"

"At the end," Mom said, "it demanded that Tessa take action against the plague of humanity. It stated that if she didn't act, namely by exterminating the bulk of the human race, that Mother Earth would rise up and take action herself."

Judah stood up, slipping his necklace back around his neck. Simone touched his arm, but he didn't look at her.

"But why take Josie?" Beech asked.

"Girl's got mad skills," Kai said from where he was leaning by the door. "Think about it."

Gretchen had been hovering in the corner behind Beech, clacking her tongue stud against her teeth. She'd met them at the hospital. Simone had called her after Judah had breathed life back into Beech. They'd brought him to the hospital to be checked out, but by the time they'd arrived, he'd refused to go the ER. All he wanted to do was find Josie. Simone wanted that too. She just wished she knew where to start looking.

"They want her to make masks," Gretchen said.

"They want her to fix the masks they've stolen," Tessa said. "All the recent thefts that have been reported have been ancient masks, all of them damaged and apparently useless."

Judah's face turned impossibly harder. "We knew. We knew that's what they wanted. What they were planning. We should've done something."

"Like what?" Tessa asked. "We did everything we could." Tessa's face contorted. "You weren't supposed to let her out of your sight."

Judah looked like he'd been gutted.

"It wasn't his fault," Simone interjected. "He tried to stop her—"

"It was my fault," Beech said, his hands scrubbing his face. "She gave herself up to save me." Gretchen ran her hand down the back of his head in the way only a mom can.

"It wasn't anybody's fault," Simone said. "There wasn't anything any of us could've done."

"We could've let him die," Judah said under his breath.

Everyone stared at him. Gretchen, angrily. Most everyone else with disbelief.

"He's got a point," Kai said.

Simone swiveled towards him, scowling. She loved him, but sometimes he could be so—harsh.

He held up his hands. "What? What do you think they're going to do with her? They're going to force her to resurrect a bunch of ancient uber-powerful gods. They're calling up the Titans." He folded his arms and leaned back. "Mass destruction and maximum body count. Score one for Mother Earth. So in the big picture, it probably would've been better to let him die,"—he notched his thumb towards Beech across the room—"because it sounds like, now, we're all going to die."

Simone hated to admit it, but the love of her life was making sense—terrible, horrible sense.

"We have to find her," Marc said.

"How?" Tessa said.

A thought popped into Simone's head. "She could—"

Judah grabbed her hand and gave it a sharp yank. She frowned up at him. He looked down at her from the corner of his eye and shook his head.

"She could what?" Tessa asked.

"Nothing..." Simone pulled her hand away from Judah's. Ouchy.

"There has to be something," Marc said, turning towards Caroline. "Some way to find her."

Caroline shook her head. "I can't think of any. Unless she has a locating charm."

They all looked at Simone.

She shook her head. "She doesn't have any charms. She wouldn't take any until I... made some for myself." She sagged, vision blurring as tears came again.

Judah put his arm around her and hugged her to him. She leaned her head against his side. He really was the best brother in the world.

"Even if she did," Gretchen said, "you've got to think they have her locked down. We all saw that earth goddess the other night. She's no fool. She'll bury Josie in the deepest darkest hole she can find and put every ounce of power into keeping her there."

"Whoever this earth goddess is, she shouldn't have much power left after what she did at the club," Marc said, still sounding like he was plotting an offensive.

Simone met Judah's glance. She pulled away from him.

"Josie thought the earth bi—"

Mom's eyebrow tilted at her. Simone pursed her lips for a second. Her mom thought that swearing was the marker of a lazy mind.

Simone started over. "She thought the goddess must be making human sacrifices."

Everyone in the room went pale, even paler than they already were.

"She was afraid that that's why they took Lily," Simone went on, "because the more powerful the sacrifice..." She didn't feel like she needed to continue. Everyone looked nauseated enough. Her own tummy twerked around inside her, shimmying like a nasty cheerleader.

Marc took off his glasses and ran his hand over his face.

"Gods," Gretchen breathed, pulling Beech closer to her.

"So there's nothing we can do?" Beech said. "Is that what we're saying?"

"I can go to the Fates," Tessa said.

Marc blanched. "No."

"Dad, I have to. They have Josie. We have to find her. The Fates can tell us where she is."

"You've never even translocated to the island. Finding the Fates on your own, Tessa . . ." Marc cupped her face in his hands. "You could be lost, forever. I've already lost one daughter today. I will not lose another."

"I can do it, Dad. It's what Josie would've done—"

"Josie. Not you. She knew the Invocation. She spent her entire life preparing—" Marc stepped back from her, gripping the bed rail, bowing his head. "We just got her back."

All of a sudden, Marc spun around and slammed his fist into the wall. Simone flinched. Marc had always been such an even-tempered guy. It hurt her heart to see him in so much pain.

Mom stood up.

"I think we should all just . . ." Her gaze swept around the room, like it was sweeping them all towards the door.

Gretchen took Beech's arm and pulled him, reluctantly, out the door. Simone followed, meeting up with Kai. She glanced back. Marc's shoulders were shaking. Mom had her hand on his back, murmuring to him. Judah and Tessa stared heatedly at each other. Then Judah turned away, propelling Simone and Kai into the hallway.

Beech tugged away from Gretchen and turned back to them. "We have to do something."

"Like what?" Judah said.

"What about the Fire—?" Simone started.

"Simone," Judah interjected, glaring at her in a way he never did. She shrank.

"What about the fire what?" Beech asked.

"Nothing," Judah said, still looking pointedly at Simone. "There's nothing we can do."

He pushed by Beech and Gretchen and left them.

Simone stared after him.

"What were you about to say?" Kai asked softly.

"Nothing." She let out a heavy breath. "It was nothing."

In the middle of the night, Simone found Judah in the back yard.

She shivered, pulling her oversized terrycloth bathrobe tight around her. Kai was crashed out in her room, snoring away. Ever since Russell had moved back home, Kai had been sleeping at her house a lot more often. Not that she minded, but Judah was so on edge these days, she didn't want Kai inadvertently setting him off.

She slid the glass door open and padded through the wet grass in her slippers to Judah's side. Kai had been with her all day. Judah had been in the exercise room, his music blaring. The same song, over and over. It didn't escape her notice that it was the song that had been playing in the car after Josie had almost drowned.

Even though the sky was overcast, the reflected light from the city was enough to see him. His skin looked gray, like ash. He glared at the sky as if he were challenging it to a fight.

"Why wouldn't you let me tell them about the fire god's symbol?" she asked. In the quiet of the sleeping neighborhood, her voice sounded brash and too loud. She lowered it. "If Josie draws it on herself again, then he might be able to—"

"We can't trust them," he said.

"Who?"

"Any of them," he said. "Including your boyfriend."

"Kai? What did Kai do—?"

"Nothing, Simone."

She flinched at his tone.

He glanced over at her, his face softening ever so slightly.

"It's not that he did anything," he said. "Or that any of them did anything. But we don't know. Someone in our tribe is a traitor. We can't give them any idea that Josie might have a way of contacting..." His gaze roved past her, like there might be someone lurking in the elderberry bushes. His voice lowered even more. "It might be her only chance. We can't risk it."

"What if she draws his mark and he doesn't come to her? We thought he was someone in the tribe, but maybe he's not. If he's not, then he might not know she's missing at all. He might ignore her—"

"He won't ignore her."

"It sounds like he wasn't very interested the last time she called," Simone said, worrying her bracelets, wishing Josie had taken a few. Not that any of the charms Simone knew could've protected Josie from being kidnapped or held against her will. Simone needed to start taking her charm-making more seriously, try making some charms with some real oomph. "Maybe he'll think she's just being annoying. You know, like when Allison used to call you all the time, before you started dating Tessa? You blocked her number."

He gave her a grim look. "It's not the same thing."

"But if we can't trust anybody else, how do we know we can trust him? Isn't that what you've been telling Josie the whole time? That she couldn't trust him? We don't even know who he is. Maybe he's working for that earth bitch."

He half-smiled. "You sound like her." His smile faded as quickly as it had appeared.

"I'm worried about her," she said, lip trembling. "You know how stubborn she is. Whatever they want her to do, she won't do it . . . they'll hurt her. They might even—"

Judah wrapped his arm around her and hugged her tightly. He was solid and warm. "We'll find her."

She wiped her nose with her sleeve and stepped back. "Don't blame yourself, okay? There wasn't anything you could've done."

His arms dropped away from her. "I could've let Beech die."

"No, you couldn't have," she said.

He crossed his arms, turning his face to the sky. "I wanted to."

She didn't take him too seriously. He was just angry that he'd failed. Judah hated to fail.

She stood next to him, tears drying on her cheeks, thinking. "I hope he doesn't go after her by himself."

He frowned. "Why?"

"Well, having his symbol on her body allows him to bypass any protective circles guarding her, right? But he could still get caught. They'll have charms to alert them to intruders, or regular old security cameras and alarms and stuff. If he goes after her alone and gets busted, then what can he do? He might be a super powerful god, but so is that psycho earth goddess. She took out a Triune. If Josie really is the key to her whole crazy plan, then she's probably going to be pissed if she catches someone trying to steal Josie back."

Judah continued to gaze upwards. "I guess we'd better hope this Fire Guy has a little sister as smart as you."

She gave him a weak smile. "Not everyone is so lucky."

He glanced over at her. "You're right. They're not." He looped his arm around her again and gave her another brief hug. "You should get some sleep."

"What about you?"

His gaze returned to the sky. It wasn't like Judah to brood. Normally, he was all plan and action.

She gave his forearm a squeeze. "Tessa will forgive you. She'll realize it's not your fault."

His gaze fell to the ground for a moment and then turned up again.

She touched his arm lightly. "She'll be okay. We'll find her."

He didn't respond. Simone left him, her heart aching. If Judah didn't have anything to say, then she knew things were really bad.

CHAPTER 26

April 9th

Vines squeezed around Josie, pinning her arms to her sides. "It takes time—" Her words were cut short as the living ropes circled, chafing, around her throat.

"You'll have time, dear," Earth Mama said. "All the time you need, don't worry. But only after I'm assured of your good faith. I'm certain you have some notion that if you dawdle long enough, your sister will find a means of rescuing you. Perhaps she has a mind to consult the Fates to locate you. As inept as she's proven thus far, who knows if she'll ever be capable of that?"

The vines tightened, making it hard for Josie to breathe. They'd slipped in behind the earth bitch after Josie had spent countless hours staring blankly at the rows and rows of boxes, each containing their own broken face of a god. Eighty-three in all. Earth Mama had been busy.

Although most of the building had been taken over by vegetation—the crumbling walls replaced by trees, the cracked and missing floors filled in with roots and lichen-covered stones, the gaping windows curtained by vines—the mask room had been renovated.

Everything gleamed. The tiled floors, the stainless steel sinks, even the white paint on the walls had a glossy sheen. The air was dry and plastic-smelling. Along one wall ran shelving full of masks. On the opposite wall, supply cabinets. Inside—clay, paper, metal, wood, tools of all shapes, even some that could've been used as weapons. But Josie had no opportunity to take one without being noticed. She'd been monitored the whole time.

Two gods stood guard in the room. Two more in the hall. In each corner, small black domes clung to the ceiling like black beetles—cameras. She'd been brought to this room and kept here since leaving Earth Mama's chamber of compost horrors.

Only after her eyes had started to droop and her stomach had gone from grumbling to sullenly aching had Earth Mama returned.

A trail of rotting sludge smeared across the pristine floors behind the earth bitch. Her trash-heap stench sharpened the dull aches in Josie's stomach into slicing pains.

"Now I feel like I need to demonstrate to you what happens if another day passes and you do nothing," Earth Mama said.

The vines suddenly cinched tight. Something in Josie's chest cracked. She screamed and gasped, almost blacking out. Then she was dropped a foot to the cold tile floor.

She landed in a heap, vision tripled, ears ringing, pain reverberating through her. Every breath felt like a hatchet blow.

"What's going on?" Fog God sounded annoyed, like he'd been awoken by Josie's scream of agony.

"What are you doing here?" Earth Mama asked.

"Checking in."

"Isn't that a bit risky?" Earth Mama asked.

Josie pushed upright. Her head spun. Tendrils of fog curled cool around her.

"Having problems?" he asked.

"Of course not," Earth Mama snapped. "We're just having a chat."

"A chat that involves bloodcurdling screams at four in the morning?" Fog God said. "Hm."

"Are you questioning me?" Earth Mama's guise grew so large her head touched the ceiling.

"That would be stupid of me," he said.

"Yes, it would." Earth Mama shrank slightly.

"But you know it's not going to work, don't you?" Fog God said. "The torture thing. Not with her."

"This isn't torture. It's aggressive persuasion."

"Right," Fog God said. "Persuade her all you want. She won't bite. And you won't get your masks repaired."

"And what would you suggest?"

Josie stared up at the bluish cloud in humanoid form, wondering who was under there and if she knew him. She was almost certain she'd met Earth Mama. The nasal pitch of her voice rang familiar, but then, Josie had met so many people over the years. Her mom had taught her lots of tricks for remembering faces, but she'd never taught Josie any for remembering voices. Josie hadn't heard any of the other gods speaking to their summoners like she had with the Fog God earlier. She'd been trying, hoping to pick up some clue about her location or some bit of information that might help her escape. But nothing.

"Fix her up, give her something to eat, and let her sleep for a while." Fog God's hollow eyes gazed down at her. "In the meantime, I'll find you some motivation."

APRIL 10TH

Her jail cell sat right next to the mask room. The cramped cell might've once been a storage closet. At least they'd fixed it up. White tile covered the floors, the walls, the ceiling. A camera was mounted in one corner of the ceiling, along with a recessed light and an air vent. She huddled on a plastic blue mat, which besides a fleece blanket and the stainless steel toilet, was the only thing in the room.

Earth Mama hadn't bothered healing her. Broken ribs, Josie assumed, as lying down was complete misery and breathing was an exercise in endurance. They brought her food: carrots, sprouts, slices of tomato, radishes. She ate everything. She knew better than to refuse. She needed to eat.

Since she'd arrived, she hadn't stopped thinking about Judah. Specifically, about the last time she'd seen him—his finger pointing at his forehead. She knew exactly what his signal had meant: call Fire Guy. But with what?

She searched the room. The light had a glass cover. That could be smashed maybe, if she could reach it. The vent had screws; she could steal those. Both could be used to cut with, but the likelihood that she would be able to reach either of them was low. Even if she could get hold of a screw or a shard of glass, she doubted she'd get a chance to use it before one of her guards caught her and then they'd know she was up to something.

As she sat there, racking her brain for some answer, her body betrayed her and stole her away into sleep.

What seemed a few moments later, but might've been hours—no windows, no watch, no phone—Granite God appeared. Beneath his guise, his hands were calloused and thick. He seized her arm and pulled her up. She stumbled after him, gritting her teeth against the explosion of pain in her side.

He shoved her into the mask room where Earth Mama waited, along with Sandstorm, who stood by the door. Behind Earth Mama was a chair. Tied to it was a lanky kid in black, a gag in his mouth, blood running down the side of his head.

Her heart dropped. "Kai."

His eyes widened when he saw her. Emphatic sounds issued from behind the cloth tied over his mouth.

Earth Mama's dirt mask had a hollow grin dug into it. "Oh, good. You do know him. I was assured that he was a friend of yours, but one can never tell with you children. So fickle in your friendships. I'd hoped to obtain that perky little girl, what's her name . . . Simone. But she was unavailable. Still, let's hope this one will serve our purposes just as well."

She motioned Granite God forward. He strode past Josie to Kai, grabbed Kai's hand, and in one quick motion, snapped Kai's little finger.

An audible crunch echoed through the room. Kai let out a wail behind his gag. His eyes slammed shut as tears spilled over, running through his eyeliner.

Josie winced. Her heart throbbed.

Granite God took the next finger and snapped it too. Kai lurched forward. The chair scraped against the tile with a metallic shriek.

Granite God reached for the next finger.

"No, wait! Stop!" Josie cried, grabbing her side against the pain.

Kai's head fell back. Tears ran freely down his face. His chest heaved. Tendons strained in his neck.

Earth Mama held up her hand, halting Granite God. "Of course, we'll stop. All you have to do to save your friend from further pain is to fix a mask." She swept her branch arm towards the shelves behind her. "Any one will suffice. And if you do, I will gladly heal the both of you. And you will both be treated quite well. And if you don't—"

Granite God broke Kai's middle finger. Kai's body pitched, but he only succeeded in rocking the chair to the side. If Granite God hadn't been there to grab the chair, Kai probably would've fallen over and cracked his head open.

"Okay," Josie said. "I'll do it. Okay? Please. Just . . . you don't have to hurt him anymore."

Kai's eyes opened again, reddened and watering. He shook his head vehemently. Even with his gag she could tell he was saying, "No. Don't."

He hadn't seen the half-rotted ribcage in Earth Mama's compost heap. Josie was more than certain Earth Mama would break every bone in his body and then drain his blood into her god's maw. And then who would be next? Simone? Beech? Her dad?

She couldn't stand there and let him be tortured, not if she could stop it.

Besides, if she started working on a mask, she might have a chance to steal something useful.

Josie shuffled over to the shelves. She didn't have to peruse the selection. One box had been calling to her from the moment she'd stepped into the room. She couldn't even see it, since it was high up in its cardboard box, but she stepped up to it.

"That one up there," she said, pointing without extending her arm. "I can't reach it."

Granite God left Kai, who was paler than usual, and took the box down for her. He carried it to the long workbench in the middle of the room. Josie followed him slowly.

He removed the lid and stepped aside. Inside was a wooden mask. A large portion of its left cheek was missing. The grain of his face was dark with age. If it hadn't been the face of a god, the wood probably would have rotted away centuries ago. She let out a painfully deep breath.

"I need a . . . tropical hardwood," she said, looking over at the cabinets of tools and supplies. "Central American, if you have it . . ."—she leaned against the table—"um, bocote, would be best."

Granite God stood there, looking like . . . well . . . granite. "Uh—"

"Bocote?" Earth Mama said in a honey-drenched voice. "As you wish, dear."

Earth Mama plunged her hands into her stomach. A squelching, sucking sound filled the room. Kai went green around the edges. Sweat dappled his face.

A moment later, Earth Mama pulled a chunk of dark, striped wood from within her guise, like she'd reached into a tree and scooped out a fistful of wood flesh. She set it down on the stainless steel table next to the box. Red-gold goo slid down the sides—sap.

"Will that do?"

Josie wanted to puke. "Yeah."

"Oh, yes," Earth Mama said, seeming to peer down at the mask. "He will do for a start. For a start." Her plump fingers slid against Josie's side. Josie tensed and grimaced as the pain redoubled under the pressure of her hands. "Allow me to thank you in advance."

"Wait, no. If you're going to heal someone, heal Kai," Josie said, sidling away from Earth Mama's fetid stench. "Please."

The open pits of the goddess's eyes widened. "You are more like Melinda than I realized. Your mother always had such a martyr complex. But don't worry, dear, I can heal both of you, quite easily."

She planted her hand against Josie's side. It was like she'd reached into Josie's body and wrenched open her chest. Josie's head swam, and then she passed out.

CHAPTER 27

APRIL 11TH
THE NEXT DAY

JOSIE'S HANDS ACHED. She wasn't sure how much time had passed. Days maybe. More like a day, probably. She had a sense, from the way her body was moving, like it was suspended in slowly hardening concrete, that it was very early in the morning.

She was covered in wood dust and shavings, glue still on her fingers.

Before she could set the repaired mask down on the table, Earth Mama swept it up.

"He's beautiful," she gushed, like he was a newborn baby. And he was beautiful.

The intricate swirls carved into his mask gleamed as if fresh cut. In fact, all she'd done was carve a replacement piece for his cheek and glued it in. But there was no sign that there had ever been a crack. The moment she'd fitted the new piece in, the mask had fused together. The new patterns matched up with the old flawlessly. Josie might've been pleased with her success, if she didn't feel like she was going to be sick.

She glanced over at Kai. He'd been gone when she'd come to. They'd brought him back a few hours ago, still tied up, still gagged, but looking better. At least his fingers seemed to be healed. As she worked, he watched her dully, slumped in his chair, looking as hopeless as she felt.

She'd quickly realized, once she'd started working, that someone was going to be standing over her shoulder at all times. Even when she went to the bathroom someone watched her, like she might flush a message down the drain to Tessa. In fact, that was one of the ways to reach the Triune—send it by water, burn it, bury it, or send it on the wind. But she didn't have any paper or anything she could write with, and she could tell that they were watching every tool she touched, accounting for it.

As she chiseled away at the wood with palm tools, she ached to slip one into her pocket, but she knew she would be caught if she tried. They were sure to search her before they let her leave the mask room.

Things were looking bleaker by the second.

She gazed at Kai. He stared back at her. His eyes blank and circled in dark shadows.

As Earth Mama admired her newest minion, Josie slid off the stool. "May I speak to him?"

Earth Mama lowered the mask. Sandstorm was with them now. The constant rasping of his guise was enough to drive her crazy, if being irritated would've done her any good, which it didn't.

"Why not?" Earth Mama said. "Mother Earth is generous. Go ahead. But don't dawdle. You have plenty of work to do."

Josie hesitated, wondering if Earth Mama would change her mind at the last minute, but she was caressing the mask again. Josie hurried over to the Kai.

She untied the knot of his gag and let it fall free. He licked his cracked lips. She crouched in front of him.

"Are you okay?" she asked.

He made a face at her.

"Sorry," she said. "Stupid question."

She went to the sink and filled the steel cup there with water, taking it to him. All the time, she could feel Sandstorm tracking her movements. By the door was a water goddess, covered in blue-green algae. The whirlpools of her eyes stayed fixed on Kai. Josie tipped the cup to Kai's lips.

"Thanks," he said after emptying the cup.

"What happened?" Josie asked in a whisper, though she knew nothing they said was private.

"Fog Dude and his brute squad ambushed me," Kai said, his voice an even lower hush. "I was on my way home from Simone's."

"How is Simone?"

His eyes flickered, pained. "How do you think?"

Josie sagged.

"Everybody's going apeshit," he said. "You went missing. The Past Eye is missing. Have you seen her?"

Josie's mind flashed to the ribcage in Earth Mama's bed of death. "No."

"Now I'm missing,"—he snorted—"but I doubt anybody's noticed that."

She touched his hand, the one that hadn't been broken. "Simone will have noticed."

His shoulders sagged. "She'll be freaking. She already was after what happened to you. Your sister wanted to go the Fates," he said, lowering his voice even more, "but your dad talked her out of it."

"Good," she said. "She doesn't know the Invocation. She would be killed attempting it."

"But weren't you going to send her to them?"

"Yeah, but I know the ritual."

"You don't think she'll try anyway?"

"I don't know," Josie said, glancing over at Earth Mama, who was having Sandstorm pull down a few other masks. She wanted to cry, but she still couldn't. She wondered if she'd ever be able to cry again.

She turned back to him. "How's Beech?"

"Alive."

She let out another long-held breath.

"He was ready to storm the castle," Kai said. "Too bad he doesn't know where it is. Do you know where we are?"

She shook her head.

"Judah's gone off the deep end too," Kai said. "He was acting extra crazy, probably from having to give Beech mouth-to-mouth."

She almost laughed. She gazed up at Kai, his long dark eyes and hard jaw. "You're not my Fire Guy, are you?"

"Sorry to disappoint you," he said with a weak side-smile.

"Actually, I'm relieved," she said. "I'm sorry that you got involved in this."

"Not like I had any choice," he said. "You think Simone was going to let me sit on the sidelines while her BFF is MIA? No way. If not for Judah, she'd probably be the one tied to this chair. He's got her on lockdown."

"Good," Josie said. "I don't want anyone else to be hurt."

"So you're just going to build them an army?"

"What other choice do I have?"

"None that I know of." He raised his eyebrow, like he was asking her if she did have another choice.

She glanced over her shoulder again. Earth Mama had arranged about a dozen boxes on the counter, like a bride picking out china patterns.

"Maybe," she murmured.

"What—?"

She shook her head and then stood up and hugged him. When she pulled back, he looked as surprised as she felt.

"If saving your life means building them an army," she said, "then that's what I'll do."

April 11th

She huddled under her blanket. She'd had to beg for a chance to sleep.

After Earth Mama had grown twice her usual size and sent her TemperMentals swirling around Josie to search for any tools she might've stolen, she'd allowed Sandstorm to push Josie back into her closet. The light overhead had dimmed, but hadn't gone out completely. The dark eye of the camera had trained on her as she curled into the corner, resting her forehead on her knees.

She had to find a way to get the fire god's symbol on her body, somehow. If she couldn't draw it, she'd have to cut it in. She knew what that would mean—having his symbol scarred into her skin would enable him to control her forever, unless he released her—but she didn't have any other choice. She had tried pressing her fingernails into her skin, but they were too short to be of any use. Again she thought about the glass covering the light, or the screws in the vent. But they would see her. They would stop her.

She moved onto her side, facing the wall. The pain in her ribs remained, more of a deep ache now than the stabbing agony of earlier. That bitch could heal. Healing was a forbidden practice, just like human sacrifice. And now Josie was building her an army of ancient gods.

The tree god Josie had repaired had been old. Really old. She wasn't even sure what kind of wood his original mask had been made from. Bocote had just been the closest thing she could think of. It seemed to have worked though. Once he was summoned . . . well, no one would doubt the power of a tree after that.

After him, she'd repaired three more—two more earth gods and a water god. They'd been easy. Too easy. She'd tried to stall, but every time she stopped working, Granite God or Sandstorm turned up, breathing down her neck. She had three more masks waiting for her, in various stages of repair. Once the plaster was dried for the molds, they would be done in a few hours. They were old too, powerful—just like the tree god, just like the fire god. And now, they were Earth Mama's.

This was so bad.

She bent her elbow under her head. She stank. She wondered if there was a shower somewhere, or if Earth Mama would refuse to let Josie bathe on principle. After all, the woman napped in a pile of compost.

She shifted, trying to get comfortable on a mat that was not built for comfort. Something scratched at her neck. She grabbed for it. Images of giant beetles and bloated maggots flashed through her mind. Her fingers touched on something smooth and hard caught in her hair.

She pulled it out. A splinter of wood.

She curled it away in her hand, holding it close to her chest.

After a few minutes, when no one appeared to take it from her, she could only assume they hadn't noticed. Not that they would expect her to carve a god's symbol onto her body anyway, not unless she was planning on sacrificing herself to him. It wasn't common for summoners to know a specific god's symbol, unless they were in possession of that god. But she wasn't a summoner. And she did know a god's symbol. The fire god's symbol.

She ran her finger over the splinter. No bigger than a toothpick. One end was ragged, but the other had a cleaner, sharper edge—sharp enough to get the job done.

Her heart quickened. Wherever she put it, the symbol needed to be hidden. She would bleed.

Her first thought was to cut into her foot, where her socks and sneakers would cover the evidence. But it would draw attention if she took off her shoes and socks and then sat huddled over her foot to work. The splinter was slender and would require a lot of pressure to break the skin. She couldn't risk snapping it before the symbol was completed.

After debating where the best place might be, she made up her mind to carve it just below her navel, hoping her underwear and jeans would obscure any blood.

Slowly, she unbuttoned her jeans and pushed the waistband down slightly.

Closing her eyes, she imagined the symbol. It leapt to her inner eye, flickering in cobalt flame. In the soft flesh just inside her hip and below her waistband, she pressed the splinter in until it hurt and then a little bit further. It had to be deep enough. It couldn't be a scratch that would fade. If there was blood, he wouldn't be able to ignore it. He couldn't.

She hoped.

Painstakingly, she began to carve his symbol into her skin.

CHAPTER 28

APRIL 12TH
THE NEXT DAY
GETTING ANTSY WITH SIMONE

"**J**UDAH!"

She tripped and almost went head over heels down the basement steps. Worse, she almost dropped her phone. Catching the railing, she took a second to compose herself. Then, clutching the phone to her chest, she walked carefully down the last three steps to Judah's bedroom door.

Before she raised her fist to knock, he opened the door. Even though it was hardly dawn, he was freshly showered, his hair sculpted in careless waves.

"Simone?"

"Look! Look!" She shoved the phone into his face.

He leaned back and took the phone from her, scowling at the message she'd received shortly before—a long series of numbers.

"What—?"

"Coordinates, Judah. GPS coordinates," she said. "He sent them. He sent them to me." She tapped the screen again and pulled up the location, then turned the map to him. "It's not even that far away."

He took the phone from her again. "How do you know—?"

"It has to be. The number that sent it to me came up as unavailable, but it has to be."

He ran his thumb over the phone. "It could be trick. It could be a trap."

"Or it could be her," Simone said. "It has to be her."

He tapped the phone a few times. His own phone buzzed in his pocket. He pulled it out and looked at it.

"Okay," he said, handing the phone back to her. "I'm going. Don't do anything while I'm gone. Don't call anyone. Not Mom. Not Kai. Got it? If I'm not back in half an hour, then call Mom, but no one else."

She squeezed her phone between her hands. "Half an hour?"

His left hand disappeared from view, when it returned, he had the mask of his air god in his hand. A fragile-looking piece of wood, delicate feathers carved into the pale surface.

"I can't translocate directly there, Simone. It might be a trap. I'll get as close as I think is safe and try to determine what we're dealing with first."

She sagged. "That sounds reasonable."

"In the meantime," he said, "go back to your room and finish whatever charms you've been slaving over for the last two days. We might actually need them."

He put the mask to his face and vanished.

Simone returned to her room.

She sat at her craft table and pulled her lighted magnifier back over the crystal she'd been etching.

The lines in the clear stone were thin and opaque, tightly woven together. Yesterday, she'd snuck into her mom's "secret" cabinet. Long ago, her mom had shown her the book containing their tribe's most powerful charms. *One day*, her mom had said, *you'll be able to produce them.*

Judah had told their mom that she should keep the book in her stash, with her mask, but their mom had claimed that wasn't safe enough. Her ring could be stolen and the tribe's charm book with it. Later, Simone had seen Judah sneak into their mom's room and had busted him with the charm book. He was horrified. Judah didn't normally break the rules, but he also couldn't resist a challenge. He did it, he'd said, just to see if he could. Simone had believed him. It was just so Judah.

Still, she'd threatened to rat him out unless he showed her how to access the hidden panel and bypass all the charms protecting it. Actually, it had turned out to be pretty simple. The key, as with all charms, was intent. So long as her intent wasn't malicious towards her tribe, all she needed were the right words, which Judah had provided, and the panel would pop right open. Their tribe's most powerful charms, hers, if she could channel them.

At the moment, her mom was scouring the state for Lily, so Simone had taken it upon herself to decide that now was the time for her to attempt to produce one of the charms. If she succeeded, the charm would allow the wearer to slip by almost any protection spell, unharmed and unnoticed, like a ghost.

She rubbed her aching shoulders, put on her safety glasses, and picked up her etching tool. She wasn't used to working in crystal. For whatever reason, her power seemed to channel best into plastic—an irony since she generally avoided plastics unless they were recycled and recyclable—but this charm was too powerful to put into plastic. She was sure that if she tried to carve it into one of her usual plastic beads, it would end up a melted mess all over her desk.

Taking a deep breath, she gazed up at the mandala on her wall for a few moments, clearing her head. Then she focused on the charm's symbol. It formed in her mind. Lines rolled out as if written by an invisible hand.

Invisible. Good word. The right word to focus her intent on.

The lines flickered in her mind, turning ghostly translucent. She hung onto that word—invisible. She switched on the engraving tool and began working. The symbols and the intent were just two parts of the whole. To finish it, she'd need to know who would use the crystal.

When she turned off the engraver and sat back, pushing the glasses on top of her head, it took her a moment to realize Judah was standing in the doorway. She jumped off her chair.

"Well?"

He licked his lips. His eyes were brighter than she'd ever seen them—blazing.

"I knew it!" She whipped off her glasses and tossed them onto her bed. "What did you see? Did you see her?"

He shook his head. "It's pretty far off the radar. I couldn't get too close, even in the air. Might've been an asylum or something, back in the day." He ran his hand over his mouth. "Most of it's overgrown, but not with native species."

"You mean like an earth goddess has been cultivating an exotic garden there?"

He nodded. "But I could see a newer truck outside. And solar panels. I brushed up against a couple protection circles. I could feel them. Hopefully, no one noticed."

A giddy rush fountained up inside of her. She bounced on her toes, her hands clasped tightly at her chest. "Josie's there. We found her. What do we do now?"

"What are you working on?" he asked.

She spun around, having completely forgotten about the crystal in those few seconds. "If it works? Invisibility charm. It should let someone sneak through protective circles."

He gazed in that intense way he had when he was thinking deeply.

"We need to decide whom we can trust," he said.

"What about Josie's Fire Guy? Shouldn't we try to get a hold of him?"

"We don't have time to stand around in a protective circle waiting for him."

Simone glanced around her room. "I do."

"Fine, you call him. I'm not waiting." He turned and started down the hall.

She chased after him. "What are you going to do?"

"I'm going to call Tessa and Mom. I'm fairly certain they're on our side." He started down the stairs. She followed close at his heels.

"What about Beech? He'll want to help."

Judah stopped at the bottom of the steps. "I don't trust him."

"You think they would've almost killed him if he was in on it?"

"I don't know."

"Whatever you're planning you're going to need help and—"

The doorbell chimed.

Judah frowned and went to it, peering through the glass panels across the top. His frown deepened as he pulled open the door.

Simone peeked around him. "Russell?"

Russell pushed back the hood of his parka. Behind him, the streets were wet and gray. Russell and Judah dueled with dark looks for a moment.

"Is Kai here?" he asked dully.

She frowned. "No."

A crease appeared in his forehead. "Do you know where he is?"

She came forward, standing between Judah and Russell, uncomfortable as she felt being caught in the midst of that tension storm.

"No. Why?"

"We haven't seen him for a while. Mom tried calling him, but he's not answering. I told her I'd stop by on my way to the gym and check on him."

That wasn't unusual. Kai ignored his mom's calls all the time. She fished her own phone out of her pocket and called him. It rang and rang and rang, then went to voicemail.

She hung up. Kai never ignored her calls. Not unless he was sleeping, in band practice, or in the shower, and he'd even been known to interrupt all three of those things for her.

"He didn't answer." Her heart started to pick up speed.

"When was the last time you talked to him?" Judah asked.

She thought back. "What day is it?"

Judah and Russell both gave her a not-very-nice look.

"Well, things have been crazy, and I haven't been sleeping," she said with a huff.

"Friday," Judah said.

"Josie disappeared Sunday and then we came back here . . ." She dug her hands into her hair. "Tuesday." Her heart stopped. She looked up at Judah. "I haven't talked to him since Tuesday afternoon, since he left here. Oh my gods."

She punched her phone's screen again, scrolling through the calls and messages. In fact, his last message was from even earlier than Tuesday because he'd been with her since they'd left the hospital after Josie's disappearance. He'd left Tuesday afternoon and said he'd call her later. But she'd passed out and when she'd woken up, she'd been so intent on the charm that she'd completely forgotten about him. She'd been about to text him when the GPS coordinates had showed up.

"Judah . . ."

He put his hand on her shoulder. "Try calling him again."

She did. He still wasn't picking up. Now her heart was jerking like a noose had been cinched around it.

Russell was on his phone too.

She tried calling his bandmates. No one was happy to be awakened, and no one had seen Kai for days.

When she finally got off the phone, she couldn't breathe.

Judah sat her down and looked her in the eye. "It's okay. Slow down," he said. "We'll find him."

At some point, Russell had come inside, closing the door behind him. He'd been calling everyone he could think of too, but no one knew anything.

"You think he ran away?" Russell asked, his jacket dripping puddles on the floor.

"No," Simone snapped. "He wouldn't leave without telling me." She clawed at her pajama pants. "Oh my gods. They took him. They kidnapped him, just like they did Lily."

Russell and Judah wore similar skeptical expressions.

"Why would they do that?" Judah asked, trying to sound reasonable.

"I don't know." Her mind pedaled faster and faster. "Maybe they needed more sacrifices, or maybe they wanted to hold him for ransom or something—"

Russell shoved his hands into his pockets, looking even more skeptical, but Judah's face was slowly changing. He stood up from where he'd been crouched in front of her.

"What?" she asked, jumping up and grabbing his arm. "What are you thinking?"

He glanced over at Russell. They had a long-standing alpha male thing going on that Simone found stupid most of the time, especially when they couldn't seem to help themselves even in times of total emergency, like when her best friend and her boyfriend had been kidnapped by supervillains.

"Maybe they did take him," Judah said.

Her insides were overheated plastic goo. "They're going to kill him, aren't they?"

"Not if Josie does what they want her to do," Judah said softly.

Simone's hand flew to her mouth. "Oh my gods, you're right. I told you she wouldn't help them willingly."

Judah nodded. "They needed someone to motivate her."

"I heard about Josie's disappearance," Russell said. "But you really think that rogue earth goddess took her?"

"We know she did," Simone said, more sharply than she knew she was capable of. "We were there."

Russell looked taken aback. "Why would they want her?"

"Why do you think? You saw what she did. You saw her repair that fire god's mask. You saw what happened at the club the other night, didn't you?"

His face hardened. "I was there—"

"Did you know they did all of that just to get Josie?" Simone asked.

His arms dug deeper into his jean pockets. "I heard something—"

"I know what everybody's been saying about Josie. But they're wrong. She's not a liar—"

Russell frowned. "I never said she was."

"Josie doesn't care about herself at all, which is totally why they had to kidnap Kai. Because she'd rather die than help that earth bitch, and she would too. The only way they'd get her to do anything would be by threatening to hurt someone else. That's how they got her to go with them in the first place." Her hand squeezed around her phone. She wanted to throw it, but stopped herself. Kai might contact her. Maybe. Please. Somehow.

"And it'll work again," Judah said grimly. "She won't let them hurt Kai."

Tears ran down Simone's cheeks. "I know," she said, looking back at her phone. "We have to do something. Now."

"But I don't understand why—" Russell started.

Just then, the back door opened. A moment later, their mom appeared, looking ragged and bleary-eyed. She dropped her hobo bag on the dining room table.

"What's going on?"

Simone went to her. "Kai's missing."

"What?" Caroline wrapped her arms around Simone, holding her tight. Simone buried her face in her mom's powdery clean smell. Nobody smelled better than Mom in times of crisis—except maybe Kai. He smelled like comic book ink and espresso and that indefinable boy smell that was all Kai and all hers.

She sobbed.

"We think they took him to . . . motivate Josie," Judah said.

"When did this happen? Why wasn't I—?"

"We just realized," Judah said. "Russell came, thinking Kai was here."

"But he's not." Simone buried her face against her mom's chest. "He's not. And now they have him tied up in that old—"

"Simone!" Judah barked.

Simone choked up, biting her lips inwards. "Sorry."

Caroline pulled Simone away from her. "Tied up where?"

"Not now, Mom," Judah said in a low voice.

"Wait a minute," Russell said, face sharp as vampire teeth. "If you know where my brother is, you'd better tell me."

Judah sneered. "Don't act like you give a shit about him—"

"Shut your face—"

"Stop this instant!" Caroline said, stepping forward.

Judah and Russell continued to posture at each other. They'd had a truce for a couple of years, but they'd been known to fight before, especially after Judah had lost that mask to Russell in the trials. Everyone knew Russell had cheated.

"Judah, if you know something about Kai's whereabouts, you will tell me right now."

"Mom, we don't know—"

"I said right now!"

Judah's lips parted and then closed. If Simone hadn't been rooted to the floor by shock, she would've turned and run from the room. She had never seen Judah defy their mom openly. Ever.

Mom's face went slack and white, like she'd been slapped by Judah's defiant silence. And then a beet-red flush started to creep up her neck.

"I got a message," Simone blurted out.

"Simone—" Normally, a growl like that from Judah would've stopped her dead.

"A message about what?" Russell demanded.

"Simone, stop talking—"

"But Kai—"

Judah turned and opened the door. "Get out," he said to Russell.

"If you know something about where my brother is—"

"We don't know anything," Judah said. "My sister's just upset. If we hear anything, we'll let you know."

Russell and Judah glared at each other for a long moment. Finally, Russell turned and left.

Caroline held up her hands. "All right. Neither of you is leaving this room until I have heard everything there is to hear." She crossed her arms. "So start talking."

CHAPTER 29

APRIL 12TH

"WHAT'S WRONG WITH HER?" Earth Mama's voice was distant, yet piercing.

"She has a fever."

"I know she has a fever! Why do you think I brought you in here?"

"I looked her over. It's likely just a virus."

"Isn't there something you can do? You are a doctor, aren't you?"

"I could try to bring the fever down, but she should be fine. Fluids, rest, the usual. We have to let it run its course. It is flu season, you know. All part of the natural order."

"Don't give me that—" Earth Mama sounded on the verge of tearing her roots out. "Get out of here before I do something we'll both regret."

Josie cracked open her eyes. The room was too white—even with Earth Mama overshadowing it. Her stink almost made Josie puke.

"Can you hear me?" Earth Mama demanded.

"Yeah," Josie said, her mouth was full of slime. How long had she been asleep? She was soaked with sweat.

"Did you hear what the doctor said?"

"Yeah." She rolled over on to her side. Earth Mama's mud face became clearer. "Can't you heal me?"

Earth Mama seemed to shrink. "I tried. Apparently, my healing powers aren't useful against the flu." She let out a low grumble. "We'll have to wait it out." She went to the door, stopping and looking back at Josie. "Feel . . . better." As she stepped out, she started barking orders. "Get in there, clean it up. Bring her water, whatever she needs."

The door slammed shut. Josie fell back into a fevered sleep.

APRIL 13TH

She woke to a cool damp cloth dabbing gently against her forehead. She squinted through the fever haze at a figure leaning over her. Her throat ached.

"Kai?"

He gave her a side-smile. "How are you feeling?"

Her tongue ran over the roof of her mouth like sandpaper across sun-scorched brick. "Once I was in Dhahran, Saudi Arabia, in June, and I discovered that asphalt has a liquid state."

"So . . . you're good then?"

"I feel like asphalt in Dhahran in June."

"Can you sit up?"

He put a hand on her back and helped her. Once she was upright, he gave her a steel water bottle. Against her palms, the metal felt like ice. She took a long drink and then another.

"Not too fast," he said. "You haven't eaten for a while."

A small ripple of embarrassment passed through her. Having her best friend's boyfriend tend to her was a bit awkward.

She wiped her mouth. "How long?"

"I don't know. It's hard to tell around here. A day?" He hooked his arms around his legs. She set the bottle aside and leaned back against the wall. So cool. She let out a sigh.

"I can't believe they let you in here," she said.

"I think they got tired of taking care of you," he said. "Since I'm not doing anything useful while you're down for the count, I guess they figured . . ." He shrugged.

She nodded. She vaguely remembered Algae Goddess helping her to the toilet at some point. Her heart stopped, thinking of the fire god's mark. Had Algae Goddess noticed?

Her fingers pressed against the burning spot near her hip. A dizzying wave of heat passed through her. Was that why she had this fever? Because of Fire Guy? Or had the wood she'd used been toxic? Maybe the wound was infected.

"Are you going to puke?" Kai asked.

She grimaced. "I don't think so. How are you?"

"I'm fine. Since you repaired those masks, the Earth Goddess has been ignoring me." He waggled his fingers, the ones that had been broken. They only looked slightly off-color now, violet-hued. "So long as I can still manage the power chords, I'll survive," he said. "But I don't think she's going to be patient about you getting back to work."

"Does she seem familiar to you?"

He frowned. "No. Do you think you know her?"

Her gaze flicked over to the camera. "I've met just about every summoner worth knowing."

"Don't worry about them," he said, tracking her gaze. "They had me stashed in the security room for a while. I heard that sand guy say one of the Earth Goddess's pet plants took out the audio cord. They should've gone wireless."

"It doesn't matter. I still don't know who she is," she said.

"Not that it matters," he said. "Who would we tell if we did know? From what I can see they've got us locked up tight."

She struggled to focus on him, but her vision kept wavering, like the rippling heat waves over the broad highways in Dhahran. "So you're just giving up?"

"I'm a lover, not a fighter."

A dry chuckle escaped her lips.

"Actually," he said, "some of the summoners have been talking to me, explaining why they're behind the dirt queen and . . ."

Her eyes narrowed. "And what?"

"And some of what they say makes sense," he said.

She stared at him. "You're joking."

He held up his hands. "Hey, you know what they say, know your enemy, or for every victory, also suffer defeat."

"Who says that?"

"Sun Tzu, *The Art of War*."

"Been prepping for battle, have you, lover?"

He side-smiled. "I read. You know, for the pleasure."

"And what have you learned about our enemy?"

"That she's a crazy bitch."

"I could've told you that."

"And she's got more followers than you might realize," he said. "I've counted thirty separate summoners. Those are just the ones I've seen."

She shook her head. "How could they be following her? Don't they know she murdered my mom? Don't they know she's been sacrificing people?"

"It's war for them, Josie. They're not messing around. They want people to die. A lot of people. That's the whole point."

She thought back to what Fog God had said about choosing sides.

Kai went on, "They think the planet is out of whack. Too many people. Too much civilization. You know, since the ancient gods have all pretty much disappeared, there's not the kind of mass destruction there used to be. Humans have adapted. Technology, medicine, all that. It's allowed a lot of people to create a whole lot of other people, and they're like a freakin' plague. This earth goddess thinks she is Mother Earth. And she's pissed. You've got to admit, she might have good reason."

"She's not Mother Earth."

"No shit. But you've been all over. You can't tell me the tribes haven't been complaining about this forever—pollution, overpopulation, deforestation, you name it. Are you really surprised that some folks in the family turned militant?"

She let her head fall back. He was right.

One of the primary complaints, wherever her mom had gone, was about the environment. Rivers disappearing, land disappearing, animals disappearing. Poison in the air, the water, the food. And he was also right that there were always a handful of

Core members who wanted to take action—violent action. That's why her mom had gone to Dhahran. A few Core members had worked their way into the oil company there. They'd basically been ecoterrorists. Instead of bombs, they'd planned on ripping the place apart with their gods. Her mom had gone to warn them to clear out, or else.

They'd cleared out.

"They may have a few good talking points," she said, "but they killed my mother. Nothing they say is of any interest to me. And beyond my personal feelings, they also murdered the Triune. According to the Covenant, their souls will be consigned to Oblivion. So however justified they feel, however happy their gods are to get a little vengeance on behalf of Mother Earth, at the end of the day, they're all fucked. And they deserve it."

He lofted an eyebrow at her. "Sounding pretty militant yourself."

She held her hand out for the rag. He passed it to her. She wiped down her forehead and her neck.

"Maybe," he said after a moment of watching her, "they're thinking about destroying the Covenant too."

She stopped sponging away the sweat, fixing on him again.

He tilted his head. "I heard some talk about how the original plan, you know, murdering your mother, was all about getting hold of the mask of the Tripartite and freeing Death."

"Yeah, she mentioned something about that to me too," Josie said, "but it's not possible."

"Sure about that?"

She scowled. The Triune could destroy a mask with the help of the Tripartite, which was surely how some of the masks in Earth Mama's collection had been broken. But many of them had been destroyed in battles with other summoners, usually ones involving divine weapons. Earth Mama certainly had some tools of the gods—the time bender, whatever she was using to blind the Eye, and ... the sword. Was the sword capable of destroying the mask of the Tripartite?

"If the Tripartite is dissolved," Kai went on, "wouldn't that dissolve the Covenant too?"

Her hands fell to the mat. "*Kuso—*"

He smirked. "You like anime?"

"How did you know that?"

"That's where everyone I know learned how to swear in Japanese."

"I'm actually fairly fluent."

"Oh yeah?"

"In more than a few languages."

"You don't act like it."

"Act like what?"

He shrugged.

"A nerd?"

"I was thinking pretentious know-it-all."

"No? How do I act?"

"Like a hardass know-it-all."

"Do I really?"

He reached out and took the rag from her, dumping more water on it from the bottle and handing it back to her. Cool rivulets ran over her wrists. A grateful breath escaped her.

"Honestly," he said, "you seem pretty lost most of the time."

She brought the rag to her face, pressing it to her eyes. They ached, like a parched throat.

"Is it that obvious?"

"Not at all."

She peeked up, meeting his calm dark eyes.

"I just happen to be extremely sensitive," he said, half-smiling. "Did you not notice the eyeliner?"

She scooted over to a cooler patch of tile. "I love anime."

"Oh yeah?"

"*Naruto* probably saved thirteen-year-old Josie's life."

"Ooo, angsty, were you? Better question. How much eyeliner did you wear?"

"You're kind of funny."

"Don't forget darkly handsome and musically gifted."

"How could I?"

"*Naruto*, huh? Why are you forcing me to like you?"

"Sorry."

He shrugged. "It's all right."

"I'm going to get us out of here," she said.

He eyed her. "You sound pretty sure of that."

"I am sure."

"You have a plan?"

She dropped her head back against the wall. Her vision swam. She closed her eyes as the room began to ripple and bend around her. "Not exactly."

He touched her knee lightly. "Don't do anything stupid, Josie. Okay? It's not worth it."

"You think they're going to keep us here like this forever? We have to get out. Eventually, they're going to kill us."

"I don't know," he said. "You're the Triune's sister. If war is coming, then having a prisoner like you to use as a bargaining chip might not be such a bad idea."

"Sun Tzu again?"

"Common sense."

"And what about you?"

He shrugged again.

"Aren't you worried?" she asked.

"How would that help?"

She pressed the rag to her forehead again, but it had grown warm in her hand and didn't offer any relief. "You sound like my mom."

A dark pulse of silence filled the tiny room.

"I'm sorry about your mom, Josie."

"Yeah—" She swallowed roughly and tried to fix on him. The edges of his lean body seemed warped, rippling. Gods, this couldn't be good. What was wrong with her? Could it be just a run-of-the-mill fever? Somehow, she doubted it. Was Fire Guy doing this to her? Punishing her for bugging him when she'd said she wouldn't? Maybe he didn't realize she'd been kidnapped. Maybe he just thought she was some pathetic teenaged girl begging for attention.

"You know something about it, don't you?" she asked. "You're a foster kid."

"I guess. My dad died before I was born. My mom had issues. She bailed."

"That's terrible."

"I'm over it."

"Really?"

"Nah." He took the rag from her again, wetting it and then placing it back in her hand. "You never really get over it. You deal with it, accept it, get on with it. But it's always there, pissing you off."

Swabbing the rag against her neck, the walls continued trembling around her, as if it was the room melting and not her.

But then, her world had been melting for a long time. Starting the day her mom had been murdered, the day her mom's blood had spilled across the floor in Brunei, everything Josie had thought was real and solid had fallen apart and flowed away like her blood.

She'd been trying so hard to hold onto to what she'd learned, to who she thought she was supposed to be, but it didn't seem to be working anymore.

When all else fails, Josie, her mom had said, *there's you.*

When Josie had been heir to the Triune, those words had made sense to her. Now she wasn't sure what to do with them. Or what to do at all.

She may not have known what was right, but she knew what was wrong. Letting Kai die here was definitely wrong. She couldn't let it happen. She wouldn't.

He raked his hands back through his hair. The black clumps stuck up like a crown's broken rays. On his fingers, even the bruised ones, he still wore his rings.

"Why didn't they take your rings?" she asked.

"They did. Then they realized my tribe didn't grant me any masks, and they gave my rings back. Courteous, don't you think?"

Her voice dropped low. "But you've passed the first trials. You can summon a god . . . can't you?" Meaning, if she could get a mask into his hands, would he be able to use it?

His eyes narrowed. "Did I mention I'm a lover, not a fighter?"

"Once upon a time, a boy named Kai was kidnapped by a psycho bitch set on destroying humanity. Do you know how that story ends?"

"Once upon a time, a girl named Josie tried to escape a psycho bitch set on destroying humanity and got the kid who-was-almost-her-friend killed in the process."

"It's not about me," she said, "it's about you. If I could get you a mask and distract them, you might be able to get away—"

"Oh, and leave you behind? What kind of dark knight would I be then, huh?"

"You could get help."

"Nice try. But we both know that's bullshit. Translocation doesn't work like that. If I could actually break out, do you really think they're going to keep you here? Even if there is only a remote possibility that I might have some way of bringing back any kind of help? Not that I could, because the only sense I have of our current location is a couple of creepy, overgrown corridors and a few sterile rooms, all of which are sure to be protected against translocating intruders. Oh, and what do you think Simone would do to me if I turned up without her BFF and with no information concerning your whereabouts?"

"I think she'd just be happy that you're okay."

His sideswiped smile returned. "For about two seconds. You know she's a black belt in tae kwon do, don't you?"

"She'll forgive you."

His smile faded. "It's not happening, Josie. Forget about it."

"What about survival of the fittest?"

"You're not talking survival of the fittest; you're saying, 'let Josie sacrifice herself for Kai.' And that ain't happening. So whatever little martyr mouse is running your wheels, you can drown it right now."

"You said it yourself. They'll keep me around—"

"Maybe," he said. "But not if you don't play along. And let me guess; the moment I'm out of here, you'll stop repairing all those masks, and how do you think that's going to go over with the blood-drinkers out there? Keeping you alive might make sense, but does Mother Earth strike you as the most stable of personalities?"

"Please, Kai—"

"Please what? It's a shitty plan, Josie. Why don't you focus on keeping your body temperature in the range of the living and leave the critical thinking to those of us whose brains aren't set to broil?"

"You have a plan?"

"I might have if you weren't distracting me with all your crazy, altruistic BS. I may wear eyeliner, but you're insulting my masculinity by suggesting I save my own ass and leave you here sick and at the mercy of the enemy. Come on."

"I didn't mean to insult your masculinity."

"Thank you."

She sunk against the mat. Was it her imagination, or had the floor started to liquefy like asphalt in Dhahranian summer?

"What are we going to do?" she asked.

"What you and I do best," he said.

She looked over at him, dubious.

"Survive."

The door opened. Granite God appeared.

"Time to get back to work," he said.

CHAPTER 30

APRIL 14TH
THE NEXT DAY

SOMETHING WAS HAPPENING TO HER. She wasn't sure if it was the fever, or if it was the mask-making, or some combination of the two. Either way, she was starting to hallucinate.

The masks were talking to her. Not the ones in possession by her guards, or even the ones she'd repaired, but the broken ones still in their boxes.

She'd been dragged back to the mask room, along with Kai, whom they didn't even bother to tie up this time. Granite God informed her that she'd get a break after she repaired another mask. She finished two and didn't get a break, unless they considered passing out on the floor in a pile of wood dust a break.

When Kai shook her awake, pouring half a bottle of water over her face and the rest down her throat, she heard a strange murmur in her ears, but she wrote it off as some background electrical hum.

She finished repairing three more masks, two of which she'd started before the fever had struck. Then, very reluctantly, she'd repaired a forest god, one made of heavy oak with a wolf face. It only needed a little glue and it was good as new. Gods with animal aspects were rare, and she was starting to understand why. Touching the snarling visage had made her stomach heave and her hands tremble. She could've sworn that it growled at her. Or that could've been the fever. She hoped it was the fever.

She'd been carving a mold for an earth god whose mask was nothing but a pile of sand, her vision growing blurry and her head spinning, when the strange hum had splintered into distinct, clear voices.

"Look at her," one said sympathetically, seeming to come from the vicinity of the top shelf. "She's hardly more than a child."

Josie stopped working, straightened up, and searched the room. Kai slumped on a chair in the far corner, eyes half open. Granite God and a murky green water god she called Swamp Creature manned the door.

"I don't care how old she is," another commented from somewhere near the lower shelf. "I'm ready to be earthbound again."

She stared at the shelves. The voice had clearly come from there. And more followed.

"And be a slave to another mortal? No, thanks," one grumbled.

"I don't know. I like humans," one said lightly.

Josie huddled back over her work, gritting her teeth, willing the masks to be silent. She might've wondered more about why she was hearing them all of a sudden or how it was even possible, but she was too exhausted and fevered to want anything more than for them to be quiet again.

"Like humans?" the second remarked. "They're stupid, they're selfish, and they stink."

"Then why are you so anxious to be controlled by one again?" the first mask asked tartly.

"You know why. If there's going to be a mass extinction, I'm not going to miss out on my share of the carnage."

"You're disgusting."

"Shut up!" Josie snapped. "No one's going to be material if I can't concentrate."

"Uh . . . Josie?" Kai's hand brushed her shoulder. "Who are you talking to?"

"No one," she muttered, turning back to the mold she'd been carving.

"Can I get you some water?" he asked.

"No . . . thanks." She sighed. "What do you think Simone's doing right now?"

The shadows around Kai's eyes darkened. "Probably cooking up some plan to rescue us."

Josie started shaving away the lump of the nose, flattening it. "Always trying to save the world." Her voice choked. "I miss her."

His face fell, taking on a bruised shade.

Swamp Creature barked at him to go sit down. He left her.

As she was waiting for the clay to dry, she started work on another mask. A rough-hewn stone mask split right down the middle. A mountain god.

"What happened to you?" she asked as she lifted both pieces of the mask out of the box.

"Ever seen an Axe of Invincibility?" the mask asked in an aloof, bass voice.

"No."

"I have."

"Are you talking to the mask?" Granite God loomed over her shoulder.

"So what if I am?" The fever was leaving her temper even shorter than normal.

"You're in the thrall of a fire god," the mountain god said, sounding amused.

She leaned closer to the inanimate, splintered stone mask. "Is that why I feel like this?"

"Probably," the mountain god said. "You'll feel however he wants you to feel."

"Tell the Goddess to come down here," Granite God said to Swamp Creature.

"But . . ."—she glanced at the door as Swamp Creature disappeared out of it—"why would he want me to feel like this?"

"Don't ask me. Fire gods are nearly as bad as air gods. Capricious hotheads."

"Hey!" a unison of voices called from the shelves.

"Are you going to fix me?" the mountain god asked. "You don't need all these tools. You're holding yourself back. Move past the limitations of your physical form. Traverse the pathways to the edge of the Beyond and bring forth my power anew into the mortal realm. Quite simple. "

"Wait." She rubbed her temple. "What?"

"Sit down," she heard Granite God say to Kai from the other side of the room.

"I think she's losing her mind," Kai said.

"I said sit down."

"She needs to rest," Kai said, assertive.

Josie was touched. She'd never felt close to Kai. He seemed to prefer it that way. But since he'd been dragged into this, he'd been surprisingly supportive. Even though she was sorry he was involved at all, it was nice to not feel so alone.

While this conversation was going on, Josie lowered her voice to a whisper. "Can he hear me? My... marked one?" Meaning her Fire Guy.

"That all depends," the mountain god said. "In your case, unlikely. You haven't been in thrall to him very long. Only in extreme instances does communication occur both ways. Normally, the master speaks and the slave listens."

"He's probably trying to send you a message," another voice offered. A sizzling, steamy voice.

"Like?" she asked.

"How would I know? He's your master. You tell me," the steamy voice replied.

"He's not my—" She stopped herself before she said anything more.

"Perhaps he means to leave you in a state that would prevent you from working," the mountain god speculated. "Since you are obviously here against your will."

"Or he's hoping if you're sick, they'll leave you alone long enough that he can come fetch you," the steamy voice said. "He really shouldn't have left something so rare and powerful just lying around for anyone to take."

"Careless," the mountain god agreed.

"Or you might just be feeling his anger," the steamy mask said. "That can happen when the summoner is lacking firm control. He might not realize what he's doing to you. If he's very unhappy you've gone missing, simply thinking about you could cause you all sorts of discomfort. You could even spontaneously combust. Messy."

"And wasteful," the mountain god added.

"Why doesn't he just . . ."—she tried to think of a way to say it without saying it. Even though she knew Kai and Granite God thought she was losing it, she couldn't risk saying too much—"take back what's his?"

"No doubt he will," the steamy voice said. "But I hope not before you've fixed me. I am next, right?"

A chorus of godly voices sounded off, all demanding that she repair them.

"I'm next!" the mountain god boomed, silencing them. "Repair me, Mask-Maker."

"They want to use you to hurt people," she said.

"And?"

"You don't even care, do you?" She lined up the pieces of the mask side by side. He was primitive and cold-looking.

"Do you remember the dinosaurs, Mask-Maker?"

"You know I don't."

"Well, I do. They ate everything in sight, shit everywhere, and thought they ruled the world too. They were wrong. Life is transient. One day, long after you're dead and forgotten, this world will cease to exist entirely. Do you care about that?"

She nudged the two halves of the mask closer together, lining up their fractured edges. "I don't know."

"You don't care. And why should you? Your life is tied to these few moments in time. You care about them and you should. That is proper. But I am a god. I have never lived and I will never die. Now fix my damned face."

"I care," the steamy god said. "Forget old stone face and fix me. Give me to your friend over there. We'll burn this whole place down with everyone in it."

"Including me?" she asked.

"You can't burn unless your master wants you to burn. You do belong to him—"

"I do not," she snapped, running her fingers over the crack in the mountain god's face, studying its flawless line.

"Oooh," the steamy voice said. "You know what *I* think?"

"I don't care."

"You're in love with him. That's why you made yourself his slave."

"That's not why. I don't even know him."

"He's a god. What more is there to know?"

"I mean the summoner."

"Mystery man, huh?" the steamy voice said. "I can help you. Fire summoners always have tells, you know."

"They do?"

"Don't listen to him," the mountain god said. "He's full of hot air. Why haven't you fixed me yet?"

"I'm studying your break. It's clean." She sat back, frowning. "You had a flaw."

"I beg your pardon."

"Your mask had a flaw," she said, tracing the crack again.

The mountain god and the steamy voice went silent. Even in her fevered state, her mind worked well enough for her to come to a revelation.

"They all do, don't they?" she murmured to the mountain god.

He didn't answer, which was answer enough.

"A weak spot," she said, touching his mask again.

She glanced over at the wolf god's mask and saw it.

A fatal flaw. A place where it would take very little force to break the mask apart. In the case of the Wolf, right across the snout. Knowledge of it materialized in her mind, just as knowledge of the gods' symbols had appeared in her mind—unbidden, inexplicable, but undeniable.

She peeked over at Granite God, who was still standing by the door. Even though she couldn't see his mask while he was in possession, she still got a feeling, like a sixth sense, where its flaw was.

Or maybe her fevered brain was giving her more hallucinations.

She turned back to the mountain god again. "You said I don't need to use tools."

"What is a tool, Mask-Maker?"

"Um ..."

"A means to an end," he answered his own question. "That is all you are. Your hands are tools. Your mind is a tool. Your soul is a tool. Why do you think you have the ability to shape the faces of the gods and the others don't? Can no other mortal carve wood or sculpt clay? What sets you apart?"

"Uh ..."

"Clearly not your keen wits."

"Hey—"

"You are connected to the Beyond, Mask-Maker. To the realm of the immortals. You must be, to see the face of a god, to bring it forth. That is all you need, the connection that is innate. Transcend your perceived limitations and create from the source, which is your very soul, and dispense with these ... tedious implements of drudges and artisans."

She ran her tongue over her parched lips, glancing over her shoulder at Granite God again. He kept glancing out the window of the door, seemingly anxious for Swamp Creature to return. Kai sat on the edge of his chair, leg bouncing with agitation.

She lowered her voice even more. "But I can't traverse the pathways. I'm not a summoner and . . . the Beyond? No mortal soul can travel to the realm of the gods."

"False," the mountain god said. "Most cannot. Many have. Believe me. But you will not have to travel into the Beyond, merely to the boundary. Summon my power to yourself, see my face, make it material."

"You mean, all I have to do is think it and I can make a mask?"

"Think? Know it. I exist. Do you know that?"

"Yes."

"Then know that I exist also in the mortal realm. Know it, so that all others will know it. See what they cannot. And make them see it. That is your power. What you see, others will also see. When you see the faces of the gods, so shall the rest of the mortal world."

She gazed at the mountain god's broken face. In her mind's eye, she could see how it would look whole. She knew what it *should* look like.

The fever haze swept back over her, blurring her vision, weakening her sense of her body, and pulling her slightly out of herself. The two images of the mountain god's mask, the one in her mind and the one before her, overlapped.

"Come, Mask-Maker," the mountain god said, "the door is open."

For a moment, she thought she was passing out again. That same sensation, loss of control, falling into herself, into darkness, rushed upon her.

But instead of blackness, she found herself surrounded by ethereal blue and fast-moving clouds. On either side of her, jagged peaks rose, snow-tipped and glittering in the light. Wind howled in her ears as it tore past, pushing and pulling at her. She no longer felt feverish, but she didn't feel cold either.

She felt thinned out, half herself—the less material half.

The wind shoved her. She stumbled onto her hands and knees, into the snow. But it wasn't cold. This moment, this place, she realized, was not entirely real.

Having grown up on an island just outside the mortal realm and not quite in the pathways, she knew the sensation of being surrounded by objects that seemed material, but that were, in fact, little more than representations of reality. Like a 3-D movie. Only her hands were actually sunk into the snow, yet without the cold or the wet. Not only was this place not entirely real, but she wasn't entirely in it either. She could feel the tug of her body, still mostly in the mortal realm, imprisoned in Earth Mama's sweatshop. Though she had escaped her body, this was not an escape. This was the means to the end.

"Mask-Maker."

She shuffled forward on her hands and knees. The wind continued to tear at her, pushing her forward, faster than she wanted. The mountain top came to an abrupt ledge—below was blackness.

At the Grand Canyon she had stood as close as she'd dared to the edge and peered down and down and down, overwhelmed, all her internal warning systems blaring at her to step back or, at least, to not move any farther forward.

The same feeling came upon her as she stared into the endless pitch below. A dizzy, surging feeling. The feeling adrenaline-junkies like Beech chased over every horizon. The feeling that death was just one wrong move away.

Below, the Beyond. The blackness had depth, like the calm surface of a swollen river, deadly currents and hidden dangers swirling beneath. All the while the wind pushed and tugged her towards the endlessness—the immortal realm of the gods—the Beyond. And sure death.

She knew Death. He was a douche. She wasn't anxious to chat with him again anytime soon.

She clung hard to the immaterial edge of the pathways and the invisible rope binding her to her body.

From the murk, a face emerged. Like the pale face of a corpse floating to the surface.

The face of the mountain god.

In the Beyond, he was much more than his broken mask could ever convey. All that was the mountain. From a distance, foreboding and awe-inspiring. Closer, breath-stealing and electrifying.

"Mask-Maker, free me."

Slowly, she reached towards the face of the god. Her fingers skimmed the surface of the Beyond—a barely perceptible barrier, like the thin swell of air between two mouths, right before they meet, not sure if they should—and then she hesitated, pulling back an inch.

She was in the pathways. The pathways of the earth gods. She was staring into the Beyond. This shouldn't have been possible. How was this possible?

"Mask-Maker!"

She flinched and scooped up the face of the god, drawing it out of the Beyond and into the pathways. And it was real.

Then she fell, plummeting straight down, slamming back into her body, back into the throbbing pulse of her fever and the stale air of her prison. She tumbled off her stool, crashing onto her back and banging her head. The fluorescent lights overhead seemed to strobe. A sickening acidic slime bulged into her throat and coated her tongue.

"Gods, Josie." Kai's voice came to her muffled and round-edged, like hearing him through a glass pressed to the wall. She felt his cool hand on her face and almost sobbed. "What the fuck?"

She blinked, focusing on him. He glanced over his shoulder furtively and then leaned over her, whispering. "What just happened? I saw . . . you like . . . ghosted out."

Before she could speak, he pulled back abruptly.

"What is going on?" Earth Mama demanded. "Get out of the way."

Kai stumbled back from Josie.

Earth Mama's fetid stench nearly shoved Josie back into unconsciousness.

"Incredible," Earth Mama said, bending closer and snatching the mask from Josie's hand.

The face of the mountain god. The face she had pulled from the Beyond.

Earth Mama ran her fingers over the mask. "Beautiful."

Josie licked her lips. Kai appeared at her side again, helping her up.

Josie's vision cleared. She fixed on Earth Mama's churning guise, the black soil was now plunging into a gaping hole at the center of her face, where her nose should have been.

No flowers, no maggots or insects, just an all-consuming sinkhole. Josie looked at the face of the goddess . . .

and saw her fatal flaw.

CHAPTER 31

APRIL 14TH

"SHE NEEDS A BREAK," Kai said. "She's delirious. She's talking to herself."

Earth Mama lowered the mountain god's mask, which she'd been admiring as if she might take it over her own. "Would you prefer to be bound and gagged again?"

Before Kai could respond, alarms sounded. High-pitched wails filled the room. Then the ground shifted and pitched as the entire building quaked.

Earth Mama stumbled, dropping the mountain god's mask.

Josie grabbed it.

Granite God reached to steady Earth Mama as the quaking continued. Boxes of masks fell from their shelves—gods shouting and complaining. One of the supply cabinets tipped and crashed. The contents spilled and skittered across the floor.

"Get off me!" Earth Mama shoved Granite God away as the tremor stopped.

"An attack?" Granite God shouted over the rumble of the earth and the crashes all around.

"Of course it's an attack," Earth Mama snapped.

"Why weren't we warned?" Granite God asked.

"Get the girl out of here!"

Granite God grabbed Josie's arm and pulled her up to her feet. The door swung open. Swamp Creature stumbled aside as Sandstorm and Algae Goddess burst in.

"You," Earth Mama barked at Swamp Creature, "the masks! As soon as they're secure, leave!"

Granite God wrapped his fat arm around Josie, pulling her through a guise that left her itchy. His belly bumped into her back. His guise weighed heavily against her. She stuffed the mountain god mask under her shirt and crossed her arms over it. Its rough edges cut into her skin.

Granite God squeezed her for a moment and then again, tighter, like he was giving her the Heimlich.

"What the—?" he muttered under his breath.

He squeezed again. She winced as her bruised ribs protested.

Earth Mama was barking more orders at Sandstorm and Algae Goddess. When she was done, she turned back to Granite God and Josie.

"Why aren't you gone yet?" she yelled.

Granite God hesitated. "I'm trying, but ... I can't."

"What the hell do you—never mind." Her fingers hooked around Josie's arm and yanked her away. "I'll take her." She wrapped her stubby arms around Josie. Her body was soft and doughy. She was much shorter than her guise.

This was Josie's chance. Maybe she could destroy Earth Mama's mask, all she needed was something—

Earth Mama shoved her down abruptly. Josie fell to the floor, almost dropping the mask.

"What the hell?" Earth Mama growled.

"I told you," Granite God said. "We can't translocate with her."

"That's not possible! What have you done?" She loomed over Josie, guise growing, shedding leaves and mud all over. TemperMentals began to appear, clouding the air as they circled and darted. "Did someone help you?" She looked towards Kai, who was picking himself up off the floor. "Did you?"

"Me?" Kai said, like he was offended by the accusation.

Earth Mama let out a shriek. Suddenly, the door flew open again. A herd of roots and vines barreled in, coiling around Josie and dragging her towards the door. When she tried to kick, they snapped down, yanking on her joints painfully.

"You!" Earth Mama shouted. "Call Gene. Tell him to get off his drunk ass and find me a helicopter."

"Kai!" Josie cried as she was dragged out of the room and down the hall.

All the while the vines continued to wrap around her, forming a cocoon. The back of her head thumped against the floor as it transitioned from concrete to earth.

Summoners were running in different directions, shouting at each other, organizing themselves.

"We're surrounded," she heard one say.

"They won't get through."

"They will if they keep at it long enough," the first said.

"Let's go."

"We can't."

"Why not?"

Their voices disappeared as they ran off and she was pulled away, around another corner, down another hall. The walls became little more than trees, the ground soft and bumpy, catching on her hair and her clothes. She knew where she was being taken—to Earth Mama's sanctuary. She only hoped she wasn't about to be sacrificed.

"Josie!" a strange voice called—at once deep and godly, and lighter, human ... familiar.

She tried to twist to see, but a root had snaked around her head and prevented her. She caught a glimpse of a god as he launched over her—a tree god. The kidnapping vegetation jerked to a halt. They began to loosen and leave her. She pushed the rest free and stumbled to her feet, clutching the mountain god's mask to her stomach.

A tree god tore roots and vines away by the fistful as they twined around him. He turned and looked at her. She recognized the godly façade.

"Beech?" She stared, stunned.

"Run, Josie!" he said as the vines began to overwhelm him. "The tribe's outside!"

She hesitated. His tree god guise was nowhere near powerful enough to compete with Earth Mama. The vines were overwhelming him. She slid the mountain god mask out from under her shirt.

"No, Beech, take off your mask!" She skipped and hopped over the writhing vines as they grappled with Beech, who was ripping them into shreds wherever his godly hands touched them.

"Sketch advice, Jos," he called.

She had almost reached him when a vine snagged her ankle. She fell hard onto her stomach.

"No, Beech, look!" She held the mask out towards him, clinging with her other hand to an inanimate root while the vine twining around her leg tugged at her. "Take it!"

The vine yanked hard. She dropped the mask as she was towed backwards.

"Josie!" he called after her.

This time she was able to twist over and sit up, seizing the slender green vine strangling her calf. She wrenched on it, but the vine clamped down harder, infused with Earth Mama's godly magic. No matter how hard she pulled, the vine only tightened, cutting off her blood flow.

She bumped along the corridor. The ground shook again. The trees swayed. Leaves whispered as they fell around her.

Her tribe was outside? How many? Who?

To make the earth shake the way it was would've taken quite a few minor gods or a single very powerful one. Her heart raced. Tessa was out there, she knew. In possession of the Tripartite. She was risking her life to rescue Josie, again. Josie ground her teeth. Tessa shouldn't have been out there. She shouldn't have come. The life of the Triune was far more important than Josie's, even if she was a mask-maker.

The wind was picking up too, howling through the branches. Thunder rumbled. What little light had been peeking through the trees began to disappear.

She ripped her fingernails bloody prying at the vine, but still it dragged her. Finally, she caught a passing tree and held on. The vine strained. Tearing pain shot up her leg. She was afraid it would rip her leg off or dislocate her hip before their tug-of-war ended, but wherever Earth Mama wanted to take her, Josie wasn't going.

As her grip faltered on the slender trunk, she spied a white triangle buried in its roots, the edge gleamed—metal. She groped for it, losing hold of the tree. The edge of the triangle cut her hand as her palm slid along it. But she didn't let go. As the vine pulled her away, its force ripped free the triangle, which, once unearthed, proved to be a rectangle. An old white sign: EXIT.

Blood smearing over the sign, she twisted around again and struggled to sit up. The vine pulled her faster. Lightning flashed through the trees. Branches whipped now. Twigs and leaves lashed at her as they were carried away on the chilly wind gusting through the corridor, stirring up the scent of rot and wet earth and . . . smoke. Was Fire Guy out there?

She jammed the sign under one of the coils of the vine and sawed viciously against it until it came loose. The vine jerked as a length of it fell away. Josie was thrown back, smacking her head on the soft earth. Quickly, she sat up again and began sawing at the remaining vine even as it pulled her away once more.

Another coil fell away. At this, the vine seemed to rethink its mission and released her, vanishing back into the trees. She flung the sign down, pushed to her feet, and raced back towards Beech.

Turning a corner, she came face to face with a wall of fog. She took a step back, right into Fog God's arms.

"Salutations, Lady Day," he said. "Let's try this again, shall we?"

Fog swirled around her. She thrashed, struggling against his hold.

"Now that's interesting," he said after a moment, grunting as she threw her elbows into his sides. "We should be half way to Shanghai right now." His hand clamped around her throat. Her lungs grasped for air as it was ripped away. "Settle down," he said. "Or this will get painful."

But before she could comply, he snatched his hand away. "Shit! You burned me."

She jammed her elbow into his stomach, loosening his grip. She tore away and ran into the fog.

More than once she slammed into a tree or tripped over a root. The ground continued to tremor, more frequently now. She could hear lightning cracking, but couldn't see it. The sweet aroma of smoke snuck through the fog to her. Finally, dizzy and lost, she stopped.

"Getting tired?" Fog God's voice was all around her.

She huffed, burning up all over. She hoped the steamy voice in the mask room hadn't been right about the spontaneous combustion thing. If Fire Guy was here, why didn't he come for her? Where was Beech?

"Why don't you just let me go?" she said. "Run away. Before you really get burned."

"It's that fire god, isn't it?" he asked. "He's helping you somehow."

Her breathing began to slow. "I don't know what—"

"Oh, wait," he said. "You tagged yourself." He let out a soft, incredulous laugh. "I don't believe it."

"Neither do I." Earth Mama emerged from the fog, a giant, three times her usual size, running with mud and sloughing off debris at record speed. Josie stumbled back as muck oozed around her feet, sucking at her.

"That's why we can't translocate her," Fog God said.

"No matter," Earth Mama said, towering over her, fifteen feet high. The back of Josie's head was practically touching her shoulder blades as she stared upwards. "We'll simply have to find the offending mark . . . and remove it."

An arm wrapped around her waist. Thinking it was Fog God, she started to struggle.

"Relax," a familiar, easygoing voice said to her.

She turned. In the mountain god's guise, Beech was all rough-cut blue stone, jagged edges, and dominating presence. Underneath, he was still Beech, warm and ropey.

Earth Mama hesitated. "Who—?"

The ground began to tremble again.

Beech's voice smiled. "Up we go."

CHAPTER 32

APRIL 14TH

I F BEECH HADN'T BEEN holding onto her, she probably would've been flat on the ground.

Beneath them, the soft soil crumbled and fell away. Everything fell away, even the fog and Earth Mama. A huge mass of rock erupted under their feet, shoving them upwards.

The spire of stone continued to build beneath them. She clung to Beech as they were propelled up at heart-stopping speed, ripping through the branches and leaving the fog below. When the ride stopped, she swayed. All around was dark cloud. A white burst blinded her. The crack was deafening. Rain pelted them. The wind pushed past them like they were standing in its way. They must've been at least fifty feet off the ground.

"Jump," he said.

"Wha—?"

He leapt, holding her to him. Another monument of stone assembled in front of them. Their feet barely touched it before he launched them again onto yet another pillar. They leapfrogged away, from stone to stone. Or Beech did. Josie hung onto him, just trying not to lose hold.

"We have to clear the protective circles!" Beech shouted to her as they bounded through the air. Below it was dark, but she tried not to look down as they sailed over the gaps. "Then we can translocate out."

"Can't we just run?" She gritted her teeth as they slammed down again.

"Too many traps," he called. "Besides, this is more fun."

Fun. Yeah, right. She teetered on the edge of a jutting precipice of stone just before they launched towards another. But, for some reason, Beech hesitated.

His momentum carried them forward anyway, off the edge. They plummeted.

"Dying so soon?" she heard the mountain god say to Beech.

Before Josie had a chance to register the fact that they were seconds from death, Beech's arms cinched tighter around her, and he pitched his weight back. Over his shoulder, through her wind-shorn vision, she could see another stone monument rising up to meet them. She tucked herself tight against Beech.

Beech slammed into the stone back first, absorbing the brunt of the impact, which wasn't nearly what it would've been if Beech hadn't been in possession. Josie's head whiplashed, but the pain was small in comparison to what could've happened. She continued to hold onto Beech as they got to their feet.

Before them a massive cliff was rising—a huge stone wall.

Their own stone pillar continued to jet upwards towards the lightning-streaked sky.

"What are you doing?" Josie cried.

"It's not me!" Beech shouted.

When the ride came to a halt, they both swayed, Josie more than Beech. Then there was a crack. The stone beneath them began to tilt.

"Wait for it!" Beech called over the rush of the wind and rumble of thunder.

"For what?" Their pillar was falling. Her feet slid on the slick stone.

"Jump, now!" Beech pushed them off before she could bend her knees. They stumbled onto a plateau, breaking away from each other. Josie managed a few steps before crashing onto her face. Heat sheared her chin, followed by a warm gush of blood.

She pushed herself up as Beech reached down for her.

"You okay?" he asked.

Rain stung her lips as she spoke. "What happened?"

Before he could answer, the stone under him gave way. He shoved her back. He fell.

"Beech!"

She crawled to the ledge, but all was fog. No sign of Beech. Her heart quailed.

"Now, let's take care of that mark," Earth Mama said from behind her.

Josie turned. Earth Mama was back to a more reasonable size. Even her guise seemed to have settled. Her gown was once again staid green grass, her arms slender, veined with fresh tendrils, multicolored flowers covered her chest. Her mask had temporarily become stone, but the rocky façade was crumbling away, revealing black dirt beneath.

"Josie," she said gently, "let's end this silliness, shall we?"

"Stay away from me."

Earth Mama's head tilted. "I'm sorry if I've seemed calloused. But there's been so much suffering, for so long. You understand that, don't you? Crimes have been committed. Justice must be served."

Josie wanted to stand up, but was so close to the edge she was afraid to. "Like the crime you committed when you murdered my mother?"

"Your mother was complacent and, quite frankly, guilty. She stood by and did nothing while many worse crimes than murder were committed. We are Core. The gods serve us so that we may protect them. When the soil is stripped, when the rivers are dry, when the forests disappear, that is theocide. Death of the gods. No crime is worse. Surely, you see that."

Josie gripped the edge of the newborn mountain, wondering if Beech had survived the fall and if she could too. She thought she could hear voices shouting nearby, but the air was so thick with wind and thunder, it was hard to tell what she was hearing.

Earth Mama stepped closer. "You know what I've most admired about you, Josie? Your conviction. You're not pliable like your sister. You know what's right and what's wrong. And so I think, deep down, you know what I'm saying is true. Even if it's difficult for you to admit it."

Josie was as far back as she dared. The wind cut up the mountain behind her, pushing against her back like a pair of hands shoving her towards Earth Mama, who was slowly moving closer. The more she spoke, the more familiar her voice sounded, but Josie's mind was too fevered, her ears too full of wind, to place it.

"All these years, the gods have been laid low," Earth Mama said, "and then a mask-maker appears. Do you think it's a coincidence, Josie? A mask-maker, one who opens the door for the gods to walk the earth and I, Mother Earth, rising now to restore the world to its proper balance? No. You know better than to believe in coincidence. Don't you? You must see that you are here now to help me do what I have been called to do."

"And what's that?" Josie asked, not that she cared.

"Save the world, hon. That's all." Earth Mama's voice was almost sweet, almost pleasant, that nasal squeak . . .

And that's when it hit her. She *did* know who Earth Mama was. "*Kuso—*"

A crack and blinding flash almost sent Josie plummeting. She landed on her back, shoulders hanging over the edge. Abs burning, she curled herself up.

Earth Mama spun. TemperMentals appeared in a fury around her. On the other side of the mountaintop, a slim form of glowing white brilliance appeared. Tessa.

Then the battle began.

Josie flattened out and rolled onto her stomach, covering her ears, blinded as lightning lanced around her, shaking the plateau. From the corner of her eyes, she could see Earth Mama swelling into a giant again. Bull-sized chunks of stone rose around Josie, scooped out by Earth Mama's will. One after another, they hurtled at Tessa. But Tessa was ready. Lightning struck one, two, three of the boulders.

Sprays of rubble showered over Josie, battering her. A fist-shaped stone struck her side. She flinched and found herself again peering over the edge of the mountain. She scrambled away as the TemperMentals flew towards Tessa, surrounding her.

If Tessa had been fully trained, fully in tune with the Tripartite, then these attacks would've been little more than a nuisance. Instead, Tessa's glow flickered. The TemperMentals surged right through her guise, like piranhas shredding a chunk of flesh. Worse, more of Earth Mama's summoners had arrived. Granite God appeared. And Swamp Creature. And Sandstorm. A dozen others. Their presence seemed to fuel Earth Mama.

More TemperMentals formed until there was a small army of phantom blurs ripping through Tessa's guise. Her light was weak enough that Josie could see Tessa's mortal form, a slip of a silhouette, under her godly guise. This was bad.

Josie searched around and found a baseball-sized rock.

Granite God swooped down on her, hauling her upright.

"I'm so sick of you grabbing me." She kicked him right in his soft belly, ripping away from his grasp.

She stumbled back, over the edge.

Falling.

Air tore at her, like it was trying to peel her apart before the ground got a chance to splatter her. The lightning and black sky grew more distant. Her heart was frantically hitting the eject button, trying to save itself.

She braced herself, she didn't know what for . . . pain, death, beyond.

Any moment, the end.

Except, she was slowing. The air turned from slicing and dicing to warm and supportive. Arms slipped underneath her. An air god. But she couldn't see him. She didn't know if he was one of Earth Mama's cronies or if he was on her side. In that moment, she hardly cared. She was just glad to be alive.

He started to take her away from the battle, away from the broken spears of lightning and the crash and clamor of the fight.

"No, no! Take me back!" she cried. "I can stop her! She'll kill Tessa! You have to take me back!"

She only hoped he was on her side.

For a moment, she hovered in midair, darkness above and below. A warm bubble surrounded her, deflecting the icy rain. She knew how crazy she must've sounded, to want to be returned to the fray when she'd just escaped it. Even she was beginning to doubt herself.

She only had a hunch really. It wasn't like she knew it would work for sure. After all, she'd never tried to destroy the mask of a god before. Normally, it took some mighty unearthly weapon or a serious godly duel. Yet she had this sense, this near-certain feeling, that if she hit Earth Mama's mask in just the right place, she could take her out.

"I have to save my sister," she said to the air god. "Please."

The summoner seemed to grumble, but then he turned them around. So he was on her side after all.

Moments later, she was back on her feet, back on the plateau, in the midst of a godly battle unlike anything the world had seen for centuries.

More summoners had appeared in the seconds she'd been gone. The rain and lightning-lashed plateau flashed, alive with conflict.

Two gods piled towards her. She lunged to the side. The invisible air god hooked her around the waist, steadying her. Where she'd stood, Granite God was slammed down, another mountain god towered over him—Beech. She had no time to feel relief. Granite God grabbed Beech, flipping him. They tumbled across the plateau, their every blow shaking the ground.

Nearby, a gray water god was spraying down Sandstorm, pushing him towards the edge. Swamp Creature was levitating, writhing and begging for mercy. Gods summoned mini-torrents, whirling dervishes of wind, cannonballs of stone, crashing into each other like waves in the sea during a storm.

At the far end of the plateau, Tessa was still under siege. Her light flickered dangerously. The lightning overhead was erratic and weak as the TemperMentals' attack drained her.

Earth Mama was as big and bold as ever, poised at the middle of the fight, giggling—a squeaky nasal laugh.

Josie pushed her wet hair away from her face. Rocks of all sizes were scattered around her, broken up by Beech and Granite God's fight. She found one of decent size, testing its weight.

She pulled away from the air god, though he seemed to be reluctant to let her go.

She rushed as close as she dared to Earth Mama.

"Lily!" she screamed.

Earth Mama turned. Josie whipped the rock at her face, at the goddess's face, aiming for her right temple.

The stone bounced off Earth Mama's temple and rolled away. Josie backed up, holding her breath.

Nothing happened.

"*Kuso.*"

Why was she surprised? All sense had told her it wouldn't work. Everything she knew, everything her mother had taught her, told her it shouldn't—it couldn't. A rock? Why didn't she just call Earth Mama nasty names? That might've hurt her feelings a little at least. Except, Josie had this feeling—an inexplicable gut instinct.

It looked like she'd been wrong.

Earth Mama's grin widened, menacingly.

Air God seized Josie's arm, like he was about to fly off with her.

Before he could take flight, the circling TemperMentals vanished.

Earth Mama's guise—of branches and mud, of roots and vines, of flowers and leaves, of life and death—disappeared.

Her mask broke and fell to the ground.

CHAPTER 33

APRIL 14TH

A PALE LUMP IN A FLOWERY SKIRT dropped to the ground. Lily.

She grasped for the broken pieces of her mask.

Behind her, Tessa's light flared and went out. She fell too, limp.

"No, no, no." Lily held the pieces of her mask up in horror. She was gaunt, hollow-eyed, the color of maggots.

Her followers, noticing her defeat, began to translocate, leaving her on her knees, clutching her broken mask, her red hair clinging to her skull like long, thick clots.

Josie stared. Even though she'd known it was Lily, it was still hard to believe. Judah had been right. There had been a traitor. Lily. Their own Past Eye. Their supposed leader.

The gray water god rushed to Josie's side. He took off his mask. Water dripped from his rimless glasses and off his bald pate.

"Dad." She threw her arms around him and hugged him tight.

"Are you okay?" he asked, pulling back so he could look her over.

"Not—"

"Stop!" someone shouted, but it was too late.

Fog swept around Lily, shrouding her. And then she was gone.

Fog God had managed to save his mom.

Across the plateau, Josie saw a crowd form around the crumpled heap that was Tessa. Josie pulled away from her dad and rushed towards them, he kept pace with her.

Beech was already with Tessa. He scooped her up.

Josie touched her sister's pale forehead. "Tessa."

Tessa's eyes fluttered. A small smile touched her lips. "I didn't puke."

"Of course not. You're the Triune," Josie said.

Dad put his mask back on. Churning gray water swirled around him. "I'll take her," he said, his godly voice deep and resounding.

Beech shifted Tessa into their Dad's arms.

Another water god appeared. This one a glittering blue ocean god. She swept off her mask: Caroline. She looked at Josie, breathless.

"Josie, are you all right?"

"I guess."

Caroline touched her head, surveying the wet and broken surface of the plateau. Rain continued to thrum down on them. But Josie hardly noticed. She was from Portland after all.

"Lily." Caroline's vibrant blue eyes darkened, filling with tears. "I wouldn't have believed it if I hadn't see it for myself."

"Neither would I," Josie admitted.

Other summoners assembled around them. The rain began to diminish, the wind to die, the clouds were black and heavy, but they too started to lighten and thin.

Josie shivered. Her fever had broken, it seemed.

Caroline took Tessa's hand. "How are you, Mother of Mothers?"

Tessa's smile widened. "I'm fine," she said, though she looked like a damp dishrag. "I'll be fine."

Josie touched Caroline's arm. "Kai. He's down there somewhere."

Caroline covered Josie's hand with her own. "We'll find him." She turned to some of the other gods, instructing them with cool authority.

At some point, Judah had appeared next to Josie.

"You survived," he said to her, like he hadn't expected to find her alive.

"She more than survived." Beech took off the mountain god mask and held it up for Judah to see. "She made a freaking sick-ass mask. This guy is seriously old school. Mountain man."

Judah didn't look impressed. "You know they're not going to let you keep that."

"Hater," Beech grumbled.

Tessa's head slumped against Dad's shoulder, into his shimmering gray guise.

"You'd better take her home," Josie said, teeth chattering.

"We're all going home," her dad said. He seemed to look from Beech to Judah.

"Don't sweat it, Papa Day," Beech said. "We're right behind you."

After a second of hesitation, her dad nodded.

In a swish of water, he and Tessa vanished.

Beech started to lift his mask to his face. "Ready to roll, Josie-pie?"

"You're not going anywhere," Judah said.

Beech looked like he was ready to resume fighting.

"You've got to put this back," Judah said, gesturing to the plateau underneath them. "And all the rest." He notched his head towards the pillars of stone still standing, now emerging as the rain cleared and the clouds broke. "You can't leave it like this."

Josie hugged her arms to her body. "He's right. What do you think would happen if people discovered a bunch of huge inexplicable stone obelisks in the middle of . . ."

"Idaho," Judah muttered.

"Really? Anyway, they don't belong here."

Beech sagged. "Lame."

"But, if it makes you feel better—"

She kissed him searchingly, hoping to find a spark. When they broke apart she knew—for sure—that it would be the last time.

"Thanks for coming for me," she said.

Beech's cheeks flushed. "Maybe you should be abducted more often, if it makes you kiss like that. But it's really Simone you should thank." He held up the crystal on the metal chain around his neck. "She made the ghost charm. I just slipped right in, through the circles and shit. No one even noticed."

He put his mask back on. "I love this guy," he said, the laidback lightness of his voice still discernable under the booming tones of the mountain god. "Guess we'd better clean up." He bounded down the mountainside.

He leapt over the edge like he was going to take flight. She shivered.

"He didn't actually rescue you, you know," Judah said. "The tribe did."

She turned to him. "It was you, wasn't it?"

His eyes narrowed.

"When I fell," she said, "you caught me."

He didn't answer.

"I thought you were done saving me," she said. "You know, ungrateful charity case that I am."

His arms crossed. His brow was difficult to read. Maybe she was just too tired, or maybe she'd forgotten how to decipher its slants and furrows while she'd been held captive. She could hope anyway.

"What? You don't have anything to say?" she asked.

He put on his air god mask again and shimmered out of view. "Let's go home."

For once, she didn't feel like arguing with him.

CHAPTER 34

APRIL 16TH
TWO DAYS LATER

WHEN THE DOOR OPENED, Josie sagged.

Judah stepped through the front door like he owned the place. But then Simone pushed past him. Her spiky hair was freshly dyed iris purple, her grin wider than ever. Josie stood up and was immediately knocked back onto the couch again by Simone's strangling embrace.

"You're alive!" she said. "Yay!"

"Thanks to you," Josie said, hugging her back, though not as crushingly.

Simone gave her another squeeze and then finally let her breathe again. "Hardly. I was here the whole time."

"Yeah, but without your charm, Beech never would've been able to reach me and who knows what would've happened?"

"Death, destruction, you know, just another Friday night in the tribe," Kai said, coming around the end of the couch. His bangs were pushed away from his face showing off his left eye which was swollen shut, purple and black. He gave Josie that half-smile. "Like it?" he asked, gesturing to the black eye.

"It suits you." Josie stood up, smiling. "I'm going to hug you now."

He winced. "Do you have to?"

"I think so." She gave him a quick hug. He patted her back awkwardly. She stepped back. "How was it?"

"Weird," he said, sidling towards the nearby chair and dropping into it.

Simone tossed a pillow at him.

He caught it. "But in a good way."

She grinned, but then there was Judah, standing there in all his superior glory. Her grin died.

He reached into his pocket and took out a phone. He held it out to her.

"What's this?" she asked.

"Your dad asked me to pick it up for you. He doesn't like the idea of you not having one," Judah stated.

She tapped the screen. "Let me guess, I'm being tracked, right?"

The eyebrow said, *You know it.*

"How are you feeling?" Simone asked. "How are your hands?"

Both of her palms were wrapped and bandaged, aching and stiff, the cuts and scrapes on them screamed when she moved too quickly.

"They're fine," she said, sliding the new phone into her back pocket with her fingertips. At this point, she was glad to be tracked.

"How's Tessa?" Simone asked.

"Okay," Josie said. "Alive. That's all that matters. Gretchen's upstairs with her now. And your mom and Nancy."

In the two days that had passed since she'd been rescued, she'd slept. She'd also taken half a dozen showers, attempting to scrub Lily's rotted stench out of her hair. It still wasn't gone completely. In the meantime, a new Past Eye had been named: Gretchen.

"Did you really take that bitch out with a rock?" Kai asked.

"I told you she did," Simone said.

"Yeah, but I want to hear it from her. Gory details please."

Josie sat on the wooden arm of the couch. "I already had to retell it ten times for the Eye this morning," she said. "I'm all out of gore."

Judah crossed his arms, standing over them. "But you knew," he said. "How?"

"Yeah, a regular rock shouldn't have taken out that earth bi . . . Lily." Simone slumped, her pixie shoulders folding in like wings. "I still can't believe it was Lily."

Josie picked at her bandages. "The Eye doesn't think I should talk about it."

"Yeah, but you can trust us," Simone said. "We're your friends."

Josie glanced at Judah. Friend? Not quite.

Still, he'd saved her more times than she was comfortable acknowledging.

She knew she should thank him. Really thank him. But every time she'd tried, the words had burned up in her mouth and turned to ash.

Anyway, she was sure he'd throw it back in her face like he had the last time. It was like he wanted her to fall all over herself, get down on her knees and wash his feet, or something equally ridiculous. Nothing was ever good enough for him.

In spite of all that, she was certain he wouldn't go gossiping her secrets. Tessa had said he hadn't wanted to get the rest of the tribe involved in her rescue at all. He'd actually made his mom promise to let him choose who would be involved in the rescue before he'd told her anything. He'd been too suspicious that there was a traitor. And he'd been right. He just hadn't realized the traitor was Lily.

She sighed, her voice lowered. "Her mask had a flaw."

Simone sat forward. "A flaw?"

Judah and Kai were watching her intensely.

She shifted, clearing her throat. "They all do."

Kai leaned his elbows on his knees. "What do you mean? All? Like every mask ever made? They can all be knocked out David-and-Goliath-style?"

"Basically."

Kai flopped back. "*Kuso.*"

He smiled at her. She smiled back.

"I didn't realize it until I was working on the mountain god's mask," she explained. "The one I gave to Beech."

"You mean when you were talking to yourself?" Kai asked.

"I wasn't talking to myself," she said. "I was talking to the masks."

"And they were talking back?"

"Actually, they started it," she muttered.

She caught Judah's eye again. He was giving her a look that said maybe she needed to go back to bed.

Kai toyed with the white shoelaces of his black sneakers. "How did you fix that mask? I was watching you." He looked up at her intensely. "I swear, you almost disappeared, like mirage-style Josie. And one minute the mask was broken and then it wasn't."

She searched around the room, like she might find an excuse not to tell them in the dark fireplace or tidy bookshelves. "It's sort of complicated. I, um ... thought it?"

Now Simone and Kai were sharing Judah's look of concern.

"I think the fever helped, in a way," she said. "It made it easier for me to ..."—she cringed as she said it, knowing what was coming—"traverse the pathways?"

Simone squeaked. Judah's arms fell away from his chest. Even Kai's swollen eye managed to crack open slightly, his other popped.

"What the hell are you talking about?" Judah demanded.

Irritation flared up in her. "Just what I said. I traversed the pathways ... went to the edge of the Beyond and just ... sort of brought the face of the god back."

They all stared at her, their mouths agape.

"But you can't say anything. Not to anybody," she said, looking back towards the kitchen. "I didn't tell the Eye or Tessa and definitely not my dad." She gave Judah an especially piercing look, since she could see the disapproval in his cool blue eyes. "I'm not even sure how I did it. And I don't plan on trying it again, it was too—"

Terrifying? Exhilarating? Unknown?

"Josie, this is ..." Simone looked up at Judah.

"Trouble," he said grimly, like he was already envisioning all the future rescues Josie would require.

"If you reached into the Beyond, that means you could bring earthbound like ... anything," Kai said, awed. "Any one of the immortal devices, even ... the Chalice of Life, the Gauntlet of Death, or ... the Book of the Other?"

"I don't know about that," she said, shrinking back.

"But . . . could you?" Kai asked.

"No, she can't," Judah said, giving Kai a deadly look.

Kai's lips pursed and he sank back, but he was eyeing Josie as if trying to pick the answer out of her head. In truth, she didn't know if she could retrieve one of the immortal devices like she'd retrieved the mountain god's mask. She had no plans to find out. The world did not need any more godly weapons lying around.

"Um, so," Simone said, breaking weakly through the tension. "Have you seen Beech?"

"Yeah, he stopped by yesterday," she said, loving Simone even more than ever.

"And what'd he think about your new tattoo?" Kai asked as if he was also helping to the change the subject.

Simone joined Josie in scowling.

"What? We can't talk about anything interesting?" Kai grumped.

"There's nothing to talk about," Josie said. "Beech is . . ." Open? Apathetic? Or just too cool to let her know that it actually bothered him when she'd told him she couldn't be his make out partner anymore? After she'd told him, he'd left pretty quickly and hadn't looked too happy. "Beech," she finished.

"Well, have you talked to . . . *him*?" Simone asked.

Josie glanced again at disapproving Judah and sulking Kai. She shook her head.

"You'd better hope he's not looking for a serving wench for his volcanic Fortress of Solitude," Kai said, his leg bouncing up and down.

"Kai, really?" Simone said.

He turned up his hands, gesturing, *What?*

"I'm sure he'll release you," Simone said, touching Josie's arm lightly. "I mean, he sent me the coordinates to find you in the first place. Without him, you'd both still be missing," she said, giving Kai a pointed look.

"You don't know it was him," Kai said. "Maybe one of Lily's faithful minions turned on her."

Josie hadn't thought of that. On her hip, the fire god's symbol was scabbed and cool. She hadn't felt any heat from it since the night she'd been rescued.

"Maybe you're right," she said.

"No, it was him," Simone said. "It had to be. He couldn't ignore what you did."

"Then why didn't he come for me himself?"

"Because he has half a brain? Maybe?" Judah offered.

She scowled at him.

"Judah's right," Simone said. "Kai told me—you were watched all the time. And the tribe is still out there trying to break through the rest of the protective circles so they can search the place."

"They're not going to find much," Kai said. "It started to fall apart while I was trying to find a way out."

"How did you get out?" Josie asked.

Kai shrugged. "Everybody bailed and just left me there. I walked out eventually."

"If Fire Guy had come for you, he risked being caught himself," Simone said. "Then you both would've been stuck."

"I guess," Josie said.

"You should be glad he hasn't come for you," Judah said. "Since you're in thrall to him, no one would be able to stop him, not even the Triune. He could take you wherever he wanted, do whatever he wanted."

"I know that," she said. "But I don't know why you're acting so smug about it, since you were the one who told me to do it in the first place." She touched her forehead. "Remember?"

He glowered at her.

"What?" Simone said. "When?"

"Considering you've been telling me this whole time that I shouldn't trust him," Josie said, her blood starting to boil in a way that only Judah seemed capable of causing, "it's completely hypocritical for you to give me—"

"I didn't mean for you to carve his symbol into your skin permanently," Judah cut in. "That's crazy."

"I didn't have a choice! You think they were going to give me a pen if I asked for one? I was a captive. I had to improvise."

"And you didn't think to use your blood as ink?" Judah asked.

Josie faltered. No, she hadn't thought of that. She could've used the splinter to draw blood and then painted the symbol on her skin. She might've had to redraw it after a while, but a symbol drawn in blood still would've caught his attention.

"You know what I think?" Judah said. "I think you wanted to put yourself in thrall to him from the very beginning."

She stood up. "No, I didn't. That's—Why would I want to do that?"

Judah crossed his arms again. "I don't know. Because you're obsessed?"

Her hands started to curl, but stopped when her wounds burst with fresh pain. For the first time since she'd returned home, she was hot again.

"Judah . . ." Simone stood up too, like she might use her black belt skills to end the argument.

"How desperate do you have to be to put yourself in thrall to a guy just to get his attention?" Judah said, running his thumb along the bottom of his chin like he was actually trying to determine her precise level of patheticness. "He blew you off. He's not interested. Why don't you just . . . get over it?"

Simone's hands were on her hips. "Judah, it is time for you to shush it."

But Judah's eyes were flickering in that terrible way that meant he was about to say something really . . .

"Unless . . ."—he smirked—"you don't think you're in love with him, do you?"

Josie was so hot, she was freezing up. "I really hate you, you know that?"

"Right," he said. "So you love this Fire Guy and you hate me, because you know both of us so well."

Her throat constricted with rage. All she could do was glare at him. She wondered if she couldn't pull the Gauntlet of Death from the Beyond after all. She knew the first person she'd send to the realm of Death with it. Why did he have to be so . . .

Right.

Truth was, she couldn't get over it. She didn't know how to get over this feeling she had—this need—just to see Fire Guy again.

If carving his symbol into her skin didn't bring him to her, what would? Judah was right. It was desperate. She was desperate. Even though she didn't know him, not his true face or even his name, the thought of not being near him again made her feel like she was falling into a frozen, lightless place she might not be able to escape from, drowning all over again.

She didn't know when it had happened, or how, but it was true; she was in love with him.

"What?" Judah said, eyes searching her face. "Nothing to say?"

"To you?" She turned away. "No."

CHAPTER 35

APRIL 16TH

OKAY, SO SHE WAS MOPING.

She'd spent the rest of the day in her room, wallowing. After another shower which finally seemed to strip the last of the garbage stink away, she'd slipped into a tank top and flannel pajama bottoms and starting whittling.

At first, her hands had ached and protested, but after a while, they'd numbed. Her dad had checked on her a few times. He kept offering her food and asking if she was all right, but after all her noncommittal responses, he gave up.

As the night filled up the windows with darkness and the house grew quiet, curls of wood shavings accumulated on her bedroom floor. Most depressing was the fact that halfway through carving, she looked down and saw a mini-mask emerging—his mask. Or some version of it. She studied the features again. If they belonged to someone she knew, she couldn't see it.

She set the carving aside, pulling her legs up and dropping her head to her knees. Judah had been right. She was obsessed. And it was pathetic.

Just when she was reaching for the light switch, ready to give in to another dream filled with falling—lately, it had been off the plateau and into the arms of Fire Guy, whom she was starting to believe she'd never see again—she felt a faint warmth, like fingertips skimming the symbol. Slowly, the warmth grew and spread.

Barefoot, she stepped over the pile of wood shavings and opened the outside door.

Her breath tremored in her lungs.

At the far end of the deck near the steps, Fire Guy stood, barely discernible from the shadows except for the flames in his eyes— pure blue.

She had to hold herself back from running to him. Walking seemed to take forever. Finally, she stood at the edge of the deck, slightly looking down at him. She didn't know how she could've thought he was Beech. He was clearly taller, assuming that his height wasn't exaggerated too much by the god's guise. She had a sense though, that he wore the guise thinly. If she were right, then his height was much closer to . . . Russell's.

Perspiration glazed over her, baking on her skin.

Neither of them said anything.

Finally, she asked, "Was it you?"

His eyes seemed to burn right through her. "What do you think?"

He didn't sound happy. She started to lace her fingers together, but they ached from whittling so she pulled them apart.

Why should he have been happy? He'd told her he couldn't see her anymore. He'd told her not to call him again. He'd told her she was threatening his control over the god. And what had she done? She'd cut his mark into her body, forcing him to take notice of her, forcing him to come to her, forcing him to grapple with the godly presence trying to seize hold of him.

"I'm sorry," she said. "I didn't know what else to do."

She reached for him. As her hand slipped through the heat of his guise, the smoke closed over her skin. The ache in her chest grew oppressive, so she could hardly breathe. Her fingers touched the bare skin of his bicep. He was letting her touch him. The ache inside of her wanted to believe it meant something.

"Thank you for telling Simone where to find me."

He moved back. Her hand dropped away, feeling the chill air creeping in around her. Judah had been right. He wasn't interested. She was making an idiot of herself. A strange sensation built around her eyes, pins and needles. Gods, was she finally going to cry?

Not now. Please.

Bad enough that her heart was in its death throes. The last thing she needed was for him to see her unleash years of built-up tears.

She looked away, towards the slim silhouettes of the cedars in the neighbor's yard.

"I'm going to release you now," he said.

She nodded, too focused on holding back the tears to speak.

"This is probably going to hurt," he said.

She nodded again. It didn't matter. She was already in the worst kind of pain she'd ever experienced. Worse even than her grief, because at least that was understandable. In some ways, grieving for her mom had made her feel stronger. It had given her purpose. Help Tessa. Stop the Earth Goddess. But this pain was nothing but confusion and senselessness, and it made her feel so weak. She could scarcely stand herself.

"I have to touch the symbol to remove it," he said.

She didn't know if he was preparing her or himself.

She set her teeth, tracing the peaks of the trees in a lame attempt to distract herself as his hand moved towards her and then touched her. His fingers grazed the skin below the hem of her tank top. She couldn't help it, a jolt passed through her. She winced, hating her body for betraying her.

His movement became brusque, like a doctor examining a patient. His hand slid under her waist band and covered the symbol, pressing firmly. Nothing seemed to happen and then . . .

She sucked a sharp breath as the heat was stolen from her.

Pain built under her skin and grew, like he was ripping away the undermost layer and vacuuming it out. She stumbled forward, grabbing his shoulder for support. Her legs trembled and gave out. He hooked her waist, holding her up. She bit down as the warmth drained from her. A low whimper escaped her, and then . . . it was over.

She sagged against him, panting and covered in cold sweat.

"Are you all right?" he asked, holding her, but just barely.

A cold sensation, like frozen razors, cut at her throat as she swallowed and pulled back, wobbling slightly. She let go of him.

"I'm fine," she said, touching the spot where the symbol had been. It felt hollow and frozen. "Thank you."

"Don't thank me," he said, like he was disgusted at the thought.

She took a sliding step back. "Are you all right?" she asked.

He was quiet. "What do you mean?"

"The god, he's not in control?"

"If he were, do you think I would've been able to release you?"

She didn't know what hurt more, the insinuation that the god still wanted her, or the implication that the summoner didn't. In her mind, they were the same, even though she knew they weren't and, in fact, was hoping that they never would be. She didn't want the summoner to lose himself to the god, even if that meant that she could be with him.

She almost didn't say it, because she knew how desperate it would sound, but she couldn't seem to stop herself.

"I can help you," she said. "I spent my entire life training to keep the Tripartite separate from myself. I could teach you what I learned. Once Tessa is better, she can take me to the island. The archives there . . . I'm sure I can find more information about manifestation, information that can help you maintain control."

His flame-blue eyes swirled like vortices. "Why do you want to help me?"

"It's my fault this is happening to you," she said. "If I hadn't made the mask in the first place—"

"Explain it to me," he said abruptly.

She hugged herself. "Explain what?"

"How you could make a mask for me when you don't know who I am?" he asked. "You know the mask looks just like me."

"I know it must, but I—"

"Maybe it's not that you don't know who I am, Josie," he said. "Maybe it's that you don't want to know who I am."

"Are you saying I should know?"

Sudden flares licked over his body and then went out again as quickly as they had appeared.

"You want to help me?" he said in a low voice. "Leave me alone."

He moved back, like he was getting clear of her to translocate.

She stepped to the very edge of the deck. "Why don't you just tell me who you are?"

He hesitated. A faint crackle filled the silence between them.

"Do you have feelings for me, Josie?"

Her heart seized up. "Ah—"

"You do, don't you?"

"I—"

"Why?" he asked.

"I don't know."

"That's not good enough."

"What do you want me to say? How can I explain something I don't understand myself?"

"It's the god you want," he said.

"No, it's not," she said before she knew what she was saying.

"I don't believe you."

"Why not?"

Another crackling silence followed her question.

Then he said, "It's the god who wants you, Josie. Not me."

Knife. Heart. Again.

She trembled. "I don't believe you."

He moved closer, close enough that the smoke of his guise swelled around her. His smoky scent, almost sweet, was like cherrywood burning. "When I showed up here tonight, what did you want to happen?"

She started to look away, but he caught her chin and held her face. His fingers were hard.

"I know what you wanted," he said. He took his hand away.

"Why are you being like this?"

"You mean being who I am? Not like the fantasy you've been dreaming up in your head? What's he like anyway? Some free-love punk like Beech?"

Did he know Beech? Did that mean he was part of their tribe after all?

"Tell me," he said. "Really. I want to know. Who is fantasy man? What's he like? What's he ever done for you?"

Tears stung the rims of her eyes. It didn't seem like there was anything she could say that would help the situation, but the words came out anyway, all on their own.

"He saved me."

The flames in his eyes seemed to freeze mid-flicker.

"Every night," she said, feeling like she was cutting herself open with each word, yet they kept slicing out of her. "Every night I'm falling, I'm drowning, I'm freezing, and ..."—a tear fell, touching her lip, salty and hot. Just one, but it hurt as if she were sobbing rivers—"every night, you're there."

Unbidden, she leaned and kissed him. Gently, briefly. The guise between them was little more than a soft breath of warmth against her cheek. He didn't kiss her back. But he didn't turn away either. She pulled back, gazing into the blue fires of his eyes.

"I know it's just a dream. I know it's not real," she said, heart catching in her throat, "but it feels real to me. So, thank you. Thank you for always being there to save me, even if it's just in my dreams."

He didn't speak. He didn't move.

She trembled all over. She wasn't sure she could stand upright for much longer. She was ready to collapse, to fall down and break down and let go. She wasn't the Triune. She never had been. She didn't need to be strong. She didn't have to put on a brave face. She didn't need to put on any face but her own. If only she knew what that face looked like.

Maybe she could reach into the Beyond and find it, like she'd found the face of the mountain god. Maybe if she found her true face, she'd be able to see the face behind the fire god's mask too.

She took a step back. Should she say goodbye? Or good luck? Or nice (not) knowing you? Or how about, thanks for breaking my heart; sorry for bothering you?

In the end, she decided it was better to just leave. Run away. As fast as she could.

She turned.

He grabbed her arm. Stepping up onto the deck, he pulled her to him.

He kissed her.

His mouth and hands were hungry on her, like they'd been craving her and were ravenous to taste her, to touch her.

And it felt wonderful to stop searching, to embrace the fire, to be consumed.

Heat and fire, that's all she remembered.

A SIMONE EPILOGUE

MAY 1ST
TWO WEEKS LATER

"AGAIN?" SIMONE SAID, glancing over her shoulder at Kai, who was passed out on her bed, snoring softly. "That's every night for the last two weeks," she said into the phone. "Are you sure he's in control?"

"Not really," Josie said.

"Did you give him the instructions for the charm we found?" Simone asked, standing up and padding out of the bedroom.

"Yeah."

"And? What did he say?" she asked as she walked down the stairs.

"We didn't talk much."

Simone flipped on the kitchen light. "I should be concerned, shouldn't I?"

"Concerned about what?" That was Josie, master evader.

"Why don't you tell me exactly what happened and then I can tell you how concerned I am," Simone said as she pulled opened the freezer and took out the pint of chocolate cherry ice cream.

"You don't have to be concerned."

"Right. But do I need to make you an anti-pregnancy charm or what?" She set the pint on the counter and took out a spoon.

Silence.

She dropped the spoon. It clattered on the tile floor. "Josie! You're not having—"

"No, I'm not . . . of course not."

Simone frowned as she picked up the spoon. "Josie, I hate to be the one to say this to you, but you don't even know who this guy is."

"I know that."

"Well?" She pried the lid off the container.

Josie sighed. "Well what?"

"You know what. It's been weeks, why hasn't he told you who he is? Hm? What does he have to hide?"

"I haven't asked him to tell me."

"So? And what?" Simone shook her head. "He should tell you whether you ask or not. And why haven't you asked? Don't you care?" She took a bite. Heaven in frozen chocolate form. Yum.

"It's not that I don't care, it's just that . . ."

She took the spoon out of her mouth. "It's just that you haven't been talking much?

More silence. Simone could read Josie's silences better than the top row of an eye chart: E. Or in this case, yes.

"And just how little talking have you been doing?" Simone said. "How close to home are we?"

"I hate baseball analogies."

"Second base?" Simone persisted.

"Which one's that again?"

Simone stabbed her spoon into the ice cream. "You're being deliberately obtuse, and as your best friend, I am offended. You are involved in a very serious intimate relationship with this guy, am I right?"

"I don't know . . ."

"How intimate?"

"Not that intimate."

"Like . . . shirt off, pants off intimate?"

More silence.

"Josie!"

"It just happened—"

"Underwear?"

"What about it?"

"On or off?"

Josie hesitated.

Simone dropped her head to the counter. "Josie . . ."

"What do you want me to say? We kiss and then there's more kissing and things just . . ."

"Josie Day, I don't believe you." And she really couldn't. She knew how quickly a relationship could progress when there were hot achy feelings involved, but Josie was usually such a control freak and so guarded. Yet she didn't seem to have any defenses up against this mystery guy. It was like she was a completely different person with him.

"Don't act so shocked. You and Kai are having sex."

"Yeah, but big difference alert: *Kai* and I. I know his name. I know what he looks like with his clothes off. You can't even see this guy under his guise. He's getting all the show and you're getting nothing."

"I wouldn't say nothing."

"Josie, I don't want to be the party pooper, but you're the one I care about, not this fire god or his summoner. It is my duty to point out to you how colossally weird it is that, considering how fast and hot this relationship is, he hasn't decided to take the mask off."

"I know who he is, Simone."

"No, you guess who he is. And the only reason you guess that is because it's who you want it to be," Simone corrected in her sternest voice.

"I don't want it to be Russell."

"Yes, you do. How many times this week have we been to the archives?"

"That's because I'm doing research."

"Uh-huh, studying his face and hair and butt."

"Which is why I'm sure it's him."

Simone frowned, poking at the ice cream listlessly. She hated to be the downer. "I'm not convinced it's Russell." She refrained from reminding Josie about the rumors concerning Russell. The latest being that he'd slept with Allison and then blown her off. Josie knew the rumors. She just didn't seem to care. "It doesn't make any sense—"

"Russell is the only one who does make sense. He knew I was repairing the mask, he knew where to find the mask after I'd repaired it—"

Simone tossed her spoon into the sink and jammed the lid back onto the container. "I guess."

"Who else could it be?"

"Maybe he's not part of our tribe at all." Simone could hope. She really didn't like Russell and not just because he was a player and had tortured Kai as a kid and had a beef with her brother... actually, those were her main reasons.

"Maybe."

"Well... since you two are taking off so many articles of clothing, have you taken the time to check out his clothes? Do you recognize them? Do they tell you anything?"

"I haven't been searching his pockets for his wallet, if that's what you're asking."

"Why not?"

"He'll tell me when he's ready, Simone."

"Uh-huh." Simone rolled her eyes as she put the ice cream away. Her appetite was gone. "Promise me you won't go any further with him until you know his real identity, for sure."

Josie hesitated again.

"Josie!"

"Okay. You're right. I promise."

Simone let out a breath. "I mean it."

"So do I."

From around the corner and down the stairs, she heard Judah call, "Simone?"

"I'd better go," Simone said to Josie. "Text me in the morning. I would wish you sweet dreams, but I already know you'll be having them."

"Ha, ha."

They hung up. Simone flicked off the light and peered down the dark basement steps.

"Judah?"

"Would you come down here?" he replied.

She plodded down the steps, which opened into the family room, squinting into the darkness.

"Judah?"

Before she could touch the light switch, a fire roared to life in the middle of the room. A human-shaped fire.

She gasped and stumbled, crashing onto her butt on the stairs and dropping her phone. The fire went out. The lights flipped on. Judah was standing over her.

"Are you all right?" he asked, helping her up to her feet.

"What the—?"

Then she saw the mask in his hand. Her mouth fell open. She grabbed his wrist, lifting the mask up to get a better look at it. Black, clay, sharp-featured.

"It's you?" She let go of his wrist. She surged up to her feet and smacked his arm, making her palm sting. "You're the Fire Guy?"

He looked like he was ready to be smacked—or worse. He backed up and then turned into the family room. Dropping the mask on the table like a baseball mitt after a lost game, he flopped onto the sofa, running his hands over his face.

She snatched up her phone and stood at the end of the sofa, arms folded. Concern and fury battled to get out first. But shock wasn't finished expressing itself.

"I don't believe this," she cried.

His hands fell into his lap. He stared at the mask as if he didn't believe it either. He looked so miserable, concern won out over fury. She sat down next to him.

"Are you okay?" Panic's turn. "Oh my gods, you're becoming manifest. Oh my gods. Are you ... you?"

"For the most part," he said, sitting forward, twisting his fist against his palm. "But it's getting harder ... I think I need your help."

She gripped his forearm. He'd always been warm, but was he warmer than usual? Or was it just her perception, now that she knew he was the Fire Guy?

"Of course I'll help you, Judah, whatever I can do ... oh gods, the charm. Josie gave you the instructions for a charm tonight. The one she found in the archives—"

He reached into his pocket and pulled out a folded piece of paper, holding it out to her. She took it and unfolded it, gazing down at Josie's meticulously copied instructions. She'd taken a long time transcribing them as clearly as she could, so he wouldn't have any trouble reading them.

"Think you can do it?" he asked.

"Maybe," she said. "I still can't believe this ..." She set the paper on the table next to the mask and then whipped around and punched him in the arm. "You're cheating on Tessa, with Josie! You—you—big jerk!"

He leaned back, not looking at her.

She stared at him. "Judah, that is just wrong and it's not like you. And"—her face began to burn remembering everything Joise had said, or not said, which was saying enough—"what are you thinking?"

His forefinger and thumb rubbed his eyes.

"You have to break up with Tessa, and you need to tell Josie who you are. Or I will."

"About that." He took a leather cord from around his neck—not his usual grounding necklace, which was now wrapped around his wrist—and looped it over her head. She touched the stone and then, realizing what it was, wished she hadn't. A secret-keeping charm. Now that she'd touched it, she was bound to keep his secret. "Judah . . ."

"You can't tell anyone," he said. "Especially not *her*."

Simone leaned towards him. "Her name is Josie, and you have been doing some very . . . naughty things with her."

He glanced at her from the corner of his eyes. "What did she tell you?"

"More than enough now that I know who she's been doing them with. And you're still with Tessa too. Ew and—" She hit him again.

"Tessa and I haven't been—" He stopped himself. "She's too busy studying to be the Triune."

"Oh, so you decided you're just going to screw around with her sister until she has more free time, is that it?"

"No."

"I hope not."

"I'm going to deal with this, Simone."

"You bet your keister you are, mister."

"Just make the charm."

"Why don't you make it? You're better at charms than I am."

"No, I'm not," he said. "You surpassed me a long time ago."

She couldn't help but feel a little flattered. Judah didn't hand out compliments unless he meant them. And he was, actually, a very skilled charm-maker, just like their mom.

"And this one's too important," he said. "It could really help me . . . clear up some things."

Again, concern took over. "Are you really okay?" she asked.

"I think so but ..." He pushed up from the couch and walked to the hidden minifridge in one of the cabinets.

"But Josie," she finished for him.

He pulled out a bottle of water, not answering as he chugged the bottle empty.

Simone covered her hands with her face and pounded the floor with her feet. "Judah, she is so in love with you."

He wiped his mouth. "She told you that?"

"She didn't have to tell me. It's obvious. Do you think she would do all the things she's doing with you if she weren't?"

"How would I know?"

"Judah!"

His face darkened. "Besides, she doesn't know who she's in love with—"

"Because you haven't told her who you are."

"Don't you think she could've figured it out, if she really wanted to?"

"She's been trying to figure it out and she's convinced it's ..." She choked up on the name.

His eyes narrowed. "Who?"

She pursed her lips.

"Simone—"

She let out a growl. "Russell! Okay? She thinks it's Russell." She slumped. "I'm sorry."

He thumped the stainless steel bottle onto one of the book shelves, shaking his head. "Russell. Right. That's exactly my point. She doesn't want it to be me, Simone. She'd rather it be anyone but me. Even ... Russell." He spat the name like it was full of rat poison.

"Well, maybe if you hadn't been so mean to her . . . gods, that's what all the fighting was about, wasn't it? You've had feelings for her the whole time, and you couldn't deal with them like a grown-up."

"I wasn't fighting with her. I was telling her the truth, and you saw how well she reacted to it."

"That's because you told it to her like a big meanie head."

"It's because *I* told it to her, Simone. She doesn't want to hear anything I have to say. The last two weeks, she hasn't even spoken to me when I'm not in possession. When I'm at the house as myself, she pretends I'm not there."

"That's because you're her sister's boyfriend. Why should she talk to you? When was the last time you even said hello to Kai?"

"That's different."

"Not for her. It's only different for you because you know the truth. Judah, that's not fair."

He crossed his arms. "You're right. That's why I'm ending it."

Her mouth dropped open. "What? No."

"I have to."

"You can't do that to her."

"Simone, I need to. I didn't want this to happen, but . . . everything gets so fucked up when I'm around her. I can't tell which thoughts are mine and which are his." He gestured to the mask. "Once you finish the charm, if it works, it should allow me to create a barrier between myself and the god. I need to stay away from Josie if I want to get this under control."

"I know you have to do it, but . . . Josie."

He was staring at the ground, stubborn-faced.

"I know you're struggling"—she choked a little—"to keep your soul. I will do whatever I can to help you. But do you seriously expect me to believe that it's only the god who wants to be with Josie? Now that I know what you've been doing with her, and the way you've been acting these last few months—"

He scowled. "What way?"

"Like a jerk! That's not like you, Judah. I mean, it is like you, a little bit, but I never understood why you were extra mean to Josie all the time—"

"I am not—"

"Yes, you are. You push her. You've been pushing her, way before you took possession of that." She pointed to the mask. "You're like an eight-year-old on the playground who can't tell a girl he likes her so he shoves her down instead."

He shook his head. "You don't know what you're talking about."

"I don't, huh? Why haven't you told Josie the truth?"

"I'm not talking about this with you, Simone."

"Yes, you are! You're about to break my best friend's heart."

"She'll get over it."

She stood up, rigid and scowling. "How long have you known you were going to stop seeing her?"

He glanced away from her.

"You were with her tonight," she said. "Like, an hour ago. And you knew you were going to end it, didn't you?" She snatched the paper off of the coffee table and shook it at him. "You are so lucky that you are my brother; otherwise, I might say some very not nice things to you right now." She stormed to the stairs, but then stopped and turned back to him. "The next time you see Josie, if she says that you even shook her hand, you will be in so much trouble."

"I'm not going to see her again," he said.

"You have to. You have to tell her in person."

He continued to stare at the floor.

She stepped back down into the family room. "Judah, you can't just . . . disappear. She loves you."

His voice was as hard as his face. "Not me, Simone. The god. I'm not disappearing. I'll still be here. I've been here the whole time. She just hasn't wanted to see me." He scooped up the mask and it vanished. He did have a secret stash. He must've made the charm himself. He walked by her towards his bedroom.

"You're just going to leave her without saying goodbye or anything? How can you do that?"

He stopped at his bedroom door. "I can't see her while I'm in possession again. If I do, I won't be able to . . ." His voice broke up, but he cleared his throat.

"There's a mission leaving next Friday, three weeks in the Rockies. I'm going. Think you can have the charm finished by then?"

Seven days?

"I'll try," she said. "But you have to—"

The door closed behind him.

She trudged back up the stairs and into her room. She sat on the edge of the bed, staring between the charm instructions and her phone. Kai rolled over and touched her back.

"Something up?" he asked in a sleepy mumble.

She shook her head, running her thumb over her phone's screen.

"Expecting a call?" he asked.

"No," she said.

In fact, she was wishing she could make a call. She wished she could call Josie and tell her the truth.

Judah was the Fire Guy.

And he was about to break her heart.

ACKNOWLEDGMENTS

I must first thank my editorial team. Renae, she is my first and best reader, fan, and friend. Chad A. Clark, fellow indie author, whose feedback and insights are invaluable. My proofreader, Kris, who wrestled my prose into submission with good humor, generosity, and grace. And my editor and partner-in-crime, Pam House Caster—she asked all the hard questions and always inspires me to get my butt back in the chair.

Thank you to all the family, friends, and teachers who have loved, encouraged, and guided me.

Finally, my boys. I had dreams before you came into my life, but it wasn't until you were in my life that my dreams actually started to come true.

WORKS BY
A.M. YATES

Summoners Series

Minor Gods: Book One
Lost Gods: Book Two
Fated Gods: Book Three

The Horizon Cycle

Shield and the Shadow
Stoneheart and the Axe
Sparrow and the Dagger

Stealer
Hunter (Stealer #2)
Unraveler (Stealer #3)

www.ingramcontent.com/pod-product-compliance
Lightning Source LLC
Chambersburg PA
CBHW031616180726
48284CB00005B/1568